About the Author

Annie O'Neil spent mo[st]... draped over the family [sofa?]... hand. Novels, baking a[nd]... angst poetry ate up most of her youth. Now, Annie splits her time between corralling her husband into helping her with their cows, listening to audio books whilst weeding and spending some very happy hours at her computer writing.

Avril Tremayne became a writer via careers in shoe-selling, nursing, teaching and public relations. Along the way, she studied acting, singing, pottery, oil painting, millinery, German and Arabic (among other things). A committed urbanite, her favourite stories are fast-paced contemporary city stories told with sass and humour. Married with one daughter, Avril lives in Sydney, Australia. When not writing or reading, she's thinking about food, wine and shoes.

Susan Carlisle's love affair with books began when she made a bad grade in maths. Not allowed to watch TV until the grade had improved, she filled her time with books. Turning her love of reading into a love for writing romance, she pens hot medicals. She loves castles, travelling, afternoon tea, reads voraciously and hearing from her readers. Join her newsletter at www.SusanCarlisle.com

Affairs of the Heart

Affairs of the Heart:
Breaking the Rules

ANNIE O'NEIL

AVRIL TREMAYNE

SUSAN CARLISLE

MILLS & BOON

First Published in Great Britain 2021
By Mills & Boon, an imprint of HarperCollins*Publishers,* Ltd
1 London Bridge Street, London, SE1 9GF

www.harpercollins.co.uk

HarperCollins*Publishers*
1st Floor, Watermarque Building,
Ringsend Road, Dublin 4, Ireland

AFFAIRS OF THE HEART: BREAKING THE RULES © 2021 Harlequin Books S.A.

Her Hot Highland Doc © 2017 Annie O'Neil
From Fling to Forever © 2014 Belinda de Rome
The Doctor's Redemption © 2015 Susan Carlisle

ISBN: 978-0-263-30023-9

MIX
Paper from
responsible sources
FSC FSC™ C007454

Printed and bound in Spain
by CPI, Barcelona

HER HOT
HIGHLAND DOC

ANNIE O'NEIL

This book goes out to – and I'm stealing her phrase here – the best friend I never met – the marvelous Nettybean. She's ALWAYS there for me and I am ever grateful. Thanks Netts – hope you don't mind having to go to an inclement Scottish Island for a big slice of gratitude pie!

xx Annie O'

CHAPTER ONE

No amount of torrential rain unforgivingly lashing his face would equal the storm brewing inside of Brodie McClellan. Not today. Not tomorrow. A month of Sundays wouldn't come close.

And yet he had to laugh…even though everything he was feeling was about as far off the spectrum of "funny ha-ha" as laughter could get. He'd seen death on a near daily basis for the months he'd been away, but this one…? This one had him soul-searching in the one place he'd longed to leave behind. *Blindsided* didn't even come close to what he was feeling.

"Hey, Dad."

He crouched low to the ground, unable to resist leveling out a small hillock of soft soil soaked through with the winter rains. The earth appeared months away from growing even a smattering of grass to cover his father's grave. It was no surprise that his brother hadn't come good on his promise to lay down some turf. It was difficult enough to drag him down from the mountains, let alone—

Enough. Callum had a good heart, and he had to be hurting, too.

Brodie dragged his fingers through the bare earth again. Time would change it. Eventually. It would become like his mother's—the grave just to the left. The one he still couldn't bear to look at. He moved his fingers behind him, feeling long-established grass. A shocking contrast to the bare earth in front of him.

Yes, time would change it. Just as it had all the graves, each one protected with a thick quilt of green. Time he didn't have nor wanted to give to Dunregan. Not after all it had taken from him.

He scanned the parameters of the graveyard with a growing sense of familiarity. Brodie had spent more time here in the past fortnight than he had in a lifetime of growing up on the island. Asking, too late, for answers to all the questions he should have asked before he'd left Dunregan in his wake.

Gray. It was all he could see. Gray headstones. Gray skies. Gray stones making up the gray walls. A color washout.

He ran a hand across the top of his father's headstone. "We'll get this place fixed up for you, Father. All right? Put in some flowers or something."

A memory pinged into his head of Callum and himself, digging up snowdrop bulbs when he'd been just a young boy. His father counting out a few pence for each cluster. He swiped his face to clear off the rain, surprised to discover he was smiling at the memory of his paltry pocket money. The small towers of copper pennies had seemed like riches at the time.

"I'll get you some snowdrops, eh, Dad? Those'll be nice. And some bluebells later on? For you and Mum. She always loved bluebell season."

He shook his head when he realized he was waiting for an answer.

"It's a bit of a nightmare at the clinic. I've had to call in a locum. It'll buy me time until I figure out how to explain to folk that it's okay. *I'm* okay."

He looked up to the skies again, unsurprised to find his mood was still as turbulent as the weather. Wind was blowing every which where. Rain was coming in thick bursts. Cold. It was so ruddy *cold* up here on Dunregan.

He pressed his hands to his thighs, stood up and cursed softly. Mud. All over his trousers.

For the few minutes it took to drive home Brodie tried his best to plumb a good mood from somewhere in the depths of his heart. He wasn't this guy. This growling, frowning man whose image he kept catching in the rearview mirror. He was a loving son. Older sibling to a free-spirited younger brother. Cousin, nephew, friend. And yet he felt like a newcomer. A stranger amidst a sea of familiarity. A man bearing more emotional weight on his shoulders than he'd ever carried before.

He pulled the car into the graveled drive in front of the family home, only to jam the brakes on.

"What the—?"

Wood. A huge stack of timber filling the entire driveway. He'd barely spoken to anyone since he'd returned to Dunregan, let alone ordered a pile of wood!

Brodie jumped out of his four-by-four and searched for a delivery note. He found it tucked under a stack of quarter-inch plywood. His eyes scanned the paper. The list of cuts and types of wood all began to slot into place, take on form…build one very particular item.

The boat.

The boat he and his father had always promised they would build.

The one he'd never been able to think about after that day when he'd come home from sailing without his mother.

Another sharp sting of emotion hit and stuck in his throat. *Today.*

All he had to do was get through today. And then tomorrow he'd do it all over again, and then one more time until the pain began to ebb, like the tides surrounding the island he'd once called home.

Kali's grip tightened on her handlebars.

The elements vs the cyclist.

Game on.

She lifted her head, only to receive a blast of wind straight in the face. Her eyes streamed. Her nose was threatening to run. Her hair…? That pixie cut she'd been considering might've been a good idea. So much for windswept and interesting. Windswept and bedraggled was more like it—but she couldn't keep the grin off her face.

Starting over—*again*—was always going to be an uphill struggle, but she hadn't thought this particular life reboot would be so *physical*!

Only one hundred more meters between Mother Nature's finest blasts of Arctic wind and a hot cup of tea. Who would win? Fledgling GP? Or the frigid forces of Scotland's northernmost islands?

Another briny onslaught of wind and sea spray sent Kali perilously close to the ditch. A ditch full of…*ugh*. One glimpse of the ice-skinned murk convinced her to swing a leg off her vintage-style bicycle and walk. A blast of icy water shot up from her feet along her legs, giving her whole body a wiggle of chills. She looked down at the puddle her ballerina flats–clad feet had landed in.

Splatterville. A shopping trip for boots and a proper jacket might be in order. So much for the romantic idea of tootling along Dunregan's coast road and showing up to her first day of work with rosy-cheeked panache. There were tulips blooming all over the place in London! How long was it going to take the Isle of Dunregan to catch up?

"Dr. O'Shea?"

A cheery fifty-something woman rode up alongside her, kitted out in a thick waterproof jacket, boots, woolen mittens, hat…everything Kali should've been wearing but wasn't. Her green eyes crackled with mischief…or was that just the weather?

"Yes." Kali smiled, then grimaced as the wind took a hold of her facial features. She must look like some sort of rubber-lipped cartoon character by now!

"Ailsa Dunregan." She hopped off her bike and walked alongside Kali, and laughed when Kali's eyes widened. "Yes. I know, it's mad, isn't it? Same name as the island. Suffice it to say, my family—or at least my husband's family—has been here a long time. *My* family's only been here a few hundred years."

Hundred?

"How'd you know it was me?"

Ailsa threw back her head and laughed. The sound was instantly yanked away by the wind. "Only someone not from Dunregan would—"

Kali struggled to make out what she was saying, her own thoughts fighting with the wind and making nothing comprehensible.

"Sorry?" Kali tried to push her bike a bit closer and keep up the brisk pace the woman was setting.

"I'm the practice nurse!" Ailsa shouted against the elements. "I get all the gossip, same as the publican, and not too many people come to the island this time of year."

Kali nodded, only just managing to keep her bike upright with the approach of another gust.

"It has its merits!" Kali shouted back when she'd regained her footing.

"You think?" Ailsa hooted another laugh into the stratosphere. "If you're after a barren, desolate landscape..." she groaned as her own cycle was nearly whipped out of her hands "...you've come to the right place!"

As if by mutual agreement they both put their heads down, inching their cycles along the verge. Kali smiled into the cozy confines of her woolen scarf—her one practical nod to the subzero temperature. Compared to the other obstacles she'd faced, this one was easy-peasy. Just a healthy handful of meters between her and her new life.

No more hiding. No more looking over her shoulder. Okay, so she still had a different name, thanks to the heaven-sent Forced Marriage Protection Unit, and there were a boatload of other issues to deal with one day—but right here, right now, with the wind blowing more than the cobwebs away, she felt she really was Kali O'Shea. Correction! *Dr.* Kali O'Shea. Safe and sound on the uppermost Scottish Isle of Dunregan.

As if it had actual fingers, the frigid tempest abruptly yanked her bicycle out of her hands, sending her into a swan dive onto the rough pavement and the bicycle skidding into the ditch. The *deep* ditch. The one she'd have to clamber into and probably shred her tights.

She looked down at her knees as she pressed herself up from the pavement. Nope! That job was done already. *Nice one, Kali.* So much for renaming herself after the goddess of empowerment. The goddess of grace might've been a better choice.

"Oh, no! Are you all right, darlin'?" Ailsa was by her side in a minute.

Kali fought the prick of tears, pressing her hands to her scraped knees to regroup. *C'mon, Kali. You're a grown woman now.*

If only...

No. Focus on the positives. She didn't do "if onlys" anymore.

"What's going on here?"

A pair of sturdy leather boots appeared in Kali's eyeline. They must go with the rich Scottish brogue she was hearing.

"You pulling patients in off the streets now, Ailsa?"

Kali's eyes zipped up the long legs, skidded across the thick wax jacket and landed soundly on... Ooh... She'd never let herself think she had a type, but this walking, talking advert for a Scandi-Scottish fisherman type with...ooh, again!...the most beautiful cornflower-blue eyes...

She swallowed.

He might be it. There was something about him that said...*safe.*

Thirtyish? With a straw-blond thatch of hair and a strong

jawline covered in facial hair a few days past designer stubble to match. She'd never thought she was one to go for a beardy guy, but with this weather suddenly it made sense. She wondered how it would feel against her cheek. Reassuringly scratchy or unexpectedly soft?

She blinked away the thought and refocused.

He was no city mouse. That was for sure. It wouldn't be much of a step to picture him on a classic motorbike, lone wolfing it along the isolated coastline. And he was tall. *Well...* Everyone was tall compared to her, but he had a nice, strong, mountain-climber thing going on. You didn't see too many men like that in London. Perhaps they were all hiding out here, in Scotland's subarctic islands, waiting to rescue city slickers taken out by the elements.

"All right, darlin'?" He put a hand on her shoulder, his eyes making a quick visual assessment, gave a satisfied nod and headed for the steep embankment. "Here, I'll just grab your bicycle for you."

Chivalrous to boot!

Strange how she didn't even know him and yet her shoulder seemed to almost miss his touch when he turned toward the ditch.

Kali's hormones all but took over her brain, quickly redressing her Knight in Shining Gore-tex in Viking clothes. Then a kilt. And then a slick London suit, just to round off the selection. Yes. They all fit. Every bit as much as his hardy all-weather gear was complementing him now. Maybe he'd just come from an outdoor-clothing catalog shoot.

"Brodie?" Ailsa called to him as he affected a surfing-style skid down the embankment toward the ditch. "She's no patient! This is Kali O'Shea. The new GP."

"Ah."

Brodie came to a standstill, hands shifting up to his hips. His bright blue eyes ricocheted up to Kali, to Ailsa and then back to Kali before he took a decisive step back up the bank.

Kali's eyes widened.

Was he taking back his generous offer?

Abruptly he knelt, grabbed the bike by a single handle and tugged it out of the ditch.

"Here you are, then."

In two long-legged strides he was back atop the embankment, handing over the bike as if it were made out of pond scum…which, now, it kind of was. In two more he was slamming the door to his seen-better-days four-by-four, which he'd parked unceremoniously in the middle of the road.

Brake lights on. Brake lights off.

And with a crunch of gravel and tarmac…away he went.

"Oh, now…" Ailsa sent Kali a mortified look. "That was no way…" She shook her head. "I've never seen him behaving…"

The poor woman didn't seem to be able to form a full sentence. Kali shook her head, to tell her that it didn't matter, nearly choking on a laugh as she did. Her Viking-Fisherman-Calendar Boy's behavior was certainly one way to make an impression! A bit young to be so eccentric, but… welcome to Dunregan!

She shook her head again and grinned. This whole palaver would be a great story to tell when— Well… She was bound to make friends at some juncture. This was her new beginning, and if Mr. Cranky Pants' sole remit was to be eye candy…so be it.

She waved off Ailsa's offer to help, took a hold of the muddy handlebars, and smiled through the spray of mud and scum coming off the spokes as she walked. She was already going to have to change clothes—might as well complete the Ugly Duckling thing she had going on.

"I am *so* sorry. Brodie's not normally so rude," Ailsa apologized.

"Who is he?"

"Don't you know?" Ailsa's eyes widened in dismay.

A nervous jag shot through Kali's belly as she shook her head. Then the full wattage of realization hit.

"If I were to guess we were going to see him again at the clinic, would I be right?"

"You'd be right if you guessed you would see his name beside the clinic door, inside the waiting room and on the main examination room."

"*He's* Dr. McClellan?"

Terrific! In a really awkward how-on-earth-is-this-going-to-work? sort of way.

Kali tried her best to keep her face neutral.

"You'll hear a lot of folk refer to him as *Young* Dr. Mc-Clellan. The practice was originally his father's, but sadly he passed on just recently." Her lips tightened fractionally. She looked at the expanse of road, as if searching for a bit more of an explanation, then returned her gaze to Kali with an apologetic smile. "I'm afraid Brodie's not exactly the roll-out-the-red-carpet type."

Kali couldn't help but smile at the massive understatement.

"More the practical type, eh? Well, that's no bad thing." Kali was set on finding "the bright side." Just like the counselor at the shelter had advised her.

She could hear the woman's words as clearly as if she'd heard them a moment ago. "It will be difficult, living without any contact with your family. But, on the bright side, your life can be whatever you'd like it to be now."

The words had pinged up in neon in her mental cinema. It was a near replica of the final words her mother had said to her before she'd fled the family home in the middle of the night, five long years ago. Taking a positive perspective had always got her through her darkest days and today would be no different.

"There's only a wee bit to go." Ailsa tipped her head in the direction of an emerging roofline. "Let's get you inside and see if we can't find some dry clothes for you and a hot cup of tea."

Tea!

Bright side.

Brodie had half a mind to drive straight past the clinic and up into the mountains to try to hunt down his brother. Burn off some energy Callum-style on a mountain bike. He was overdue a catch-up since he'd returned. And it wasn't as if he'd be seeing any patients today anyway.

She would.

The new girl.

He tipped his head back and forth. Better get his facts straight.

The new *woman*.

From the looks of Dr. O'Shea, she was no born-and-bred Scottish lassie, that was for sure. Ebony black hair. Long. *Really* long. His fingers involuntarily twitched at the teasing notion of running them through the long, silken swathe. He curled them into a fist and shot his fingers out wide, as if to flick off the pleasurable sensation.

There was more than a hint of South Asia about her. Maybe... Her eyes were a startling light green, and with a surname like O'Shea it was unlikely both of her parents had been Indian born and bred. He snorted. Here he was, angry at the world for making assumptions about him, and he was doing the same thing for poor ol' Kali O'Shea.

When he'd received the email stating a Dr. O'Shea was on her way up he had fully been expecting a red-headed, freckle-faced upstart. Instead she was strikingly beautiful, if not a little wind tousled, like a porcelain doll. With the first light-up-a-room smile he'd seen since he didn't know how long. Not to mention kitted out in entirely inappropriate clothing, riding a ridiculous bicycle on the rough lane and about to begin to do a job he could ruddy well do on his own, thank you very much.

He slowed the car and tugged the steering wheel around in an arc. He'd park behind the building. Leave Kali and Ailsa guessing for a minute. Or ten, given the strength of the gusts they were battling. Why did people insist on riding bicycles in this sort of weather? Ridiculous.

He took his bad mood out on the gear lever, yanking the vehicle into Park and climbing out of the high cab all in one movement.

When his feet landed solidly on the ground it was all too easy to hear his father's voice sounding through his conscience.

You just left her? You left the poor wee thing there on the side of the road, splattered in mud, bicycle covered in muck, and didn't lend a hand? Oh, son... That's not what we islanders are about.

We islanders... Ha! That'd be about right.

And of course his father, the most stalwart of moral compasses, was right. It *wasn't* what Dunreganers were about.

He scrubbed at his hair—a shocker of a reminder that he was long due for a trip to the barber's. He tipped his head up to the stormy skies and barked out a laugh. At least he was free to run his hand through his hair now. And scrub the sleep out of his eyes. Rest his fingers on his lips when in thought...

Not that he'd done much of that lately. A moment's reflection churned up too many images. Things he could never un-see. So it was little wonder his hair was too long, his house was a mess and his life was a shambles ever since he'd returned from Africa. The only thing he was sure of was his status on the island. He'd shot straight up to number one scourge faster than a granny would offer her little 'uns some shortbread.

He slammed his car door shut and dug into his pocket for the practice keys, a fresh wash of rain announcing itself to the already-blustery morning. The one Ailsa and Dr. O'Shea were still battling against.

Fine. All right. He'd been a class-A jerk.

To put it mildly.

He'd put the kettle on. A peace offering to his replacement. *Temporary* replacement, if he could ever convince the islanders that he wasn't contagious. Never had been.

Trust the people who'd known him from the first day he'd taken a breath on this bleak pile of rocks and earth not to believe in the medical clearance he'd received. A clearance he'd received just in time to be at his father's bedside, where they'd been able to make their peace. That was where the first hit of reality had been drilled home. And then there had been the funeral. It was hard to shake off those memories just a fortnight on.

His brother—the stayer—had received the true warmth of the village. Deep embraces. Claps to the shoulder and shared laughter over a fond memory. Only a very few people had shaken hands with him. Everyone else…? Curt nods and a swift exit.

He blamed it on his time in Africa, but his heart told him different. No amount of time would bring back his mother from that sailing trip he'd insisted on taking. No amount of penance would give the island back its brightest rose.

He had thought of giving a talk in the village hall—about Africa, the medicine he'd practiced, the safety precautions he'd taken—but couldn't bear the thought of standing there on his own, waiting for no one to show up, feeling more of an outsider than he had growing up here.

He shoved the old-fashioned key into the clinic's thick wooden door and pushed the bottom right-hand corner with his foot, where it always stuck when the weather was more wet than cold.

The familiarity of it parted his lips in a grudging smile. He knew this building like the back of his hand. Had all but grown up in it. He'd listened to his first heartbeat here, under the watchful eye of his father. Just as he had done most of his firsts on the island. Beneath his father's ever benevolent and watchful eye.

And now, like his father and his father before him, he was taking over the village practice in a place he knew well. *Too* well. He grimaced as the wind helped give the door a final nudge toward opening.

Without looking behind him he tried to shut it and met resistance. He pushed harder. The door pushed back.

"You're certainly choosing an interesting way to welcome our new GP, Brodie."

Ailsa was behind him, trying to keep the door open for herself and—yes, there she was...just behind Ailsa's shoulder—Dr. Shea.

Dr. *O*'Shea?

Whatever. With the mood he was battling, he was afraid she'd need the luck of the Irish and all of...whatever other heritage it was that he was gleaning.

"Hi, there. I'm Kali." She stepped out from behind Ailsa and put out a scraped hand.

He looked at it and frowned. Another reminder that he should've stuck around to help.

She retracted her hand and wiped it on her mud-stained coat.

"Sorry," she apologized in a soft English accent. One with a lilt. Ireland? It wasn't posh London. "I'm not really looking my best this morning."

"No. Well..."

Brodie gave himself an eye roll. Was it too late to club himself in the forehead and just be done with it?

"Ach, Brodie McClellan! Will you let the poor girl inside so we can get something dry onto her and something hot inside of her?" Ailsa scolded. "Mrs. Glenn dropped some homemade biscuits in yesterday afternoon, when she was out with her dogs. See if you can dig those up while I try and find Dr. O'Shea a towel for all that lovely long hair of hers. And have a scrounge round for some dry clothes, will you?"

"Anything else I can do for you?" he called after the re-treating figure, then remembered there was still another woman waiting. One not brave enough to shove past him as Ailsa had. "C'mon, then. Let's get you out of this weather."

Kali eyed Brodie warily as he stepped to the side with an actual smile, his arm sweeping along the hallway in the manner of a charming butler. Hey, presto! And...the White Knight was back in the room. Sort of. His blue eyes were still trained on the car park behind her, as if the trick had really been to make her disappear.

Kali quirked a curious eyebrow as she passed him. Not exactly Prince Charming, was he? *But, my goodness me, he smells delicious.* All sea-peaty and freshly baked bread. With butter. A bit of earthiness was in there, too. An is-lander. And she was on his turf.

She hid a smile as she envisioned herself helming a Viking invasion ship, a thick fur stole shifting across her shoulders as she pointed out to her crew that she saw land. A raven-haired Vikingess!

Unable to stop the vision, she mouthed, *Land-ho!* with a grin.

Oops! Her eyes flicked to Brodie's. His gaze was still trained elsewhere. Probably just as well.

She looked down the long corridor. A raft of closed doors and not much of a clue as to what was behind them.

"Um...where should I be heading?"

"Down the hall and to your left. First door on your right once you turn. You'll find Ailsa there in the supplies cup-board."

Brodie closed the outside door and rubbed his hands to-gether briskly, his body taut with energy, as if someone had just changed his batteries.

He had a lovely voice. All rich and rolling *r*'s and broguey. If he weren't so cantankerous... She tilted her head to take another look. Solid jawline, arrestingly blue eyes bright with drive, thick hair a girl could be tempted to run her fingers through.

Yup! Brodie McClellan ticked a lot of boxes. He might be a grump, but he didn't strike her as someone cruel. In fact he seemed rather genuine behind the abruptness.

She envied him that. A man who, in a split second, came across as true to himself. Honest. Even if that honesty *was* as scratchy as sandpaper. Her eyes slid down his arms to his hands. Long, capable fingers, none of which sported a ring. *Huh*... A lone wolf with no designs on joining a pack.

She shook her head, suddenly aware that the lone wolf was speaking to her, though his eyes were trained on his watch.

"So...you'll want to get a move on. I'll just put the kettle on and see you in a couple of minutes so I can talk you through everything, all right? Doors open soon."

He turned into a nearby doorway without further ado. Seconds later Kali could hear a tap running and the familiar sound of a kettle being filled.

Note to self, she thought as her lips twitched into yet another smile, *civilities are a bit different up here.*

None of the normal *How do you do? I'm Dr. fill-in-the-blank, welcome to our clinic. Here's the tea, here's the kettle, put your name on your lunch if you're brave enough to use the staff refrigerator, and we hope you enjoy your time with us, blah-de-blah-de-blah.*

Dr. Brodie McClellan's greeting was the sort of brusque behavior she'd expect in an over-taxed big-city hospital. But here in itsy-bitsy Dunregan, when the clinic wasn't even set to open for another...she glanced at her waterlogged watch...half hour or so... Perhaps he *wasn't* too young to be eccentric. She was going to go with her original assessment. Too honest a human to bother with bog standard social niceties. Even though social niceties were...*nice.*

A clatter of mugs on a countertop broke the silence, followed by some baritone mutterings she couldn't make out.

Well, so what if her new colleague wasn't tuning up the marching band to trill her merrily into her first shift? She'd faced higher hurdles than winning over someone who had obviously flunked out of Charm Academy.

Kali leaned against the wall for a minute. Just to breathe. Realign her emotional bearings. She closed her eyes to see if she could picture the letter inviting her to come to Dunregan. She'd been so ridiculously happy when it had arrived. With so much time "at sea" it had been a moment of pure, unadulterated elation. When the image of the letter refused to come, she pulled her phone out of her pocket so she could pull it up from her emails.

The screen was cracked. Shattered, more like it.

Of course it is! shouted the voice in her head. *It's the least you deserve after what you've done. The trouble you've caused your mother. Your little sister.*

She pressed her hands to her ears, as if that would help silence the voice she fought and fought to suppress on a daily basis.

She huffed a sigh across her lips and looked up to the ceiling. Way up, past the beams, the tiled roofing and the abundance of storm clouds was a beautiful blue sky. And this…? This rocky, discombobulated start was one of those things-could-only-get-better moments. It *had* to be. This was her shot at a completely fresh start. As far away from her father's incandescent rage as she could be.

"Kali, are you—" Ailsa burst into the corridor. "Darlin', did Brodie just leave you standing here in your wet clothes? For heaven's sake. You would've thought the man had been raised by wolves!"

An eruption of colorful language burst forth from the kitchen as Kali eyed the long-sleeved T-shirt from a three-years-old charity run. That and a pair of men's faded track pants were all Ailsa had managed to rustle up.

"Brodie's," Ailsa had informed her.

Her first instinct had been to refuse, but needs must and all that…

Kali stopped for a moment as the soft cotton slid past her nose and she inhaled a hint of washing powder and peat. A web of mixed feelings swept through her as the T-shirt slipped into place boyfriend-style. Over-sized and offering a hint of sexy and secure all at once. She shook her head at her dreamy-eyed reflection in the small driftwood-framed mirror.

It's a shirt! Get over it.

"When are we going to get this blasted kettle fixed?"

Blimey. Had the walls just vibrated?

"Cool your jets, Brodie. For heaven's sake, it's not rocket science. You *do* know how to make a cup of tea, don't you?"

Ailsa's voice whooshed past the bathroom as she went on her way to the kitchen, her tone soothing as the clink and clatter of mugs and spoons filled out the rest of the mental image Kali was building.

"Stop your fussing, will you?" Brodie grumbled through the stone walls.

"Let *me* have a look," Ailsa chided, much to Kali's amusement. Then, after a moment, "I'll need to get some dressing on that, Dr. McClellan."

"Oh, it's Dr. McClellan now I'm injured, is it?"

"Brodie. Dr. McClellan. You're still the wee boy whose nappies I changed afore you jumped up on my knee, begging me to read you stories about faeries and cowboys over and over, so hush!"

Kali's smile widened as the bickering continued.

Local Doctor Defied by Feisty Kettle:
Nurse Forced to Mollify GP with Bedtime Stories.

Was that the type of story the local newspaper would run? The population on Dunregan wasn't much bigger than some two thousand or so people, and if memory served she was pretty sure that number accounted for the population surge over the summer months. The *hospitable* months.

"For heaven's sake, Ailsa! Stop your mithering. I don't need a bandage! It's not really even a burn!"

"Well, that's a fine way to treat your head nurse, who has twenty years experience on *you*, Brodie McClellan!"

Kali chalked one up to Ailsa.

"But it's a perfectly normal way to treat my auntie who won't leave well enough alone!"

Brodie's grumpy riposte vibrated through the wall. Kali was relieved to hear Ailsa laugh at her nephew's words, then jumped not a moment later when a door slammed farther along the corridor. *Crikey.* It was like being in a Scottish soap opera. And it was great! No-holds-barred bickering, banter and underneath it all a wealth of love. The stuff of dreams.

Her family had never had that sort of banter— *Stop-stop-stop-stop-stop.* Kali deftly trained her hair into a thick plait as she reminded herself she had no family. No one to bicker with, let alone rely on. Not anymore.

Turn it into a positive, Kali.

The other voice in her head—the kind one, the one that had brought her out of her darkest moments—came through like the pure notes of a flute.

There's always *a bright side.*

Good. Focus on that. Turn it into a positive... Not having a family means I'm free! Unencumbered! Not a soul in the world to care about me!

The familiar gaping chasm of fear began to tickle at Kali's every confidence.

Okay. Maybe a positive mantra was going to be elusive. For today. But she *could* do it. Eventually. And realistically there was only one mantra she really needed to focus on:

K.I.C.K.A.S.S. Keep It Compassionate, Kind and Supremely Simple.

It had kept her sane for the past five years and would continue to be her theme song.

She tightened the drawstring on the baggy pants and gave her shoulders a fortifying shake. Who knew? Maybe she could get someone with bagpipes to rustle up a tune!

The piper's "K.I.C.K.A.S.S. Anthem."

Hmm. It needed work.

Regardless, the rhythm of the words sang to her in their own way. They were her link to sanity.

She jumped as a door slammed again. Hearing no footsteps, she thought she might as well suck it up and see what was going on out there. No point hiding out in the toilet! In less than thirty minutes she'd be seeing a patient, and it would probably be a good idea to get the lie of the land.

Kali cracked the door open and stuck her head out—only to pull it right back in when Brodie unexpectedly stormed past. If he'd had a riding cloak and a doublet on he would have looked just like the handsome hero from a classic romance.

Handsome?

She was really going to have to stop seeing him in that way. Rude and curt was more like it. And maybe just a little bit sexy Viking.

He abruptly turned and screeched to a halt, one hand holding the other as if in prayer, his index fingers resting upon his lips. His awfully nice lips.

Stop it! You are not to get all mushy about your new boss. Your new, very grumpy boss. You've been down that road and had to leave everything behind. Never again.

She stood stock-still as Brodie's eyes scanned her from top to toe. A little shudder shivered its way along her spine. His gaze felt surprisingly…intimate.

"That's one hell of a look, Dr. O'Shea."

As Brodie's blue eyes worked their way along her scrappy ensemble for a second time Kali all but withered with em-

barrassment. Snappy comebacks weren't her forte. Not by
a long shot.

"Once I get a lab coat on it should be all right."

Nice one, Kali.

"Sure." Brodie turned and resumed his journey to the
front of the clinic. "I'll just get the patient list."

Kali did a skip-run-walk thing to catch up with his long-
legged strides.

"Would you like me to take a look?"

"That's generally the idea with a patient list."

Kali blew out a slow breath, her eyes on Brodie's retreating back as she continued race-walking to keep up with
him. Touchy, touchy! She was next to certain he wasn't
angry with *her*, but there was a bagpipe-sized chip on that
shoulder of his.

"I meant your hand."

Brodie stopped short and whirled around. Kali only just
skidded to a halt in time not to run into his chest. Which,
given how nice he smelled, wouldn't have been too bad a
thing, but—

"I'd have thought you'd be too afraid."

"Wh-what?" Kali instinctively pulled back at Brodie's
aggressive response. She'd been afraid before. Terrified,
actually. For her life. And she'd survived.

She pressed her heels into the ground. If she could
make a last-minute exit out of an arranged marriage under
the threat of death she could deal with a grumpy thirty-
something doctor with a self-induced kettle burn.

"I've dealt with difficult patients before," she continued
levelly, her eyes on his hand. Meeting his gaze would only
increase the heated atmosphere. "I'm sure we'll come out
all right in the end."

"Difficult patients with Ebola?"

Brodie thrust his hand forward and with every pore of
strength she could muster Kali held her ground. She had no

idea what he was talking about, but she was not—absolutely, positively *not*—going to start out her new life fearfully.

"Aren't you going to touch it?"

He thrust his hand straight into her eyeline—millimeters from her face. What *was* this? Some sort of hardcore newcomer test? Whatever it was, she was not going to be frightened by Brodie McClellan or anyone—ever again.

Brodie watched, amazed, as Kali stood stock-still, seemingly unfazed by his ridiculously aggressive behavior. She took his hand in hers, one of her delicate fingers holding open his own as they instinctively tried to curl round the injury. It was the first time he'd been touched by someone outside of a medical exam in weeks, if not months. The power of it struck him deeply.

Kali's delicate touch nearly released the soft moan building in his chest. He couldn't—*mustn't*—let her see how much this single moment meant to him. He looked at her eyes as they moved across his hand. Diligent, studied. Their extraordinary bright green making them almost feline. More tigress than tabby, he thought.

Moments later, as he exhaled, he realized he'd been holding his breath while Kali was examining him with clinical indifference—examining the burn mark he'd all but shoved directly in her face. It wasn't a bad burn. His pride had been hurt more than his hand. Her touch had been more healing than any medicine. Not that he'd ever tell her. She'd be off soon. Like all the good things that came into his life. Just passing through.

Her long lashes flicked up over those green eyes of hers meeting his inquisitive gaze head-on. Could she see how strange this was for him? Being treated as if he *weren't* a walking, talking contagious disease? No. It ran deeper than that. She was treating him compassionately. Without the stains of his past woven through her understanding of who he actually was.

"That's all you've got?"

"I'm sorry?" Brodie near enough choked at her about-face, bring-it-on attitude.

"Ebola?" She scoffed. "That's your best shot?"

Now it was Brodie's turn to be confused. Was she trying to double bluff him?

"I get a bit of hazing, Dr. McClellan. The less than warm welcome, the mocking about this ridiculous outfit. But seriously...?" She snorted a *get real* snort, took a step back, her hand still holding his, and gave him a smile wreathed in skepticism. "That's your best shot at getting me to high-tail it back to the mainland, is it? Ebola?"

CHAPTER TWO

BRODIE PULLED HIS hand out of Kali's and received an indignant stare in response.

"What? Now I'm not fit to see to a first-degree burn? I am a qualified GP, I'll have you know."

This time there was fire behind her words. *She was no pushover.* He liked that. Decorum ruled all here on Dunregan and it had never been a good fit for him. It was what had forced him to head out into the world to explore who he could be without That Day branded onto his every move.

Enough with the bitterness, McClellan. You're not a teenager anymore.

"No, that's not it at all." Brodie waved away her presumption, opting to get over himself and just be honest. "I think the booking agency might not have been entirely forthright with you."

"What are you talking about? Four weeks—with the possibility of an extension. What's there to know beyond that?" Her forehead crinkled ever so slightly.

"I…" Brodie hesitated, then plunged forward. No point in beating round the bush. "I've recently finished my twenty-one-day clearance after three months working in an Ebola hospital. In Africa," he added, as if it weren't ruddy obvious where the hospital had been.

Three countries. Thousands dead. He'd wanted to make a difference. Needed to make a difference somewhere—

anywhere—before coming back here. And he had done. Small-scale. But he'd been there. A pair of hazmat boots on the ground in a place where "risky" meant that sharing the same air as the person next to you might mean death. Only to come back and face a sea of incriminating looks.

Is this what you had in mind, Dad? Making me promise to work on the island for a year after you'd gone so I could be reminded how much of an outsider I am?

He shook off the thought. His father had been neither bitter nor vengeful. It had been his fathomless kindness and understanding that had driven the stakes of guilt deep into Brodie's heart.

"Hmm…"

Kali's green-eyed gaze remained steady apart from a blink or two. Could she see the inner turmoil he was fighting? Filial loyalty over a need to cut loose? To forge his own path.

Kali's voice, when she finally spoke, was completely neutral. "Guess they *did* leave that bit out." She considered him for a moment longer. "I am presuming you wouldn't be here if you hadn't had the all clear so…it does beg the question: what am I doing here if you're good to go?"

"Ah, the mysteries of life in Dunregan begin to reveal themselves." This was the part that rankled. The part where Brodie found himself slamming doors, spilling boiling water and leaving unsuspecting GPs with their muckcovered bicycles by the side of the road on a stormy day.

"Some of—*most* of the patients are *concerned*…about being seen by me." Total honesty? *All* of them. Fear of catching Ebola from Ol' Dr. McClellan's son had gripped the island.

Or…the thought struck him…maybe they had simply preferred his father and were using the Ebola scare as an excuse to refuse his treatment. Now, *that* hurt.

He cleared his throat. One step at a time.

"Even though you've had the all clear?" Kali's voice remained impartial. She was fact gathering.

"Right. Apparently most folk round here don't put much faith in the Public Health Office's green light." He snorted derisively. "And to think of all the viral infections I've treated here. Rich, isn't it?"

He stopped himself. He was going to have to check the bitter tone in his voice. Yeah, he was angry. But he was hurting much more than he was spitting flames. And to add on moments like these—moments that reminded him why he wanted more than anything to live somewhere else. Oh, to be anonymous!

"I'm going to presume, as someone who has also taken the Hippocratic oath, that you wouldn't have returned to your practice until you felt well and truly able to."

Despite himself, he shot her a look. One that said, *Obviously not. Otherwise I wouldn't be so blinking frustrated.*

"Don't shoot the messenger, Dr. McClellan! I wouldn't be doing my job if I didn't check with you."

"Fair enough."

And it was. It just felt...*invasive*...being questioned again. And by someone who hadn't been through the post-Ebola wringer as he had.

Kali might be a fully qualified GP, but her face was unlined by personal history. With skin that smooth, no dark circles under her eyes, excited to be working in *Dunregan*... She had to be green around the ears.

"What are you? Two...three days out of med school?"

She looked at him as if he'd sprouted horns. The rod of steel reasserted itself.

"Old enough. Apart from which, I don't really think that's any business of yours."

"No." Might as well be honest. "You just look—"

"Yeah, yeah. I know." She all but spat the words out, crossing her arms defensively across her chest. "Baby-faced."

"Not exactly what I was going to say," Brodie countered. *Arrestingly beautiful* would've been more accurate. Her smooth skin was entirely unweathered by life, but now that he was paying more attention the wary look in her eyes spoke of wisdom beyond her years.

"Well…" She adopted a tone one might use for toddlers. "I'm a fully fledged grown-up, just like you, so you can rest easy, Dr. McClellan."

"Brodie," he countered with a smile.

He was warming to Kali. The more they spoke the more it seemed they might be two of a kind. Quick to smart when someone hit the right buttons. Slow to trust. A well-earned friendship if you ever got that far.

"Well, guess you're just lucky. Good genes from your parents, eh?"

She stiffened.

More sensitive territory, from the looks of things. Maybe her relationship with *her* family was as terrific as the one he had with his. One wayward brother, a meddling auntie and a godsend of a niece who'd stepped in at the reception desk when his "loyal" long-term sidekick had flown the coop. Okay…so they weren't that bad. But right now he was feeling a bit more me-against-the-world than he liked.

"So…you were working in Africa…?"

Score one to Kali for deftly changing the topic!

"Right, sorry." Brodie regrouped with a shake of his head. "Okay—long story short: I did the work through Doctors Without Borders who—as I'm sure you will appreciate—have some pretty rigorous safety systems in place for this sort of thing. I was lucky enough to be working in one of the newly built facilities. Upon my return to the UK…" he glanced at the date on his phone "…which was about five weeks ago, I went to a pre-identified debriefing under the watchful eye of Public Health England."

"PHE? I know it." Kali nodded for him to continue before noticing Ailsa coming down the corridor, her arms laden with patient files.

"Oh, Dr. O'Shea! Glad to see you in some dry clothes. If you'd just like to hang yours on the radiator in the tea room at the back there—where we came in—they should be dry in no time. I'll see about finding you a white coat as well, but folk don't stand too much on formality here. What you have on now will do just fine."

Ailsa squeezed between the pair of them on her way to her office, giving Brodie a bit of a glare as she did. He gave her a toothy grin in return. He knew he was a pain in the bum, but that was what number one nephews were for!

Ailsa Dunregan was a brilliant nurse. And a vigilant auntie. It meant more than he could say that she hadn't fled the coop like the rest of his staff. Well, the receptionist. Best not get too hysterical.

He returned his focus to Kali. All gamine and sexy looking in his castoffs. Who knew a scrubby T-shirt and joggers could look so...rip-offable?

He gave his head a quick shake. Kali was showing professionalism. Now it was his turn.

"Okay, the clinic is going to be opening soon so—in a nutshell—there's a twenty-one-day incubation period. I stayed near a PHE-approved facility and did the following: I took my temperature twice a day, called my 'fever parole officer,' did a full course of malaria prophylaxis, because malaria symptoms can mimic Ebola symptoms. Any hint of a fever and I was meant to isolate myself and call the paramedics—like that doctor in New York. Who also got the all clear, by the way," he added hastily.

"Where did you do all this?" Kali asked.

"I stayed in London so that I was near an appropriate treatment center should any of the symptoms have arisen, and I spoke regularly with hospital staff just to triple-check everything I was experiencing was normal."

She quirked an eyebrow.

"It makes you paranoid. Hemorrhagic fever ain't pretty." He checked his tone. Kali hadn't said a word of judgment. She wasn't the enemy. Just a GP doing her job. *His* job. Whatever.

He started over. "Three months in protective gear, vigilant disinfections and then nothing. I'd never realized how often people sneeze on public transport before." He tried for a nonchalant chortle and ended up coughing. *Sexy.* Not that he was trying to appeal to Kali on any level other than as a doctor or anything.

"Right." Kali took back the conversation's reins before his thoughts went in too wayward a direction. "I take it you've spoken with everyone? The islanders?" she clarified.

He swallowed. *Not in so many words...*

Kali watched Brodie's Adam's apple dip and surge, her eyes flicking up to his in time to see his gaze shift up to the right. So *that* was his tell.

She was hoping he hadn't felt her fingers shaking earlier when she had held his palm in hers. Countless self-defense courses hadn't knocked the infinitesimal tremor out of her hands. But when Brodie had thrown the Ebola grenade into her lap years of medical training and logic had dictated that she'd be fine. Instinctually she knew that she had a jacked-up instinct for survival. It had never come to that, but if she needed to fight for her life she had the skills to give it her all.

"Depends upon what you mean, exactly...by 'spoken with.'" Brodie's gaze returned to hers, his fingers dropping some air quotes into the space between them. As their eyes met—his such a clear blue—she wondered that anyone could doubt him. They were the most honest pair of eyes she had ever seen. She felt an unexpected hit of disappointment that she wouldn't be here in Dunregan longer than a few weeks.

She shook her head, reminding herself they were in the middle of a pretty important conversation.

"So, you've not held a town hall meeting or anything like that?"

Just the look on his face was enough to tell her he hadn't.

"Maybe you've had an article in the...what's the local paper?"

"The *Dunregan Chronicle*."

"I'm asking, not telling," she reminded him when his tone lurched from informational to confrontational. "Have you had anything published? An article? An interview?"

"No, I've been a bit busy burying my father, amongst other things," Brodie snapped, instantly regretting it.

Quit shooting the messenger, idiot!

He gave Kali an apologetic glance. "I thought the ever-reliable gossip circuit on the island would cover all of my bases. Which it did. Just not in the way I'd thought."

"Look. If it's all right, I'm going to stop you there," Kali jumped in apologetically. "I'm really sorry to hear about your father. Now—not that the nuts and bolts of how this island works aren't interesting—I really need to get a handle on how things work right here." Kali flicked her thumb toward the front of the clinic. "If you're happy to meet me after the clinic's shut I'd love to hear all about it. Your work in Africa," she qualified quickly. "It sounds fascinating."

"It was an unbelievable experience. I'll never forget it."

Wow! The first person who'd actually seemed interested!

"So..." She gave her shoulders a wriggle, as if to regroup.

A wriggle inside *his* shirt, with more than a hint of shoulder slipping in and then out of the stretched neckline. A tug of attraction sent his thoughts careening off to a whole other part of his—er—brain? Another time, another place?

Focus, man! The poor woman's trying to speak with you.

"If I was in your shoes I wouldn't want me here either. It's *your* practice! But I'm here to help, not hinder."

He nodded. Wise beyond her years. Those green eyes of her held untold stories. He'd been wrong to think otherwise.

"Can we shake on it?" She thrust her hand forward, chin jutted upwards. Not in defiance, more in anticipation of a problem.

He put his hand forward—the one he hadn't burned—for a sound one-two shake.

"Are we good?"

"Yes, ma'am?" He affected an American accent and gave her a jaunty salute.

Her eyes narrowed a bit.

Okay, fine. He blew that one.

"We're good. I'll steer clear of tea duty."

She furrowed her brow at him in response.

Quit being such a jerk. Like she said, she's here to help!

She shifted past him in the corridor, leaving the slightest hint of jasmine in her wake. "I should probably go introduce myself up front."

"Yes—yeah. On you go. Caitlyn's my niece and is about as much of a newcomer to the clinic as you are."

"Excellent." Kali gave him a polite smile. "She and I can forge into unknown territory together, then. And don't worry about the tea. I'm more of a coffee girl."

Her tone was bright, non-confrontational.

"We've not given you much of a welcome, have we?"

Kali rocked back on her heels with a squelch, not looking entirely sure how to respond until she saw the edges of Brodie's lips tweak up into a slow but generous grin.

"Ailsa's great!" Kali shot back with her own cheeky grin. Adding, "I've yet to make a decision on the boss man…"

"He's a real piece of work." Brodie was laughing now. "But he's good at his job."

"I don't doubt that for a minute."

And he could see she meant it. He *was* a good doctor. A little shy on bedside manner, but—

"Oh, and as for that hand of yours—you probably don't

need a bandage, but it might be a good idea to put some topical sulfonamide antibacterial cream on there. Although, as you probably know, some new studies suggest it might actually lengthen the healing time."

Brodie gave a grin as Kali shrugged off her own advice before tacking on, "I'm sure you know what's best, Old Timer…" as she pushed through the swinging door into the front of the clinic.

Kali gave as good as she got. Just as well, given his zigzagging moods.

Brodie put his hand to the door to talk Caitlyn and Kali through their intro but stopped at his aunt's less than subtle clearing of her throat.

"And what can I help you with on this fine day, my dear Auntie?"

"You're not thinking of going in there and looming over Caitlyn, are you?"

"No."

Yes.

"Give the girl a chance. She's only just out of school and she doesn't need her uncle hovering over her every step of the way."

"What? Do you think I might accidentally breathe too much in the reception area and frighten away even more patients?"

"Brodie McClellan." Ailsa wagged a finger at him. "You'd best think twice about pushing so hard against the support system you have. Caitlyn's here until she starts university in September—but after that… Only a few months for you to make your peace with everyone. Including…" she steeled her gaze at him "…Dr. O'Shea. She's here to *help*, might I remind you?"

"Help for something that's not actually a problem?"

"You know what I mean, Brodie. C'mon." She gave his shoulder a consoling rub. "You can't blame folk for being nervous. And besides, you're only fresh back. It'll give you time to settle back in. Mend a couple of fences while you're at it."

She gave him her oft-used Auntie Knows Best stare.

He could do as she suggested. Of course he could. Or he could go back home and pack his bag and head back on another Doctors Without Borders assignment until Kali was gone.

A hit of protectiveness for his father's surgery took hold. Unexpected.

Or was it curiosity about Kali?

Interesting.

He leaned against the wall and gave his aunt his best I'll-give-it-a-try face.

"So, after all the miraculous recoveries of the bumper-to-bumper patients we normally have over the past couple of weeks, do you think they'll come flooding back now that we have Kali here?"

"Most likely."

His aunt had never been one to mince words.

"So what am *I* meant to do? Just twiddle my thumbs whilst Kali sees to folk?"

"I suspect she'll need some help. You would be showing her the *good* side of yourself if you were to talk her through a patient's history. Give her backup support if she needed it. Prove to her you're the lovable thirty-two-year-old I've had the pleasure of knowing all my life instead of that fusty old curmudgeon you showed her this morning. I'll tell you, Brodie—I didn't much like seeing that side of you. It's not very fetching."

"Fine." He pressed back from the wall with a foot. "Maybe it'd be best if I just leave well enough alone. Let you two run the show and I'll—I don't know—I'll build that boat I always had a mind to craft."

The words were out before he could stem them.

"You mean the one your father always wanted to build with you?" Ailsa nodded at the memory, completely unfazed by his burst of temper. "That's one promise you could make good on. Or you could put all of that energy you've got winging around inside of you helping out the new doctor who's come all the way up here to get you out of a right sorry old pickle. Then make good on the *other* promise you made to your father."

They both knew what she meant.

"I'm here, aren't I?"

"That's not what I meant, nor your father and you know it, Broderick Andrew McClellan."

Brodie had to hand it to her. Whipping out all three of his names—that was fighting talk for Ailsa.

She pursed her lips at him for added measure, clearly refusing to rise—or lower herself—to his level of self-pity. And frankly he was bored with it himself. He'd never been one for sulky self-indulgence. Or standing around idly doing nothing.

He had twiddling his thumbs down to a fine art now. Not to mention a wind farm's worth of energy to burn. He gave the wall a good thump with the sole of his boot.

Ailsa turned away, tsking as she went back into her office to prepare for the day. Which would most likely be busy now that Kali was here.

"It's not like I was away having the time of my life or anything!" he called after her.

She stuck her head out into the corridor again, but said nothing.

"People were dying in droves!"

"Yes, you were an incredibly compassionate, brave man to go and do what you did—and it's a shame folk here haven't quite caught up with that. But with you looking like you've got the weight of the world on your shoulders it's little wonder you've become so unapproachable."

"Unapproachable! *Me?*" He all but bellowed it, just as Kali walked into the hallway—only to do an immediate about-face back into the reception area.

Ailsa gave him an I-told-you-so look. Brodie took a deep breath in to launch into a well-rehearsed list of the things wrong with Dunregan and her residents, and just as quickly felt the puff go out of him. It would take an hour to rattle off the list of things wrong with *himself* this morning, let alone address the big picture.

For starters he'd been rude to Kali. Unprofessional. Then had thrown a blinkin' tantrum over a burn that had happened solely because he'd been slamming around a kettle of boiling water in a huff because he had to tell yet *another* person why he was toxic.

The word roiled round his gut.

He wasn't *toxic*! He was fit as a fiddle set to play for an all-hours fiddle fest! But he knew more than most it ran deeper than that. How to shrug off the mantle of the tortured laddie who'd sailed out on a handmade skiff with his mum, only to be washed ashore two hours later when the weather had turned horribly, horribly fierce?

He knew it was a miracle he'd survived. But he would've swapped miracles any day of the week if only his mother could have been spared.

"You know, Ailsa…"

His aunt gave him a semi-hopeful look when she heard the change in his tone.

"A second pair of hands round this place would be helpful longer term, wouldn't it? Female hands. You're wonderful—obviously—but Dad always spoke of having a female GP around. Someone not from Dunregan to give the islanders a bit more choice when they need to talk about sensitive issues."

As he spoke the idea set off a series of fireworks in his brain. New possibilities. With Kali on board as a full-time GP he wouldn't have to kill himself with office hours, out-of-hours emergency calls, home visits and the mountain rescues that cropped up more often than not during the summer season.

Not that he minded the work. Hell, he'd work every hour of the day if he could. But working here was much more than ferrying patients in and out for their allotted ten minutes. And if he was going to make good on his deathbed promise to his father to work in the surgery for at least a year he wasn't so sure doing it alone would get the intended results...

His grandfather and his father had prided themselves on being genuine, good-as-their-word *family* doctors. Their time and patience had gone beyond patching up wounds, scribbling out prescriptions and seeing to annual checkups. Here on Dunregan it was personal. Everything was. It was why his father's premature death from cancer had knocked the wind out of the whole population. Everyone knew everyone else and everything about them.

Sharing the load with Kali might be the way he'd get through the year emotionally intact. Maybe even restore some of his tattered reputation. Everyone who'd ever met his father thought the world of him. John McClellan: treasured island GP.

The same could not be said of himself.

Ailsa eyed him warily. "You're not just saying this to get out of the promise to your father, are you?"

"No." He struggled to keep the emotion out of his voice. A bedside promise to a dying father... It didn't get more Shakespearean than that.

"Well, my dear nephew, if you're wanting Dr. O'Shea to stick around you best check she's not already legged it out the front of the clinic. You need to show her the other side of Brodie McClellan. The one we all like."

She gave his cheek a good pinch. Half loving, half scolding.

He laughed and pulled her into her arms for a hug.

"What would I do without you and your wise old ways, Auntie Ailsa? I've been a right old pill this morning, haven't I?"

"I'm hardly old, and there are quite a few ways I could describe your behavior, Brodie—but your way is the most polite." Ailsa's muffled voice came from his chest. "Now…" She pushed back and looked him square in the eye. "Let me get on with my day, will you?"

As she disappeared into her office so, too, did the smile playing across his lips. Here he was, blaming the islanders for the situation he was in, when truthfully all his frustration came from the fact that he loved his father and his work and right now the two were at odds. Not one part of him was looking forward to the year ahead.

Truthfully? He needed Kali O'Shea more than he cared to admit. If he could convince her to stay she might be the answer to all his prayers. A comrade in arms to help him get through the thicket of weeds he was all but drowning in.

He jogged his shoulders up and down.

Right. Good.

Time for what his father had called a "Starty-Overy, I've Done A Whoopsy." His behavior this morning had been childish. He might as well give it the childish name. Then start acting his age and focus on winning over the mysteriously enigmatic Dr. Kali O'Shea.

Kali tapped at her computer keyboard a second time. Then pressed Refresh. And again.

Weird.

There didn't seem to be anyone next in the queue. She stuck her head round the corner into the office where Brodie had been lurking… Okay, not exactly lurking. He'd been "on hand" in case she needed any information. But it had felt like lurking.

"Hey, does the computer system get jammed sometimes?"

"All the time is more like it," he answered with a smile.

Her stomach grumbled. Kali's hand flew to cover it, as if it would erase the fact it had happened.

"Er…"

"Hungry after only seeing three patients?" Brodie teased.

"Something like that. I was too excited for my first day at work to eat breakfast."

"Only fifteen more patients to go before lunch!"

"Or…" She drew out the word and thought she might as well push her luck. "I do seem to recall an offer of a cup of tea and a biscuit."

He blinked, dragging a tooth across one of those full lips of his. Distracting. *Very* distracting.

"Would you like it if I put on a pinny and pushed a wee cart along to your office for delivery, Dr. O'Shea?"

A flush of embarrassment crept up her cheeks. He was an experienced doctor. Her superior. Had she pushed that envelope too far?

"Ach, take that nervous expression off your face, Dr. O'Shea. I'm just joshing you." He stood up from his desk and gave her shoulder a squeeze. "A nice cup of tea is the least I can do an hour after I promised it."

He dropped her a wink and her tummy did a flip. The sexy kind.

Oh, no. Not good. Not good at all.

"Right, well… I guess I better check with Caitlyn who's next." She gave the door frame a rap, as if that was the signal for action. Then didn't move.

"Anything good this morning?"

"Depends upon your definition of 'good,'" she replied with a smile. She liked this guy. He was a whole load nicer than Dr. McCrabby from this morning. "A prenatal check, a suspected case of the flu—which thankfully wasn't more than a really bad cold—and a check on a set of stitches along a feisty four-year-old's hairline. Rosie Bell, I think her name was."

"That's her mother. The daughter is Julia."

"Right—that's right. I mean, of *course* you know it's right—you know everyone." She stopped herself. She was blathering. "The stitches were just fine. She had them put in on the mainland, at the hospital, there…so…that was a quickie. Everyone has been incredibly welcoming…"

So much for no more blathering.

A shadow darkened Brodie's eyes for a moment. He abruptly slipped through the doorway and headed down the hall. "Best go get my pinny on and leave you to it, then, Dr. O'Shea."

"Thank you," she said to his retreating back, wishing the ground had swallowed her up before she'd opened her big mouth.

But it was the truth. Everyone *had* been really welcoming and it felt amazing! Never in her adult life had she been part of a community, and this place seemed to just…*speak* to her.

Her tummy grumbled again.

Dinner.

She would ask Brodie to join her for dinner and then maybe she would stop saying the wrong thing all the time. Fingers crossed and all that.

"Who's next, please, Caitlyn?" Kali stuck her head into the receptionist's room, willing herself onto solid terrain. Seeing patients was the one thing in the world that grounded her. Gave her the drive to find some place where she could settle down and play a positive role in her patients' lives.

"Sorry, Dr. O'Shea… I've been trying to send it through on your computer screen. I've not yet got the hang of the system with all of these patients showing up like this."

Kali peeked beyond Caitlyn and out into the busy waiting room.

"It's not normally like this?"

"Well…" Caitlyn used her feet to wheel herself and her chair over to Kali, lowering her voice to a confidential tone. "Since I started last week it's all been mostly people here to see Auntie Ail—I mean, Sister Dunregan. But most of the people who canceled appointments when Unc—Dr.

McClellan came back seem to have all magically turned up now they've heard you arrived…"

"I only got in last night."

"Aye, but you were on the public ferry, weren't you?"

Kali nodded. It was the only way onto the island unless you owned a private helicopter. Which she most assuredly did not.

"Word travels fast round here."

Kali laughed appreciatively as the outside door opened and another person tried to wedge her way onto the long window seat bench after giving Caitlyn a little wave in lieu of checking in.

"Hello, Mrs. Brown. We'll see what we can do, all right? You might have a wee wait," Caitlyn called.

"That's fine, dear. I've brought my knitting."

"So people are just coming along and trying their luck?" Kali's eyes widened.

"Something like that." Caitlyn nodded. "No harm in trying, is there? Hey!" Her eyes lit up with a new idea. "I bet you'll get in the paper!"

Kali felt a chill jag along her spine and forced herself to smile. "Well, I doubt me being here is *that* big a deal."

"On *this* island? You'd be surprised what turns up in the paper. There was a notice put in when my hamster Reggie died."

She pulled her chair back up to the window that faced the reception area and started tapping at the computer keyboard to pull up the next patient's information.

Kali crossed her fingers behind her back, hoping that her arrival on Dunregan didn't warrant more attention than a full waiting room. *That* she could deal with. Public notice? No. That would never do. So much for unpacking her bags and staying awhile.

"Oh! Dr. O'Shea—I'm such an airhead. Sorry. Would you

mind seeing Mr. Alexander Logan first? He's just come in and says it's an emergency. He didn't look all that well…"

"Absolutely." Kali nodded.

Medicine. And keeping her head down. Those were her two points of focus. Time to get on with medicine.

CHAPTER THREE

"ALEXANDER LOGAN?" Kali swung open the door leading into the waiting room.

"Aye, that's me." A gentleman with a thick shock of gray hair tried to press himself up from the bench seat, flat cap in one hand, cane in the other. "And you are…?"

"Dr. O'Shea. I'm the new—the locum doctor."

"With a name like O'Shea and those green eyes of yours I'm guessing you must be Irish." He grinned at her, eyes shining.

Kali hoped he didn't see the wince of pain his question had elicited. He wasn't to know that her mother—her *ballast*—with her distant Irish connection was the only reason she was alive.

"My wife was Irish. Feisty."

Just like her mother.

"She sounds like a great woman," she replied with a smile, grateful to dodge the question about herself. "You all right there, Mr. Logan? Would you like a hand standing up?"

"Oh, no—well, a bit." He looked up at her with a widening smile. "Yes, those eyes of yours remind me of Tilly, all right."

Kali hooked her arm through his, relieved to feel him put a bit of his body weight on her arm. "Shall we try and work our way to the exam room?"

"Oh, sure. Not as quick on my—" He lifted his hand to

his mouth, as if he were waiting for a sneeze to arrive. When the sneeze came, he stumbled forward, losing his grip on his cane as he fell, then let out a howl of pain.

Half the people in the waiting room lurched forward to lend a hand as Kali tightened her grip on his elbow and shifted an arm round his waist.

She heard the swinging door open behind her.

"Sandy?" It was Brodie.

"I'm all right...just me hip."

He was clearly the opposite of all right, but as Brodie stepped forward to help support Mr. Logan Kali could feel the older man press closer to her.

"No, no..." Mr. Logan gave a little wave of his hand. "It's all right, Brodie. I've got Dr. O'Shea here, seeing to me."

Kali was surprised to see fear in the man's eyes. No one in that waiting room looked healthier than Brodie McClellan. The man was a veritable poster boy for the ruggedly fit.

"I was just—" Brodie began, then gave up. "Caitlyn, can you call Ailsa and have her help Mr. Logan into the exam room? I'm guessing your hip is giving you gyp again, Sandy?"

"Aye, well..."

That was all the older man would allow. Kali couldn't figure out if that was a standard Scottish response or if he was trying to breathe less now that Brodie was in the room. Out of the corner of her eye she saw one of the other patients bring a tissue to her lips. The sea of helping hands had been withdrawn entirely.

She was surprised to realize she was feeling indignant. On Brodie's behalf. She'd known within minutes of meeting him that he wouldn't compromise someone's health...well, maybe in *quite a few* minutes... Even so, the man meant no harm. Quite the opposite, in fact.

"If you two have a history, I'm happy for you to see Dr. McClellan, if you prefer," Kali offered. Might as well try to build bridges out here in the public eye.

"Oh, no dear." Mr. Logan put more of his weight on Kali. "You understand, Brodie—don't you? I wouldn't want to seem rude to Dr. O'Shea, when she's gone to all this trouble to come up here to Dunregan." His eyes flicked between the two doctors. "Would I, Dr. McClellan?"

It was an apology. Not a question.

"Of course not, Mr. Logan." Brodie dropped the informal abbreviation he'd used earlier and grabbed a couple of antiseptic wipes from the counter before bending over to pick up the man's cane. He gave it a visible scrub along the arch as he did.

Kali's eyes flicked to Ailsa as she entered the room, watching her assess the situation before taking the cane from Brodie with a bright smile. He disappeared into the back of the clinic before Kali could catch his eye. Get a reading on how much the incident had hurt. She would've felt it if it had happened to her, and she didn't even know these people.

"Oh, dearie me, Mr. Logan," chirped Ailsa. "It looks like your new hip isn't quite playing ball, is it?"

"It's been fine, but Bess and I were walking along Ben Regan—"

"Away up on the cliffs?"

"Aye, well… Going up was all right, but the going down part… Well, it's just not felt quite right since then."

"Are you up to the journey down the corridor, Sandy? Any sciatic pain before you went on your walk?"

"No, no. I did that flexing test thing Brodie showed me the last time." He shot a guilty look at the space Brodie had vacated.

"Did you feel the hip come out of the socket?" Kali asked.

"Just now? Aye, that I did."

Ailsa shot Kali a look which she interpreted as, *Are you up to doing a hip relocation?* Kali nodded, her lips pressed grimly together. Mr. Logan wasn't exactly light.

"With the two of you lassies helping me, I should be fine

to get to the room." Mr. Logan gave them each a grateful smile.

Not two or three steps into the corridor he sneezed again and all but crumpled to the floor.

"Well, all right, then, Mr. Logan." Kali nodded at Ailsa as she spoke. "I guess we'll get to it right here, if that's okay."

"Anything…" he huffed out. "Anything to stop the pain."

Kali straightened both of the gentleman's legs out onto the corridor floor—one was visibly shorter than the other—taking a glimpse up to his face as the left knee refused to unbend. The color was fading from Mr. Logan's cheeks and his breath was coming in short, sharp pants.

"Mr. Logan? It looks like you've got a posterior dislocation here. I'm just going to take your leg—"

"Do whatever you need to do quickly, lassie!" Mr. Logan panted.

"Ailsa—Mrs. Dunregan—Nurse—" Kali stumbled over the words—she still wasn't up to name etiquette in this place where everyone knew everyone. "Would you mind holding Mr.—Sandy's head steady?"

"I'd probably be best holding down his pelvic bones for you when you do the reduction," Ailsa corrected gently. "Mr. Logan and I aren't going anywhere. You go on and get whatever medication you need."

"Right." She shot a look over her shoulder, as if some medication would magically appear, then whispered, "I've only ever done this procedure with a patient under general anesthetic in surgery."

"But you've done it?" Ailsa's voice was low.

"Yes, but…"

"We don't have a hospital on Dunregan, dear. Mr. Logan's had a hip replacement, so he's got an artificial ball joint. You'll need to perform a reduction of the dislocated hip prosthesis, okay? Sooner rather than later. You'll be fine," she added with a reassuring smile.

Kali rose and jogged to the exam room she'd been using to find Brodie, hands sheathed in protective gloves, filling a syringe with something.

"Morphine." Brodie pinched the syringe between two fingers, handing it to her with the needle still capped. "And you will probably also want to give him this."

"Which is...?" Kali hoped the panic she was feeling wasn't as obvious as it felt.

"Midazolam. For sedation." He handed her the syringe with a gloved hand. "Are you sure you're good with this?"

"Yes, of course," she answered—too swiftly.

"So you've done a hip relocation in these circumstances?"

Not in the strictest sense of the words.

She looked up at Brodie's face. Was he doubting her or offering reassurance? There was kindness in his eyes. He gave her a *go on* nod.

"I've got it. I'm good." She gave a firm nod in return, convincing herself as much as Brodie. This was just another one of those moments when life wasn't giving her much of a choice. Her patient had specifically requested her as his doctor, and it seemed Brodie was in her corner.

"Any special tips for Mr. Logan's hip?" She hoped the question wasn't a giveaway that her brain was short-circuiting.

"Nope."

Brodie turned back to the sink to peel off his gloves and wash his hands. Or to ignore her.

Both?

So much for being in her corner! She stared at his back, tempted, just for a moment, to stick out her tongue at him. She wasn't *that* long out of med school and, whilst she *had* done a reduction before, she certainly hadn't done one under these circumstances.

Well, tough. That was what she had and she would just have to cope.

"Are you going to do the reduction or do you need help?"

Brodie didn't turn around, his question rising only slightly above the sound of running water. It was difficult to tell if his tone was kind or frustrated.

"It's not as if there's anyone else we can ring, is there?" Kali asked rhetorically, instantly wishing she hadn't when his shoulders stiffened.

Open mouth…insert foot. The poor man's father wasn't long gone and he was having just about the worst period of mourning a son could go through. He had her compassion.

"I'm good. I've got it." She spoke to his back again, shook herself into action and took a careful look at each of the syringes she held. Brodie had labeled them.

A tray appeared in her eyeline, preset with alcohol prep pads, tape and a blunt-end needle already attached to a high-flow extension tube with a four-way stopcock. Her eyes flicked up and she gave Brodie a grateful smile. His neutral expression gave nothing away—but his actions were clear. The man was meticulous. And his patient's welfare was paramount. Otherwise he wouldn't be here—hovering, checking she was up to snuff. Which she'd better get busy proving she was.

"Thanks for doing the syringes. And the tray. Everything."

She didn't catch his mumbled reply as she picked up her pace to get back to her patient.

"You'll need these as well."

Kali turned as Brodie reappeared in the corridor with a box of gloves, a roll of hygiene paper and a paper blanket.

Ailsa took them from him, then asked Brodie to let Caitlyn know what was happening so she would stop sending people through for a moment.

Kali tugged on a pair of gloves, taking the time to focus.

Mr. Logan's breaths were deeply labored and his face was contorted with pain.

"All right, Mr. Logan, we're going to have to give you a couple of injections—"

"Just get on with it, already," he gasped. "I can't bear it much longer and Bess is in the car."

"Your dog will be just fine, Mr. Logan. We can always get Caitlyn to check on her." Ailsa took charge again. "Just lay still for a moment, Sandy, so we can get some of this painkiller into you. You've not got any allergies, have you?"

"What? No, no. I'm fine."

Ailsa took an antiseptic swab off the tray Brodie had prepared and rubbed it along Mr. Logan's left arm. Deftly she inserted the needle, holding the extension tubing out for Kali to put the syringe on. They watched as the morphine left the tubing and went to work, combatting Mr. Logan's acute pain. Kali carefully injected both the morphine and the midazolam, trying to think of something to chat with him about to monitor the effects of the painkiller.

"And how is Bess these days, Sandy?" asked Ailsa, coming to her rescue.

"She's getting on, like me." Sandy chuckled, a slight wince creasing his forehead as he did so.

"And are you still spoiling her rotten?"

"I don't know what you're talking about," he replied with a soft smile. "No point in going daft over a dog, is there?"

"Course not, Sandy. Even such a loyal one like Bess." Ailsa slipped her fingers to Sandy's wrist before whispering across to Kali, "There's a monitor in the exam room there—the one Brodie's in. Would you mind—?"

"Absolutely. No problem." Kali glanced at her watch as she rose. She could tell by the gentle slurring in Sandy's voice that the painkiller was kicking in…they would just need to wait a few more moments.

Brodie met her at the doorway, portable monitor in freshly gloved hands.

"You're not just standing there earwigging, are you?" Kali quipped.

"Hardly." Brodie's brows tucked closer together, his eyes lighting with a flash of barely contained anger.

Frustration. That was all it was. She'd feel the same.

Kali took the monitor with a smile of thanks.

After Mr. Logan's voice had become incredibly sleepy in response to her questions about how he was feeling, followed by a soft snore, she felt confident to go ahead with the maneuver.

"We're going to have to take your trousers off, Mr. Logan."

Another snore and a soft grunt was her response.

"I think you're all right to proceed, dear." Ailsa smiled.

One look at his face was proof that Sandy Logan didn't care if they dressed him up to look like the Easter bunny as long as his hip was fixed in the process. He wore a goofy grin and was definitely seeing the brighter side of life as the painkillers did their work.

Kali straddled Mr. Logan and raised his hips as Ailsa swiftly tugged off his trousers, offering soothing words of consolation as she did so. Mr. Logan's smile remained intact, his eyes firmly shut.

"Posterior or anterior?" Ailsa asked Kali.

Just one look at the inward pointing knee and foot indicated posterior. For good measure Kali examined the hip, trying to keep her touch as light as possible. The ball joint was very obviously protruding to the rear.

"Posterior." Her years of training took over. "The lower limb will need to be flexed, adducted and internally rotated."

"That's right," Ailsa said, as if her memory had needed jogging as well. If she hadn't been such a great nurse, Kali would've recommended she take up a career in acting.

Kali bent Sandy's knee, tucked her arm in the crook and, with a nod of her head, indicated that Ailsa should begin applying pressure to the hip as she pressed her heels into the floor and, with a fluid tug and a moan from the semiconscious Mr. Logan, the hip shifted back into place.

Her eyes met Ailsa's and they both laughed with delight.

"I did it!"

"Well done, Dr. O'Shea."

"Nice work."

Kali started at the sound of Brodie's voice. He'd been watching?

"Well…" She shrugged off the compliment. Being in the spotlight had always made her feel uncomfortable.

"Shall we get him onto a backboard and let him have a rest in one of the overnight rooms?" Ailsa asked—the question aimed more at Brodie than Kali.

"Good idea. I'll go get the gear."

"You've got overnight rooms?"

Not a nine-to-five surgery, then. Good. The more all-consuming things were here, the less time she'd have to think about the past. The family she'd left behind. The arranged marriage she'd narrowly avoided.

"A couple." Ailsa nodded. "They're always a good idea, with the weather up here changing at the drop of a hat and…" she nodded at their patient "…for situations like this."

"Thank you."

"For what?" Ailsa looked up at her in surprise.

"You know—for all the help with this. It's all a bit…" As she sought the right word Brodie came back into the corridor with a backboard.

Ailsa gave Kali's arm a squeeze before clearing away the tray of medical supplies, detaching the monitor pads and making room for Brodie to slip the backboard under Mr. Logan at Kali's count.

"Right…" Brodie looked down at the soft smile on Mr. Logan's face. "Glad to see another happy patient. Shall we get him moved before he wakes up and sees I've had anything to do with this?"

"Thank you." Kali looked straight into his eyes. She needed him to know she meant it. "For everything."

"Not a problem. Lift on three?"

He counted at her nod and as they walked Mr. Logan down the corridor she heard Brodie softly laugh to himself.

"What's so funny?"

"I forgot to make your tea."

Three o'clock in the afternoon and still not one patient. Plenty for Kali—but not one had come to see him.

Brodie was about as close to tearing his hair out as he'd ever been. He'd finally managed to remember to make cups of tea, only to find Caitlyn had just done a round for everyone. Terrific. He couldn't even get that right!

Brodie was beginning to get a good understanding of how innocent people on the run must feel.

Criminal.

Here he was, healthy as a professional athlete—he knew that because the doctor monitoring him had expressed envy at his level of fitness—and all for what? To lurk around his own surgery in the desperate hope of picking up a few medical crumbs?

At least Kali was getting a good feel for how the surgery worked. She had a smile on her face every time he saw her. Which would be good if he wasn't so desperate for something to do! There was only so much surfing the internet a man could do. He hardly thought this was what his father had meant when he'd made his final request: *Just one year, son. Just give it one year.*

If—and this was a big if—people were just giving him grieving time, didn't they know he'd be far better off grieving by making good on his promise to his father to run the surgery for a year?

Or maybe... No. *Would* he? Would his father have told folk to do this? Give him wide berth?

No. He shook his head resolutely. His father had always championed him. There were few things he was certain of, but his father's undivided loyalty was one of them.

A message pinged through on his office computer. He looked at the screen hopefully, despite his best efforts to remain neutral.

Mr. Donaldson—urgent.

A patient?

It was almost silly how happy he felt. A *patient*! He was out of his chair and on his way to Reception before Mr. Donaldson—a long-time patient of both himself and his father—had a chance to change his mind.

When he opened the door his heart sank.

"Dad, are you absolutely sure?" Mr. Donaldson's daughter, Anne, had her back to Brodie and hadn't seen him come in.

"Of course I'm sure. He's my doctor," Mr. Donaldson insisted.

"But…" Anne looked across at Caitlyn—presumably to get some backup—only to find the receptionist was busy on the phone.

Shame, thought Brodie. He would've been curious to see how she reacted to this. He checked himself. The fact Caitlyn had taken the job showed her support. Never mind that she was family and could do with the money. She didn't let fear override her common sense. Or, he conceded, her nan's say-so.

"Now, Mr. Donaldson. What can I do for you today?"

Anne all but recoiled at the sound of his voice, her arm moving swiftly up to cover her mouth.

"You're all right, Anne." Brodie forced himself to stay calm. "I've been cleared. I'm not contagious."

"Oh, I know, Brodie—Dr. McClellan. It's just—" She stopped speaking, her eyes widening in horror—or embarrassment. She widened the gap between the fingers covering her mouth. "It's just that poor nurse who went where you did in Africa is back in hospital…"

Ah…he'd seen the headlines on the internet. Must've hit the broadsheets as well. That explained the hands and arms covering people's mouths. Fresh media scares about recurrences and isolation units and that poor, poor woman. Her courage and generosity was going heavily unrewarded.

"I saw that." Brodie shook his head. "And I was very sorry to hear it. But I can absolutely assure you that is not the case with me."

"Brodie, I would get up to greet you, but…" the elderly gentlemen interjected, pointing at his foot.

Brodie's eyes widened at the sight. A blood-soaked rag was wrapped around the middle of his foot.

"Is that just a wool sock you're wearing there, Mr. Donaldson?"

"Sure is. My foot would've had a boot on as well, but my daughter, here, said you were likely to cut it off and I wasn't going to let that happen. I only just bought them five years ago. Still got miles to go in them yet."

"Dad!" Anne jumped in, forgetting to shield her mouth. "The boot's got a gaping great hole in it now your turf spade's gone through it. It couldn't have done your foot one bit of good to be yanked out of your boot after you pulled the spade out of it."

"You put a turf spade through your boot and into your foot?"

Brodie couldn't help but be impressed. Wielding a spade with that sort of strength would have taken tremendous power. Then again, at eighty-five years of age Mr. Donaldson showed few signs of succumbing to the frailty of the elderly. *Vital* was just about the best description Brodie could conjure.

"Aye, that I did, son—no need to broadcast it round the village."

"I'd take it as a compliment, Mr. Donaldson. Let's get you into my exam room, shall we?" He moved to help him up just as Kali entered the waiting room with a patient's chart.

"Are you coming, Anne?" Mr. Donaldson turned to see if his daughter was behind them.

Brodie saw Kali catch the look of horror on Anne's face at the suggestion.

"Can I help?" Kali stepped forward without waiting for an answer, offering another arm for Mr. Donaldson to lean on. Brodie gave her a grateful smile.

This was tough. He'd had a few other doctors warning him something like this might happen, but he'd just blown it off. Dunregan was his *home*! He hadn't expected a victory parade—but having people frightened of being treated by him…? It seared deeper than he'd ever have anticipated.

"Thank you, dear." Mr. Donaldson's fingers wrapped round Kali's forearm. "I'm sure you're busy, but you wouldn't mind, would you?" He raised his voice as they were leaving the waiting room. "Explaining to my daughter that John McClellan's son is *not* going to give me or anyone else who sets foot on Dunregan the plague."

Brodie's eyebrows shot up. An unlikely champion! He had known Mr. Donaldson his whole life, but they certainly weren't close. Then again…he didn't know how many hours of chess had passed between Mr. Donaldson and his father down at the Eagle and Ram. Thousands. Most likely more.

"I'd be delighted to," Kali replied. "Public health is one of my areas of interest."

"As well it should be." Mr. Donaldson nodded approvingly. "Now, you do know, dear," Mr. Donaldson continued, putting his paper-skinned hand atop hers as they inched their way along the corridor, "that Brodie, here, is one of the island's most eligible bachelors?"

"Well, that *is* news!" Kali's eyebrows shot up and…was that a fake smile or real one?

"Yes, it's absolutely true. Isn't that so, Brodie? Most of the suitable girls have already been married off, and we know he will need someone who's a bit of a brainbox to keep him interested. So…"

He didn't wait for an answer. Brodie was too gobsmacked to intervene. Since when had Mr. Donaldson been made the Matchmaker of Dunregan?

"You cannae go far wrong if you marry a Scot, Dr. O'Shea. They're loyal, truehearted...and, of course, if you're into strapping laddies our Brodie here looks very nice when he's all kitted out in his kilt."

"I—I will take you at your word on that," Kali replied, her expression making it very clear she wasn't interested.

"Mr. Donaldson—" Brodie was goldfishing, trying to search for the best way to cut this conversation short. His romantic escapades—and that was about as far as he'd ever taken any of his relationships—were things he'd always kept very close to his chest. Talking about it so openly made him feel about twelve!

"Brodie, why don't you invite Dr. O'Shea, here, along to one of our Polar Bear outings? They're great fun and a wonderful way to really get to know one another. I've seen more than a few Polar Bear weddings!" He hooted at the memory, then chided Brodie, "And it's been some time since we've seen you down at the beach."

Something in the neighborhood of ten years!

"We should just be taking a left here, Mr. Donaldson." Brodie tried to steer his patient and the conversation firmly off the topic of marriage. He had more than enough on his plate without worrying about getting a fiancée as well.

Not that Kali would be a bad choice, but—

His eyes caught hers. Her expression gave little away. If not the slightest hint of *Uh-uh...you can keep your Scottish yenta.*

"So, Dr. O'Shea," Mr. Donaldson continued, clearly enjoying himself, "you'll do me the favor, please, of going back out there and informing my daughter and the rest of that mob that I've not set to with a fever or anything, won't you?"

"I'll do my best, Mr.—"

"Donaldson. And my daughter is Anne. Now, which way am I going, son?"

"To the left, Mr. Donaldson," Brodie repeated with a shake of his head and a smile. Life on a small island, eh?

Kali looked perfectly bemused, and who could blame her? Not on the island twenty-four hours and already she was being set up by the locals. He sniggered, thinking of how animals always tried to widen the gene pool when their numbers dwindled. Maybe Mr. Donaldson was trying to increase the population of Dunregan. *Ha!*

Kali shot him a look. Whoops. Had that been an outside laugh?

"Later…" he stage-whispered. "I will explain everything later."

If she was going to carry the lance for him regarding the Ebola virus he owed her. As for the whole eligible bachelor thing… Well… At least Mr. Donaldson didn't think he was going to catch the plague.

"Where do you want me?"

"Just over here, Mr. Donaldson. Kali, would you mind helping me get our most loyal and truehearted patient up onto the examination table?"

"Oh, son. Don't go about trying to set *me* up with this young lassie because I've embarrassed you. That's what old people *do*. It's our specialty. My courting days are over. Mrs. Donaldson was more than enough woman for me," Mr. Donaldson scolded as he eased himself up onto the table. "Let's look at this foot, if you don't mind. What a silly old codger! I was away with the faeries when I was cutting the peat and there was a two-hour wait to see Dr. O'Shea. All this silliness going on over you and the Ebola nonsense…" He shook his head at the madness of it all. "As if someone could contract Ebola on an island this cold!"

He looked at the pair of them for agreement that his hypothesis was a good one.

"Well, it doesn't really work like that…" Brodie began reluctantly.

"Ach, away! I know perfectly well how it works, Brodie McClellan. I was trying to make a joke. Your face is more somber than most folk look at a funeral! Yours, too, dear."

He gave a little cackle and patted Kali's hand as she helped him shift his legs up onto the examination table.

"You go on out there, dear, and please explain—very loudly—to my daughter that no one is catching Ebola on this island if Dr. McClellan says so. John McClellan's son would do no such thing."

Brodie looked away, surprised at the hard sting of emotion hitting him.

Even after he'd passed his father was still looking after him.

He cleared his throat and refocused his attention when he felt Kali shift her gaze from Mr. Donaldson's twinkling eyes up to him. There was something almost anxious in her expression. Something he couldn't put his finger on. And just as quickly it was gone, replaced by a warm, generous smile.

"It would be my very distinct pleasure to answer any of your daughter's questions, Mr. Donaldson."

"Thank you very much. All right, then, dear. Leave us men folk to inspect my idiocy. I'd like to get it bandaged up so I can get the rest of the peat in without the whole of Dunregan knowing I rent my foot in half."

Kali left the room, throwing a final smile over her shoulder at the pair of them. A smile that awoke an entirely new set of sensations in Brodie. He'd done little to nothing to deserve the understanding she'd shown him today.

"Aye, she's a right fine lassie. Isn't she, Dr. McClellan?"

"What?" Brodie turned his attention back to Mr. Donaldson.

"You're not suggesting I'm losing my eyesight as well, are you, son?"

"Absolutely not, but—"

"But nothing. When someone like that arrives on the island, you take notice."

They both turned to look at the closed door, as if it would offer some further insight, but no. It was just a door, covered in various and sundry health notices and how-to sheets. No lessons in romance, or changing terrible first impressions.

Brodie closed down that thought process. Kali wasn't here to be wooed. Or won. And he had a patient!

"Right, Mr. Donaldson…when was the last time you had a tetanus booster?"

CHAPTER FOUR

"It's nothing fancy, but the pub does good, honest food."
Brodie loaded Kali's bike onto the rack atop his four-by-four
in a well-practiced move. She put her arms up in a show of
helping, but he'd clearly done this before.

"I'd rather that than a bad meal of fripperies!"

Brodie laughed as he tugged the security straps tight.
"I'm not entirely sure if fripperies are a food group, but I
can assure you, you won't get any up here." He opened the
car door for her with a slight bow. "Madam?"

Kali felt herself flush, instantly thanking the short days
for the absence of light. She climbed in and busied herself
with the seat belt buckle to try and shake off an overwhelming urge to flirt. Her gut and her brain were busy doing bat-
tle. She *never* wanted to flirt with people…and now she was
getting all coquettish with Mr. Disagreeable. Ridiculous!

Probably just her empathy on overdrive. The man had
had a tough day. It was natural to want to comfort someone
who was hurting, right?

An image of Brodie laying her across a swathe of sheep-
skin rugs in front of a roaring fire all but blinded her. She
clenched her eyes tight, only to find Brodie hiding behind
her eyelids—peeling his woolen jumper off in one fluid
move, his lean torso lit only by the golden flicker of flames.

Was this what *choice* was? The freedom to choose who
you loved?

Loved?

Pah! Arranged marriage was how things worked in the world she'd grown up in. Love was…a frippery. Icing on the cake if your father's choice for your intended turned out to be a good match. Unlike hers. She shuddered at the thought.

Love.

The island air must be giving her brain freeze or something.

She yelped when the driver's door was yanked open. Brodie jumped in and banged his door shut with a reverberating clang.

"The catch on the door is a bit funny," Brodie explained with an apologetic grin. "Suffice it to say Ginny's seen better days."

"Ginny?"

"This grotty old beast."

"Ah…" she managed, still trying to scrub the mental image of her dark past and a half-naked Brodie out of her mind's eye.

Perhaps Mr. Donaldson had put one too many subconscious ideas into motion. This sort of thing had never happened to her in Dublin. Then again…she tipped her head against the cool window as Brodie fired up the engine…in Dublin she'd never felt entirely safe. Up here…

"Now, I should warn you…" Brodie began cautiously.

What? That you've got three girlfriends on the go and the idea of another is repellent?

"Yes?" Kali asked in her very best neutral voice.

"I haven't exactly been to the pub since this whole stramash kicked off."

"Stramash?"

"Sorry. It's Scots for a rammie."

"Still not following you." Her smile broadened. She could listen to Brodie talk forever. All those rolling *r*'s and elongated vowels with a pair of *the most* beautifully shaped lips forming each and every— Oops! Tune in!

"A bit of bother. Or in this case a *big* bit of bother."

"We could always go somewhere else."

Brodie threw back his head and laughed. It was a rich, warm sound. Kali liked the little crinkles that appeared alongside his blue eyes.

Another time, another place...

Another lifetime was more like it. Not with the steamer trunks full of baggage she was hauling around.

"Darlin', this time of year there really *isn't* anywhere else. It's the Eagle and Ram or a fish and chips takeaway from Old Jock's. That's yer choices." He tacked on a cheesy grin for added salesmanship.

"I'm happy with whatever you choose."

"Well..." He gave her a duplicitous wink. "Shall we risk the pub and see if the Ebola public-awareness campaign you kicked off with Anne Donaldson has had any effect beyond the reaches of our humble clinic? It's a bit warmer than a picnic table outside Old Jock's."

Kali nodded, grinning at his choice of words.

Our clinic.

It had a nice ring to it. Chances were slim he'd meant anything by it, but the words warmed her. Not just because her hormones had decided to kick into action and turn her tummy into a butterfly hothouse, but because she'd never had a chance to be a part of anything in that way before. Put down roots.

Dunregan was the first place she'd been that had absolutely no connection to her past. It was why she'd applied for the so-called hardship post. Safe place was more like it. There was no way her father could find her here, up in the outer reaches of Scotland's less populated islands.

"Right." Brodie pulled the four-by-four in front of a low-slung stone building. "Here goes nothing!"

Moments later Brodie was pulling open a thick wooden door to reveal a picture-postcard pub. The Eagle and Ram was duck-your-head-under-the-beams old. Being short was an advantage here—unfortunately for Brodie. Kali took in stone walls as deep as her arm. A clientele who looked as though they'd known the place since the rafters were green. A landlady robust enough to turf out anyone who wasn't playing by the rules.

She turned her head at the sound of male voices coming in from the back door. Nope. Scratch the chaps-only presumption. There was a varied clientele. A group of young men kitted out in all-weather gear were clustered round the bar, greeting the landlady familiarly, jokes and banter flying between them and the chaps with flat caps already at the bar. And a couple of ruddy-cheeked women elbowing past the rowdy crew to order drinks.

And then...a complete hush as all eyes lit upon Brodie.

"All right, lads?" Brodie stepped into the room with a broad smile. His physical demeanor looked relaxed, although Kali thought she could hear a tightness in his voice.

Her eyes flicked to a nearby table where a newspaper's headline screamed out the poor nurse's recurrence of Ebola.

A few of the men nodded and a couple of muttered "all rights" slid onto the floor and pooled around their ankles, as if weighing everyone down with the lack of truth in them. The atmosphere was tense. Quite the opposite of all right.

"I've brought the new GP along—Dr. O'Shea—to meet you. Thought I'd give her an Eagle and Ram welcome."

Kali was half-hidden behind Brodie, and felt like hiding herself entirely behind his broad back. She hated the limelight. But something told her she needed to step up and be seen—no matter how much it frightened her. This moment wasn't about *her*.

"Right you are, Brodie." The fifty-something woman came out from behind the bar and stood between them and the ten or so men around the bar. "You're looking well."

"Thank you, Moira. I am feeling fit as a fiddle."

"So I hear. It's the *English* Health Authority, is it? Cleared you to come away back up to Dunregan?"

"That's right."

"The Scottish Health Council no good for you, then?" Her face was serious but her tone carried a teasing lilt.

Brodie nodded, clearly appreciative of what was going on. An impromptu public forum. With pints of beer.

"What do the Scots know about getting sick? Healthy as oxen—the lot of you." His eyes scanned the crowd, then returned to Moira. "Excepting the odd run-in with a peat spade. I take it you've spoken with Anne, then?"

Ding! A lightbulb went on in Kali's head. Moira bore an uncanny resemblance to Anne Donaldson.

"Oh, aye. She rang after she brought Dad back from the clinic. We heard all about it. And about Dr. O'Shea answering all of Anne's questions." The landlady's words were loaded with meaning.

Brodie raised his eyebrows. "Well, good. Your father'll heal up in no time. And there'll be no mention of him coming to the clinic." He tapped his finger on the side of his nose with a *got it* gesture. "That peat came in without incident, right?"

Moira nodded and grinned. "Understood. Good to see you looking so chipper...and healthy. Especially with all you've been through after your father passing and everything—right, boys?"

There was a fresh wave of murmurs and nods—and focus was realigned on what really mattered. To Brodie, at the very least.

"Now, what do you say you two go over by the snug and I'll bring you some nibbles? The fire's on."

Kali followed Brodie's gaze. The snug was way across the other end of the pub and could be closed off with a very thick door.

"I suspect you two'll be talking business, and you won't

want us butting our noses in while you get to know each other a bit better," Moira clarified.

Kali got a whiff of matchmaking about the suggestion rather than using the snug as an isolation room. What *was* it with these people and pairing her off?

"That'd be grand, Moira. After you, Kali." Brodie stepped to the side and put out his hand for Kali to lead the way.

She felt her cheeks go crimson, with all pairs of eyes trained on her. *Just smile!* She forced her lips to tip upwards and met one or two sets of eyes. She received nods and a couple of hellos as she passed.

How could walking across a room take an eternity? Her eyes shifted to the floor. The thick wooden planks were covered every now and again with old tin signs. A brand of beer here. A vegetable vendor there. It felt like walking over history while making history. She had no doubt this moment would be talked about.

A headline popped into her head:

Ebola Doc Enters Pub for First Time with Blushing Bride...

Locum! *Locum.* She'd meant to say locum. In her head. Where she was busy lecturing herself in turbo speed.

She felt the color in her cheeks deepen as she scuttled to enter the snug ahead of Brodie. Being in the public eye wasn't ideal when very inappropriate thoughts were charging through her head.

"Oh, look," Brodie stage-whispered. "How romantic! We get it all to ourselves!"

It wasn't until she whirled around to face him, a positively goofy smile of expectation lighting up her features, that she realized he was aiming the comment to the crowd of earwiggers over at the bar.

Now officially mortified, she sank into a cushioned

bench seat across from the huge inglenook fireplace, feigning total absorption by the flickering flames. Looking into those crystal clear blue eyes of his just might tip her over the edge.

A bit prickly? Definitely. But his edginess had a depth to it. Like an errant knight slaying dragons only he could see.

"What can I get you to drink?"

Kali nearly jumped in her seat. "You're going to go back out there?" Her fingers flew to her lips. She hadn't meant to say that out loud.

"Absolutely." Brodie gave a wide grin, as if energized by the thought of going back into the lion's den. "Moira's laid the groundwork for my reentry into society here at the pub. And I owe a debt of thanks to you for your handiwork at the clinic today, so no point in turning this into an 'us and them' situation, eh?"

She nodded. Absolutely right. The less acrimony, the better.

See? Errant knight. She gave a satisfied sniff of approval.

"Besides…" He dropped a duplicitous wink. "Now that you've seen all there is to see of the bright lights of Dunregan, I'm guessing the sooner you get back to civilization the better. Am I right?"

Hmm…okay. So he could do with a few tweaks.

"I'm sure I could bear to stay for the duration." She had to force a bit of bravura to her tone. The thought of losing her job before she'd barely begun brought home just how many eggs she'd unwittingly put into the Dunregan basket.

All of them.

Brodie tilted his head, taking a none-too-subtle inspection of the impact of his words. "Easy there, tiger. I'm not doubting your staying power." He laughed. "This is nothing to do with your GP skills. You've proved, beyond a doubt, you can hold your own at the clinic. I just can't imagine why anyone would want to stay up here if they didn't have to."

She pasted on a smile.

It's the first time I've felt safe in years.

"Hey…"

Brodie reached across the table, covering her hand with his. The warmth of his hand worked its way through hers, sending out rays of comfort.

"Honestly, Kali. It was just a joke. If you think I can go in there, order a couple of drinks and change the minds of all those knuckleheads in one night, you're in for a surprise. Apart from being emotional Neanderthals, these folk are stubborn. They put mules to shame."

She managed an appreciative snort. "Sounds like the voice of experience."

"Who knows?" He withdrew his hand and shrugged. "They might take so much of a shine to the new GP you'll be stuck here forever."

Kali chewed on her lip, preventing too broad a smile from breaking out. "Would a wine spritzer be all right?"

"A few shots of whiskey would be more understandable after the day you've had," Brodie intoned, his eyebrows doing an accompanying up and down jig.

"What? You mean sorting out the irascible Young Dr. McClellan? Child's play." She arched an eyebrow expectantly.

"Got it in one!" Brodie laughed appreciatively.

What was going on with her? She didn't flirt. Or behave like a sassy minx. And yet…

Suffice it to say her tummy was alight with little ribbony twirls of approval.

"Hold that thought. I'll just get the drinks. Wish me luck?"

He dropped another one of those slow-motion, *gorgeous* winks, sending the ribbony twirls into overdrive.

"Thank you."

Oh, gross. Did you just coo?

Brodie quirked an eyebrow. "Not a problem."

When he had safely disappeared out of the snug, Kali

buried her head in her hands with a low groan. What was going *on* with her? She'd have to have a little mind-over-matter discussion with herself later on. All by herself in the dinky stone cottage she'd rented. The one that didn't strictly have any heat. Or much in the way of windows. But there was a nice sofa!

Hey, she reminded herself, it's home. For this month, at least, it's home.

"So..." A wine spritzer slid across the table into her eye-line a few moments later. "Let's hear it, then."

She sat up, pleased to see Brodie looking unscathed by his trip to the bar.

"Hear what?" Kali took a sip of her spritzer.

"Your life story."

She tried her best not to splutter, and if he'd noticed, Brodie gave nothing away.

"Oh, nothing much to tell." She trotted out the practiced line whilst feeling an unfamiliar tug to tell him the truth.

"I doubt that," Brodie retorted amiably.

"Nothing out of the ordinary," she lied. "Childhood, medical school and now a locum position up here."

It was staggering how much had happened in between each of those things. Her father's vow to avenge the family's honor when she'd backed out of the match he'd made for her. The terrifying flight for her life with a fistful of cash. So much...*too* much...for a young woman to carry on her shoulders. If it hadn't been for the government's ability to give her a new identity—

Enough.

Those were her stories to keep safely hidden away.

"Is that a bit of an Irish accent I detect?" Brodie wasn't giving up.

"Yes." She nodded. "I did my medical degree in Dublin." That much was true.

"But you grew up in England?"

She nodded, taking a deep drink of her spritzer.

"No matter what I do, or what corner of the world I find myself in, I can't seem to shake my accent." Brodie shook his head as he spoke.

Why would he want to? Brodie's accent was completely and totally gorgeous. Which she wasn't going to tell him, so best change the subject.

"So...you've traveled a lot?"

"Some." He nodded. "Lots, actually. Unlike everyone else who was born and raised here, I couldn't wait to get off the island."

"Why?"

"Is it so hard to believe?"

"Yes!" Kali nodded her head rigorously. "I think Dunregan's great."

"Aye, well..." His eyes shot off to that faraway place she couldn't access. "You don't have history here."

Fair enough. She had her own history, and no one was going to pry that from her.

"Where have you traveled?" she asked.

"Everywhere I could at first."

"At first?"

"My father always hoped I'd take over the clinic after medical school, but I..." He paused for a moment searching for the right words. "I struggled to *settle* here."

There was a reason behind that. That much was clear. One only he would decide when to reveal.

Kali was about to say something, but clamped her lips tight when Brodie continued without prompting.

"I'd do stints here, to help relieve my father. The job is bigger than one man's best. Especially during tourist season. But over the winter I kept finding myself volunteering abroad. Orphanages, refugee camps needing an extra pair of hands, villages without access to hospitals." He laughed suddenly, his eyes lighting up. "I used up the paltry first aid kit the agency gave us in my first couple of weeks away! Got my dad to send more supplies along whenever I changed country…"

His eyes shifted to the fire, his brow crinkling as something darker replaced the bright acuity of the happy memory.

Kali pulled him back to the present with a question about his work in Africa. Then another. And before she knew it their conversation had lifted into something effortless and taken flight.

Time slipped away with stories shared and anecdotes compared as their mutual passion for medicine carried them away from whatever had encumbered them during the day into the undefinable giddy excitement that came from meeting a—*a soulmate.*

Kali froze at the thought, her gaze slipping to Brodie's hands. His fingers loosely circled his pint, one index finger shifting along the dewy sheen of condensation as he told her about his grandfather and the crew of men he'd corralled into helping him build the stone clinic in exchange for some of his wife's shortbread. It was how folk did things up here, Brodie was saying. Together. Always together.

And she'd spent her entire adult life alone.

Was a soulmate something she even deserved after leaving her mother and sister behind with her father?

"…and then, when he retired up to the mountains, the key was passed on to my father," Brodie concluded with an affectionate smile. "I don't know if I've told anyone the whole story in one go before. You must've bewitched me with your beguiling ways!"

Kali laughed shyly, her eyes flicking up to meet Brodie's. When their gazes caught and meshed she felt her body temperature soar as the magnetic pull of attraction multiplied again and again, until she forced herself to look away and pretend it hadn't happened.

"So, you coming back here to run the clinic is kismet, really, isn't it?"

She saw him blink away something. A memory, perhaps. Or a responsibility he had neither asked for nor wanted.

She tried again. "Or was it more preordained?"

"Something like that." He took another drink of his pint, eyebrows furrowing. "Look, Kali…while I'm on a bit of a very uncharacteristic 'tell all' roll, I think you should know something—something about *me*. Because you'll no doubt hear it at some point while you're here and I'd rather you heard it from me."

Her heart lurched to her throat as her chin skidded off her hand. Had he felt it, too? The click of connection that made her feel as if she could find sanctuary in telling him who she really was?

She sat as still as she could, her fingers woven together in front of her on the wooden table as he began.

"When I was about ten I went out on a sailboat with my mother. Begged her, actually. She and I hadn't been out since my kid brother had been born." He cleared his throat roughly. "Long story short: the weather turned nasty. Our boat got overturned. I made it back. My mother didn't."

Kali's fingers had clenched so tightly as he spoke her flesh had turned white with tension.

"Oh, Brodie. I am *so* sorry."

He shook his head. "No, I didn't tell you for your pity. I just want you to understand why sticking around this place isn't top of my list."

"Then why are you here? If there are so many bad memories?"

"A promise." He circled his fingers round his pint, weaving them together on the far side and moving them back again. "To my dad. He loved it here so much and wants—*wanted*—the same for me. So he asked me to stay for a whole year. No trips, no inner-city assignments, a year solid on the island. And I think he wanted someone—family—to be here to look after Callum. My brother," he added.

"And after the year is up—was he expecting you to close the clinic or hand it on to someone else?"

Was this where she came in?

"Ha! No." Brodie smiled at her as if she were an innocent to the world of hard knocks, then his expression softened. "I suppose it was his not very subtle way of hoping I'd fall back in love with the place."

"How's that working out for you?" Kali chanced in a jokey tone.

"Absolutely brilliantly, Dr. O'Shea! Nothing like winning over the people you've kept at arm's length all your life with a nice little Ebola scare." He raised his glass and finished his pint in one long draught.

"You know…" Kali said after they'd sat for a minute in silence. "What's happening here…with you, the islanders… it's really quite exciting."

Brodie couldn't help but laugh. "You've always got a positive spin on things, don't you, Kali? Is this excitement you speak of manifesting itself in the way nary a soul would step foot in the clinic until you arrived, or in the way they've stuck us in this room where no one hardly ever goes except to read the paper in a bit of peace?"

"See—that's where you've got it all wrong."

Her green eyes shone with excitement, as if she had a huge secret she was about to share. If anyone else had told him he'd got it wrong he would've bridled. But coming from Kali…?

It seemed completely bonkers, but he felt closer to her after just a handful of hours than he had near enough anyone outside of his family.

Beguiled or bedeviled?

He didn't know what it was, but he was spilling private thoughts like it was going out of style. And a part of him felt…*relief.* As if with the telling of his story he'd somehow lessened the levels of internal pain it caused.

"I don't mean it in a bad way, Brodie. It's just—you're taking the reaction of the villagers incredibly personally. Which, obviously, it would be hard not to. *But*," she continued quickly, before he could jump in to protest, "it seems to me people are using the Ebola thing as an excuse."

He grunted a go-on-I'm-listening noise.

"Now that I know why you don't want to be here, I get it. That's a lot of weight to carry on your shoulders for something you surely realize wasn't your fault."

She held up her hand again, making it clear he was going to have to hear her out—gutsy beguiler that she was.

"Perhaps—and this is just a *perhaps*—everyone here thinks you've turned your back on *them*. Your job is to help people. Help them at a time when they're feeling weak, or frightened or downright awful. And if you add a bit of fear into the mix…fear that you won't be around when they've entrusted you with their private concerns…"

"It makes for a pretty poisonous pill," he finished, seeing his plight from an entirely new angle. "I see where you're going with this," Brodie admitted with a nod.

He was so intent on ticking days off the calendar to get through the year he was blinded to everything else. But he wanted to fulfill his promise honorably—so until he took full control of the clinic he couldn't mark a single day off the calendar. He scrubbed at his hair and jiggled his empty pint glass back and forth. Maybe that was why everyone was refusing to see him. So he could never turn over the hourglass and begin the countdown.

He gave her an impressed sidelong look. "You sure you didn't specialize in psychology?"

"Positive."

Kali flushed as their eyes met. A sweet splash of red along the porcelain lines of her cheekbones. She was a beautiful woman. And smart.

Frustration and anger had eaten away at his ability to be compassionate. Show the people he'd known his entire life the same care and attention he'd given each and every patient he'd treated abroad. The same care and attention they'd shown him when first he'd lost his mother and then again when his father had passed. Even if they weren't all huggy-kissy about it.

Anonymous plates of scones had been delivered. Stews heated up. Distance kept…

"You're quite the insightful one, Dr. O'Shea."

"Well…" She drew a finger round the base of her wine glass. "We've all had hurdles to jump. I know how frustrating it can be when it seems like no one is on your side. You against the world, sort of thing. But it's not exactly as if you're powerless to change things, is it?"

Something told Brodie she was talking about something a world away from what *he* was experiencing. An instinct told him not to push. His were the only beans getting spilled tonight.

"I get the feeling you have an idea or two about how I can win the hearts and minds of my fellow islanders." Brodie leaned forward, rubbing his hands together in a show of anticipation.

"I do!" she chirped, enthusiasm gripping her entire body. "GPs are at the forefront of the medical world as far as a community like this is concerned, right? They're authority figures, really."

Brodie nodded. He'd always pictured his father as the authority, but now he supposed that baton had been well and truly handed over.

"And what do you see me doing with all of this authority?"

"Well…it sounds like you've had some amazing experiences overseas. You combine that with your local knowledge and you've got an amazing opportunity for public outreach. To teach people firsthand what's going on in the world beyond the sensationalist headlines." She picked up a discarded copy of the nation's favorite rag and held it in front of him like a red cape to a bull. "Make them wise, not re-actionary. From Ebola to...to Zika virus."

"What? Quell their fears about Ebola, only to get every-one up in arms about every mosquito arriving on their hal-lowed shores being laden with the Zika virus? Now *there's* an idea?"

Kali swatted at the space in between them, taking his words as he'd meant them. In jest. With a healthy splash of affection.

The strangest feeling overtook him as he watched her speak. He was no spooky-spooky sort, but meeting Kali felt meant to be. Their long talk, which had all but emptied the pub, seemed like a homecoming of sorts—as if they'd been cinching the loose strings of a relationship they'd let fade and were now eager to rekindle.

Her own voice came to him in the perfect way to de-scribe the sensation.

Kismet.

And then he realized she was still talking about public awareness.

"You know what I mean. The only reason people are being funny about you is because they don't understand. About Ebola. Why you don't like it here. And, frankly, I'm a little on their side with that one. You're keeping them at arm's length. It makes you scarier."

"Loveable, approachable me?" Brodie put on his best teddy bear face. "I come across as *scary*?"

"Yes! Exactly!" She grinned, her smile lighting up those green eyes of hers from within.

Funny how a guy could take an insult when it came from a woman with such a genuine smile.

"Luckily I've already learned your bark is worse than your bite," Kali replied regally.

She was obviously enjoying herself. The young medi-cal disciple offering words of wisdom to the block-headed Scottish doctor.

"So…how do you suggest I open my arms to people who don't even want to breathe the same air as me?"

"Get a gas mask," she replied with a straight face.

He stared at her, waiting to see if she'd break.

She didn't.

"A gas mask? That's your big idea."

Kali burst into gales of laughter, tears of delight filling the rims of eyes now flecked with golden reflections of the fire.

"Sorry, sorry…" She swallowed away the remains of her giggles, pressing her lips together in an attempt to regroup. "Look. You don't have to do it alone. I'm happy to go to bat for you."

"So soon?" He feigned astonishment, though in truth he was genuinely touched.

"Oh, it's more for me than you," she replied with mock gravitas. "I don't know if you noticed, but there's an awful backlog of patients to see. Time is of the essence, Dr. McClellan."

Brodie grinned. Couldn't help it. Probably his first genuine smile since he'd lost his father. "Anyone told you your enthusiasm is infectious, Miss O'Shea?"

"That's *Dr.* O'Shea to you," she riposted with a shy smile.

He tipped his head to the side and looked at her with fresh eyes.

Strikingly pretty. Petite, but not fragile. Thick mane of black hair framing the soft outlines of her heart-shaped face. And those eyes…

He'd better watch it. This whole two-peas-in-a-pod thing had *wrong time, wrong place* written all over it.

"So, what do you say?" He rubbed his hands together briskly. "We take on the islanders one by one, or gather them all up in a stadium and do it warlord-style?"

"I was thinking more softly, softly—kitten-style."

"You think I'm up to being a *kitten*?" Brodie snorted as Kali feigned imagining him as a kitten.

"Maybe more of an alley cat. With an eye patch and a broken tail."

"Ah—so we'll have a cat fight at the end?"

"*Purrr*haps," she purred, completely capturing his full attention.

Her lips were parted, chin tilted up toward his, eyelids lowered, half cloaking that mystical green-eyed gaze of hers as a thick lock of hair fell along her cheek. He was itching to shift it away, feel the peachy softness of her skin.

Brodie readjusted as his body responded.

Kali had just shape-shifted from beautiful to downright sexy.

And an instant later...the shutters closed.

Kali's gaze had gone from inviting to *stay away* in an actual blink of the eye.

He chalked up another reminder about barriers as she tugged on her coat, pulling the zip right up to her chin.

She wasn't here to stay. Nor was he.

Kali threw her coat on top of the duvet, shivered, then grabbed her suitcase and shook the whole pile of clothes along the bed in a line stretching the length of her body.

Her fire-making skills, as it turned out, were not great. Thank goodness she'd convinced Brodie to let her ride her bicycle home in lieu of a lift, otherwise she'd have no body heat at all! Not that he hadn't put up a fight.

He'd insisted. She'd insisted more firmly. Said it was all part of the rugged island adventure she'd been banking on when she took up the post. She tugged on a pair of tights and zipped a fleece over her layers of T-shirts and jumpers, acutely aware that an online shopping spree was growing increasingly essential.

Her eyes flicked over to the bedroom door. Firmly shut. Front door? Dead-bolted. Checked twice. She'd never let anyone walk, drive or cycle home with her in the past five years. The fewer people who knew where she lived the better. And yet...

How many times had she been tempted to blurt out her life story tonight?

Too many.

How many times had she let herself wonder...*what if*?

Each time she'd caught herself staring at Brodie's lips was how many.

Too many.

This was a working relationship. Not an island romance.

Apart from which, Brodie wanted nothing to do with Dunregan and she...she wanted *everything* to do with it. Just one day here was as appealing as one day with her "intended" had been repellent.

She huffed out a sigh of exasperation, eyes widening as she did.

Was that her *breath*?

She pulled up the covers, trying to keep the pile of clothes balanced on top of her, and snuggled into the fetal position. Shivering created body warmth.

She giggled. Now she was just being silly. But it felt good. She hadn't been plain old silly in...*years*. Perhaps it was the cold, or the delicious lamb stew she'd virtually inhaled at the Eagle and Ram. She felt warm from the inside. A cozy glow keeping the usual fears at bay.

She was safe here in Dunregan. And, for tonight at least, she couldn't wipe the smile off her lips if she tried.

CHAPTER FIVE

TOO LATE, BRODIE saw the beginning of the end. It was a miracle the wood had stayed atop his four-by-four this far.

"Nooooooooo!"

The planks of wood were crashing and slithering all over the place. Smack-dab in front of the clinic.

He glanced at his watch.

Kali would be there soon. No doubt expressing her despair at yet another way he'd made her time at the clinic less than straightforward.

Three days in and she seemed a more regular part of the place than he ever had. Correction. Than he had ever *felt*.

Big difference.

He nudged a bit of wood with his foot and shook his head.

Woodworking was a class he really should have taken when he'd had the chance. He'd scoffed at his brother's choice at the time. Now he was beginning to see the advantages of having learned some practical skills. Or having stuck around so he could've built the blasted thing with his father, a man as at home with a hammer as a stethoscope.

He heard a throat clearing on the far side of his car.

Kali.

Kali trying desperately not to laugh.

She'd been keeping him at a courteous arm's length after their strangely intimate night at the pub, so it was nice to see that smile of hers.

"New project?" she asked, barely able to contain her mirth.

"Aye. I'm sure you will have noticed just sitting round the clinic waiting for patients to magically appear hasn't worked quite the treat I'd hoped."

She made a noncommittal noise, turning her head this way and that, obviously trying to divine what the pile of wood in front of her—*his*—clinic was meant to be.

"It's a boat."

"Ohhhh…" She nodded. "I can see that now."

"Ha-ha. Very funny."

"No, I mean it." She sidled up beside him, crossed her arms and gave the hodgepodge pile of wood a considered look before pointing to one of the shorter cuts. "That's the pram, right?"

"The prow," he corrected, the language of boats coming back to him as if it were genetically embedded.

"And you're building this here because…?" Kali tactfully changed the subject.

"I was rehashing our talk the other night—about public awareness and all that—and I thought, how can I get through to everyone island-style?"

"And this is what you came up with?" Kali gave him a dubious look.

"I told you—it's a boat." He frowned at the pile of wood. "Or it will be once word gets out I'm trying to make one. The folk here can't resist giving advice when it comes to building a boat."

"And that means you're staying?"

A jag of discord shot through him at the wary note of hope in her voice. He'd heard it often enough in his father's voice each time he'd returned. The thought of disappointing Kali bothered him, but he wasn't there yet. In that place where settling down—setting down *here*—felt right. Might not ever be. That was why he'd decided to get out of the clinic, where they had been warily circling each other after that night of so much connection. No bets taken as to why he was building the boat right next door to the clinic, though.

It was Kali. One hundred percent Kali.

He scrubbed his jaw and tried to look like a model citizen.

"I was thinking more along the lines of the public health campaign first."

She gave him a sidelong glance. One he couldn't read. One that made him wonder if she could see straight through his bluster.

"This is your master plan to convince people you don't have Ebola?"

"Who could resist such a rugged, healthy-looking soul?" Brodie looked off into the middle distance supermodel-style. Sure, he was showing off, but the reward was worth it.

A shy grin.

Each of Kali's smiles was like a little jewel—well worth earning.

He struck a bodybuilder pose to see if he could win another.

Bull's-eye.

A fizz of warmth exploded in Kali's belly. Then another. *Would he just stop doing that?*

"Well? What do you think? Irresistible or repugnant?"

Brodie's blue eyes hit hers and another detonation of attraction hit Kali in the knees. What *was* she? Twelve? *Regroup, girl. This man has danger written all over him.*

"Well...you're not exactly repugnant..."

Brodie threw back his head and laughed. "Touché."

He dropped her a wink. Another knee wobbler.

"Serves me right for floating my own boat." Brodie's eyes scanned the higgledy-piggledy pile of wood. "Or not, as the case might be."

Kali gave him a quick wave and hightailed it around the back of the building and into the clinic.

Despite her best efforts to keep her nose to the proverbial grindstone…to see patients and race her bicycle back home to her icy cold house…she knew she was falling for Brodie. Fast.

It scared her. But as unsettling as it felt it also felt good. A little *too* good.

He wasn't hanging around. It was easy enough to see the boat was a project with a timeline and once that was done… *Poof.*

Goodbye, Romeo.

Or, more accurately, goodbye, Kali. Brodie would win the hearts of Dunregan back in no time and then there'd be no need for her here. Before she knew it, it would be time for her to begin again.

"Kali?" Ailsa called to her from the tea room as the back door shut with its satisfying click and clunk. "I've just put the kettle on. Milk and no sugar, isn't it?"

"Got it in one!" She grinned despite the storm of unwelcome thoughts.

"Are we going to be blessed with my nephew's presence today?" Ailsa popped her head round the corner and gave Kali an exasperated smile.

"He's out front," Kali answered. "Building a boat."

Ailsa's eyebrows shot up. "Aye?"

Kali nodded, keeping her own expression neutral.

"Well…"

It was a loaded word. Suspicious. Loving. Expectant. Curious.

Kali couldn't help but smile. She might not have much time here, but at the very least she was becoming much more fluent in Scots!

"Kali! First patient's come early!" Caitlyn called from the front office. "Will you be all right to take a look?"

"It would be my pleasure," she replied, accepting the hot cup of tea Ailsa had just handed her. "Let's get this show on the road."

* * *

"Someone's up with the lark."

A woman in her early thirties spun round at the sound of the bell ringing above the door, her face lighting up with a smile when she saw it was Kali.

"The usual?"

Kali grinned. This was the third morning running she'd relished the warmth and sugary sweet air of the Dunregan Bakehouse. This first "thawing station" on her bicycle ride into work. It had nothing to do with the fact they also made the fluffiest scones she'd ever tasted. And with lashings of the fruitiest, raspberriest jam in the world. She'd bought treats for everyone at the clinic each day since she'd discovered the place.

"I'm Helen, by the way."

"Nice to meet you. I'm Kali—"

"O'Shea," finished Helen with a laugh. "If you haven't found out already, word travels fast in Dunregan. By my count, you've been here about a week now."

"Only three more to go!"

The words were double-edged. She didn't want to leave. Little bits of her heart were already plastered about the small harbor town. Once she got a chance to explore some more she was sure the rest of it would follow suit.

"I guess you'll know my being here is actually a bit pointless. With Brodie having the all clear." It was hardly subtle, but they'd passed that point.

"I thought he'd given up doctoring to build that boat of his?"

Kali pulled a face. To say Brodie was making a success of turning the pile of planks into a boat would be...very kind. He'd eventually brought all the wood over and laid it out in a completely indecipherable series of piles in the open shed next to the clinic. Some nails had gone in. Some nails had been pulled out. The piles remained.

"I'm no expert on boat building myself, but I get the

feeling medicine is more of his forte," she said as tactfully as she could. "But it keeps him busy while he waits for his patients to feel more comfortable about coming back to see him."

Helen laughed conspiratorially, but Kali saw a generous dose of compassion in her brown eyes.

"I don't think I ever saw him near the woodworking classes at school. Complete and total brainbox." Distractedly she added a couple more scones to the box she was filling. "You know, I have an idea of someone who could lend a hand. In the meantime..." She flicked the lid shut, putting a Dunregan Bakehouse sticker in place to seal it as she did so. "I've got something special for you to try."

She put up her finger to indicate that she'd be back in a second and disappeared into the back.

"Me?" Kali whispered to the empty room, a giddy twirl of anticipation giving an extra lift to her smile. She knew it was silly, but the gesture made her feel—*better* than welcome. As if she were part of something. A community.

"Right. Give this a taste." A piece of toast appeared in her eyeline. Thick cut, oozing with butter and a generous smear of soft cheese. "You're all right with goat's cheese?"

"Absolutely. I love it." Kali took the bread and was three bites in before she remembered Helen was expectantly waiting for a response. "This is the most delicious thing *ever*," she said through another mouthful. "Ever!"

"Really?" Helen's eyes glowed with happiness. "It's a new bread I've been working on. Hazelnuts and a mix of grains for all the island's health nuts. I'm still debating about raisins. But it's locally produced cheese so I thought I might put it on the board as a lunch offering. What with you being an outsider, I thought you'd give an honest response."

"It's completely yummy."

And thanks for the reminder that I don't belong here. Surprising how much it stung.

"Thanks, Dr. O'Shea."

"Kali," she corrected firmly. They were around the same age. And on the off-chance that she were to stay...

Don't go there. As long as your father is alive, you'll always live a life on the run.

"Thanks, Kali. It means a lot. And don't worry about Brodie's boat. We'll get him sorted out—island-style."

Mysterious. But positive! Kali left the bakery with a wave, feeling a bit unsettled. Could a place do that to someone? Or, she thought, as an image of Brodie flickered through her overactive brain, was it a person that was unsettling her?

"Look who made it all the way up the hill today!" Brodie applauded as Kali dismounted from her bicycle with a flourish. "A mere week on the island and you're a changed woman!"

Kali flushed with pleasure, glad her cheeks were already glowing with exertion.

"It has helped that the wind isn't quite so—"

"Hostile?" offered Brodie.

"Exactly."

Kali smiled at his choice of word, but now she officially needed to get indoors as soon as possible. No heat again in her house meant riding her bicycle and the pit stop at the bakery were the only ways she got warm in the morning. It was absolutely freezing! Which did beg the question...

"How many layers are you wearing?"

"You like?"

Brodie did a little catwalk strut for her. Man, he had a nice bum. A nice *everything*. Even if it *was* covered in a million layers of down and fleece.

"You'll do."

Understatement of the universe!

"So how is Operation Public Awareness going?"

"Well, in terms of gathering in the crowds, you can see how well *that's* going." He swept his arm along the length of the empty street.

"Mmm…could be the weather?"

"Or could be they just prefer you," Brodie replied, his tone lighter than a week ago, when even mentioning the cotton bud delivery had been enough to set him off. Keeping her distance had been easier when he was all grumbly.

This Brodie… All rugged and tool wielding… *Yummy.*

"What's in the magic basket today?"

Brodie leaned toward the wicker basket he had helped Kali attach to the front of her bike with a whole pack of zip ties. Suffice it to say his stitches were better than his DIY skills.

"Wouldn't you like to know?" She protectively covered the box with her hand, eyes sparkling with excitement.

For a split second Brodie envied her the purity of emotion. Every joy he experienced seemed to come with conditions. Obligation after obligation, intent on dragging him down.

Although lately…

"Don't open it yet." He nodded at the box. "I bet I can sniff it out. I've got a nose that knows…" He tapped the side of it with a sage nod.

Kali laughed, dimpling with the simple pleasure of silly banter.

"It's definitely not bridies hiding in there."

She shook her head, lips pushed forward in a lovely little *guess again* moue.

"Too early for hot cross buns…"

"Correct again." She nodded. "That you're wrong, that is."

"Scones." He took a step back. "That's my final answer."

"Is it, now?"

The *guess again* moue did a little back and forth wiggle.

Suggestive. Very, very suggestive.

She unpeeled the sticker to reveal a pile of fluffy scones.

Then snapped the lid shut again before he could get his hand in there to steal one.

"Uh-uh." She wagged a finger at him. "These are for later. For *everyone*."

"You know, you've got to stop spoiling us like this."

"Why?" She looked at him like he was nuts.

"We just might get used to it."

"We?" she countered, with a flirty shift of the hips.

"Me," he admitted, not wanting to put words to the feeling of emptiness he knew was inevitable once she left.

"Go on, now." He shooed her off. "Run off to your lovely warm clinic whilst I freeze to death out here with my pile of wood."

"Take your time," Kali teased. "Gives me more time to steal all of your patients!"

Her grin disappeared instantly at the sight of Brodie's defenses flying into place, blue eyes snapping with anger.

"I'm perfectly happy to come in and see patients. It is, after all, *my* name on the clinic."

The words flew at her like sharp arrows and just as rapidly her own walls of protection slammed down.

Too soon.

She'd let herself believe in the fairy tale too soon.

"I'm perfectly aware it's a temporary posting, all right? I just—" She looked away for a minute, trying to ward off the sting of tears.

She'd been too keen. Too enthusiastic about settling in. Brodie's sharp reaction served her right. She'd fallen hook, line and sinker for the friendly island welcome. The frisson she'd thought existed with Brodie. Her heart had opened up to give too much faith too soon. Trusting people was always a mistake—how could she not know that by now? After everything she'd been through?

Fathers were meant to look after their daughters. Care for them. Protect them. It had never occurred to her that he would choose a man with a history of violence to be her husband. Perhaps her father had fallen for the smooth public demeanor her "intended" had down to a fine art. The one that hid the fact he saw nothing wrong with hitting her to get what he wanted. Her hand flew to her cheek as if the slap had happened yesterday.

She stamped her feet with frustration and forced herself to look Brodie in the eye. It was what people who were in control of their lives did. Met things head-on.

They stood there like two cowboys, each weighing up whether or not it was safe to holster their weapons.

From the looks of Brodie's expression—a virtual mirror of her own—Kali was fairly certain they were both wishing they could swallow back their words.

Had she been this touchy when she went to the Forced Marriage Protection Unit and pleaded for a new identity? She'd been so consumed with fear and a near-primal need to survive she didn't really have a clue *what* sort of impression she'd given. If Brodie was feeling half the trauma she'd experienced, it was little wonder his temperament was whizzing all over the place.

"I didn't mean to stake some sort of claim on your clinic."

"And I didn't mean to sound like such an ass."

She watched as Brodie raked his long fingers through his thatch of wayward blond hair.

He met her questioning gaze head-on. "Start again... *again*?"

There it was. That melt-her-heart-into-a-puddle smile.

"Sounds good," she managed, without too much of a waver in her voice.

"Shall I make you a cup of tea?"

Kali couldn't help it. She burst out laughing. "The solution to everything? No, thanks, you're all right. I don't want to stand in the way of a man who's got a boat to build!"

Brodie shook off her refusal and commandeered her bicycle, hooking his free arm through hers as he did so, turning them both toward the clinic door. A small step in the right direction to start afresh.

"Now, then, Dr. O'Shea, if I can't make you a fresh cup of tea, I'm not going to be much good at building a boat, am I?"

"I suppose not." Kali giggled. "But how long is this going to take? It did take you about five hours to make me one on my first day."

"Well, lassie…" He increased his brogue, rolling his *r*'s to great effect, mimicking his auntie Ailsa. "Can you afford me a second chance to make you a nice cuppa tea within the hour, accompanied by a wee bit of Mrs. Glenn's delicious shortbread?"

"That would be lovely." Kali smiled up at him, eyes bright, cheeks flushed with the cold and the cycle ride.

Brodie found himself fighting an urge to bend down and kiss her. But getting attached to Kali when he had no idea what his own future held… *Bad idea.*

He unhooked his arm from hers, focusing on getting her bicycle into the stand at the back door. Wooing the locum was probably *not* what his father had had in mind when he'd hoped his son would fall in love with the island.

Besides, Kali wasn't here for an island fling—she was here to do a job. *His* job! And it rankled. Perhaps he wouldn't go inside with her after all.

"Right, then, here you are, Dr. O'Shea. Enjoy your day in the clinic. I've got a boat to build!" He gave her a silly salute he didn't quite feel just as Ailsa poked her head through the door.

"Oh, there you both are. I've been wondering if it was just me who was going to run this place today. Kali, you look like you've just been pried out of an iceberg!"

Brodie took a closer look. "Are you shivering?"

"No. Not really." Kali's lips widened into a wince, only succeeding in making her shivering more obvious.

"Oh, for heaven's sake!" cried Ailsa. "Come in out of

the cold, would you? I've just put the kettle on. I'll make us all a nice cuppa tea. And perhaps some of Mrs. Glenn's delicious shortbread."

Kali and Brodie shared a glance, bursting into simultaneous laughter.

Ailsa waved them off as if they'd each lost their wits. "Ach, away with the pair of you. Now, hurry up so I don't heat up the outdoors more than the clinic."

Kali gathered together the day's files, tapped them on the top and sides so they all aligned, then picked them up to give them a final satisfying *thunk* on the desk.

There.

She'd done it.

Another full day of seeing patients—and, she thought with a grin, it had all gone rather swimmingly.

Brodie had been in and out of the tea room, reading various instruction manuals for an ever-growing array of tools. She'd chanced a glance out into the large shed when he'd come in for a cuppa and had smiled at the untouched pile of wood. But she wouldn't have a clue how to build a boat, so she would be the last one to cast aspersions.

Her phone rang through from the reception line.

"Hello, Caitlyn, are you all ready to close up shop for the day?"

"I am, but I was wondering if you wouldn't mind seeing one last patient. Mr. Fairways has popped in. Says his hearing aid is acting up."

"Wouldn't he be—" Kali was going to ask if he'd be better off seeing a hearing specialist, but remembered there was no hospital. "Absolutely." It wasn't as if she had anything else to do. "I'll come out and get him."

She pushed through the door into the waiting room, where a wiry gentleman—an indeterminate fiftysomething, wearing a wax jacket and moleskin trousers—was leaning on the counter, speaking with Caitlyn. He looked familiar to her, but that was hardly likely seeing as she'd only been on the island for a week.

"Mr. Fairways?"

He continued to regale Caitlyn with a blow-by-blow account of the weather. Was that feedback she was hearing? She walked toward him. Yes. There was definitely feedback coming from one of his hearing aids.

"Mr. Fairways?" She touched his shoulder.

"Ah, hello there." He turned to reveal a pair of deep brown eyes and the most wonderful mustache Kali had ever seen outside of a nineteenth-century photo. Or…had she seen him before? There was something familiar about him she couldn't put a finger on.

"So you're the mad spirit who's come up to join us on our fair isle?"

Kali smiled. "Something like that. I understand you're having a problem with your hearing aid?"

A screech of feedback filled the small waiting room.

"What was that, dear?"

Caitlyn stifled a giggle. Kali shot her a horrified look. She couldn't *laugh* at the patients!

"I said, I understand you're here about your hearing aid?"

"I can't quite understand your accent, dear. I'm here about my hearing aid." He glanced at the window facing the street. "I see Young Dr. McClellan is taking a hand to building that boat."

"That's what he says." Kali smiled, then hid her flinch at another piercing hit of feedback.

"What volume do you have your hearing aid on, Mr. Fairways?"

"Eh?"

"The volume?" Kali turned an invisible volume control near her ear.

"Oh, it's up as high as it'll go! It was getting harder to hear so I ramped it right on up."

"That might be your problem."

"Eh?"

Caitlyn out-and-out laughed. Kali hushed her, but not in time for Mr. Fairways not to take notice.

"Oh, you'll want to watch it, lassie." He teasingly waggled a finger in front of the receptionist's eyes. "You might be bonny now, but soon enough you'll be all old and wrinkly like me—eyes not working so well, ears packed up and wondering what on earth people are talking about."

"Ach, away." Caitlyn waved off his comment with a youthful grin. "You're hardly an old codger, Mr. Fairways. My great-gran's about twice your age. You're obviously doing something funny to those hearing aids of yours, though, with the amount of bother they're giving you."

"Since the day I was born, lassie. Since the day I was born."

"So you've *always* had hearing aids?" Kali asked.

"Aye, well…"

Kali smiled. She was getting used to the Scots' all-purpose response. Never giving more information than absolutely necessary. She was hardly one to quibble with the tactic.

"Why don't you come down to my office and we'll take a look?"

A few minutes later Kali had eased down the volume on her patient's hearing aids, syringed his ears and clipped away the long hairs that had accrued outside his ear canal. Once he had the hearing aids safely back in place Kali spoke at a normal volume.

"There doesn't seem to be anything wrong with the hearing aids so far as I can tell, Mr. Fairways, but it's a good idea to keep your ears as clear of hair and wax as you can."

"I know, dearie, but with no one to keep myself dapper for I sometimes forget."

"Well, you're always welcome to come along and see me." As the words came out of her mouth she realized they weren't true. This was temporary. Just like so much in her life had been. Temporarily safe. Temporarily happy. Temporarily a normal woman doing her dream job with a hot Viking building…something or other just outside.

"Aye, well…" Mr. Fairways's brow crinkled with concern.

"Let's make you an appointment with the audiologists next time they're on the island. Unless you usually go to the mainland for this sort of thing?"

"Oh, no. I stay here. I'm the honorary mayor of Dunregan, and it wouldn't do for me to be leaving willy-nilly. I'm happy here. On the island," he qualified, as if that weren't obvious.

"Right, then, so I'll check with Dr. McClellan about the audiologists and we'll get in touch."

"Fine." Mr. Fairways gave a satisfied nod, but made no move to leave.

"Is there anything else you want to talk about?"

"No, no…not really—it's just that…"

"Mmm…?" Kali nodded that he should feel free to speak.

"I just noticed Brodie doesnae have a proper base set up for his A-frames. He won't be getting the right sort of balance on the skiff if he's doing it that way."

Kali's grin widened. "Mr. Fairways, I am afraid everything you just said flew straight over my head. I'm about as landlubbery as a girl can get!"

"Well, if you could let Brodie know—"

Kali put up a hand. "I'm afraid I'm going to have to stop you there. I am quite certain anything you tell me would be lost in translation. How about you tell him yourself on your way out?"

She watched him consider the idea. Neutral territory… A way to tease away the groundless fears…

"Oh, I wouldnae want to get in his way or anything."

"You wouldn't be," she assured him. "I think he'd quite like it. Especially since you'd be doing him a double favor."

"How's that, then?"

"Well…" She leaned forward conspiratorially. "So many people don't seem to understand he's been given the all clear as far as his health and his time in Africa are concerned."

"Oh?" Mr. Fairways' fingers twiddled with the end of his handlebar mustache. "Is that right?"

"Absolutely." She crossed her heart and held up two fingers. "Girl Scouts' honor."

"Aye…there was some talk about it at the Eagle and Ram."

Kali checked a broad grin. *That* was where she'd seen him before. The pub!

"Given that you're the mayor of the island—"

"Oh…" Mr. Fairways tutted, a modest smile on his lips. "Only *honorary*, dear. We don't go for too much pomp and ceremony up here."

"Well, even so, it seems to me you have the islanders' respect, so if you were to be seen speaking with Brodie… you know, just giving him a few pointers…it might put a lot of people's minds at ease." She paused while he took in the information. "I've seen Brodie's medical paperwork myself. If you like, I can show you."

"No, dear, no. That won't be necessary. I saw him at his father's funeral. Didn't want to interfere, is all." He pushed himself up to stand. "I think I might head on out and have a word with Brodie now. No need to take up any more of your time."

"It was my pleasure, Mr. Fairways."

He gave her a nod and a smile as he tugged on his overcoat. "You'll do well here, lassie—with a smile like that. And sensible, too. Who knows? We might make an islander of you yet?"

From your lips, Mr. Fairways…

"You take care of yourself, then, Mr. Fairways." Brodie gave a wave as the sprightly fellow headed off down the road toward the pub for his evening pint, flat cap firmly in place.

Would wonders never cease?

Mr. Fairways…standing right out there in the middle of the street…chatting with him about boat mechanics. He'd been the first one to cancel his appointment when Brodie had returned to Dunregan. It had felt like being struck by a battering ram. Only to be hit again and again as one by one his patients had dropped off the appointment list like flies.

Had it been the Ebola or had it been an unofficial mourning period?

It had been easier to blame the nonexistent contagion rather than face up to years of pushing people away. With his father gone, he might have finally succeeded in pushing near enough everyone away.

Except his auntie. Stoic Ailsa. Unflappable at the worst of times. She was the only one who could tease Callum out of the mountains. Something *he* needed to put a bit more energy into, with all this unexpected free time.

"Did you get your advice, then?"

"Kali!" Brodie turned abruptly. "Sorry, I was miles away. What was that?"

"Mr. Fairways was saying something about props or frames—"

"Kali O'Shea…" He took a step toward her. "You didn't have anything to do with Mr. Fairways suddenly turning into a chatterbox, did you?"

"Oh, no. Nothing like that. He was just interested in your project, and I didn't have a clue what he was talking about, so I thought—"

"Kali," Brodie interrupted with a knowing smile, "you are about as transparent as a glass of water."

She grinned, the smile lighting up her eyes. Was that a dimple on her cheek?

"Well, whatever you did or didn't say…thank you." He pulled a tarp over the pile of wood and began to organize his tools into some newly purchased boxes. "I'm not going to hold my breath for everyone to come back tomorrow demanding an appointment with me, though."

"Well, isn't that the mad thing about life? You just never know." She raised her eyebrows and tacked on, "Do you?" for added emphasis.

"I suppose."

If he could get back to work at the clinic then the ticker would start on his promise to his father, he could wipe his hands clean of his past, move on with the future and…and Kali would be gone.

He wasn't quite ready to give her up just yet.

"Don't you worry, Kali. Things work at a glacial pace up here. Besides, what would you do if I were hogging all the patients? Your contract is for a month, and if you weren't busy at the clinic—"

"I'm sure I could think of a load of things to keep me occupied."

"In Dunregan? You must be joking!" Then again…he could think of a number of things to do with Kali to keep her occupied.

Uh…where did that come from?

"Of course Dunregan," Kali replied emphatically, blissfully unaware of his internal monologue.

What would she want with someone who hauled around baggage as oversized as his anyway?

"There's this Polar Bear Club I still have to find out about," Kali continued enthusiastically, "and I've discovered there's no need to go to the tourist office. The patients have told me about so much more. There's the cake-baking club, hiking up in the mountains, fell running—"

"You're a runner?"

Kali nodded, his question jolting her back to another time and place. She'd never give up running. It was her escape.

"Good call." Brodie interrupted her silent musings. "Running is one thing I missed about being here. The mountain tracks are out of this world. Just the views alone are worth the burn."

"Finally!" She forced on a cheery smile. "Something you like about the island."

"Ach…" He waved away her playful gibe. "There's plenty I like about the old lump of rock. Doesn't mean I have to stay here till my bones are creaking, does it?" He gave her a sly grin. "So…given that we've established neither of us are going to be here forever…maybe you and I could go for a run sometime before you go back?"

"That'd be great!" Her smile faltered a bit.

"Or not. If you prefer running alone."

"No, no. A run together would be great."

There was something in her response Brodie couldn't put a finger on. She wanted to stay? She didn't like running with other people? She didn't like being with him? None of the puzzle pieces fit quite right.

She leaned her bicycle on her hip and rubbed her hands together, blowing on them even though they were kitted out in a new pair of mittens.

"I see you've been to the shops for a bit of warm-weather gear."

"Yes!" She nodded with a self-effacing laugh. "I think I must've spent my entire month's salary on a Dunregan wardrobe, but I'll finally be warm tonight."

"You're joking, right?"

She shook her head.

"Doesn't the heating work where you are?"

"Um…not really. But it's fine. Although my fire-making skills could do with a bit of improvement."

"I could show you. I'm all wrapped up here." Brodie gave the shed a final scan and flicked off the overhead lighting. "Where is it you're staying again?"

"Oh, it's fine. Honestly. It's just a small cottage, and I've got loads of warm clothes now. As long as I wear all of them I'm cozy as a teapot."

"Kali. Which cottage?" he pressed.

"It's fine—honestly."

He wagged a finger at her. "I think you've been in Dunregan long enough to know it doesn't take a man long to figure out every single thing there is to know about a person if he sets his mind to it. I can have a word with your landlord, if you like. Who is it you're renting your cottage from?"

"Seriously…" Her voice went up a notch. "I'm absolutely fine!"

Kali looked anything but fine. There was near panic in her voice, and even through the descending murk of the early evening it was more than apparent that any happiness had drained away from her eyes. A need to protect her overrode his instinct to back away.

"Hey, you're all right," he said gently.

He checked an impulse to pull her in for a hug when her body language all but shouted, *Back off!*

"I'm not trying to pry, Kali. I'm just trying to help you. Make sure you don't freeze to death while you're busy covering my back."

"So which is it, then? I'm covering your back or taking over?"

"Easy there, tiger! What's going on? This isn't just about dodgy heating, is it?"

"Sorry, sorry. It's just been…" Her voice trailed off.

"A long day. I know. A long week. And you've done well." Again he fought an impulse to tug her in for a protective hug.

She grabbed the handlebars of her bicycle. "I'll see you tomorrow, then."

"No, sorry… Kali, I can't let you go back to a house with no heating. Let's get your bike atop the four-by-four, then I'll get you home and we'll build you a fire."

Kali eyed him warily, then shook her head. "Sorry, I don't mean to make such a fuss." She held her bike out for him to put on top of the four-by-four.

"Too many boyfriends chasing you round London?"

"Something like that."

Even in the dark he saw her lips tighten. There *had* been something. He was sure of that now. Something that made her wary of letting people know where she lived. Letting a *man* know where she lived?

Whatever it was, he wasn't going to pry it out of her tonight. He'd build her a fire and leave her to it. He, of all people, should understand a person's desire to keep things close to their chest.

CHAPTER SIX

"So it's not just me, is it?" Kali was almost pleased to see Brodie struggling as much as she had with getting the fire to light.

No. *Pleased* wasn't the right word. *Relieved* was more like it. Proof she wasn't useless at looking after herself.

Not that it covered over all the fuss she'd made about him knowing where she lived. Behaving like she had only drawn attention to the fact she had something to hide. And the whole point of coming up here had been because it had seemed safe. A place where she could finally stop the relentless need to check over her shoulder.

Years of medical school in Ireland had felt safer...but her mother had an Irish connection. One she had always been terrified her father would investigate. Perhaps the passage of time had softened his anger.

"It appears not, Dr. O'Shea," Brodie replied, leaning back on the heels of his work boots. "I've got a guess as to why it isn't working, though."

"Why's that?"

"This is a summer cottage."

"Why would that mean the fireplace wouldn't work? It's not like summer is tropical up here."

He raised an eyebrow.

"Well, it isn't."

Brodie turned his focus back to the fire. "It could be

loads of reasons, but my guess is the top cap was knocked off the chimney and your flue has been stuffed with leaves, or a birds' nest, so you've no longer got a draw. Easy enough to fix, but only with the right tools. We can get Jimmy Crieff to take a look tomorrow, but tonight…" Brodie's tone changed from informational to nonnegotiable. "You're coming home with me."

"I'm *sorry*?" she protested, but just as suddenly realized there was a part of her that felt relief. Someone to look after her. And not just anyone. Someone who made her feel safe.

"I'm not going to let you stay here in the freezing cold, am I? What sort of man would I be, leaving you here all alone to catch pneumonia?" He put on a jaunty grin. "Then we'd have to get another locum in to cover for the locum, who is covering for the doctor, who would have to learn how to make chicken soup."

Kali felt herself relaxing. "So would it be a good idea for me to offer to make dinner tonight in thanks?"

"Throw a few things in a bag," Brodie ordered before she could rescind. "I'll get the car warmed up while you get your things together."

She went to her bedroom, a bit astonished at how easy it was to go along with the plan. As if her trust in Brodie was innate. The first person in—years, really. *Years.*

Her mother had been right. *"Have faith,"* she had whispered, pressing some money into Kali's hand before hugging her one last time. "One day you will find a man you love and trust, and your lives together will be *good.*"

Kali pressed her eyes shut tight, too late to prevent a couple of tears from popping out. Maybe that was what linked her to Brodie. Two pseudo-orphans, hoping for a safe harbor from all that had passed before.

"You grew up *here*?" Kali could hardly believe her eyes.

Even in the darkness it was easy to see the McClellan family house had a substantial footprint. When Brodie flicked on the lights as they entered what she saw took her breath away.

The design was a stunning combination of modern with a healthy nod of respect to the traditional stone buildings speckled across the island. The house was almost Scandinavian in design, with an equal division of glass, wood and stone. Thick oak beams soared up to the roof, supporting vast floor-to-ceiling windows. The central wall of thick stone gave the house a solid grounding.

While the view wasn't visible now, Kali imagined being in the house, particularly in the summer, would feel like being part of the environment that surrounded it. Wild. Protective. Free.

She was so caught up in absorbing all the details of the house she barely heard Brodie when he answered her.

"I was born in one of the cottages you might've seen on the seafront, near the ferry docks, but when my parents found out my brother was coming along a few years later—he was a surprise—they put an unexpected inheritance toward building this place."

"Tell me about your brother."

The subject brought a light to her eyes that it had never brought to his own.

"The wayward McClellan! Never met a mountain he didn't like." He tried to affect a comic voice to cover up how he really felt. His kid brother—Callum. The brother constantly disappearing off, only to be returned hours later by a friend or a neighbor, twigs in his hair, moss on his jumper, an unapologetic grin on his face. The brother he could have looked out for a whole lot better than he had.

"He sounds interesting."

"He is that," Brodie agreed. And he meant it. "He's on the mountain rescue squad…does test rides for off-road cycle companies all over Europe. First-class nutter."

"He sounds like fun."

That was one way to put it.

"He doesn't live here with you?"

"No. Well…sort of. He comes down when he needs things. A twenty-seven-year-old man trapped in the habits of a teenager. But mostly he stays in his but 'n' ben up in the mountains."

"His *what*?"

"A cottage. It's basically two rooms. One for sleeping in and one for all the rest. Kind of like the one you're staying in, but with a working fireplace and all his mountain bikes. He comes down every now and again to stay. And steal." He jiggled his eyebrows up and down.

Brodie's show of brotherly consternation couldn't mask the obvious love he had for Callum. What Kali wouldn't give for just one day with her sister. To make sure she was safe. Ensure her father's fury hadn't shifted to her when Kali had fled.

She forced herself to focus on the house. Wood. Stone. Glass. Deep-cushioned sofas inviting a person to come in and stay awhile. A huge hide on the flagstones in front of a large open fireplace. Highland cow? It was certainly hairy enough.

"It's so different from all of the other houses here." She lowered her voice, speaking in the hushed tones one used in a church. "It's absolutely beautiful."

"Aye, well…"

Kali giggled. Spell broken. She could see in Brodie's eyes there was an untold story nestling there amongst the throwaway line. "Is that something all of you Scots say— or just the islanders?"

"I think you'll find it's most Scots. Our rich and varied dialect hard at work! Now, then…" Brodie rubbed his hands together. "Let's get you a room, shall we? And then we'll see about getting something rustled up for tea."

Brodie took Kali on a high-speed tour of the rest of the house. An expansive kitchen, a pantry the size of her flat in

Ireland, a cozy snug with a television, and, toward the rear, a more formal sitting room and a huge swirl of a staircase leading up to the bedrooms.

He showed Kali to one of the two guestrooms his parents had had built—styled to make the guests feel like they were in a tree house—and brushed off Kali's compliments, muttering something about seeing her down in the kitchen after she'd had a chance to settle in.

As he walked back down to the kitchen Brodie tried to see the house though Kali's eyes. Time had dulled the memory of just how amazing they'd all thought it was as they'd seen it coming together, stone by beam, by slate. There was no question about its appeal. But it was weighted with just about every single reason he found it hard to stay in Dunregan.

Putting down roots. Family. Commitment. All things he was quite happy to put on hold. Indefinitely. And yet showing Kali around had tapped a pretty deep well of pride... and affection. She had a way of bringing out the positive... and it felt good. Healing.

Kali swooped into the kitchen, layers of clothes peeled off to reveal a simple flowery button-up blouse and a swishy little skirt, her delight still wholly undisguised.

"It's so warm in here!"

"My parents had the house built with under-floor heating. It keeps the place pretty cozy, even in winter."

"You mean spring, right?"

"It might be spring where *you're* from, darlin'—but Dunregan doesn't acknowledge spring for at least another month. If you're lucky."

"No matter how hard you try, you're not going to convince me to see the downside of living here, Brodie."

"An eternal optimist, aren't you?"

It would've been so natural to reach out and tug her in close to him. Snuggle into the nook between her neck and the silky swoosh of hair cascading over her shoulder.

"Something like that." Kali's green eyes flicked away for a second, then back to his. "Did your parents design this place?"

"My mother. She was an architect and this was her third child. Her words, not mine," he added hastily. He might have issues to spare, but no one had begrudged her the passion she'd had for their family home.

"It's really gorgeous."

Brodie stuck his head into the refrigerator, making a show of rifling through the cluster of packets to see what would go together. He could hardly bear to think of all the buildings his mother would have designed if she'd lived.

"Guess I forget to stop and appreciate it," he mumbled from the refrigerator, not believing his own words for a second.

He missed her every single day. Had never understood why his father and brother hadn't turned on him after her death. Logic dictated that squalls were tempestuous things. Sometimes one side of the island would see the crueler side of Mother Nature whilst the other side carried on none the wiser. But he knew she wouldn't have been out there at all if it hadn't been for him.

Being here, living in this house, was a penance of sorts. One he'd be doing for the rest of his days, no matter where he was. Being on Dunregan in the family home minus the family just made it more…acute.

He pulled a couple of things out of the refrigerator and followed Kali's gaze.

"She did all this herself?"

"Not entirely. It is the interwoven dreamchild of my architect mother and the beautiful craftsmanship of my never-met-a-tool-I-didn't-like father."

"Did the skill base skip a generation?" Kali teased gently.

"Just a child. Callum got the handy genes," Brodie conceded, a smile playing on his lips as he looked at the house afresh.

Having Kali here gave him an unexpected bolstering of strength. The ability to see his family from a loving perspective rather than one tainted with the guilt and sorrow he'd hauled around all these years. It also brought back the unexpected intimacy he'd felt on That Night at the pub. As if he'd opened another door to himself he would normally have kept locked tight.

What was it he'd felt?

Kismet.

Just as his parents' relationship had been. Predestined. Two like-minded souls bucking staid ways and setting new trends on their beloved Dunregan.

At least his mother had seen the house finished. Lived in it three years with her "flock of boys," as she'd called them all.

And his father! The iron rod of strength in that man was unparalleled. Only heaven knew how he'd done it, but his father had treasured that house, *and* his sons, every hour he'd lived. A testament to his love for his wife and family.

"Right!" Brodie clapped his hands together and surveyed the pile of food on the kitchen counter for a moment. Enough memory lane. Time to focus on the present. "How do you feel about chicken stroganoff?"

"Never heard of it," Kali replied, accepting the bundle of vegetables Brodie was handing her.

"That's because…we are going to invent it." He flashed her a smile. "If it's really good we could always call it Chicken *à la* O'McClellan?"

What a difference an hour made! Between the music blaring away on the stereo, the food sizzling on the stove-top and the quips they were slinging at each other, Kali felt as if she'd entered an alternative universe. Or maybe the house was enchanted. Being here with Brodie felt like…*home.*

She tried to squelch the thought instantly, for fear of jinxing it.

"Turn it up!" Brodie called from across the broad flagstone kitchen.

"I just did!" she shouted above the already-blaring pop tune.

"Even more! I *love* this song!" he called, hands either side of his mouth, his voice barely audible above the volume. *"Let's dance!"*

He jumped and twisted his way into the middle of the room and let loose. Arms flying in the air, hair taking flight with his accelerated movements, his face a picture of pure abandon.

Kali didn't need to be asked twice. How often had she let herself just...*be.*

She started slowly at first. Hips taking on the beat of the music, eyes closing as she let her practical self float away while her body tuned in to the rhythm. She began to lose track of time and place. It was an old pop song. One that had been popular when she was a teenager, living at home with her mum, dad and sister. When trust had been a given and fear something other people felt. It said nothing but *happy* to her.

She raised her hands above her head and began to twirl as her arms took on a life of their own—obeying nothing but the rhythm of the song as it filled her, from head to toe, with joy.

When she opened her eyes she felt Brodie's eyes on her in an instant. There was a look in them she hadn't seen before and she let herself be drawn in by the magnetism of the bright blue. They danced and whooped and by some sort of silent agreement their movements became more synchronized. The sway of their hips matched each other's, their breath was coming in deep, energized huffs.

And then without either of them seeming to notice the music changed. Their movements changed with it. Slow, sensual, instinctive. Brodie was close now. Incredibly close. She looked up into his face, felt their shoulders still gently swaying back and forth, back and forth, in a cadence that almost demanded intimacy.

He slipped his broad hands onto her hips and tugged her in, closer to him. "May I have this dance?"

His eyes were a bright blue, lit up by an accelerated heart rate and—she was sure of it now—a mutual attraction.

A shower of untethered electricity lit up parts of Kali she hadn't known existed. Her breasts were hyperaware of the satin and lace of her bra. The soft swoosh of skin just below her belly button could feel where the lace lining of her panties shifted and smoothed against her skin—almost as if Brodie was tracing his finger just out of reach of her most sensitive areas.

She felt one of his hands slide up her back as the other sought to weave his fingers through hers, then held her close enough to his chest that she could feel his heart beat.

Everything about the moment felt forbidden. And inevitable. She could feel her hair shifting back and forth along her shoulders as Brodie's hand swept down her back to her waist. The shift of his fingers over the curves between her breasts and hip elicited hypersensitive tingles, as if she were being lit up from within.

If she had thought she knew what being touched by a man was like before, she knew for certain she had had no idea until now. Each infinitesimal movement of Brodie's fingertips, hips, even his breath spoke to her very essence.

He untangled their fingers and tipped her chin up as he lowered his lips to meet hers. Tentative at first. A near-chaste kiss. Then another. Longer, more inquisitive. His short beard was unbelievably soft. Kali's fingers crept up to trace along his jawline as his hands cupped hers. Her lips parted, wanting more than anything to taste and explore his full lips.

A soft moan passed between the pair of them—she had no idea where it had started or how it had finished—she was only capable of surrendering to the onslaught of sensations: on her skin, inside her belly, shifting and warming, further, deeper than she'd ever experienced. She felt delicate and protected in his arms. And utterly free to abandon herself to the erotic washes of heat and desire coursing through to her very core.

Already her lips were feeling swollen. In one swift move she felt Brodie tuck his hands under her buttocks, pull her up to his waist and swing her round to the countertop. She couldn't help it. She tipped her head back and out came a throaty, rich laugh she hardly recognized as her own.

Brodie nuzzled into her exposed neck, kissing the length of it with the periodic flicker and tease of a nibble or lick. Kali felt empowered to give herself up to nothing other than feeling and responding, touching and being touched.

Brodie's fingers teased at the hem of her jumper, shifting past her singlet and touching bare skin. Never before had she understood the power of a single caress.

As his hands slipped along her waist and on to her back she wove her fingers through his thick blond hair, tiny whimpers of pleasure escaping her throat as his thumbs skidded along the sides of her breasts.

"Are you okay with this?" Brodie's voice was hoarse with emotion.

"Very," she managed. And she meant it. This was entirely mutual.

He cupped her chin in one of his hands and drew a long, searching kiss from her.

"Want to see the room I grew up in?"

She managed a nod, her brain all but short-circuiting with desire.

Brodie took her hand as she jumped off the countertop and, laughing, she reached out to turn off the stove with the other. Dinner could wait.

Dinner would have to wait.

Giggling like a couple of teenagers, they ran up the stairs. The music shifted as they took the steps in twos, this time to a gentle male voice lazily singing along to the simple melody of a guitar.

"You're sure you're sure?" Brodie looked over his shoulder as they hit the landing. "It won't be weird for you or anything? Working together?"

"If we'd listed all the things that are weird about this we probably wouldn't have kissed in the first place," Kali replied, more for her own reassurance than Brodie's.

"That, my lovely, is a very good point." He pulled her in close to him for another long, deeply intentioned kiss.

My lovely.

The words trilled down her spine. She couldn't remember a single time when she'd been called lovely before. She'd had the odd med school romance, but nothing had stuck. No one had brought her to life in the way Brodie had. And for the next few hours at least she was his—all his. Gladly. Willingly. *By choice.*

And it felt amazing.

Kissing and touching and exploring, and with a frantic dispensing of winter clothes, they eventually made their way to a doorway flung open with grand finesse by Brodie, before he hooked a hand onto her thigh and tugged her legs up and around his waist again.

"Mind your head," he cautioned—unnecessarily, as she'd lowered her lips to taste his yet again.

There was only a deep purple singlet and a lace-edged bra between them. Brodie's shirt had disappeared somewhere between the bottom of the stairs and the top, and his body heat was beginning to transmit directly to Kali, stoking her hunger for more.

"What if I were to throw you on the bed and have my wicked way with you?" Brodie pulled back, eyes crackling with anticipation.

"Go on, then," she dared him, hardly believing the words

were coming out of her own mouth as she spoke. "Finish what you started."

More tigress than tabby was right.

The sexual tension igniting between the pair of them was the most intense thing Brodie had ever felt with a woman. He loved holding Kali's petite body, feeling the weight of her thick hair on his hands as he spread his fingers across her back. If he'd ever thought her timorous, he was being set straight now. This was alpha with alpha. Each using their personal advantages to bring the other pleasure.

He took one hand and shifted it lower, to cup one of her buttocks, and then half threw, half laid her upon his bed. Seeing her stretching to her full length as she hit the deep blue of his duvet, he felt another surge of desire.

"Protection?" she asked softly, pulling her ebony hair into one hand and twisting it into a spiral.

He stood, mesmerized, like a man who was seeing a goddess for the very first time. She looked up at him, eyes heavy lidded and sexier than ever. *Definitely more tigress than tabby.* With a fluid whoosh of her hands she fanned her hair out across her shoulders.

"On it." He turned to check his chest of drawers, then whipped around. "Don't move... I want you to stay exactly as you are."

Kali blinked once, as if processing the thought, and then again, as though she'd made her decision. "What are you waiting for?"

Socks flew everywhere as Brodie searched the top drawer for the little foil packets he vaguely remembered putting in there after he'd cut yet another relationship short. All he could think of right now was Kali, and giving her the most pleasure a woman could have. His fingers struck gold and he turned round with a flourish.

Her beauty near enough sucker punched him. He was the moth and she was the flame. Her fingers were teasing at the spaghetti straps of her singlet.

"Stay still," he whispered, easing himself onto the bed beside her.

He wanted to be the one to slip the fabric up and over her head. To tease the hooks away from her bra, freeing her breasts to his touch, his kisses. He wanted to give her a night of undiluted pleasure.

Kali obliterated his moment's hesitation as she wriggled close to him, rucking up the soft fabric of her top as she moved. Skin against skin. Lips exploring. The tip of her tongue slowly circling the dark circle of his nipple. Her fingers and his fought with his belt buckle and won. Each move, each discovery, only increased Brodie's desire to be with her. Tenderly. Passionately.

He rolled on top after yanking his trousers off, his forearms holding part of his weight above her soft-as-silk body as he sought her eyes for permission to continue. There was no question now of how much he wanted her. She must feel it, too, as she pressed and shifted against the length of his erection.

A nod and a smile were all he needed. And exactly what he received.

Slowly. He would take his time. This was a woman worth taking his time over, and he wasn't going to risk missing a single square inch of Kali O'Shea.

CHAPTER SEVEN

CONTENT DIDN'T EVEN begin to cover how Kali felt. This
was the sixth…no, the seventh day she and Brodie had decided her place was too cold to stay in and she had accidentally on purpose ended up in his bed. Sure, they were both
being a little coy about it during "office hours"—but here
in bed? *Mmm…* A whole new world of trust and intimacy
had woven its invisible threads, linking them in a way she
hadn't imagined possible.

She stretched like a cat, reveling in the contrast of her
skin against Brodie's body. She felt soft and pliable whilst
he… *Whoo!* He was all muscle and strength. A spray of
fireworks went off in her belly when she remembered their
night together. If she had a trophy, she'd hand it to Brodie
for his skills in the art of lovemaking. She had never, ever,
in her limited romantic history, felt as amazing as she had
with the man who had protectively held her in his arms all
night long.

"Is that you up?" Brodie murmured.

She pushed herself up on her elbows and gave his cheek
a kiss.

"Yup! Rise and shine—we've got another big day of
work ahead of us!"

"Already?" Brodie put his arm around her shoulder and
tugged her back in to nestle alongside him.

Sweet monarch of the glen, that man smells good!

"Guess we'd better get you fed and watered, then," he murmured after a few minutes.

"What? Like a horse?" She whinnied and asked for coffee in her best horse voice.

"Is that how you win everyone over?" he intoned.

"Something like that. You should hear my duck voice."

"Go on, then."

She asked for toast with butter in her duck voice. She'd used it countless times to entertain her little sister when she'd been in the toddler indefatigable *"Again!"* phase.

Kali fought with the sobering fact that her sister would be a young woman now. Completely changed.

The shard of reality all but shattered the undiluted joy she'd been feeling over the past week. Nights of old-fashioned fun and frisson with just about the most gorgeous man she'd ever laid eyes on.

Okay, fine. *The* most gorgeous man she'd ever laid eyes on.

"Impressive." Brodie pulled himself up to sit, making sure a pillow was tucked beneath her head as he did so. "I'll give you a pound for every patient you see using only that voice." His light tone showed he was oblivious to her shift of mood.

Live in the moment, Kali. It's the only thing you have in your power.

"I think I'll use my Dr. O'Shea voice and save all my other voices for you."

"Well, that's very generous." He popped a kiss on her forehead. "So many hidden talents, Kali! I wonder what other hidden treasures I'll uncover over the next two weeks."

"Two?" she squeaked. *Was that it?*

"Just under, actually." He frowned. "Not so long now, my little whip-poor-will."

Kali bit into the inside of her cheek. There it was again. The reminder that she wasn't staying. She turned away from Brodie, snuggling into the warmth of his embrace so he couldn't see the complex emotional maze she was navigating. It seemed absolutely mad...but a mere fortnight here on Dunregan with Brodie and she felt the safest and happiest she had since she'd left the family home all those years ago.

It was the first time she'd felt whole. As if Kali O'Shea was a real person and not a name she'd had to invent so she could never be found by her father and the man he'd arranged for her to marry.

Brodie made a contented *mmm*...noise and tugged her in closer. It was almost ridiculous how good she felt with him. A crazy thought entered her head. She knew that if in some mad turn of events Brodie were to ask her to stay, she would say yes.

Her gut, heart, the *tips of her toes* were telling her that this feeling she was experiencing right now—this deep, instinctive peace she was feeling—was the elusive "it" she'd heard so much about when people spoke of love.

Which, of course, was utter madness.

Particularly given the fact they'd all but been living in a self-contained lust cocoon, all safe and cozy, tucked away from the world and all its problems. Problems just waiting to be dealt with...

She heaved a silent sigh, turned around to face Brodie. His eyes opened just enough to give her a flash of their cornflower-blue brightness before shutting with heavy-lidded contentment. She traced a finger along his cheekbone and bounced it to his lips. Eyes still closed, he gave her fingertip a kiss. A kiss she transferred to her own lips with a smile. He rolled over to face the window and she cuddled into him for a cozy spooning. His body and her body matching with a made-in-heaven perfection.

It was probably just as well she only had a couple of weeks left on Dunregan. Getting too attached would only mean lying to this gorgeous man beside her. There was no way she was going to burden him with the complexities of her past. The family she'd been forced to leave behind. The father who had irrevocably betrayed her trust.

Brodie abruptly flung the duvet to the side, as if cued by the universe to remind her how fleeting their time together was.

Only two more weeks.

He leaped out of bed and she rolled into the warm spot he'd left behind as he stood at the windows, facing the expansive sea view.

"Is that snow?"

"Oh, my gosh!" Kali scrambled out of bed, pulling on Brodie's discarded rugby jersey, and joined him, expertly stuffing the dark thoughts to the back of her mind.

Outside the window, big fat flakes were floating down from a gray sky completely unencumbered, ultimately finding purchase on a bit of slate, the deep green tines of a fir tree, or the dock she could see stretching out to the edge of the bay the house had been built on. It would take some time for a thick blanket of snow to build up—but the still beauty of the scene took her breath away.

"How beautiful…"

"Always see the bright side of things—don't you, my little Miss Sunshine?"

If only you knew!

"It's mesmerizing to watch."

"And dangerous."

"*You* always see the dark side of things, don't you, Mr. McGloomy?" Her lips twitched.

Brodie held her gaze as if daring her to break character. Soon enough her lips broadened into a wide smile.

"I suppose so. But with you here…" He tugged her close, wrapping his arms around her so that they both faced the wintry scene. "It's impossible not to see what's right with the world."

If she could preserve this moment in time she would.

Together they stood, enjoying the wintry scene, before

a clock somewhere down on the ground floor bonged out the fact that it was high time for them to get ready for work.

"Back to reality?" Kali quipped—not really minding a jot. If this could be her everyday reality she would take it in an instant.

"Right, my beauty. We'd best get a move on." Brodie dropped a kiss on top of Kali's head. "All those sick people for you to see, and I've got to figure out how on earth to build a boat."

"I'm sure there's a video on the internet," Kali teased, disappearing into the bathroom.

She stopped when the reflection of a woman caught her eye in the mirror. A happy, tousle-haired woman, her lips peeled apart in a wide smile.

It was, she realized with a start, herself. The woman she never thought she'd have a chance to be. Plain ol' happy.

"That's an interesting approach."

"Johnny! I didn't see you there."

Brodie put down the sander and wiped his brow with his forearm before shaking hands with his old classmate. It might have been snowing all morning, but he was feeling the satisfying warmth that came from physical labor.

"I was just going to clamp the…uh…the sheer clamp to the front bit. The bow."

"You've not really got a clue, have you, Brodie McClellan?" Johnny asked with a friendly guffaw. "I've built nine of these skiffs since you took yourself off to get your fancy medical degree, and I can spot a man who doesn't have the first idea how to put together a boat from a mile off. Had to run up here from the docks to set you straight."

"Why'd you have to build so many? None of them watertight enough to float?" Brodie gibed back.

He'd missed this. Just being able to blether with his schoolmates. The folk who knew him best. Although Kali was coming up a very close second…

"All of them, you cheeky so and so," Johnny mocked, quickly starting the one-two, one-two fist jabs of a man ready to clock another one in the jaw.

"So, are you going to stand there waiting for a fight that's not going to help, or are you going to help me?"

Brodie handed him a clamp. Not that he knew if it would be useful, but it was to hand.

"I'm guessing they didn't teach you anything useful like shipbuilding down at your medical school, then?" Johnny teased the clamp expertly into place and put together two bits of the boat Brodie had thought would forever remain apart.

"Right before the diseases of the liver lecture," answered Brodie with a grin.

Johnny ran a practiced hand along the golden grain of the planks and started reorganizing them into a more recognizable pattern. A boat shape.

"So, it's looking like your trip to Africa didn't kill you, then," he said, after a few moments of turning Brodie's "workshop" into something that actually *looked* like a workshop.

"Nope. You're stuck with me."

Johnny looked up from the woodpile, mouth agape. "For good? You've moved back to the island?"

Brodie's gut instinct was to laugh facetiously. But the hint of hope in his friend's eyes made him check himself. Johnny was a through and through islander. And, truthfully, the idea of staying, whilst not exactly growing on him, was distinctly more appealing than it had been a few weeks ago.

"You've definitely got me here for the foreseeable future." Brodie chose his words tactically. He still had an out if he wanted one.

"That's good to hear." Johnny nodded his approval. "We always thought you'd bugger off to some exotic country for good once your dad passed."

"We?"

"Helen and I. You remember Helen from school?"

"Of course I do! Seared into my brain, the lot of you." Brodie mimed branding his brain. "Looks like she's keeping you well fed."

"Aye, that'd be about right." Johnny patted his gut appreciatively. "Her steak bridies won me over years ago. I can't get enough of them. It's what inspired her to start the bakery. She makes a mountain of them every Hogmanay, remember?"

"I don't think I've been to yours on New Year. Not since you shacked up with Helen anyway."

"Hey, that's my wife you're talking about. I made an honest woman of her."

"Well, congratulations to you both! Belated, they may be, but no less heartfelt." Brodie shook his friend's hand, genuinely happy for him.

"No one's made you bend *your* knee, then?"

"No," Brodie answered quickly. Too quickly. He'd been too busy trying to outrun his past ever to think about starting a future. A flash of Kali lying in his bed, hair fanned out on the pillow, came to him. If he were the type to settle down…

Johnny examined the wood again, giving it another once-over with hands that had known more than their share of physical labor. "We reckoned none of us were good enough for you—that's why you had to go off seeking your fortune elsewhere."

Brodie shook his head. "No, that's not even remotely true, Johnny. I'm just—" He looked up to the dark skies, still ripe with snowfall, and sought the right words. "I suppose I just wanted to see what the world had to offer."

"And now, like a wise man, you've come back to Dunregan. The home of Western civilization!"

They laughed together, their eyes taking in the tiny village hardly a stone's throw from the clinic. Butcher, baker and a newsagent/post office/coffee shop on one side. Pub, grocery and a charity shop supporting the Lifeboat Foundation on the other. And, of course, the Dunregan Bakehouse. What more did a village need?

"What's the wee girl like? The locum you've got in for all the folk who still think you've got the touch of death about you?"

"Ha! You never minced words, did you, Johnny? Kali? She's fine. Great, in fact."

In more ways than one.

Memories of their nights together were very likely the reason why he had made next to no progress on his skiff. Since when had he become a daydreamer?

"Well, I guess I'll find out in a minute."

"Everything all right?"

Johnny nodded. "Just a wellness checkup for my diabetes. It's pretty much under control now, but Helen always badgers me into coming for these annual checkups."

He gave a *women, eh* harrumph, and turned toward the clinic.

"Good to see you, Brodie. Perhaps we'll catch up at the pub one of these nights, eh? And I'll come along and lend you a hand on that boat of yours later this afternoon, if you're still here. Make sure you don't sink when you put her out to sea."

Johnny winced the moment the words were out of his mouth.

"Oh, mate, I'm *so* sorry—I didn't mean—"

For the first time in he didn't know how long, Brodie took the joke at face value. It *wasn't* a dig about his mother and the dark course their sailing trip had taken.

"Not to worry. I could do with your wise counsel. It's an excellent idea." And he meant it. "See you soon?"

"Soon." Johnny nodded affirmatively.

They shook hands again and Brodie watched him disappear into the clinic.

It was good of Johnny to stop by and have a word. He'd

been so engrossed in his sanding he wouldn't have noticed if his old school pal had walked straight on by. But that wasn't the Dunregan way. You saw someone you knew— you stopped and you chatted. People looked after each other as they had done in small communities like this from the dawn of time. Tribal.

He watched his breath cloud and disperse as he huffed out a laugh. He would bet any amount of money this was the type of moment his father had been hoping he would have when he'd made him promise to stay. Clever sod. It was easy enough to stay at arm's length from the people he'd grown up with when he was thousands of miles away. But receiving offers of help on a boat he didn't have a clue how to build…? That was humbling. And it was starting to tease away at the very solid line he'd drawn between himself and those who'd chosen to stay.

He felt his phone vibrate in his pocket before the ring sounded. He tugged it out and took a look at the screen, eyes widening when he saw who it was.

"Callum?" He stepped out of the shed, moving his eyes up to the mountains as if he could see his brother. "What's going on?"

"There's been a wreck."

"What kind of wreck?" Brodie felt his heart rate surge. Was his brother all right?

"I'm fine," Callum said, as if reading his mind. "But you better get up here—with help if you can—the Taywell Pass road."

"What's happened?"

"The snow's right thick up here and a lorry towing a huge load of logs has jackknifed, taking out two oncoming cars as he went. One's flipped and the other is on the edge of a wee loch. Get the fire brigade up as well. We'll need the Jaws of Life. And make sure you've got tow ropes in your four-by-four."

"Do you have your medical kit on you?"

"Only the small bag. I was taking a new bike for a ride down the mountain in the snow."

"Have you got your four-by-four? We can put patients in it if necessary."

"No, just the bike."

Brodie heard his brother give a sharp gasp.

"Callum, are you all right?"

"Fine. Quit your fussing and get up here."

Brodie headed toward the rear entrance of the clinic.

"Right. Ten, twenty minutes max—I'll be there with reinforcements."

"Make it fast, Brodie. The truck driver's in a bad way. Probably internal bleeding. And there's a wee laddie trapped in one of the cars as well."

"Did you ring the air ambulance?"

"Not yet. I wanted to find out your ETA."

"Give them a ring. At least as a heads up."

"Aye—just get a move on, Brodie."

He didn't need telling twice. His brother had said he was fine, but there was something off in his tone.

Brodie hung up the phone and yanked open the clinic door. In a matter of moments he'd got Caitlyn to cancel the rest of Kali's appointments, put Ailsa in charge of ringing the volunteer fire brigade and coordinating with the ferry captain in case they needed to hold the ship for patients needing hospital care.

He grabbed his own portable medical kit and loaded a couple backboards and everything else he thought would be useful in the cab of his vehicle.

"Where do you want me?"

Kali appeared at the back of the clinic, her new winter coat zipped right up to her chin.

"Passenger seat for now. We can fold down the seats in the back if we need to transport anyone."

"Is there not an ambulance?"

"You're looking at it." Brodie pulled a blue light attached

to a wire out of his glove box and clamped it to the top of his four-by-four.

"Brodie?" Johnny stuck his head out through the back door of the clinic. "I hear you're wanting the fire brigade?"

"Aye." Brodie jumped into the four-by-four.

"That's me."

"What happened to Davie Henshall?"

"Retired, pal. See you up there as soon as I get a couple of the other lads together. Won't be long."

He waved them off and disappeared back into the clinic, only to be quickly replaced by Ailsa running to Kali's side of the car.

"Here you are, dear." She handed over three flasks. "Hot water if you need it. There's tea bags and sugar and things in the glove box."

"Thanks, Ailsa." Brodie leaned across Kali whilst shifting the car into gear. "We'll give you an update when we get there."

As he hit the road, driving safely but with intent, Brodie could feel his suspicions increase. The call from his brother ran in his head on a loop, refusing to offer up any clues. He would've told him if something was wrong. Wouldn't he...?

Even to think of suffering another loss constricted his throat. That was what this island did. Take and take and take.

He swore softly under his breath.

Stop thinking like a petulant teenager. Life's not perfect anywhere and Dunregan's no different. It's the home your parents loved as much as they loved each other. And you. You're alive. Practicing medicine, which you love. There's a beautiful woman sitting right next to you who could light up your life for the rest of your days if you let her. Now, go find your brother.

Concentrating didn't begin to describe how deep in thought Brodie looked. He was navigating the snow-covered roads with the dexterity of someone who could've walked the island blindfolded. The landscape seemed a part of him. Even more so right now.

"You all right?" Kali finally broke through the deepening silence in the car.

"Fine. We'll be there in just a couple of minutes. I was just trying to work through how we'll sort everyone."

"Triage, you mean?"

"Yes."

"You must be used to this sort of thing with all of the work you've done out in the field. With Doctors Without Borders."

"Mmm-hmm."

Brodie wasn't giving anything away. She wasn't going to lower herself by getting insecure, but this Brodie was an entirely different one from the sexy man who'd pinned her against the wall in the supplies cupboard earlier that morning for a see-you-at-lunchtime snog. Maybe this was Work Brodie, and she was confusing his refusal to engage in conversation with his concentration over what was to come.

She glanced across at him. Jawline tight. Eyes trained on the road. No guesses as to what was going on in his head.

"This'll be my first accident," Kali said.

Brodie shot her a sharp look.

"Outside a clinic or a hospital, I mean," she quickly qualified.

"You'll be fine. A bit less equipment and no nurses to fetch things, but with the help of the fire crew—they've all got basic paramedic skills—you'll be fine."

He shot her another look, one exhibiting a bit more of the Brodie she knew off duty.

He gave her thigh a quick squeeze. "Sorry, Kali. My brother's up in that mess, and he said he was fine but I have a bad feeling."

"In what way?"

"He's trained in mountain rescue—basic paramedic

stuff—but he didn't sound like he was doing anything. Normally he would've called while he was doing fifteen things as well as talking to me. One of those rare multi-tasking males." He gave a weak smile. "Hold up—I think I see them up ahead."

Kali nodded. She got it now.

Family.

The one thing you could never escape. They were woven into your cell structure.

Brodie pulled his four-by-four to an abrupt halt and scanned the scene. Not good. The opposite, in fact. He was out of the cab and crunching across ankle-deep snow toward the stationary vehicles in an instant.

"Callum?" His voice echoed against the hillsides, then was absorbed by the ever-thickening snow.

Kali appeared by his side, all but dwarfed by the large medical kit slung over her shoulder.

"Here." He took a hold of the free strap. "I'll take that. Can you grab the backboards off the roof? *Callum!*" he called again, his tension increasing.

The name reverberated from hillside to hillside, leaving only the hushed silence of snowfall.

He jogged to the logging truck, where there were huge lengths of freshly sawn trees splayed hither and yon, and climbed up to the cab. The driver was slumped over the wheel. Brodie yanked open the door and pressed his fingers to his pulse point. Thready. But he was alive.

"All right there, pal? Can you hear me?"

No answer. The driver's airbag had deployed, bloodying his nose. He could've easily knocked his head on the side window and concussed himself.

"Here's the backboard. Where do you want me?" Kali looked up at him from the roadside.

Brodie used the high step of the cab to scan the site. As his brother had described, there was a car twenty or so meters away at the edge of the loch, and one flipped onto the roadside just a few meters beyond.

He jumped down from the cab.

"Let's do a quick assessment then board up whoever needs it. Get blankets to everyone. *Callum!*"

Nothing.

They ran toward the overturned vehicle and knelt at the windows.

A woman hung, suspended by her seat belt, looking absolutely terrified.

"Madam, are you all right?"

"My boy!" she screamed, hands pressed to the roof of the car. "Can you get my boy out? Billy! Are you all right, darling? Mummy's just here."

"Hello, in there."

Brodie kept his voice calmer than he felt. The accident victims he could deal with. Not hearing from his brother... A sour tang of unease rose in his throat.

He saw the woman trying to release the catch on her seat belt. "I'm Dr. McClellan. We'll help get you and your boy out of the car, but can you keep your seat belt on, please? Don't try to undo it. You could hurt your neck. What's your name?"

"Linda. Linda Brown. Billy—can you hear Mummy?"

Kali tried to pull the rear door open on the driver's side, where a toddler was hanging from his child seat. "I can't get it open!"

"The roof must've been crushed when the car flipped." Brodie gave the door a tug as well, his foot braced against the body of the vehicle. No result. "Can you run down and check the other car while I get these two out?"

The whine of a siren filled the air. The fire department.

"Go on." Brodie waved to Kali to get to the other car while he pulled out his window punch. "Linda, can you cover your face, please? I'm just going to break Billy's window—all right?"

"What about Billy's face?" the panicked mother asked.

"I'll do my best—he should be all right, but we really need to be getting him out."

He held the tool to the window and pressed. The glass shattered but remained intact. Brodie stuck the slim tool into a corner of the window to make a small hole, then tugged as much of the glass away from the boy's face as he could. It fell away in a sheet, exactly where Brodie needed to kneel. He ran over to the backboard and tugged it into place by the window, grabbing his run bag as he did so.

He unzipped his medical kit and raked through the supplies, his fingers finding the neck braces by touch as he tried to find a pulse on the boy's neck.

Yes!

Three out of three so far.

Where the hell was his brother?

"How is he? Is he all right?" called Linda.

"I've got him. He looks good on the outside, but we'll have to wait and see if he's sustained any internal injuries."

Linda began to cry softly, a low stream of "No, no, no…" coming in an unrelenting flow.

Brodie rucked up the boy's shirt. He could see the sharp red marks from the seat belt, but no swelling that would indicate internal bleeding. He'd need tests. X-rays. Everything he didn't have here. The boy needed a proper hospital.

Had Callum called the air ambulance? Could it even fly in this weather? The snow had managed to thicken in the space of ten minutes, shrouding the surrounding mountains and hillsides in cloud.

C'mon, little brother. Throw me a sign you're okay.

"Brodie?"

Johnny appeared by his side, kitted out from head to toe in his all-weather firefighting uniform. Brodie blinked and for an instant saw the young redhead he'd used to play footie with as a youngster. That young lad had been replaced by a man who was ready for action.

"Tell us what you need."

Brodie quickly ran through instructions to get the truck driver out onto a backboard—but not before he'd had a neck brace applied. Then he'd need checks on internal bleeding, heart rate, blood pressure—the usual stats for an extraordinary situation.

"Can you help me get Billy's mother out of the car so we can get the two of them into a warm vehicle?"

"On it, mate."

Brodie looked toward the car by the loch and couldn't see anyone around it. Where had Kali disappeared to?

He forced himself to be still for a moment, to crush the growing panic. He'd dealt with thousands of people fearing for their lives in Africa. He could do this.

"Brodie?" Johnny tapped his leg. "We've got this if you want to go down to the other car."

"Thanks, pal. I'll do that. Extra blankets and things are in the back of my four-by-four."

Brodie took off at a jog, quickly ratcheting his pace up to a run when the details of the scene became clear. The front of the estate car was completely concertinaed. If anyone was alive in there it would be a miracle. He could hear barking. Dogs in the back? Had to be. There weren't any running around free.

He reached the front of the car, a seventysomething woman inside. The crash's first fatality.

The barking began again in earnest, as if the dogs sensed their owner had been killed. He made a mental note to ring the vet, see if he could come out as well.

He raced to the other side of the car. There was Kali, kneeling next to the mangled remains of a bicycle and...

Oh, no, no, no...

"Callum?"

CHAPTER EIGHT

BRODIE DROPPED TO his knees beside Kali, barely taking in the stream of information she was efficiently rattling off. Something about the car beginning to roll into the loch, Callum skidding on his bicycle in an attempt to get it behind the wheel to try and stop it, and not being able to unclip his bicycle shoes from the pedals before the car started rolling. Possible lacerations or puncture. Bones crushed.

His own observations took over as he absorbed the sight of his brother's pale face and contorted torso, only just visible outside the edge of the vehicle. Limited to zero blood flow would be going to his legs. Muscle damage. Tissue damage. Possible paralysis. He'd seen worse. So much worse. But seeing Callum like this sent shock waves of hurt through him. Pain unlike anything he'd ever experienced.

He forced himself to swallow down the emotion before he spoke. "Hey, little brother."

Callum, his head resting on a heat blanket Kali had put under him, tried to crane his neck to see Brodie better, despite the handlebars of his bicycle pinning his chest to the ground.

"Ach, no, Callum. Don't move your head. Why isn't he in a neck brace?" he snapped at Kali.

"He's not complained of any neck pain," Kali replied gently.

He knew the tone. The one he'd used with countless family members of patients. The one that said, *You're missing the big picture, so why don't you take a big breath and—*

"It's his leg, Brodie. I've not administered anything for the pain yet. Until we see what's going on under there it'll be like working in the dark," Kali stated simply. She pulled a phone out of her pocket and wiggled it in his eyeline. "Your Aunt Ailsa's rung your brother's phone here. She couldn't get through to you. An air ambulance is on its way. There is only one that can risk it in this kind of weather."

"How long?" Brodie wished he could take the bite out of his tone, but this was his *brother* they were talking about.

"Ten…maybe fifteen minutes?"

"Right." He cursed up at the sky, then checked his watch. "I suppose they didn't manage to stop the last ferry?"

"No." Kali shook her head, putting up a hand to cut off Brodie's reaction. "But Ailsa rang round and finally got hold of the captain. He's going to drop everyone and come back with a couple of ambulances. Then he'll make the trip back to the mainland."

Brodie nodded, taking in the enormity of the gesture. These were islanders pulling together to help each other. Lives woven together in good and bad. *This*, he suddenly realized, was what island life was about. Being there. Each person doing what they could to enrich and strengthen the vital community.

Brodie gave Kali's hand a quick squeeze. One that he hoped said, *I know I'm being an ass, but help me get through this.* He felt her squeeze back. It was all the sign he needed.

"All right, little brother…let's take a look, eh?"

He shifted to his hands and knees, the snow sending the cold straight through his trousers. But that was nothing compared to what his little brother must be feeling, with half his body trapped underneath that car.

The scene was impossible to break down into simple components. Just a mesh of metal, bicycle wheels, winter clothes and his brother's legs. Everything was indiscernible except the ever-increasing pain on his brother's face.

He shook his head, trying to keep his expression light as he faced his brother. "What have you done, you numpty? Why didn't you say you were in a bit of bother yourself when you rang?"

Brodie tried his best to keep his tone loving. Funny how anger and love wove together so tightly when a person was terrified.

"I wasn't when I rang. I was freewheeling down the mountainside and saw it all happen. Got down as soon as I could, checked out everyone and then saw Ethel's car going backwards toward the loch."

"Ethel?"

"The woman driving this car." He tried moving an arm to indicate the front of the vehicle, only to cry out in pain. "I—had—to—stop—it—" he panted.

"The world's first human cribbing." Brodie gave him an impressed smile. No need to point out the obvious flaws in the plan.

"I think my bike trail days might be on hold for a while. Always happens when I leave the refrigerator door open." Callum laughed before another wince of pain took over.

Brodie shot a look at Kali. His brother was talking nonsense and—as man-childish as he was—he had never been a babbler.

He gave his brother's arm a rub and felt Callum's body beginning to be consumed by shivering. Could be the cold. Could be shock.

"Kali, have we got a couple more blankets?"

"You bet." She nodded and ran back to the car to retrieve them.

"Callum. How are you feeling, mate? You still with me?"

Callum shut his eyes, but spoke with deliberation. "There weren't any blocks out here, and I wasn't going to let the dogs go into the loch to drown on top of everything…" His voice began to lose what little strength it had.

"You saved them, pal."

He gave his brother's shoulder a gentle squeeze as his eyes traveled the length of his body to his leg, pinned beneath both his cycle and the back wheel of the estate car. Any number of things could be going wrong underneath that mess. If a spoke had jammed into his leg when the car had moved it might easily have pierced a posterior tibial or fibular artery.

"Talk me through what you feel." Brodie's eyes were on his brother.

"Done that." His brother's eyes flicked up in Kali's direction. "Little to no sensation below the knee. Clear of injury other than a strain in the back from such a kickass move!" Callum finished, with a grin that rapidly shape-shifted into a grimace.

"Okay, superhero—we know you're the coolest kid on the block. Any light-headedness?" Brodie's tone was all business.

"Yeah—but there's a blinkin' car on top of me, bro. I'm hardly going to feel great."

"Since when do you talk like one of the boys in the hood?" The words were out before he could stop them.

"Since when did *you* start caring?"

Callum shot. Callum scored.

"Blankets?"

Kali's voice broke through the silence Brodie couldn't fill. Her bustle of action—swiftly wrapping the specialized heat blankets around Callum's torso—was a welcome cover for the surge of guilt threatening to drown Brodie. He was going to get his brother out of this, and he didn't know how but he was also going to make things up to him. Some way. Somehow.

"Kali…" Brodie lowered his voice. "We need to get this car off him."

"Absolutely. But I haven't done a thorough check inside because I saw Callum first. And the car will definitely go into the loch if we pull him out right now. The car could be the only thing holding him together..." Kali countered, not unreasonably.

She was right. If Callum began to bleed out before they had proper medical supplies there, or a means to get him to an operating theater... The very thing that was threatening his life could be keeping him alive.

"Can you get the dogs?"

"What?" Brodie leaned in closer to hear his brother.

"The dogs...in the back of the car."

Callum flicked a familiar pair of blue eyes toward the rear of the vehicle. Sometimes it was like looking in a mirror.

"On it."

Brodie knew his brother would do anything to help an animal before a human. The man should've been a vet, but that would've meant he had to leave the island for five years' training. And that was never going to happen.

He wouldn't rest easy now unless he knew the dogs were sorted.

The back of the car was undamaged, so the hatch top easily rose when Brodie unlatched it. Two enormous dogs leaped out of the vehicle, one landing with a sharp yelp. A broken leg? Brodie scanned the car for their leashes and easily found them, along with a bag of treats tucked into a side compartment. It was all precious time away from his brother, but Kali was there, assessing and treating him. He trusted her.

He tried unsuccessfully to get the dogs to sit... If the Newfoundlands would just play ball...

"Brodie?"

Kali's voice stopped him in a near-successful attempt at getting the leashes onto the dogs.

"Could you bring the dogs over? Your brother wants to say hello."

"I'm not the ruddy dog whisperer in the family," he grumbled, and only just stopped his eyes from rolling. His brother was in serious trouble here. Time to quit playing the despairing older brother.

One limping, one resisting, Brodie finally managed to get the dogs over to his brother, where they immediately turned into entirely different beasts, licking Callum's face, gently placing their paws on his shoulders as if petting him. These three weren't strangers. They shared a warmer relationship than he did with his own brother, and the hit of shame was hard to shrug off.

But he had to do his best. There was an accident scene to sort. The air ambulance crew would need a situation report when and if they arrived. With the weather closing in they would be lucky. And Linda and her son would need some extra care, not to mention the truck driver. This car needed lifting and towing away from the loch, and the poor soul who was inside needed extracting.

"It's Ethel."

Kali was looking up at him. He shook his head, not understanding.

"Your brother says it's Ethel *Glenn* inside. These are *her* dogs."

His mind raced to connect the dots and in an instant he made the link. Ethel Glenn and her famous shortbread. The long-term widow had stayed up in the croft she and her husband had lived on long after his death some twenty years ago. The villagers went to her, instead of the other way round. She guarded that rickety old croft like an explorer staking a claim on an island full of treasure. Peat and stone. Impossible to make a living on. He'd never understood the draw.

"Brodie?" Johnny jogged over beside them. "We've got the chap in the lorry boarded up. He's not looking too bad."

The interruption was exactly what Brodie needed to knock him back into action. Working in an emotional daze wasn't going to help any of these people—least of all his brother.

"Anyone keeping an eye on him for cardiac fallback?"

"No, he seems fine."

"If he really got a bash from that airbag—his nose was bleeding, right?"

"Yeah, it's broken. It'll need resetting."

Brodie nodded. "He'll need some scans. If he was within ten inches of that thing when it deployed it won't present now, but we'll want to check for aortic transection, tricuspid valve injuries, cardiac contusions. There's a raft of things that could still go wrong."

"Got it. I'll get one of the lads to keep an eye out. We've got Linda and Billy in our rig, getting warm. Again, nothing obvious—but from what you've said it sounds like they'll be needing a trip to the hospital as well. What now?"

The entire scene crystallized into a series of steps they would need to take as a team. Brodie gave Johnny a grim but grateful smile, then rattled off a list of assignments for everyone, taking on communications with the air ambulances and patient checks for himself. Kali was to continue monitoring his brother, while the remaining fire lads prepared the vehicle on top of Callum for removal.

It couldn't have been more than ten minutes before they all heard the whirr and thwack of the bright yellow helicopter's rotors as it began its descent.

Kali had been running on pure adrenaline, each moment passing with the frame-by-frame clarity of a slow-motion film—Brodie the confident director, able to shift from patient to casualty to fire crew to dog handler and back again.

It was a blessing that the crash had happened on the broad stretch of valley where it had, making the helicopter landing possible. Snow, time and limited visibility were the enemies. Every person present was a hero, pushing themselves to the limit to turn a bad situation into something better.

"Where do you want me?" Kali asked when Brodie appeared on her side of the car.

"Stay where you are. The crew will work around you." He lowered his voice. "He all right?"

She nodded. Callum's eyes were closed, but he was resting rather than unconscious. It had to be tough, seeing your sibling like this. It was exactly why she'd stayed away from her family. To keep them safe from harm. The violence her father had threatened... She shuddered away from the fearful thoughts that kept her up at night. She just had to have faith. Faith that her mother and sister were all right.

"We're good," she said with a firm nod.

"You warm enough?" Brodie took a half step forward and drew a finger along her jawline. The distance she'd thought he'd put between them on the way to the crash evaporated entirely.

Times like this prioritized things. She knew that better than most.

She nodded, giving the palm of his hand a soft kiss. The move was totally unlike her, but why the hell not? From the moment she'd stepped off the ferry onto Dunregan she'd felt a change was afoot. She cared for Brodie and she was going to show it. If it backfired then so be it. She'd just have to learn to cope with a whole new level of heartbreak.

Brodie's hand cupped her chin, tipping it up toward him so she could see the gratitude in his eyes. Her heart cinched...then launched into thunderous thumps of relief.

Her instinct had been right.

The intimacy of their moment was snapped in two as the air ambulance doctors jogged toward them with their own backboards and run bags.

On Brodie's signal, the fire department volunteers began preparing the vehicle to be raised and then towed away from Callum and the loch's edge.

"I'll grab hold of the bike," Brodie called as the noise of the rescue crews increased. "We don't want it yanked away from Callum's leg. If any of the spokes have pierced through we could easily make it worse. Straight up—and only then do you pull the car forward. Got it?"

A chorus of "Aye" and "You got it" filled the air as lines were attached to the mangled front of the vehicle. All the clamps and foot pump lifts were put in place. A hush descended upon the team.

Brodie knelt down by Kali, his fingers automatically shifting to his brother's neck to check for a pulse. She didn't envy him. Not one bit. The intensity of the ache in her heart shocked her, cementing the need to shake it off and focus on Callum.

The car was lifted in seconds, and the cycle went with it, its metal twisted into the undercarriage of the vehicle and—as Brodie had suspected—not one but two spokes had been jammed into his brother's leg. Callum's scream of pain at the release hit the sides of the mountains, pulsing back and forth as each person flew into action.

"All right, let's get him out from under here and onto the scoop stretcher," Brodie called. "Can somebody trench it into the snow so there's not too much movement for him?"

A blur of activity took over. Everyone was acting on well-practiced instinct and skill. Everyone was hiding their dismay at the wreckage that was Callum's leg.

"Compound fractures to the tibia and fibula," one of the doctors said unnecessarily.

"He's got an arterial bleed." Kali jumped forward, pinching the geyser of blood with her gloved hands. "Can I get a clamp?"

"On it," replied one of the air medics, raking through his run bag.

"We're also going to need blood, IV and morphine." She ticked off the list with her other hand.

"Not before splinting him," Brodie interjected. "If you're

injecting into the muscle he will feel everything during the splinting."

"Do you have any inhalable diamorphine?" Kali asked the air medic. "He's losing consciousness, so swallowing anything is out of the question."

"Right you are." He handed Kali a clamp and set to mining another part of his bag for supplies.

"Callum? Stay with us, pal. I'm here with you." Brodie held a hand to his brother's face. "Nonresponsive," he muttered, using his other hand to give Callum a brisk sternal rub with his knuckles. "His blood type is A positive. You can give him A positive and negative and O positive and negative. Can we get a defib machine over here?"

"They're using it on the truck driver. He just coded."

Brodie cursed, giving his brother another sternal rub. "C'mon…c'mon! Show me something, here."

Kali flinched in unison with Brodie at Callum's searing scream of pain as they began the messy splinting process. It was a sorry thing to be thankful for—but at least he was alive. The leg was a mess. Months of rehab were in his future. Pins. Bolts. Who knew what other hardware he'd need?

"I'm his brother," Brodie told the crew as they each took a handle of the stretcher and walked as steadily as they could across the frozen ground toward the chopper. "If there's room, I'd like to come along."

"I'll send one of my guys with the two less urgent cases. The mother and child can go on the ferry, so there's room."

"How's the lorry driver? Did he make it through the resus?"

"Only just" was the grim response as they reached the helicopter, where the truck driver was being strapped in. "Definitely something dodgy going on with his heart. He'll need seeing to straight away."

Brodie glanced at his watch, then at Kali. "Will you be taking the ferry as well?"

"Don't you trust my guys?" the head of the aircrew said with a joshing smile.

"Nothing like that, mate. I think I'll just need to see a friendly face in a couple of hours with the way things are going."

Brodie's eyes locked with Kali's. More passed between them in that single moment than ever had before. The feelings all but tearing her heart in two were shared.

Kali was entirely speechless. What a moment to realize she was in love! Her entire body surged with energy. She felt she was capable of doing anything now that she knew how Brodie felt about her.

"We need to load up!" one of the paramedics called from the helicopter. The rotors were already beginning to swirl into action.

Brodie dug into his pocket and handed her a set of keys, his gloved hand giving hers a quick squeeze. "Go in convoy with the lads from the fire station. They'll help with the transfer to the ambulances. I will try to meet you on the other side. If not—I'll see you at the hospital. Ailsa will meet you at the docks as well, no doubt."

Kali nodded, the to-do list in her head growing, turning into vivid detail and then action.

She ran across to the fire truck, where Linda and Billy were keeping warm, just as the helicopter took its first tentative moves to lift and soon soared off, skidding across the white landscape. She stopped to watch it go, taking away the man she was giving her heart to, having no idea what would happen next.

"Doc?"

Kali whipped around to see Johnny holding the two dogs on leads.

"Are you able to drop these two by the vet's?"

"Yeah, absolutely. Um…" Two big furry faces looked up at her expectantly. They were like small yetis!

"We'll give you a hand loading them up. If you could

bring your car here it would save this one's leg an unnecessary journey?"

"Yes, absolutely!" Kali jumped into action—embarrassed to have held them up. "I'll be right behind you in a second."

And right behind you, Brodie, she added silently, with a final glimpse at the helicopter before it completely disappeared from sight.

"I'll come check on you soon, all right?"

Kali waved as Linda and Billy were wheeled off on their gurneys for a full set of scans and X-rays. Bumps and bruises were a definite. She held up a set of crossed fingers that there wasn't going to be anything else.

"Can we get you anything, Dr. O'Shea? A coffee or tea? I think you might be stuck on the mainland tonight."

The charge nurse was halfway out of her station before Kali's brain kicked back into action. The long day was beginning to show.

"No, I'm good, thanks. Just directions to where I might find another one of the patients who came in on the air ambulance."

"Reggie Firle?"

"No." Kali shook her head. "He was the lorry driver. He's all right, though?"

Best not let the heady combination of lust and love cloud her priorities. Patients. They were number one right now.

"Yes, he's fine. In Recovery, where they are monitoring his heart. So it's…" She ran her finger along the patient list.

"Callum McClellan."

"Oh, yes!" The nurse's finger hit the name at the same time as she spoke. "The one with the doctor brother."

The extremely gorgeous doctor brother, whose existence is eating all of my brain particles.

"Yes."

A more politic answer, she thought, given the circumstances.

Turned out the hour-long ferry ride had given her *way* too much time to think…overthink…and then to worry. Was she thinking she was in love too soon? Reading far too much into *that look*?

She sucked in a deep breath. It was *carpe diem* time.

She nodded and smiled as the nurse gave her directions to the surgical department, where Callum was currently undergoing the first of several surgeries. Her breath caught in her throat. Poor guy. Doing his best to save the dogs, the car, dear old Ethel's remains and now—courtesy of a bicycle shoe—compromising his own future. His life.

The relief Brodie felt when he saw Kali walk into the surgery unit threatened to engulf him. Weighted to the chair he'd only just sat down in, he finally felt able to succumb to the emotions he'd been struggling to keep at bay. He was raw. More so than he'd ever been. And the thought of letting someone see him this exposed was terrifying.

One look at Kali and he knew he shouldn't have worried. The soft smile, the compassion in her eyes, the outstretched arms all said, *You won't have to go through this alone.* As she wordlessly came to him he tugged her in between his knees, his arms urgently encircling her waist when she pulled his head close to her and hit after hit of untethered emotion finally released.

"Want your coffee straight up or with a splash of artery-hardener?" Kali held the small pitcher of cream aloft, poised to pour.

"With a dram of whiskey, but that's a no-goer," Brodie replied, his eyes searching just a little hopefully round the deserted hospital canteen for a bar. Kali's ever-present optimism must be catching.

"Artery-hardener and some not very appetizing biscuits

it is, then, sir!" She handed him a paper cup, with cream still whirling its way through the steaming liquid, and wiggled a packet of vending machine ginger biscuits in front of him that looked as though they could have been made in the last century.

"The middle of the night seems to have its advantages round here."

He put his arm round her shoulder, biscuits and coffee held aloft in his other hand. Being close to Kali was healing. Touching her was downright curative.

"How's that?" She smiled up at him with an *oops* shrug after losing half of her biscuit in a too-deep dunk.

"Lots of sofas to commandeer."

He steered her toward a dimly lit corner of a waiting room not too far from surgery and sank into the well-worn cushions. The stories they could tell…

"I used to dream of working in a place like this."

"Oh, yeah?"

"Well," he qualified, "not exactly like *this*. Inner city. Busy. Never-get-a-moment's-rest busy."

"I thought you preferred international work?" She toed off her thick-tread boots and tucked her feet up underneath her.

"I really love it. Doctors Without Borders does amazing work. But the idea of being part of a city I know and helping people there—being part of something…"

"Like being part of the community on Dunregan?"

"Touché!" He raised his coffee cup and took a noisy slurp, because he knew it sent a shiver down her spine. But she was right. "This sort of thing does put a lot in perspective."

"Gives you different priorities?"

She wasn't asking. She was telling.

"That sounds like the voice of experience."

Kali's green eyes flicked up to the ceiling, then did a

whirl round the room. "Suffice it to say when the unexpected happens for me it all boils down to family."

"The family you never talk about?" He was feeling too worn by the day's events to mince words.

She shook off his question and put one of her small hands on his cheek. He pressed into as she said, softly but deliberately, "Today is about you and your family."

Brodie put his coffee down. Another wave of emotion was hitting him and there would be spillage. Literal and figurative.

"I—I could've done so much more..."

"What do you mean? You did everything you could today."

"Not today. His whole life!" He scrubbed both hands through his hair. "*I'm* the reason he didn't grow up with a mother, and then I couldn't even stick around to be a big brother for him. I just let him go feral. What kind of a person does that?"

Kali let the words percolate and settle before softly replying, "The kind who hasn't forgiven himself for something that isn't his fault?"

"But it *is*! Was..." He still couldn't believe she wasn't able to see why the blame lay solidly at his feet. He'd *begged* his mother to go out with him that day.

Kali pulled back and folded her hands in her lap, her index finger tapping furiously, the rest of her completely still.

"The only thing you can change," she said at last, "is the future. That is completely in your control."

"Who turned *you* into a sage little Buddha?" He nudged her knee with his own.

"Ohhhh..."

Her lips pressed together and did that little wiggle that never failed to make him smile.

"Let's just say life's had a way of regularly shoving me

into the Valuable Lesson department." She tipped her head onto his shoulder.

"Oh, yeah?" He wove his fingers through hers and leaned his head lightly on top of her silky black hair. "What's today's valuable lesson, then?"

"Sticking together," she said without a moment's hesitation. "Through thick and thin."

"This being the thin?"

He could feel her head nod under his.

"This being the thin."

They both stared blankly out into the room. The beeps and murmurings from the wards were more of a white noise than a frenetic addition to the chaos of the day. Callum's surgery shouldn't take too much longer. Then they'd have a much better idea of what lay ahead of him.

Brodie's thumb shifted across Kali's and he took a fortifying inhalation of her wildflower-and-honey-scented skin.

A sudden hit of clarity came to him. He stayed stock-still for risk of shaking the perfection of it away. Kali was right. He *was* in charge of his future—and she, he knew in his heart, was the missing piece of the puzzle.

"Kali? Have you got anything booked after this gig? The locum post on Dunregan?"

"Not yet."

"Would you consider staying?"

He felt her sharp intake of breath before he heard it.

"You mean at the clinic?" Her voice was higher than usual.

He kept his eyes trained on the double doors of the surgical ward, but continued.

"At the clinic, yes. I don't know how long I'm going to need to be here at the hospital, but..." This was the hard part. The part that scared him silly. "Would you stay with me? Give up your igloo of a cottage? Come stay with me? At home?"

Okay—so it was a little open-ended. It was no proposal, but...

Her fingers, so tiny in amongst his own, squeezed his tightly. But she didn't say a word.

"It's not much of an offer, is it? Stay with a messed-up guy, with a messed-up brother, on an island with a whole lot of messed-up history to untangle."

He laughed. Life had finally pinned him into a corner, forcing him to deal with everything head-on—and, oh, he wished Kali would stay here by his side. He knew he'd have to do the fighting on his own, but knowing that she'd be there waiting for him... He felt his heart skip a beat. Was this how deeply his father had felt for his mother?

"Kali," he said quickly, before she could answer, "I'm not sure what I'm offering you, but...please don't go."

He turned, pressed his lips softly to hers, words suddenly too flimsy for what he needed to communicate. She returned the kiss. Gently...silently.

They sat there for a moment, forehead to forehead, the world around them dissolving into a blur of white noise and shadows. He felt closer to her now than he had when they had made love. Those intimate moments they'd shared? Sheer beauty. But right now...? This...this was the stuff true love was made of.

"Yes," she finally whispered. "I'll be here for you as long as you need me."

CHAPTER NINE

Missing you.
Can't wait to see your beautiful eyes again.
Just dreamed of holding you in my arms.

KALI GAVE A loved-up sigh, forcing herself to put her mobile phone down. She and Brodie had been texting like moonstruck teens since she'd left the mainland three days ago. In spite of all the difficult moments they'd shared at the hospital, these messages were like little drops of heaven.

Ailsa knocked on her office door frame, mugs of tea in hand. "How many are you up to now? I heard Caitlyn put another call through a few minutes ago."

"I can't believe there hasn't been a nationwide alert!" Kali looked at her growing list of volunteers.

"You don't need an alarm system here on Dunregan. Telephones and a trip down to the Eagle for a pint do the trick fast enough." Ailsa slid a mug of tea onto Kali's desk and perched on the edge. "Here you are, dear. You'll need this."

Kali ran her finger along the list. "So...how do you think I should work it? Brodie's insisting on staying for the next few days, while Callum's still in Intensive Care."

"He's not in Recovery yet?" Ailsa's eyes widened.

"No. He's been in and out of surgery for the past two days." She cleared her throat, trying to keep the emotional fallout at bay. "And this morning Brodie was pretty concerned about his blood pressure. Callum lost a lot of blood before they got him into hospital with the arterial bleed and they were talking about bringing him back into sur—" She choked on the word, unable to continue.

"Hey, now. Our Callum's strong as an ox. If anyone can pull through it's that lad." Ailsa pulled her up and into a warm hug. "Brodie tells me you were an absolute rock. That he couldn't have got through the past couple of days without you."

Kali pulled back, tears streaming down her face. "He said that?"

"'Course he did, love." Ailsa reached across the desk and tugged a tissue out of the ever-present box and handed it to her. "And if I were a betting woman I would guess things are running a bit deeper than that."

Kali felt red blossom on her cheeks.

Ailsa laughed. "I might be well into middle age, darlin', but do you think I haven't seen the sparks between you two?"

"It's not— Well, it's…"

Of all the times to be at a loss for words!

"It is what it is," Ailsa filled in for her. "But you be careful. This is quite a time of turmoil for Brodie, and I love my nephew to bits but I've never known him to be into much of anything for the long-term except for his work."

A fresh wave of tears threatened to spill over onto Kali's cheeks.

"Ach, away." Ailsa pulled her in tight again for a lovely maternal hug. "I'm not saying Brodie will let you down. I'm just saying mind your heart. We've all really taken to you and we'll hate to see you go."

"Brodie's actually asked me to stay on."

"As a partner in the clinic? He'd been talking about it before you came, but I didn't think he meant it." A look of happy disbelief overtook Ailsa's features. "Are you *sure* we're talking about my Brodie? The errant nephew of mine who won't commit to dinner in a couple of hours' time—that Brodie?"

"The very same. But—" Kali quickly covered herself, not wanting to get too excited. "He wasn't specific about the clinic. I presume he just meant until Callum's out of hospital and things are back to normal."

"There's no such thing as 'normal' for Brodie, Callum *or* Dunregan for that matter, love."

Kali's brain was pinging all over the place. And her heart was thudding so loudly she was surprised it wasn't boinging out through her jumper, cartoon-style.

"Are you saying it's best if I leave?"

"Oh, heavens no!" Ailsa looked horrified. "Absolutely not, Kali, love. I'm just an interfering auntie. What happens between you and Brodie is none of my business. You're about the best thing that has happened to him ever since the poor lad's mother died. I'm only saying he's never been settled here. Not in his heart. But these past few weeks I've seen you take to the community here like a duck to water." She sighed. "I suppose I'm saying make sure you know what you want. Brodie and the island don't necessarily come as a package."

Kerthunk.

Could hearts defy the most intricate internal structuring and actually plummet to the pit of your stomach?

That was what it felt like. A best day and a worst day colliding midchest and sinking like a lead weight. Taking all of the air in her chest with it.

Kali looked down at the list of names she'd compiled on her desk, feeling genuine fatigue creeping in and replacing the positive energy that had been keeping her afloat.

Brodie had asked her to stay! Not as his wife or anything, but he'd asked her to *stay*. And here was a list of people all willing to help him as he transitioned from globe-trotter to islander. A *list*! A list in black-and-white of at least two dozen people who'd rung her up this morning, volunteering to take stints of time with Callum so Brodie could get some rest.

She pulled the papers off the desk and forced a bright smile. "I guess we'd better get cracking on putting this rota together before the patients start coming. There's a busy day ahead."

"That there is," Ailsa agreed. She knocked her knuckles against the door frame, as if chiding herself. "Don't let me get you down, Kali. I'm just an overcautious Scot. You might be pleased to hear that Johnny was looking to head over to the mainland soon, to stand in for Brodie so he can come back and get a fresh change of clothes."

Kali's eyes lit up, but she did her best to contain her smile as Ailsa disappeared out into the corridor.

Perhaps Ailsa was right. She wasn't being cautious enough. Wasn't looking after the heart she'd so hoped to set free up here on this beautiful, wild island.

She closed her eyes and there was Brodie, clear as day. All tousled hair and full lips parting in that smile that never failed to send her insides into a shimmy or seven. She guessed it was time to venture into unknown territory yet again, because closing her heart to Brodie... An impossibility.

"C'mon. Budge over. I need a bit of normal." Brodie pulled a chair up next to Kali's as she looked through the afternoon's patients, wanting to make sure she'd crossed her i's and dotted her t's...or was it the other way round? Brodie must be just as tired as she was. It had taken four days for Callum to get out of ICU. He had been lucky, his doctors had cautioned. *Very* lucky.

She pulled a folder from the top of her ever-growing pile and scanned it.

"All right, then, Doctor. How's about a 'normal' case of toe fungus?" She hung air quotes round the *normal*.

"If it's who I think it is…" Brodie flashed her a quick smile "…it's perfectly normal."

She held up the file so he could see.

"Bingo! Got it in one!" Brodie clapped his hands together happily. "That chap needs to develop a better friendship with his washer-dryer."

"Or just buy some fresh boots and start over?"

They laughed, not unkindly, while Kali made a couple of notes, then moved on to the next patient.

Together they worked through the dozen or so patient files—Brodie offering a bit of insight here, Kali making her usual meticulous notes. The atmosphere between them was perfect. Warm. Companionable. No—even better than that. *Loving.*

She could've sat there all day with him, doing her best to keep the odd hits of panic at bay. Panic that what she was feeling whenever they were together wasn't real. Panic that she didn't deserve such happiness.

Ailsa's words kept echoing in her head… *Brodie and the island don't necessarily come as a package.*

"When are you going to be done?" Brodie's sotto voce tone sent shivers down her spine as his hands spread out across her back in search of her bra strap. "I want to get you up on the exam table and do some examining of my own."

"Someone's in a good mood." Kali nudged him away with her elbow while she tried to input some information into the computer system.

"Someone's too busy working to indulge me," he teased, tickling her side to no effect.

He sat back in his chair and assessed her.

"Someone else is ignoring very important paperwork." Kali didn't want to be under the microscope right now. Not with the zigzags of emotions she was experiencing.

"Are you putting patient care over your—?" He stopped for a moment, his eyes flicking up to the left in the telltale sign that he was searching for the right thing to say.

"My what?" Kali asked, trying her absolute, very, very best to keep her tone light.

"Boyfriend sounds stupid, doesn't it? And partner always sounds too clinical for me. Too businessy."

Brodie turned her round in her wheelie chair and tugged her closer toward him so that he could lay a deeply satisfying, sexy-as-they-come kiss on her lips.

Uh-oh! Boy, was she in trouble!

He pulled back and feigned a detached inspection, silently chewing a few words round in his mouth before sounding them out into her office.

Seafaring Lothario, main squeeze and *plus one* were rejected outright. "Man-friend?" he tried, to Kali's resolute horror.

"Or..." He pulled back even farther, eyes firmly glued on hers. "You don't look entirely happy, here. Have I jumped the gun?"

"No!" Kali all but shouted, then forced herself to turn her own volume down. "No, I think it's sweet."

"Sweet?" Brodie recoiled. "I thought you liked me because I was all silent and broody and muscly. A pensive Viking."

"Oh, definitely!" Kali was giggling now, fears laid to rest. At least for now. "You're my pensive Viking."

"You don't have a whole string of us out there, do you?" Brodie pulled her in again, dropping kiss after kiss on her lips. "A doctor in every port?"

"As if."

She returned one of his kisses with the ardor of a Viking mistress whose man had only just returned from months at sea. Shirts became untucked, fingers started exploratory journeys, backs arched, soft moans unfurled out of throats receiving naughty nips and licks as hands squeezed and caressed and—

A knock sounded.

Kali and Brodie hastily tugged everything back into

place that should be in place, still giggling when Ailsa opened the door with a wary expression.

"I'm not interrupting anything here, am I?"

"No, Auntie Ailsa. What can we do for you?"

"I've got some patients."

"Already? I thought I had another twenty minutes." Kali's eyes flicked to the clock to double-check.

Ailsa stood back from the door frame and in bounded two very familiar furry beasts, one with a bright pink plaster on her leg.

"Hamish! Dougal!" Kali dropped to her knees, only to be covered in big slobbery kisses.

She'd been visiting the vet's on a daily basis, sending photos to Brodie to show to Callum to prove that Ethel's—now his—beloved dogs were being taken care of.

"Glad to see it's such a happy reunion." Ailsa smiled down at her, before squaring her gaze with Brodie's. "Now, you're sure you're all right to have these two massive bear cubs running round your house until your brother is well enough to look after them?"

"Definitely." Brodie nodded solidly whilst Ailsa's stern expression remained unchanged.

"I know Kali's willing to help, and we can rely on her, but the onus is on *you*, Master McClellan. No swanning off to Africa, or whatever exotic location takes your fancy, with these two relying on you."

Brodie looked down at the two dogs, their big eyes now locked on him. Hopeful. Gleaming. And between them, of course, was Kali. The most beautiful face in the world. Her green eyes were filled with the same glint of hopeful anticipation. One that cemented his decision.

"Yes, Aunt Ailsa." He nodded soberly. "You have my word."

"Well, then…" She gave a brisk *that's done* swipe of her hands. "That's good enough for me. Now, will you be bringing them to Ethel's funeral? I'm fairly certain Callum said she stipulated in her will that they be there."

"That's this Friday, isn't it?" Kali asked, her arms still around her new furry companions.

Ailsa nodded.

"It's a shame it's so soon. Callum would've been the best one to speak."

"Could we get him to do a video link on someone's phone or tablet?" Kali suggested.

"That's a good idea." Brodie nodded as the idea took shape. "Or maybe—as we can't do the pyre until Ethel has been cremated—we could wait until he's back. Even if he's on crutches or in a wheelchair we can wheel him down to the beach before we set the boat alight."

"I'm sorry?" Kali looked like she was choking on the image he'd painted.

"Didn't Callum tell you?"

"The last time I saw him he was so high on painkillers he mostly talked about putting Ethel in a boat and setting it on fire, then shoving it out to sea. I thought he was just away with the faeries."

"Nope. Not in the slightest." Brodie shook his head, and his aunt nodded along with him. It was one of the island traditions he had actually always loved. A traditional Viking funeral. "It won't be completely traditional, because I think Health and Safety have something to do with it. But Ethel requested that her ashes be put out to sea Viking-style. I think she traced her lineage back to the Norse gods, or something mad, and she always was a bit of an old battle-ax…"

An idea shot through him like a jolt of electricity.

"What if I got some of the lads to help me finish my boat and we used that instead of one of those smaller model-types? It would take a couple of weeks, and that would hopefully buy Callum the time to get out of hospital."

"Oh, no—Brodie. Not that one." Ailsa shook her head disapprovingly.

"Why not?" He looked between the two astonished women as if it was perfectly obvious that he should send his handcrafted boat out in a burning pyre of flames.

"Don't worry, ladies. Leave it with me. Ethel will go out in style!"

"Mmm…this is my favorite part of the day." Kali stretched luxuriously, using Brodie as ballast for her small frame as she twisted and wiggled herself from early-morning sleepy to fresh-faced awake.

"And why's that, my sweet little raven-haired minx?" Brodie had a pretty good idea why, but he wanted to hear Kali say it anyhow.

"Calm before the storm."

"Which storm is that? The patients who can't get enough of you? The boatbuilding brigade? The two larger-than-life dogs we've been looking after until my softie of a brother can walk again? Do you want me to keep going?" he asked when she started giggling.

"I don't see them as storms—they're just…life."

"You're *my* calm." Brodie tugged her in so he could give her a smooch on the forehead.

"Hardly!" Kali protested, accepting the kiss anyway, tip-toeing her fingers up along his stomach until they came to rest on his chest. "Does that make you the storm?"

"It's not as if I've brought much tranquility into your life."

They both laughed as Brodie began to tick off the number of things that had happened since his return to Dunregan, and Kali dismissed each of them as insignificant.

"If you'd actually *had* Ebola this would've been a very short-lived romance."

"That's true. And you'd have had to die as well, since we've been snogging ourselves silly."

"How very *Romeo and Juliet* of us!"

"Except my family doesn't hate your family because you

keep them all secret and locked up in your little Kali hide-away," Brodie teased.

He felt Kali instantly stiffen beside him. Bull's-eye on the sore subject, and he hadn't even been trying!

He propped himself up on an elbow and drew a finger along her jawline, compelling her to meet his gaze. "Sweet-heart… I don't know why you don't talk about your family, but if you ever need to talk about it—about them—we both know you've helped me a lot with mine…"

Kali put on an impish grin—one that didn't make it all the way to her eyes—gave him a quick peck on the lips and then skittered out from under his arms.

"We've got to get a move on. I want to get the dogs walked before I go to the clinic." She wrapped herself up in his hugely oversized dressing gown, looking like a ter-rycloth princess in her ceremonial robes. "Today's the big day."

"Ethel's ceremony! And getting Callum back from hos-pital, of course. Do you think we should make up the down-stairs bedroom for him or just let him bed down with the dogs?"

Kali smirked at him and pointed at the linen cupboard down the hallway.

"Well, we'd best crack on, love." He shooed her out of the bedroom. "Hie thee to the shower, lassie. I'll not have you entering the clinic smelling like anything less than a dewy rose."

Brodie fell back into the pile of pillows when he heard the shower go on, glad to have put a smile back on Kali's face. He'd let it slide this time. But now that he realized what an idiot he'd been to turn his back on his family he really hoped she would open up to him about hers. Good or bad, they were worth coming to terms with.

He'd thought he didn't need his family. What had never occurred to him was how much they'd needed *him*. They hadn't been trying to suffocate him. They'd just been trying to love him. And for the first time since his mum had passed he was beginning to believe he was *worthy* of their love.

Just a few days more and he would find out if he was worthy of Kali's.

He rolled over to the far side of the bed and tugged open the drawer of the bedside table, where he'd hidden the tiny green box he'd brought back from the mainland after his last trip to see Callum. He flicked open the box and smiled… one perfect solitaire. All that was left to do now was find the perfect moment.

"Are you sure you're comfortable?" Kali tucked an extra blanket over Callum's knees. Tartan, of course. Over the tartan of his kilt.

"I'm not geriatric. I'm simply…transitioning to bionic. It's a process," Callum grumbled good-naturedly, swatting her hands away. "If that brother of mine could learn to steer this thing better I might not have shouted so loud when we hit that bump."

"What's that about my driving?"

Brodie sidled up, also kilted-out to the nines, slipping a warming arm across Kali's shoulders. She loved the "everydayness" of the gesture. How protected she felt. Secure.

"Your driving is absolutely wonderful, big brother." Callum grinned.

"That's what I thought you were saying. How's the leg?"

"As I was saying to the beautiful Dr. O'Shea—"

"Hey, watch it," Brodie interrupted, his fingers protectively tucking Kali a bit more possessively under his arm. "I saw her first."

"I know… I know!" Callum held his hands up in the surrender pose. "Seriously, though. Thanks to you two and your stellar calls on my leg, I want you to know I am *feeling* bionic. Even if it will take six months to test run all the new hardware inside it. You'll get front-row seats to the inaugural run, if you can bear looking after me that long."

"Don't worry, Callum. We'll be here to watch you take the first tenuous steps all the way to your first hill run." He gave Kali's arm a little rub. "Won't we, love?"

Kali smiled and nodded, hiding as best she could the hint of anxiety this glimpse into their mutual future had unleashed. She had never planned for the future. Never been able to. The fact that she'd made it through medical school was little short of a miracle.

And her little-girl hopes of falling in love and marrying the man of her dreams one day... Her father had shown her just how much of a nightmare that sort of dream could become.

"Hey, you." Brodie nestled in to give her a peck on the cheek. "Everything all right?"

"Absolutely." She gave him a wide smile. One filled with every ounce of gratitude that she had for having him in her life at all. "I was just thinking—do we have your brother parked in the best place to give his eulogy?"

"Celebratory remembrance, Kali! Ethel would've hated the idea of a eulogy," Callum cut in. "And here was me, worried you'd put me at the end of the dock so Brodie could push me off. What do you think, Kali? You've got to know this wayward beast over the past couple of months...are his intentions honorable?"

Her eyes widened and zipped from Callum's to Brodie's. One set of cornflower-blue eyes was filled with laughter, whilst Brodie's... Was that panic she saw? Whatever it was, it sent her stomach churning.

"Relax, Kali. I'm just messing with you." Callum laughed heartily. "Wow! Take a look at the crowds. I don't think I've ever seen the beach this crowded. Do you think I'll be needing a microphone?"

"Don't worry, little brother. Your dulcet tones are plenty loud enough."

* * *

Brodie would've punched his brother's lights out if he hadn't already been laid up in a wheelchair. Trust him to near enough let the cat out of the bag before he'd even had a chance to propose. It wasn't as if Kali had professed her undying love for him or anything. Or said she wanted to stay on Dunregan forever. Something he could picture himself doing. Especially tonight.

He finally saw what his father had wanted him to see. A place where people came together to help. Yes, they knew your secrets, and whether or not your shortbread was better or worse than the woman's next door. But they were a united front in the face of adversity and—in tonight's case—the celebration of a life fully lived. People were absolutely flooding the broad arc of a beach.

Tall torches were secured in the sand every five meters or so, the flames adding a warm glow to the scene. Up above them the stars were out in force, and even though it was freezing cold he felt warmer in his heart than he had in years. Being here with the woman he loved, his brother and his extended family—virtually the entire population of Dunregan—all gathered together to send off Ethel Glenn in about the most dramatic fashion possible. It was heaven-sent.

Kali lit the first candle on Callum's say-so. The atmosphere was hushed, a mix of tears and laughter as everyone remembered Ethel in their own way after Callum gave a simple but loving speech in memory of the woman who had touched each of their lives—if not with her deep understanding of the island, then with her excellent command of shortbread.

Within minutes the sky was filled with scores of Chinese lanterns. Hamish and Dougal each raised their furry head to the skies and howled their farewells.

"Brodie?" Callum prompted, when a few moments had

passed and another collective silence was upon them. "Will you do the honors?"

Brodie stepped forward, his eyes solidly on the boat he had built with the unfettered help of the community. Young and old had gathered to craft her, and for just an instant he felt remorse at the decision to set her alight. But there'd be time to build another one. And he couldn't think of a more appropriate send-off for a woman who had embodied the very essence of the place he was now proud to call home.

"This boat—*The Queen Ethel*—she's a project that's been—" He stopped, feeling the choke of emotion threatening to overwhelm him.

He looked to Kali and gathered the strength he needed from her beautiful green eyes and warm smile.

"This boat was built by many hands. The wood—grown on Dunregan, ordered by my father—has been lovingly crafted—"

"You mean put together with sticky tape?" Johnny shouted from the crowd.

A ripple of laughter lifted the mood, bringing a smile to Brodie's lips.

"Near enough, mate. That and plenty of glue. A thank-you is definitely required for Johnny's long-suffering wife, Helen, for keeping all of us chaps in bridies, scones and raspberry jam for the duration."

He patted his air-inflated stomach, to the delight of the crowd.

"But seriously—and I do mean this from the bottom of what most of you know to be my very wayward heart—this boat would not exist without all of you."

He reached out to Kali and gave her hand a squeeze, buying himself a moment to swallow another surge of emotion.

"We all know I couldn't think of enough reasons to leave this island as a teen—but, having seen the world and come back home... I can assure you all that Ethel exemplified all of the reasons to stay. Will you all charge your glasses, please, as we offer up a toast and a farewell to our dear friend, Ethel Glenn?"

Callum handed Brodie the flaming torch he'd been holding throughout his brother's speech. Brodie raised it aloft as the sound of bagpipes began. Another man untied the boat and with an almighty shove set her out to sea, with the torch Brodie flung in the very center of the craft.

Collectively everyone held their breath as a huge whoosh of flame took hold of the boat and it was transformed into an otherworldly Viking craft.

Huzzahs and shouts of delight filled the air, and for a few moments Kali stood spellbound by the sight of the boat floating out to sea. By the contrast of the billowing flames reaching up to the heavens and the foamy crash of waves against the hull of the boat.

Out of the corner of her eye she saw motion. An awful lot of motion. Her eyes shifted closer to the shore.

Was that…?

Were those…?

Had they really…?

Her fingers flew to her mouth in disbelief.

Scores of islanders were flinging off their clothes and jumping—some in old-fashioned swimsuits, others completely stark naked—into the sea! Including, she saw with complete amazement as a kilt landed in her arms, Brodie!

Kali laughed and laughed. She'd heard all sorts of people mention the Polar Bear Club, but until this very minute she'd had no idea what they were talking about. With all the white bums bobbing about in the sea, children and adults alike shrieking with delight at the frigid arctic temperatures, the scene had the undeniable feel of a party.

Ethel's boat was quite a distance out now, the fire illuminating the effervescence of the waves with a golden tinge. Completely magical.

Kali could imagine living here until the end of time. Yes, there would always be a hole in her heart where her mother and sister had lived. Maybe over time she could make it a warmer place. A sacred place where she kept them safe, preserved in a time before she'd known the cruel twists life could sometimes take.

"Here you are, love. Mind giving me a hand?" Ailsa materialized by her side with an enormous bag overflowing with huge fluffy towels.

"Wow! Did a spa go out of business or something? These look amazing!"

"We held a charity do a couple of years back, after folk kept misplacing their towels along the beach. This way the swimmers come out, they towel off, get a warm drink—see the table set up over there by the shore?—and everything goes down to the pub for washing the next day."

"The pub?"

"Aye, they've got one of those big industrial washing machines because of the rooms and the little cabins they let over the summer. That was their donation. Scrubs and suds."

Kali grinned at the wording. If it was possible for her to like Dunregan even more, it was happening.

She stopped for a second, shifting up her chin as if it would help her hear better. Just out of earshot she heard a sharp, frightened call. A woman.

"Jack!" shouted the voice. *"Jaaaack!"*

Kali knew that tone.

Fear.

Complete and utter fear.

CHAPTER TEN

FROM WHERE SHE STOOD, atop the pier, Kali quickly linked the voice with a woman, eyes frantically scanning the sea and the crowded beach, her voice growing more and more strained amidst the loud party atmosphere.

The atmosphere which had just seemed so festive turned abruptly discordant.

The sea water would be warmer than the air—which was just hovering at freezing—but Kali knew cold water like that could kill a child in seconds.

"Ailsa…" She touched her arm and whispered, "Can you go help that woman there? Search along the beach for her child. I'll look in the water."

Ailsa's eyes widened with understanding and she quickly ran down to the beach, pulling people along with her as she went, somehow mysteriously silencing the bagpipes along the way.

Kali forced herself to remain steady, her eyes systematically working along the first few meters of the shoreline.

"Take the dogs." Callum's voice cut through her concentration.

"Sorry?"

"Ethel's dogs," Callum repeated, handing her the leashes. "They're water rescue dogs."

Of course! That would explain why Ethel had been heading to the loch in the dead of winter to "play" with her dogs.

A siren sounded, bringing the whoops and chatter to a complete halt.

Kali's eyes flicked back to Callum.

"That's the lifeboat rescue siren."

"Who's in charge?"

"Johnny. He probably set the siren off. Go." Callum shooed her away. "I know you want to help."

The cove abruptly became a floodlit area, with shocked faces standing out in sharp relief against the night as they regrouped, turning from revelers into a focused search party. Boats appeared, their searchlights fanning this way and that along the broad reaches of the cove.

The beach spanned a good two or three kilometers. What had seemed a cozy and protected arc shifted into a shadowy, borderless expanse.

"Kali?"

She whirled around at the sound of Brodie's voice. A rush of emotion overwhelmed her heartbeat for an instant when he appeared—safe—towel in one hand, dry suits in the other.

"I'm going out in one of the boats." He rapidly scrubbed the sea out of his hair. "Here's a dry suit. I'd like to take one of the dogs out on the boat with me. The suit will be a bit big, but do you mind suiting up and going with Dougal along the shoreline?"

She nodded, slotting all the information into place. "Absolutely."

Seconds morphed into minutes.

The calling of the little boy's name—Jack was a mischievous four-year-old who'd slipped the protective grip of his mother's hand—rang out again and again.

Kali was hyperaware of how precious each passing moment was. If Jack had run into the water hypothermia was a threat. Children had a higher ratio of surface area to mass than adults, causing them to cool much faster. But there was a plus side. Cold water would instantly force his body to conserve oxygen—it would slow down the heart instead of stopping it and would immediately shift blood to vital parts of the body. The brain. The heart. Particularly in children.

Kali felt a surge of energy charge her as the community turned from being mourners to a mobilized search and rescue team.

"Here. Let me make sure you've got these sealed up properly."

Brodie shifted and tugged the bright orange neoprene suit she'd pulled on, sealing her into a cocoon of body heat. Something that poor little child, if he were in the sea, wouldn't have.

Brodie locked his bright eyes to hers. "Jack's wearing a sky blue puffer jacket. He has hair the color of your suit— all right?" He dropped a distracted kiss on her forehead. "See you soon. Be safe."

"You, too," she whispered to his retreating figure, extra glad for the company of the warm shaggy dog beside her.

"Right, Dougal." She gave his head a good rub. "Let's go to work."

Kali saw him at a distance, and Dougal made the same link a lightning-fast second later. She blew on her whistle as hard as she could and ran so fast her lungs burned with the exertion.

Jack was farther down the beach than she would've believed possible. Whether he'd been caught in a crosscurrent or had wandered off and then been sucked under by a wave they'd probably never know. All that mattered now was getting the tiny figure out of the water.

Dougal reached Jack, instantly grabbing a hold of the hood of his coat. Kali swam as hard as she could. The tide was stronger than she'd anticipated, but she got there. Her toes were unable to touch the sea floor. Jack's pallor was a deathly blue white. It was impossible to check his pulse, but she knew he was hovering somewhere between life and death.

She took the life ring attached to Dougal's safety line and got it round Jack as best she could, ensuring his head was above water, blowing her whistle again and again in between choking on mouthfuls of briny seawater.

Just when her toes had managed to gain purchase on the sea floor she saw Brodie arriving, poised at the helm of a speedboat, its searchlight all but blinding her. With a Herculean effort, and a well-placed nose-nudge from Dougal, she managed to hoist the little boy out of the water and into Brodie's waiting arms.

Someone else's arms reached out to pull her in. She waved off the offer, needing to slosh through the water back to the shore. Just a few minutes alone, to walk off the shakes of adrenaline now shuddering through her.

The speedboat whizzed off to the pier, where a team of people were already on standby to receive the tiny patient.

Something in her gut told her the boy would live.

Something in her heart clicked into a place she'd long dreamed of.

She knew where she belonged.

She was irrevocably part of the island now. Sea, sand, sky—the entire package felt imbedded in her in a way she'd never believed possible. And she would do everything in her power to hold it tight.

Brodie checked the boy's pulse again, shaking his head when he felt nothing. "Can someone grab the pelican cases from my four-by-four?" he shouted, to no one in particular.

They appeared by his side moments later, along with a huge pile of dry towels, blankets and clothing. He could see feet jostling and hear the murmur of the crowd shifting and changing, but his focus remained steadfastly on his hands, clasped together, delivering the steady cadence of compressions required to bring Jack's heart back to life.

"The air ambulance is going to be at least an hour. They're just finishing another call. What do you need me to do?"

Kali dropped to her knees on the other side of Jack, the AED in her hands.

"He's not responding. Severe hypothermia. Body temperature twelve degrees below normal." He kept his voice low. The anxious keening of the boy's mother still came in waves of sound above them.

"Twenty-five Celsius? You've got a thermometer that registers temperatures that low?"

Brodie nodded. "Have to up here. Unfortunately this sort of thing isn't unusual."

It was how his mother had died. He more than most knew the importance of warming this child in the safest way possible.

"We need to get some fluids inside him. I don't want to use the defibrillator until we're inside."

"If the ambulance is going to be a while, should we get him to the clinic?"

"Yes, but he's going to need constant CPR." Brodie was panting. He'd already been administering CPR for over ten minutes, and the intensity of his focus was beginning to take a toll. "Can you help me intubate?"

"Absolutely—then let's get him on the biggest backboard we have and I'll ride it."

"I've got a surfboard right here," someone called.

"Great." Brodie nodded. "Get the board." His eyes flicked up to meet Kali's. The steady green gaze assured him that they had this—as a team.

Swiftly, efficiently, they intubated Jack and then transferred him to the board. Kali straddled the small body and took over CPR while Jack compressed the airbag providing oxygen to the little boy's lungs.

"Steady, lads," Brodie cautioned as six men lifted the board on his count. "Precious cargo."

His eyes were on Kali, whose expression was one of utter focus on the child. She was in a class of her own. He would count himself lucky to have had her in his life at all, let alone for the rest of his life. He made a silent promise to propose sooner than later.

"Fluids?" Kali threw him a questioning look.

"Nothing warm enough to put into a drip. Everything will have gone cold in the car."

"Warmer than his body?"

He nodded. It was a good point. They'd have to warm him gradually. Anything else would be too much of a shock to the small body that had already been traumatized.

"All right, lads? Slide them in as steady as you can."

The trip to the clinic passed in a blur of CPR, pulse checks, IV insertion, airway checks and temperature monitoring.

"It's not looking good, is it?" Jack's mother asked tearfully. She was leaning over the seat into the back of the car, where Kali was still carrying out CPR.

"I read about a case of a two-year-old..." Kali huffed between compressions. "Fell into an icy river—must've been in it for half an hour at least. They performed CPR for over an hour and a half. Between that, fluids and other warming methods they got him back."

"But was he all right? You know..." Jack's mother asked, not wanting to put words to everyone's concern. Irreparable brain damage.

Kali nodded. She thought so, but wasn't 100 percent. She wanted to offer hope, but knew there was a degree of caution required in all hypotheticals.

"We're here," Brodie said unnecessarily as the vehicle slowed to a careful halt.

He'd thrown the keys to one of the lads. CPR was tiring. If Kali needed to be relieved he wanted to be by her side to help.

"Kali, if you grab the IV bag I'll take over."

Again, the concentrated blur of saving someone's life had shifted everything else out of his consciousness. If they could just get...

"We've got a pulse!" Kali finally said, a few minutes after having hooked Jack up to the monitoring system. "It's weak, but we've got one."

A collective sigh of relief released the taut tension in the exam room, where Jack's family had anxiously been looking on.

"Will you be needing the ventilator?" Ailsa appeared in the doorway.

"Thanks, Ailsa. Yes. It'll make it easier for the little guy to breathe, and maybe we can get some aerosol medication in him."

Brodie curled his fingers into a loose fist and gave Jack a quick sternal rub. He felt a twitch of a response. Heard a cough, then a gag.

"Quick! Let's get him in the recovery position."

He and Kali quickly shifted Jack onto his side, a stream of seawater gushing out of the little boy's mouth as they did so, and a wail of relief from his mother filled the room.

They'd done it. They'd brought him back to life.

Kali gave Brodie a happy nod, her lips shifting in and out of her mouth as she tried to keep the emotion at bay. He felt it, too. Deep in his heart. All he wanted to do was pull Kali into his arms, but they weren't out of the woods yet.

"Right, guys. We're still fighting the hypothermia. Anyone have word on that air ambulance?"

Kali gave him a soft smile as a new flurry of activity began to whirl around them. They would do this. Together.

"Look who's on the front page!" Brodie flourished the *Dunregan Chronicle* in front of Kali.

She felt the blood drain from her face in an instant. She could hear Brodie happily chattering away, but his voice was only coming to her in the odd hit of vowels and consonants she couldn't put together. She blinked hard, forcing herself to concentrate on what he was saying.

"Craig thinks it's so good the nationals might pick it up. It's already all over the internet—so some of the international papers might run it."

Her breath came out in short, sharp huffs.

"What's wrong?" Brodie sat down beside her, laying the paper down on the round table in front of her. "I think it's an amazing shot. You should be proud."

"I am—it's not that—I just…"

She stared at the photograph in disbelief. A picture of the moment she and Dougal had hoisted the near-lifeless body of little Jack into the lifeboat was printed in full color—her face was utterly unmistakable. She was struck by the confidence, the passion she saw in herself. The complete antithesis of the fear she felt welling within her now.

"Hey, babe." Brodie slid a hand across her back in a slow circular motion. "What's wrong with being the heroine of Dunregan for a day? It's well deserved."

"Everything!" The word came out as a wail as years of fear came to the fore. Hot tears poured down her cheeks, and the back and forth *no, no, no* shaking of her head flicked them onto the paper, instantly blurring the ink.

"Kali, you're scaring me. What's going on?"

She turned to him, knowing that this might be one of the last moments when Brodie's belief in her was absolute. The moment she'd been dreading had finally arrived. The moment when she had to explain to Brodie that the Kali he knew…was a fiction.

"Come here."

He held open his arms but she couldn't move. The weight in her heart was rendering her motionless except for her head, which persisted with its shaking. *No, no, no.*

"Right." Brodie pushed back from the table and headed toward the kitchen counter. "I'm making you a fresh cup of tea—and then, Kali O'Shea, you are going to tell me exactly what has got you so—"

"I'm not Kali O'Shea."

The words were blurted out before she could stop them and they seemed to assault Brodie physically. His blue eyes clouded, steady blinks shuttering them from her view every few seconds, and his body became absolutely rooted to the spot.

"Who are you, then?"

Ice water ran through her veins. All she could hear in Brodie's voice was the betrayal he had to be feeling. She pressed her fingers together to stop their shaking and forced herself to tell him the story.

"My birth name is Aisha Kalita."

Brodie folded his arms across his chest, as if protecting himself from what she was about to say. She didn't blame him. This was a blindsider. A trust breaker. So it was now or never if she was going to win his trust again.

"My father is originally from India. He is...very *traditional...*"

In a monotone, Kali heard herself telling Brodie about her naively happy childhood, the support her parents had given her in her quest to become a doctor.

"So what happened?"

"He arranged a marriage for me. My father."

"What?" Brodie all but shouted the word.

The dogs came scrambling in from the lounge, where they had been lolling in the morning sun, big furry heads shifting from Brodie to Kali, waiting to see who needed them most.

Kali sat rigidly as Brodie digested the news, her hand distractedly giving each of the dog's heads a rub.

"Sorry, Kali. Please. Go on."

The clinical tone of his voice sent another chill of fear through her. She swallowed and forced herself to tell the story that had been told out loud only once, five years earlier at the Forced Marriage Protection Unit.

"My father had been planning it for months, but none of us knew about it. Not my mother or sister—"

"You have a sister?"

She shook her head yes, and continued. If she didn't get it all out now...

"It was someone from my father's hometown. A man highly esteemed for his business acumen—but not for his morals. My father organized for me to marry this man and secured a visa for him in England."

She choked back a sob.

Brodie came toward her, stopping himself halfway, as if undecided about whether or not to comfort her. Her heart physically hurt. For him, for herself, for the lies she'd been forced to tell and for the life she'd thought she could have.

She put up a hand. "Please. Let me finish."

He pulled out a chair on the opposite side of the table and nodded for her to continue. It was impossible to tell what was happening behind those pure blue eyes of his. She prayed to everything she could think of that he would be empathic. Compassionate. Forgiving.

"I was completely clueless. My father brought him over to dinner one day and then later made my sister and mother leave the room with him so that it was just the two of us. He wasted no time in telling me how the marriage would work. Who would be in charge. That I would have to shelve my medical degree and do something more...something that would give me more time to look after him. When I protested and said I would only go ahead with the marriage if I were able to complete my medical studies he—"

A ragged sob escaped her very core.

"He hit me. The rest of it happened horribly fast. My father was in the room in an instant, apologizing—can you believe it?—*apologizing* to this man for my behavior. When he left I begged my father to be released from the union. He said the only way I could escape the marriage—humiliating him as I had—was death."

Brodie's hand shot across the table. He needed to touch her. Comfort her. Aisha… Kali—whatever her name was—she was the same woman she'd been ten minutes ago. If there was any way he could have taken back his initial reaction he would have.

Kali slid her own hand across the table, then retracted it.

"What happened next?" Part of him didn't want to know, but it was imperative he heard the full story.

"In the middle of the night my mother came to me with a small amount of money and an address for a distant relative in Ireland. She said I should seek her out if I absolutely must—but if it were possible to just go. Never speak of them or think of them again."

In a rush she blurted out the rest. The tremors of fear juddering through her body as she'd stuffed a handful of clothes into a small backpack. The fearful silence in the house as they'd tiptoed to the back door, terrified of waking her father. The tears she'd been unable to shed as she'd hugged her sister and mother goodbye that one last time.

"And then I just began to run."

Brodie itched to hold her. Ease away the pain. But she had to finish. He could see the determination in her eyes.

"I stayed at a cheap hostel the first night. And then—because I didn't want anyone to know where I was, especially if my father was going to go on the hunt for me—I spent my days in London's biggest hospitals. Just reminding myself why I had chosen to become a doctor. I spent my nights in the waiting room of an ER until a nurse finally figured out something was wrong and helped me contact the Forced Marriage Protection Unit. They helped me with a new identity. But with the invention of Kali O'Shea I had to let my mother and sister go."

Brodie felt his throat go dry, his body physically aching

for her. He'd left his family of his own accord. A selfish decision by a teenager blinded with grief and anger after a tragic accident. But Kali...? She'd been betrayed by her own father and forced to live apart from the people who could have comforted her most.

"And you've never been back?"

"Never." Her eyes were wide with disbelief, though she was the one who'd lived with the pain, the reality of a life lived in fear. "I moved to Dublin so I could feel close to my mother's relatives. It was a weak link—but it helped, believe it or not."

"That's why you picked the name O'Shea?"

"No." Kali finally looked across at him, her beautiful green eyes shining with vitality. "It was the name of the nurse who helped me that night. Helped me to find the FMPU and make a fresh start. Become who I'd always thought I could be."

She was so much braver than he had ever imagined. Stronger.

Brodie couldn't restrain himself anymore. He was pulling her into his arms before he could stop himself, running his fingers through her hair, holding her tight to his chest so she could weep long pent-up tears of grief, fear and loss.

"My beautiful, brave Kali...Aisha," he corrected, then laughed awkwardly. "What do you want me to call you?"

"Kali," she answered without hesitation. "It's the name I chose because I thought it would give me strength. And it has. And," she added, looking at him as if she hardly believed he was still there, "I *have* become who I thought I could be. Thanks to you, to Ailsa—everyone here on Dunregan."

"But mostly me, right?" he teased gently.

"Mostly you." Her fingers pressed into his.

"You've never looked for them? Your family?" Brodie asked, leading her out to the sofa in the lounge, where they nestled into a big pile of humans, dogs and cushions.

"I was far too frightened the first couple of years. There were enough scary stories of retribution killings to keep me as far away from my father as I could. Though I worry about my mum and sister. Every day I worry that my father turned his anger on them."

She shook her head, suddenly looking overwhelmed with exhaustion.

"Are you—are you okay with this? With me?"

"Are you kidding?" Brodie shook his head in disbelief. "Obviously it's all a bit of a shock, but I love you, Kali. I don't think having a different name changes who you are and what you mean to me."

Kali blinked, her teeth biting endearingly into her lower lip as she did so. "You *love* me?"

"Of course I do. What did you think? I go parading around Dunregan with every beautiful woman who shows up here?"

"I—uh—"

"Don't answer that." Brodie laughed, scooching along the sofa so he could hold her in his arms. "I love you, Kali O'Shea, and I will do everything in my power to ensure you're never put in harm's way. You have my word."

He dropped a kiss onto the top of her head, enjoying the weight of her body as she slowly let herself relax into his embrace.

They were words he'd never said to a woman before.

I love you.

And they were words he meant from the bottom of his heart. The only thing left to do was rustle up the most romantic setting he could and propose.

"Kali?"

It was Brodie, gently knocking on the door to her office.

"You left your mobile in the staff room and it rang. I hope you don't mind, but I answered it for you."

"Who is it?"

A jag of fear ran through her. It had been twenty-four hours since the photo had gone public and she'd heard nothing so far.

"Is it a man or a woman?" she whispered, more to herself than Brodie. She would never forget the malice in her father's voice. Not as long as she lived.

"A woman," Brodie said with a smile, his blond hair shining in the late-morning sun coming through the back door. "I think you'll want to take it. It's a Mrs. Kalita."

Tears leaped to her eyes as one set of fingers popped to her lips and the other to her chest, as if trying to hold her heart inside.

Her entire body shook with anticipation as she reached forward to accept the phone from Brodie. She had to hold it with both her hands as she took it from him, the tremor in her fingers was so strong.

Over five years. It had been over five painfully long years.

Brodie took a step back, dismay furrowing his brow. He mouthed a question. *Want me to stay?*

She shook her head, no, then quickly changed it to yes. Brodie was part of her life now. No more secrets.

She took a big breath and lifted her fingers off the phone's mouthpiece. "Hello?" Her voice was barely audible.

"Aisha?" The familiar name came down the line, the voice causing her tears to spill over. "Aisha, is this connection all right? Can you hear me?"

Kali nodded silently, only just remembering to speak the word she hadn't allowed herself to say out loud for over half a decade…

"Mummy-ji?"

CHAPTER ELEVEN

KALI SET DOWN the phone in disbelief.

She was free!

She felt herself go into autopilot—stepping away from her desk, only just remembering to give Brodie's hand a little squeeze, blindly taking the handful of steps to the small kitchen, filling the kettle, listening to it come to a boil as she had on her very first day here.

She watched, almost as if she were someone else, as her hands reached for mugs, opened the tea canister, fingers deftly, knowingly, going about making cups of tea for everyone. An extra splash of milk for Ailsa, a sugar-even-though-she-knew-she-shouldn't for Caitlyn, strong builder's tea for herself and, of course, leaving the tea bag in the longest for Brodie, and adding just a few drops of milk… one…two…three…four.

Four weeks.

Four weeks of living on the sanctuary of Dunregan. Embracing the life here every bit as much as it had embraced her. And now she could just…go…?

"Hey, you."

Brodie slipped into the tearoom behind her. Kali felt the warmth of his hands shifting along her hips and lacing loosely around her waist. The inevitable tremor of desire skittered down her spine as he nestled into the crook of her neck to give her a smattering of soft kisses along her neck.

She murmured instinctively, tipped her head toward his, loving his scent, his touch, the fact that she knew how to make his tea and which side of the bed he slept on—and the instant she turned around to clink mugs with him felt a cascade of tears begin to pour down her face.

"Oh, hey, now…" Brodie's face was wreathed in concern. "What did she say?"

He took Kali's mug of tea and set it on the counter.

"It's my parents…my family," she choked out as the wash of tears grew thicker.

"So that was her?" His voice tightened, concern woven through each word. "Your mother?"

She managed a nod.

"And…?" He tugged a hand through his hair, losing his knit cap in the process, his eyes completely locked on her. "Kali, are they—have they been hurt in any way?"

She shook her head, no, and forced herself to calm down. Happiness came in so many forms, and the flood of tears streaming freely down her cheeks were tears of pure joy.

At last.

"They're safe." She hiccuped and laughed. "Sorry, it's just…"

"Pretty overwhelming?" Brodie finished for her.

She nodded, and blew out a slow breath before beginning to explain what she'd just learned from her mother. "They're living in Ireland, near the village where her relatives are. My sister's great. She's—" Her eyes filled with tears again. "She's training to be a doctor."

"Like her big sister?" Brodie clapped his hands together.

"Yup." She felt a burst of pride taking shape in her heart, then a shot of sorrow. "My dad…" She shook her head at the enormity of putting all of these sentences together. "My dad…he—he is divorced from my mum and lives in India now. He's become a *monk*."

Her eyes widened in wonder.

"He spent one year solid looking for me, and my mother

said the rage and anger all but killed him. He returned home one night and nearly hit my sister when she stood up to him—told him to leave me be. It was then that he broke down, told my mother he just couldn't live with the shame of how he'd behaved. So…now he's a monk in a religious sanctuary somewhere in India."

"So…" Brodie began tentatively. "It's all good?"

"I've just been so scared they wouldn't have been able to get on with their lives, you know? I so wanted to write to them, tell them to please carry on with everything as if I was still with them, because they were with *me*." She clasped her hands to her heart. "Every step of the way I brought them with me."

"Of course you did." Brodie laid a hand atop of hers, as if to cement what she'd said.

Brodie rubbed his hands along her arms and pulled her in for a hug—but not before she saw a hit of anxiety flash across his face.

She pressed her fingertips into his back, loving the strength of feeling and connection passing between them. Of all the people in the world she could share her news with—the most joyous news she could ever imagine—this was the one she wanted. The man she could imagine a future with.

She felt his chin shift along the top of her head, his hand brushing her hair back from her tearstained face, his fingertips tracing along her jawline before tugging her back into his chest for a tight, long-held embrace. She stood, so grateful just to breathe and listen as their hearts began to beat in synchronicity.

As their breathing shifted and changed, each of them taking on the enormity of the news, she sensed a shift in Brodie's mood. He was happy for her—she didn't doubt that. But there was… She tipped her head up to take a look at his face. There was anxiety creasing his forehead, shifting the crinkles alongside his eyes into winces of doubt and worry.

"So." Brodie abruptly pulled back from their embrace and put on a bright smile. "I guess this means you'll be leaving us."

"Well, I—" Kali scraped her nails along her scalp, as if it would help clear the jumble of thoughts. "I have to go to them."

"Of course." Brodie nodded as if he were agreeing with a patient about a need to get a second opinion on an unusual condition. "You must."

The coolness in his voice physically chilled her. She knew him well enough to know this was Brodie in protection mode, and as much as it pained her she understood completely. If she had been in his shoes she would have done the same.

"Brodie?" Callum flicked off the television. "Stop pacing, would you? She'll be back."

"It's been over a week now."

"You've texted. And called."

"I know. But everything's going great for her! She's having the time of her life."

"Aren't you happy for her?"

"Of course I am!" Brodie shouted, then checked himself. "Of course I am. It's just…"

What if I never see her again?

"I don't think Kali is the type to just leave a man hanging," Callum replied calmly, and his voice was an echo of their father's.

Since when had his kid brother become the mature one?

Brodie wheeled around. "What makes *you* so sure?"

Callum's lips twitched as he unsuccessfully held back a snigger.

"Oh, go ahead. Get a good laugh in, why don't you? Enjoy it while you can because—because…" He threw up his hands.

Helpless. He felt absolutely and utterly helpless. Maybe

he should go chop wood or something. If he knew where the ax was that was exactly what he would do.

"Brodie…" Callum looked his brother straight in the eye. "You may be many things—but the last thing you are is someone who gives up."

Brodie harrumphed.

Callum laughed openly this time, giving his brother a playful jab with one of his crutches.

"Why don't you go down to the docks?"

"What on earth for?"

"There's a boat coming in." Callum checked his watch. "I have something on there I need you to get."

"So I'm your slave boy now?"

"Hardly!" Callum laughed again. "But I think you'll like this delivery." He aimed the remote at the television, feigning a renewed interest in the show neither of them had been watching. "It'll make you a lot easier to be around, that's for sure."

"What is it? Earplugs so you don't have to listen to me wallowing anymore?"

Callum pushed his lower lip out and jigged his chin back and forth. "Something along those lines. Go." He pointed toward the door. "And take the dogs while you're at it."

"What is it, Dougal?"

Brodie could barely keep a hold of the huge dog's leash as passenger after passenger walked off the boat. Deliveries always came last.

Dougal jumped up with a joyful woof and broke free of Brodie's hold. Hamish dragged Brodie along with him, across the gangplank and onto the boat, where they near enough clobbered someone to the ground. Wagging tails, whines of pleasure—this was no stranger.

"Dogs! What are you—?" Brodie shook his head in disbelief when he caught a glimpse of green eyes amidst the furry bodies. "Kali?"

Flat out on the ferry deck, being covered in dog licks, was Kali, her face wreathed in smiles. Brodie elbowed past the dogs and helped to pull her up, pulling her tightly into his arms.

"What are you doing here?"

She pulled back from the embrace and smiled shyly up at him. "I thought I would come home…"

"Are you asking or telling?" Brodie wasn't going to take any chances here.

"A bit of both, I guess." Kali wove her fingers through his and scooped up one of the dog's leashes, handing him the other. "Fancy a walk on the beach?"

A few minutes later Brodie, Kali and the dogs piled out of the four-by-four onto the beach. The ride had been largely silent. Just two people grinning at each other as if it were Christmas morning. From the deep hits of magnetic connection each of his smiles brought, Kali knew she'd made the right decision.

"So…seeing your family again…" Brodie began tentatively, unlooping the dogs' leashes from around their necks, watching them race out to the shoreline for a swim.

"It was amazing," Kali answered honestly. "My sister is incredible and my mother—strongest woman I know."

A rush of tears filled her eyes. It *had* been amazing. To be with her family. To find the inner peace she'd long sought.

"And how was it to be back in Ireland?"

It was impossible not to hear the worry in Brodie's voice. Worry she never wanted him to feel again. "It was great, because my family is there, but home…" Her lips parted into a broad, hopeful smile. "*This* is home." She scanned the beach, then laid a hand on Brodie's chest. "*You* are home."

She felt the whoosh of release from Brodie's chest.

"I'm pretty happy to hear that."

"Just 'pretty happy'?" She grinned up at him.

"Relieved—over the moon—ecstatic." He threw a few

more words out into the ether for added measure until they were both laughing.

He cupped her face in his hands, tilting it up to his for a long-awaited kiss. *Passionate* didn't even begin to cover it. As their lips touched, sparks of desire burst throughout Kali's body. Her arms smoothed along his chest, up and around his neck, and her feet arched up onto tiptoe. She could feel Brodie's arms tighten around her waist, pulling her in close to him, close enough for her to feel his heart racing as fast as her own.

Minutes, hours could have passed for all she was aware. Nothing mattered—nothing existed outside of Brodie.

"I love you, Brodie McClellan." Her lips shifted and whispered across his as she spoke.

"I love you, too, my little one."

He loosened his hold on her, then held her out at arm's length, a serious expression taking over the wash of desire they had both succumbed to.

"I have something to ask you. Something I probably should've asked before you left."

"Oh?" Kali's eyes widened. It was difficult to tell if it was going to be good or bad.

She held her breath as Brodie reached into his jacket and tugged out a small box. He held it between them, flicking the lid up with his thumb. The soft spring sunshine set the diamond alight, glinting and sparkling like the sea.

"Kali O'Shea—would you do me the honor of marrying me?"

He dropped to one knee, holding the diamond up between them.

She stared, openmouthed.

"Kali?"

"Yes!" She nodded and laughed, dropping to her knees so she could smother him with kisses. "Yes! A thousand times yes!" She kissed him again and again then abruptly pulled back. "We're staying *here*, right?"

"As long as you're happy with that."

"Are you mad? There is no place I would rather be. As long as you don't mind a nutty Indian family with bonkers Irish accents coming to visit."

"As long as they're happy having mad Scottish in-laws."

"They'll love you." Kali tackled him to the sand, stealing kiss after happy kiss. "But not quite as much as *I* love you."

"You think?" Brodie wiggled his eyebrows up and down.

"I *know*." Kali smirked back, before wrapping her arms around her future husband and giving him a soft kiss. "There isn't a soul out there who could love you more than me."

"Good." Brodie held her tight to him, the sound of the waves swooshing back and forth only magnifying the joy he felt. He dabbed a finger on her nose. "So, which name do you want on the surgery door? O'Shea? Kalita?"

"McClellan," Kali answered solidly. "The Doctors McClellan."

* * * * *

FROM FLING
TO FOREVER

AVRIL TREMAYNE

This book is dedicated to my fellow writer PTG Man and Dr. John Sammut with many, many thanks for the generous medical advice. Thanks also to Dr. John Lander and Dr. Hynek Prochazka. Any errors that snuck in despite their best efforts are mine, all mine!

I would also like to acknowledge the amazing Angkor Hospital for Children (AHC)—a non-profit pediatric teaching hospital that provides free quality care to impoverished children in Siem Reap, Cambodia. All the characters, settings and situations in FROM FLING TO FOREVER are fictional—however, during the course of my research, I learned so much from AHC, which has provided over one million medical treatments, education to thousands of Cambodian health workers, and prevention training to thousands of families since it opened in 1999. You can find out more about the hospital at www.angkorhospital.org

CHAPTER ONE

WEDDINGS.

Ella Reynolds had nothing against them, but she certainly didn't belong at one. Not even this one.

But her sister, Tina, had insisted she not only attend but trick herself out as maid of honour in this damned uncomfortable satin gown in which there was *no* stretch. Add in the ridiculous high heels and hair twisted into a silly bun that was pinned so tightly against her scalp she could practically feel the headache negotiating where to lunge first.

And then there was the stalker. Just to top everything off.

She'd first felt his stare boring into her as she'd glided up the aisle ahead of her sister. And then throughout the wedding service, when all eyes should have been on the bride and groom. And ever since she'd walked into the reception.

Disconcerting. And definitely unwanted.

Especially since he had a little boy with him. Gorgeous, sparkly, darling little boy. Asian. Three or four years old. Exactly the type of child to mess with her already messed-up head.

Ella looked into her empty champagne glass, debating whether to slide over the legal limit. Not that she was driving, but she was always so careful when she was with her family. Still… Tina, pregnant, glowing, deliriously happy, was on the dance floor with her new husband Brand—and not paying her any attention. Her parents were on the other side of the room, catching up with Brand's family on this rare visit to Sydney—and not paying her any attention. She was alone at the bridal table, with *no one* paying her any attention. Which was just fine with her. It was much easier to hold it all together when you were left to yourself. To not let anyone see the horrible, unworthy envy of Tina's pregnancy, Tina's *life*.

And—she swivelled around to look for a waiter—it made it much easier to snag that extra champagne.

But a sound put paid to the champagne quest. A cleared throat.

She twisted back in her chair. Looked up.

The stalker. *Uh-oh.*

'Hi,' he said.

'Hello.' Warily.

'So...you're Ella,' he said.

Oh, dear. *Inane* stalker. 'Yep. Sister of the bride.'

'Oh.' He looked surprised. And then, 'Sorry, the accent. I didn't realise...'

'I speak American, Tina speaks Australian. It does throw people. Comes of having a parent from each country and getting to choose where you live. I live in LA. Tina lives in Sydney. But it's still all English, you know.' Good Lord—*this* was conversation?

He laughed. 'I'm not sure the British see it that way.'

Okay—so now what? Ella wondered.

If he thought she was going to be charmed by him, he had another think coming. She *wasn't* going to be charmed. And she was *not* in the market for a pick-up tonight. Not that he wasn't attractive in a rough sort of way—the surfer-blond hair, golden tan and bursting muscles that looked completely out of place in a suit was a sexy combination. But she'd crossed the pick-up off her to-do list last night— and that had been a debacle, as usual. And even if she hadn't crossed it off the list, and it hadn't been a debacle, her sister's wedding was not the place for another attempt. Nowhere within a thousand *miles* of any of her relatives was the place.

'Do you mind if I sit and talk to you for a few minutes?' he asked, and smiled at her.

Yes, I do. 'Of course you can sit,' she said. Infinitesimal pause. 'And talk to me.'

'Great.' He pulled out a chair and sat. 'I think Brand warned you I wanted to pick your brains tonight.'

She frowned slightly. 'Brand?'

He smiled again. 'Um…your brother-in-law?'

'No-o-o, I don't think so.' Ella glanced over at Brand, who was carefully twirling her sister. 'I think he's had a few things on his mind. Marriage. Baby. Imminent move to London. New movie to make.'

Another smile. 'Right, let's start again and I'll introduce myself properly.'

Ella had to give the guy points for determination. Because he had to realise by now that if she really wanted to talk to him, she would have already tried to get his name out of him.

'I'm Aaron James,' he said.

Ella went blank for a moment, before the vague memory surfaced. 'Oh. Of course. The actor. Tina emailed me about a…a film?' She frowned slightly. 'Sorry, I remember now. About malaria.'

'Yes. A documentary. About the global struggle to eradicate the disease. Something I am very passionate about, because my son… Well, too much information, I guess. Not that documentaries are my usual line of work.' Smile, but looking a little frayed. 'Maybe you've heard of a television show called *Triage*? It's a medical drama. I'm in that.'

'So…' She frowned again. 'Is it the documentary or the TV show you want to talk to me about? If it's the TV show, I don't think I can help you—my experience in city hospital emergency rooms is limited. And I'm a nurse—

you don't look like you'd be playing a nurse. You're play-ing a doctor, right?'

'Yes, but—'

'I'm flying home tomorrow, but I know a few doctors here in Sydney and I'm sure they'd be happy to talk to you.'

'No, that's not—'

'The numbers are in my phone,' Ella said, reaching for her purse. 'Do you have a pen? Or can you—?'

Aaron reached out and put his hand over hers on the tiny bronze purse. 'Ella.'

Her fingers flexed, once, before she could stop them.

'It's not about the show,' he said, releasing her hand. 'It's the documentary. We're looking at treatments, mosquito control measures, drug resistance, and what's being done to develop a vaccine. We'll be shooting in Cambodia pri-marily—in some of the hospitals where I believe you've worked. We're not starting for a month, but I thought I should take the chance to talk to you while you're in Syd-ney. I'd love to get your impression of the place.'

She said nothing. Noted that he was starting to look im-patient—and annoyed.

'Brand told me you worked for Frontline Medical Aid,' he prompted.

She controlled the hitch in her breath. 'Yes, I've worked for them, and other medical aid agencies, in various coun-tries, including Cambodia. But I'm not working with any agency at the moment. And I'll be based in Los Angeles for the next year or so.'

'And what's it like? I mean, not Los Angeles—I know what— Um. I mean, the aid work.'

Ella shifted in her seat. He was just not getting it. 'It has its highs and lows. Like any job.'

He was trying that charming smile again. 'Stupid ques-tion?'

'Look, it's just a job,' she said shortly. 'I do what every

nurse does. Look after people when they're sick or hurt. Try to educate them about health. That's all there is to it.'

'Come on—you're doing a little more than that. The conditions. The diseases that we just don't see here. The refugee camps. The landmines. Kidnappings, even.'

Her heart slammed against her ribs. Bang-bang-bang. She looked down at her hands, saw the whitened knuckles and dropped them to her lap, out of Aaron's sight. She struggled for a moment, getting herself under control. Then forced herself to look straight back up and right at him.

'Yes, the conditions are not what most medical personnel are used to,' she said matter-of-factly. 'I've seen the damage landmines can do. Had children with AIDS, with malnutrition, die in my arms. There have been kidnappings involving my colleagues, murders even. This is rare, but...' She stopped, raised an eyebrow. 'Is that the sort of detail you're looking for?' She forced herself to keep looking directly into his eyes. 'But I imagine you'll be insulated from the worst of it. They won't let anything happen to you.'

'I'm not worried about that,' Aaron said, with a quick shake of his head. Then, suddenly, he relaxed back in his chair. 'And you don't want to talk about it.'

Eureka! 'It's fine, really,' she said, but her voice dripped with insincerity.

The little boy Ella had seen earlier exploded onto the scene, throwing himself against Aaron's leg, before the conversation could proceed.

'Dad, look what Tina gave me.'

Dad. So, did he have an Asian wife? Or was the little boy adopted?

Aaron bent close to smell the small rose being offered to him.

'It's from her bunch of flowers,' the little boy said, blinking adorably.

'Beautiful.' Aaron turned laughing eyes to Ella. 'Ella, let me introduce my son, Kiri. Kiri, this is Tina's sister, Ella.'

Kiri. He was Cambodian, then. And he'd had malaria—that was Aaron's TMI moment. 'Nice to meet you Kiri,' Ella said, with a broad smile, then picked up her purse. 'Speaking of Tina and flowers, it must be time to throw the bouquet. I'd better go.'

She got to her feet. 'Goodbye Aaron. Good luck with the documentary. Goodbye Kiri.'

Well, that had been uncomfortable, Ella thought as she left the table, forcing herself to walk slowly. Calm, controlled, measured—the way she'd trained herself to walk in moments of stress.

Clearly, she had to start reading her sister's emails more carefully. She recalled, too late, that Tina's email had said Aaron was divorced; that he had an adopted son—although not that the boy was Cambodian, because *that* she would have remembered. She'd made a reference to the documentary. And there probably had been a mention of talking to him as a favour to Brand, although she really couldn't swear to it.

She just hadn't put all the pieces together and equated them with the wedding, or she would have been better prepared for the confrontation.

Confrontation. Since when did a few innocent questions constitute a confrontation?

Ella couldn't stop a little squirm of shame. Aaron wasn't to know that the exact thing he wanted to talk about was the exact thing she couldn't bring herself to discuss with anyone. Nobody knew about Sann, the beautiful little Cambodian boy who'd died of malaria before she'd even been able to start the adoption process. Nobody knew about her relationship with Javier—her colleague and lover, kidnapped in Somalia and still missing. Nobody knew because she hadn't *wanted* anyone to know, or to worry about her. Hadn't wanted anyone to push her to talk about things, relive what she couldn't bear to relive.

So, no, Aaron wasn't to be blamed for asking what he thought were standard questions.

But he'd clearly sensed something was wrong with her. Because he'd gone from admiration—oh, yes, she could read admiration—to something akin to dislike, in almost record time. Something in those almost sleepy, silver-grey eyes had told her she just wasn't his kind of person.

Ella's head had started to throb. The damned pins.

Ah, well, one bouquet-toss and last group hug with her family and she could disappear. Back to her hotel. Throw down some aspirin. And raid the mini-bar, given she never had got that extra glass of champagne.

Yeah, like raiding the mini-bar has ever helped, her subconscious chimed in.

'Oh, shut up,' she muttered.

Well, that had been uncomfortable, Aaron thought as Ella Reynolds all but bolted from the table. Actually, she'd been walking slowly. Too slowly. Unnaturally slowly.

Or maybe he was just cross because of ego-dent. Because one woman in the room had no idea who he was. And didn't *care* who he was when she'd found out. Well, she was American—why *would* she know him? He wasn't a star over there.

Which wasn't the point anyway.

Because since when did he expect people to recognise him and drool?

Never!

But celebrity aside, to be looked at with such blank disinterest...it wasn't a look he was used to from women. Ella Reynolds hadn't been overwhelmed. Or deliberately *under*-whelmed, as sometimes happened. She was just...hmm, was 'whelmed' a word? Whelmed. Depressing.

Ego, Aaron—so not *like you.*

Aaron swallowed a sigh as the guests started positioning themselves for the great bouquet toss. Ella was in the thick of it, smiling. Not looking in his direction—on purpose, or he'd eat the roses.

She was as beautiful as Tina had said. More so. Staggeringly so. With her honey-gold hair that even the uptight bun couldn't take the gloss off. The luminous, gold-toned skin. Smooth, wide forehead. Finely arched dusky gold eyebrows and wide-spaced purple-blue eyes with ridiculously thick dark lashes. Lush, wide, pouty mouth. No visible freckles. No blemishes. The body beneath the figure-hugging bronze satin she'd been poured into for the wedding was a miracle of perfect curves. Fabulous breasts—and silicone-free, if he were any judge. Which he was, after so many years in the business.

And the icing on the cake—the scent of her. Dark and musky and delicious.

Yep. Stunner.

But Tina had said that as well as being gorgeous her sister was the best role model for women she could think of. Smart, dedicated to her work, committed to helping those less fortunate regardless of the personal danger she put herself in regularly.

Well, sorry, but on the basis of their conversation tonight he begged to differ. Ella Reynolds was no role model. There was something wrong with her. Something that seemed almost…dead. Her smile—that dazzling, white smile—didn't reach her eyes. Her eyes had been beautifully *empty*. It had been almost painful to sit near her.

Aaron felt a shiver snake down his spine.

On the bright side, he didn't feel that hot surge of desire—that bolt that had hit him square in the groin the moment she'd slid into the church—any more. Which was good. He didn't want to lust after her. He didn't have the time or energy or emotional availability to lust after anyone.

He turned to his beautiful son. 'Come on, Kiri—this

part is fun to watch. But leave the bouquet-catching to the girls, huh?'

We're not going down that road again, bouquet or not, he added silently to himself.

CHAPTER TWO

ELLA HAD BEEN determined to spend a full year in Los Angeles.

But within a few weeks of touching down at LAX she'd been back at the airport and heading for Cambodia. There had been an outbreak of dengue fever, and someone had asked her to think about helping out, and she'd thought, *Why not?*

Because she just hadn't been feeling it at home. Whatever 'it' was. She hadn't felt right since Tina's wedding. Sort of restless and on edge. So she figured she needed more distraction. More work. More…something.

And volunteering at a children's hospital in mosquito heaven is just the sort of masochism that's right up your alley, isn't it, Ella?

So, here she was, on her least favourite day of the year—her birthday—in northwest Cambodia—and because it *was* her birthday she was in the bar of one of the best hotels in town instead of her usual cheap dive.

Her parents had called this morning to wish her happy birthday. Their present was an airfare to London and an order to use it the moment her time in Cambodia was up. It was framed in part as a favour to Tina: stay with her pregnant sister in her new home city and look after her health while Brand concentrated on the movie. But she knew Tina would have been given her own set of orders: get Ella to rest and for goodness' sake fatten her up—because her mother always freaked when she saw how thin and bedraggled Ella was after a stint in the developing world.

Tina's present to Ella was a goat. Or rather a goat in Ella's name, to be given to an impoverished community in India. Not every just-turned-twenty-seven-year-old's cup of tea, but so totally perfect for this one.

And in with the goat certificate had been a parcel with a note: 'Humour me and wear this.' 'This' was sinfully expensive French lingerie in gorgeous mint-green silk, which Ella could never have afforded. It felt like a crime wearing it under her flea-market gypsy skirt and bargain-basement singlet top. But it did kind of cheer her up. Maybe she'd have to develop an underwear fetish—although somehow she didn't think she'd find this kind of stuff digging around in the discount bins the way she usually shopped.

A small group of doctors and nurses had dragged her out tonight. They'd knocked back a few drinks, told tales about their life experiences and then eventually—inevitably—drifted off, one by one, intent on getting some rest ahead of another busy day.

But Ella wasn't due at the hospital until the afternoon, so she could sleep in. Which meant she could stay out. And she had met someone—as she always seemed to do in bars. So she'd waved the last of her friends off with a cheerful guarantee that she could look after herself.

Yes, she had met someone. Someone who might help make her feel alive for an hour or two. Keep the nightmares at bay, if she could bring herself to get past the come-on stage for once and end up in bed with him.

She felt a hand on her backside as she leaned across the pool table and took her shot. She missed the ball completely but looked back and smiled. Tom. British. Expat. An...engineer, maybe? *Was* he an engineer? Well, who cared? Really, who cared?

He pulled her against him, her back against his chest. Arms circled her waist. Squeezed.

She laughed as he nipped at her earlobe, even though she couldn't quite stop a slight shudder of distaste. His breath was too hot, too...moist. He bit gently at her ear again.

Ella wasn't sure what made her look over at the entrance to the bar at that particular moment. But pool cue in one hand, caught against Tom's chest, with—she realised in one awful moment—one of the straps of her top hanging off her shoulder to reveal the beacon-green silk of her bra strap, she looked.

Aaron James.

He was standing still, looking immaculately clean in blue jeans and a tight white T-shirt, which suited him way more than the get-up he'd been wearing at the wedding. Very tough-guy gorgeous, with the impressive muscles and fallen-angel hair with those tousled, surfer-white streaks she remembered very well.

Actually, she was surprised she remembered so much!

He gave her one long, cool, head-to-toe inspection. One nod.

Ah, so he obviously remembered her too. She was pretty sure that was not a good thing.

Then he walked to the bar, ignoring her. *Hmm.* Definitely *not a good thing*.

Ella, who'd thought she'd given up blushing, blushed. Hastily she yanked the misbehaving strap back onto her shoulder.

With a wicked laugh, Tom the engineer nudged it back off.

'Don't,' she said, automatically reaching for it again.

Tom shrugged good-humouredly. 'Sorry. Didn't mean anything by it.'

For good measure, Ella pulled on the long-sleeved, light cotton cardigan she'd worn between her guesthouse accommodation and the hotel. She always dressed for modesty outside Western establishments, and that meant covering up.

And there were mosquitoes to ward off in any case.

And okay, yes, the sight of Aaron James had unnerved her. She admitted it! She was wearing a cardigan because Aaron James had looked at her in *that* way.

She tried to appear normal as the game progressed, but every now and then she would catch Aaron's gaze on her and she found it increasingly difficult to concentrate on the game or on Tom. Whenever she laughed, or when Tom let out a whoop of triumph at a well-played shot, she would feel Aaron looking at her. Just for a moment. His eyes on her, then off. When Tom went to the bar to buy a round. When she tripped over a chair, reaching for her drink. When Tom enveloped her from behind to give her help she didn't need with a shot.

It made her feel…dirty. Ashamed. Which was just not fair. She was single, adult, independent. So she wanted a few mindless hours of fun on her lonely birthday to take her mind off sickness and death—what was wrong with that?

But however she justified things to herself, she knew that tonight her plans had been derailed. All because of a pair of censorious silver eyes.

Censorious eyes that belonged to a friend of her sister. Very sobering, that—the last thing she needed was Aaron tattling to Tina about her.

It was probably just as well to abandon tonight's escapade. Her head was starting to ache and she felt overly hot. Maybe she was coming down with something? She would be better off in bed. Her bed. Alone. As usual.

She put down her cue and smiled at Tom the engineer. Her head was pounding now. 'It's been fun, Tom, but I'm going to have to call it a night.'

'But it's still early. I thought we could—'

'No, really. It's time I went home. I'm tired, and I'm not feeling well.'

'Just one more drink,' Tom slurred, reaching for her arm.

She stepped back, out of his reach. 'I don't think so.'

Tom lunged for her and managed to get his arms around her.

He was very drunk, but Ella wasn't concerned. She'd been in these situations before and had always managed to extricate herself. Gently but firmly she started to prise Tom's arms from around her. He took this as an invitation to kiss her and landed his very wet lips on one side of her mouth.

Yeuch.

Tom murmured something about how beautiful she was. Ella, still working at unhooking his arms, was in the middle of thanking him for the compliment when he suddenly wasn't there. One moment she'd been disengaging herself from his enthusiastic embrace, and the next—air.

And then an Australian accent. 'You don't want to do that, mate.'

She blinked, focused, and saw that Aaron James was holding Tom in an embrace of his own, standing behind him with one arm around Tom's chest. How had he got from the bar to the pool table in a nanosecond?

'I'm fine,' Ella said. 'You can let him go.'

Aaron ignored her.

'I said I'm fine,' Ella insisted. 'I was handling it.'

'Yes, I could see that,' Aaron said darkly.

'I was,' Ella insisted, and stepped forward to pull futilely at Aaron's steel-band arm clamped across Tom's writhing torso.

Tom lunged at the same time, and Ella felt a crack across her lip. She tasted blood, staggered backwards, fell against the table and ended up on the floor.

And then everything swirled. Black spots. Nothing.

The first thing Ella noticed as her consciousness returned was the scent. Delicious. Clean and wild, like the beach in winter. She inhaled. Nuzzled her nose into it. Inhaled again. She wanted to taste it. Did it taste as good as it smelled? She opened her mouth, moved her lips, tongue. One small lick. Mmm. Good. Different from the smell but…good.

Then a sound. A sharp intake of breath.

She opened her eyes. Saw skin. Tanned skin. White next to it. She shook her head to clear it. Oh, that hurt. Pulled back a little, looked up. Aaron James. 'Oh,' she said. 'What happened?'

'That moron knocked you out.'

It came back at once. Tom. 'Not on purpose.'

'No, not on purpose.'

'Where is he?'

'Gone. Don't worry about him.'

'I'm not worried. He's a big boy. He can take care of himself.' Ella moved again, and realised she was half lolling against Aaron's thighs.

She started to ease away from him but he kept her there, one arm around her back, one crossing her waist to hold onto her from the front.

'Take it easy,' Aaron said.

A crowd of people had gathered around them. Ella felt herself blush for the second time that night. Intolerable, but apparently uncontrollable. 'I don't feel well,' she said.

'I'm not surprised,' Aaron replied.

'I have to get home,' she said, but she stayed exactly where she was. She closed her eyes. The smell of him. It was him, that smell. That was…comforting. She didn't know why that was so. Didn't care why. It just was.

'All right, people, show's over,' Aaron said, and Ella realised he was telling their audience to get lost. He said something more specific to another man, who seemed to be in charge. She assumed he was pacifying the manager. She didn't care. She just wanted to close her eyes.

'Ella, your lip's bleeding. I'm staying here at the hotel.

Come to my room, let me make sure you're all right, then I'll get you home. Or to the hospital.'

She opened her eyes. 'Not the hospital.' She didn't want anyone at the hospital to see her like this.

'Okay—then my room.'

She wanted to say she would find her *own* way home *immediately*, but when she opened her mouth the words 'All right' were what came out. She ran her tongue experimentally over her lip. *Ouch*. Why hadn't she noticed it was hurting? 'My head hurts more than my lip. Did I hit it when I fell?'

'No, I caught you. Let me…' He didn't bother finishing the sentence, instead running his fingers over her scalp. 'No, nothing. Come on. I'll help you stand.'

Aaron carefully eased Ella up. 'Lean on me,' he said softly, and Ella didn't need to be told twice. She felt awful.

As they made their way out of the bar, she noted a few people looking and whispering, but nobody she knew. 'I'm sorry about this,' she said to Aaron. 'Do you think anyone knows you? I mean, from the television show?'

'I'm not well known outside Australia. But it doesn't matter either way.'

'I don't want to embarrass you.'

'I'm not easily embarrassed. I've got stories that would curl your hair. It's inevitable, with three semi-wild younger sisters.'

'I was all right, you know,' she said. 'I can look after myself.'

'Can you?'

'Yes. I've been doing it a long time. And he was harmless. Tom.'

'Was he?'

'Yes. I could have managed. I *was* managing.'

'Were you?'

'Yes. And stop questioning me. It's annoying. And it's hurting my head.'

They were outside the bar now and Aaron stopped. 'Just one more,' he said, and turned her to face him. 'What on earth were you thinking?'

Ella was so stunned at the leashed fury in his voice she *couldn't* think, let alone speak.

He didn't seem to need an answer, though, because he just rolled right on. 'Drinking like a fish. Letting that clown slobber all over you!'

'He's not a clown, he's an engineer,' Ella said. And then, with the ghost of a smile, 'And fish don't drink beer.'

He looked like thunder.

Ella waited, curious about what he was going to hurl at her. But with a snort of disgust he simply took her arm again, started walking.

He didn't speak again until they were almost across the hotel lobby. 'I'm sorry. I guess I feel a little responsible for you, given my relationship with Brand and Tina.'

'That is just ridiculous—I already have a father. And he happens to know I can look after myself. Anyway, why are you here?' Then, 'Oh, yeah, I remember. The documentary.' She grimaced. '*Should* I have known you'd be here now?'

'I have no idea. Anyway, you're supposed to be in LA.'

'I was in LA. But now— It was a sudden decision, to come here. So it looks like we've surprised each other.'

'Looks like it.'

Aaron guided Ella through a side door leading to the open air, and then along a tree-bordered path until they were in front of what looked like a miniature mansion. He *would* be in one of the presidential-style villas, of course. He didn't look very happy to have brought her there, though.

'How long will you be in town?' she asked, as he un-locked the door.

'Two weeks, give or take.'

'So, you'll be gone in two weeks. And I'll still be here, looking after myself. Like I've always done.' She was pleased with the matter-of-factness of her voice, because in reality she didn't feel matter-of-fact. She felt depressed. She blamed it on the birthday.

Birthdays: misery, with candles.

'Well, good for you, Ella,' he said, and there was a definite sneer in there. 'You're doing such a fine job of it my conscience will be crystal clear when I leave.'

Hello? Sarcasm? Really? Why?

Aaron drew her inside, through a tiled hallway and into a small living room. There was a light on but no sign of anyone.

'Is your son with you?' she asked. *Not that it's any of your business, Ella.*

'Yes, he's in bed.'

'So you've got a nanny? Or is your wife—?' *Um, not your business?*

'Ex-wife. Rebecca is in Sydney. And, yes, I have a nanny, whose name is Jenny. I don't make a habit of leaving my four-year-old son on his own in hotel rooms.'

Oh, dear, he really did *not* like her. And she was well on the way to actively disliking *him*. His attitude was a cross between grouchy father and irritated brother—without the familial affection that would only just make that bearable.

Aaron gestured for Ella to sit. 'Do you want something to drink?'

Ella sank onto the couch. 'Water, please.'

'Good choice,' Aaron said, making Ella wish she'd asked for whisky instead.

He went to the fridge, fished out a bottle of water, poured it into a glass and handed it to her. She didn't deign to thank him.

She rubbed her forehead as she drank.

He was watching her. 'Head still hurting?'

'Yes.'

'Had enough water?'

Ella nodded and Aaron took the glass out of her hand,

sat next to her. He turned her so she was facing away from him. 'Here,' he said tetchily, and started kneading the back of her neck.

'Ahhh…' she breathed out. 'That feels good.'

'Like most actors, I've had a chequered career—massage therapy was one of my shorter-lived occupations but I remember a little,' Aaron said, sounding not at all soothing like a massage therapist.

'Where's the dolphin music?' she joked.

He didn't bother answering and she decided she would *not* speak again. She didn't see why she should make an effort to talk to him, given his snotty attitude. She swayed a little, and he pulled her closer to his chest, one hand kneading while he reached his other arm around in front of her, bracing his forearm against her collarbone to balance her.

She could smell him again. He smelled exquisite. So clean and fresh and…yum. The rhythmic movement of his fingers was soothing, even if it did nothing to ease the ache at the front of her skull. She could have stayed like that for hours.

Slowly, he finished the massage and she had to bite back a protest. He turned her to face him and looked at her lip. 'It's only a small tear. I have a first-aid kit in the bathroom.'

'How very *Triage* of you, Aaron.' He looked suitably unimpressed at that dig.

'Just some ice,' she said. 'That's all I need. And I can look after it myself. I'm a nurse, remember?'

But Aaron was already up and away.

He came back with a bowl of ice and the first-aid kit.

Ella peered into the kit and removed a square of gauze, then wrapped it around an ice cube. 'It's not serious and will heal quickly. Mouth injuries do. It's all about the blood supply.'

Not that Aaron seemed interested in that piece of medical information, because he just took the wrapped ice from her impatiently.

'I promise you I can do it myself,' Ella said.

'Hold still,' he insisted. He held the ice on her bottom lip, kept it pressed there for a minute.

'Open,' he ordered, and Ella automatically opened her mouth for him to inspect inside. 'Looks like you bit the inside of your lip.' He grabbed another square of gauze, wrapped it around another cube of ice and pressed it on the small wound.

He was looking intently at her mouth and Ella started to feel uncomfortable. She could still smell that heavenly scent wafting up from his skin. Why couldn't he smell like stale sweat like everyone else in that bar? She blinked a few times, trying to clear her fuzzy head.

Her eyes fell on his T-shirt and she saw a smear of blood on the collar. Her blood. Her fingers reached out, touched it. His neck, too, had a tiny speck of her blood. Seemingly of their own volition her fingers travelled up, rubbing at the stain. And then she remembered how it had got there. Remembered in one clear flash how she had put her mouth there, on his skin. She felt a flare of arousal and sucked in a quick breath.

He had gone very still. He was watching her. Looking stunned.

CHAPTER THREE

'Sorry,' Ella said. 'It's just... I—I bled on you.'

'Ella, I don't think it's a good idea for you to touch me.'

'Sorry,' Ella said again, jerking her fingers away.

Aaron promptly contradicted himself by taking the hand she'd pulled away and pressing it against his chest. He could actually *hear* his heart thudding. It was probably thumping against her palm like a drum. He didn't care. He wanted her hand on him. Wanted both her hands on him.

He could hear a clock ticking somewhere in the room, but except for that and his heart the silence was thick and heavy.

I don't even like her. He said that in his head, but something wasn't connecting his head to his groin, because just as the thought completed itself he tossed the gauze aside and reached for her other hand, brought it to his mouth, pressed his mouth there, kept it there.

Okay, so maybe you didn't have to like someone to want them.

He really, really hadn't expected to see her again. She was supposed to be in LA. Their 'relationship' should have begun and ended with one awkward conversation at a wedding.

And yet here he was. And here she was. And he had no idea what was going to happen next.

When he'd walked into that bar tonight and seen her

with that idiot, he'd wanted to explode, drag her away, beat the guy senseless.

And he *never* lost his temper!

He'd been so shocked at his reaction he'd contemplated leaving the bar, going somewhere else—a different bar, for a walk, to bed, anything, anywhere else. But he hadn't.

He'd only been planning on having one drink anyway, just a post-flight beer. But nope. He'd stayed, sensing there was going to be trouble. She'd laughed too much, drunk too much, Tom the idiot engineer had fondled her too much. Something was going to give.

And something definitely had.

And of course he'd been there smack bang in the middle of it, like he couldn't get there fast enough.

And then his arms had been around her. And she'd snuggled against him. Her tongue on his neck. And he'd wanted her. Wanted her like he'd never wanted anyone in his life.

And it had made him furious.

Was making him furious now.

So why was he moving the hand he'd been holding to his mouth down to his chest, instead of letting it go?

His hands were only lightly covering hers now. She could break away if she wanted to. Bring him back to sanity. *Please.*

But she didn't break away.

Her hands moved up, over his chest to his collarbones then shoulders. Confident hands. Direct and sure.

He stifled a groan.

'You don't want me.' She breathed the words. 'You don't like me.' But her hands moved again, down to his deltoids, stopping there. Her fingers slid under the short sleeves of his T-shirt, stroked.

This time the groan escaped as his pulse leapt.

Ella moved closer to him, sighed as she surrounded him with her arms, rested the side of her face against his chest then simply waited.

He battled himself for a long moment. His hand hovered over her hair. He could see the tremor in his fingers. He closed his eyes so the sight of her wouldn't push him over the edge. That only intensified the sexy smell of her. Ella Reynolds. Tina's *sister*. 'I can't,' he said. 'I can't do this.' Was that his voice? That croak?

He waited, every nerve tingling. Didn't trust himself to move. If he moved, even a fraction...

Then he heard her sigh again; this time it signalled resignation, not surrender.

'No, of course not,' she said, and slowly disentangled herself until she was sitting safely, separately, beside him.

Whew. Catastrophe averted.

'A shame,' she said. Her voice was cool and so were her eyes as she reached out to skim her fingernail over his right arm, at the top of his biceps where the sleeve of his T-shirt had been pushed up just enough to reveal the lower edge of a black tattoo circlet. Her lips turned up in an approximation of a smile. 'Because I like tattoos. They're a real turn-on for me. Would have been fun.'

He stared at her, fighting the urge to drag her back against his chest, not quite believing the disdainful humour he could hear in her voice, see in her eyes. Wondering if he'd imagined the yielding softness only moments ago.

At Tina and Brand's wedding he'd sensed that there was something wrong with her. It had made him uncomfortable to be near her. Made him want to get away from her.

He had the same feeling now. Only this time he couldn't get away. He would be damned if he'd let Tina's sister stagger home drunk and disorderly, with a pounding head and a split lip. *Oh, yeah, that's the reason, is it? Tina?*

Ella shrugged—a dismissive, almost delicate gesture. 'But don't worry, I won't press you,' she said calmly. 'I've never had to beg for it in my life and I won't start now, tattoos or not.'

She stood suddenly and smiled—the dazzling smile that didn't reach her eyes. 'I'd better go,' she said.

'I'll take you home,' he said, ignoring the taunt of all those men she hadn't had to beg. None of his business.

'I'll walk.'

'I'll take you,' Aaron insisted.

Ella laughed. 'Okay, but I hope we're not going to drag some poor driver out of bed.'

'Where are you staying?'

'Close enough. I can walk there in under ten minutes.'

'Then we'll walk.'

'All right, then, lead on, Sir Galahad,' Ella said lightly, mockingly.

And that was *exactly* why he didn't like her.

Because she was just so unknowable. Contrary. Change-able. Ready to seduce him one moment and the next so cool. Poised. Amused. They made it to the street without him throttling her, which was one relief. Although he would have preferred a different relief—one for inside his jeans, because, heaven help him, it was painful down there. How the hell did she *do* that? Make him both want her and want to run a mile in the opposite direction?

Ella led off and Aaron fell into step beside her, conscious of her excruciatingly arousing perfume. The almost drug-ging combination of that scent, the damp heat, the sizzle and shout of the street stalls, the thumping music and wild shouts from the tourist bars, was so mesmerisingly exotic it felt almost like he was in another world. One where the normal rules, the checks and balances, didn't apply.

The minutes ticked by. A steady stream of motorbikes puttered past. A short line of tuk-tuks carrying chatty tour-ists. Jaunty music from a group of street musicians. Sounds fading as he and Ella walked further, further.

'Needless to say, tonight's escapade is not something Tina needs to hear about,' Ella said suddenly.

'Needless to say,' he agreed.

A tinkling laugh. 'Of course, you wouldn't want it getting back to your wife either. At least, not the latter part of the evening.'

'Ex-wife,' Aaron corrected her. He heard a dog barking in the distance. A mysterious rustle in the bushes near the road.

'Ah.' Ella's steps slowed, but only very briefly. 'But not really ex, I'm thinking, Sir Galahad.'

Aaron grabbed Ella's arm, pulling her to the side of a dirty puddle she was about to step into. 'It's complicated,' he said, when she looked at him.

She pulled free of the contact and started forward again.

'But definitely ex,' he added. And if she only knew the drug-fuelled hell Rebecca had put him through for the past three years, she would understand.

'Oh, dear, how inconvenient! An ex who's not really an ex. It must play havoc with your sex life.'

She laughed again, and his temper got the better of him. The temper that he *never* lost.

'What is wrong with you?' he demanded, whirling her to face him.

She looked up at him, opened her mouth to say—

Well, who knew? Because before he could stop himself he'd slapped his mouth on hers in a devouring kiss.

Just what he *didn't* want to do.

And she had the audacity to kiss him back. More than that—her arms were around him, her hands under his T-shirt.

Then he tasted blood, remembered her lip. Horrified, he pulled back. 'I'm sorry,' he said.

She ran her tongue across her lower lip, raised her eyebrows. '*Definitely* would have been fun,' she said.

'I'm not looking for a relationship,' he said bluntly. And where had that come from? It seemed to suggest he *was* after *something*. But what? What was he after? Nothing—nothing from her.

It seemed to startle her, at least. 'Did I ask for one?'

'No.'

'That's a relief! Because I'm really only interested in casual sex. And on that note, how fortunate that we're here. Where I live. So we can say our goodbyes, and both pretend tonight didn't happen. No relationship. And, alas, no casual sex, because you're married. Oh, no, that's right, you're not. But no sex anyway.'

'I should have left you with the engineer.'

'Well, I would have seen a lot more action,' she said. She started forward and then stopped, raised her hand to her eyes.

'What is it?' Aaron asked.

'Nothing. A headache,' she answered. 'I'll be fine.'

'Goodbye, then,' he said, and turned to walk back to the hotel.

A lot more action! Ha! Aaron was quite sure if he ever let himself put his hands on Ella Reynolds she wouldn't be able to think about another man for a long time. Or walk straight either.

But he was not going to touch her, of course. *Not.*

Ella made her way to her room, cursing silently.

Her head was throbbing and her joints were aching and she longed to lapse into a thought-free coma. She'd just realised she'd contracted either malaria or dengue fever. She wasn't sure which, but either way it sucked.

But when she'd taken two paracetamol tablets and clambered into bed, praying for a mild dose of whatever it was, it wasn't the pain that made the tears come. It was shame. And regret. And a strange sense of loss.

Aaron James had wanted her. Ordinarily, a man wanting her would not cause Ella consternation. Lots of men had wanted her and she'd had no trouble resisting them.

But Aaron was different. He'd kissed her like he was

pouring his strength, his soul into her. And yet he'd been able to fight whatever urge had been driving him.

Why? How?

She manhandled her pillow, trying to get it into a more head-cradling shape.

Not looking for a relationship—that's what he'd said. How galling! As though it were something she would be begging for on the basis of one kiss. All right, one *amazing* kiss, but—seriously! What a joke. A relationship? The one thing she *couldn't* have.

Ella sighed as her outrage morphed into something more distressing: self-loathing. Because she was a fraud and she knew it. A coward who used whatever was at her disposal to stop herself from confronting the wreck her life had become since Javier had been kidnapped in Somalia on her twenty-fifth birthday.

She'd been in limbo ever since. Feeling helpless, hopeless. Guilty that she was free and he was who-knew-where. In the year after his kidnapping she'd felt so lost and alone and powerless she'd thought a nervous breakdown had been on the cards.

And then she'd found Sann in a Cambodian orphanage, and life had beckoned to her again. Two years old, and hers. Or so she'd hoped. But he'd been taken too. He'd died, on her twenty-sixth birthday.

And now here she was on her twenty-*seventh* birthday. Still in limbo, with no idea of what had happened to Javier. Still grieving for Sann.

Panicking at the thought of seeing an Asian child with an adoptive parent.

Unable to entertain even the thought of a relationship with a man.

Pretending she was calm and in control when she was a basket case.

Her life had become a series of shambolic episodes. Too many drinks at the bar. Getting picked up by strange men, determined to see it through then backing out. *Always* backing out, like the worst kind of tease, because no matter how desperate she was to feel *something*, the guilt was always stronger. Coping, but only just, with endlessly sad thoughts during the day and debilitating dreams at night.

She knew that something in her was lost—but she just didn't know how to find it. She hid it from the people she cared about because she knew her grief would devastate them. She hid it from her colleagues because they didn't need the extra burden.

And she was just...stuck. Stuck on past heartbreaks. And it was starting to show.

No wonder Aaron James abhorred the idea of a 'relationship' with her.

Ella rubbed tiredly at her forehead. She closed her eyes, longing for sleep, but knowing the nightmares would come tonight.

Dr Seng slapped his hand on the desk and Aaron's wandering mind snapped back to him. 'So—we've talked about malaria. Now, a few facts about the hospital.'

Kiri had been whisked off to do some painting—one of his favourite pastimes—on arrival at the Children's Community Friendship Hospital, so Aaron could concentrate on this first meeting.

But he wasn't finding it easy.

He had a feeling... A picture of Ella here. Was this where she was working? He wasn't sure, but he kept expecting her to sashay past.

Dr Seng handed over an array of brochures. 'Pre-Pol Pot, there were more than five hundred doctors practising in Cambodia,' Dr Seng said. 'By the time the Khmer Rouge fled Cambodia in 1979 there were less than fifty. Can you imagine what it must have been like? Rebuilding an entire healthcare system from the ground up, with almost no money, no skills? Because that's what happened in Cambodia.'

Aaron knew the history—he'd made it his business to know, because of Kiri. But he could never come to terms with the brutal stupidity of the Khmer Rouge. 'No, I can't imagine it,' he said simply. 'And I'd say this hospital is something of a miracle.'

'Yes. We were started by philanthropists and we're kept going by donations—which is why we are so happy to be associated with your documentary: we need all the publicity we can get, to keep attracting money. It costs us less than twenty-five dollars to treat a child. Only fifty dollars to operate. Unheard of in your world. But, of course, we have so many to help.'

'But your patients pay nothing, right?'

'Correct. Our patients are from impoverished communities and are treated free, although they contribute if they can.'

'And your staff…?'

'In the early days the hospital relied on staff from overseas, but today we are almost exclusively Khmer. And we're a teaching hospital—we train healthcare workers from all over the country. That's a huge success story.'

'So you don't have any overseas staff here at the moment?'

'Actually, we do. Not paid staff—volunteers.'

'Doctors?'

'We have a group of doctors from Singapore coming in a few months' time to perform heart surgeries. And at the moment we have three nurses, all from America, helping out.'

'I was wondering if…' Aaron cleared his throat. 'If perhaps Ella Reynolds was working here?'

Dr Seng looked at him in surprise. 'Ella? Why, yes!'

Ahhhhh. Fate. It had a lot to answer for.

'I—I'm a friend. Of the family,' Aaron explained.

'Then I'm sorry to say you probably won't see her. She's not well. She won't be in for the whole week.'

Aaron knew he should be feeling relieved. He could have a nice easy week of filming, with no cutting comments, no tattoo come-ons, no amused eyebrow-raising.

But…what did 'not well' mean? Head cold? Sprained toe? Cancer? Liver failure? Amputation? 'Not well?'

'Dengue fever—we're in the middle of an outbreak, I'm afraid. Maybe a subject for your next documentary, given it's endemic in at least a hundred countries and infects up to a hundred million people a year.'

Alarm bells. 'But it doesn't kill you, right?'

'It certainly can,' the doctor said, too easily, clearly not understanding Aaron's need for reassurance.

Aaron swallowed. 'But…Ella…'

'Ella? No, no, no. She isn't going to die. The faster you're diagnosed and treated the better, and she diagnosed herself very quickly. It's more dangerous for children, which Ella is not. And much more dangerous if you've had it before, which Ella has not.'

Better. But not quite good enough. 'So is she in hospital?'

'Not necessary at this stage. There's no cure; you just have to nurse the symptoms— take painkillers, keep up the fluids, watch for signs of internal bleeding, which would mean it was dengue haemorrhagic fever—very serious! But Ella knows what she's doing, and she has a friend staying close by, one of the nurses. And I'll be monitoring her as well. A shame it hit her on her birthday.'

'Birthday?'

'Two days ago. Do you want me to get a message to her?'

'No, that's fine,' Aaron said hurriedly. 'Maybe I'll see her before I head home to Sydney.'

'Then let's collect Kiri and I'll have you both taken on a tour of our facilities.'

It quickly became clear that it was Kiri, not Aaron, who

was the celebrity in the hospital. He seemed to fascinate people with his Cambodian Australian-ness, and he was equally fascinated in return. He got the hang of the *satu*—the graceful greeting where you placed your palms together and bowed your head—and looked utterly natural doing it. It soothed Aaron's conscience, which had been uneasy about bringing him.

They were taken to observe the frenetic outpatient department, which Aaron was stunned to learn saw more than five hundred patients a day in a kind of triage arrangement.

The low acuity unit, where he saw his first malaria patients, a sardine can's worth of dengue sufferers, and children with assorted other conditions, including TB, pneumonia, malnutrition, HIV/AIDS and meningitis.

The emergency room, where premature babies and critically ill children were treated for sepsis, severe asthma, and on and on and on.

Then the air-conditioned intensive care unit, which offered mechanical ventilation, blood gas analysis and inotropes—not that Aaron had a clue what that meant. It looked like the Starship *Enterprise* in contrast to the mats laid out for the overflow of dengue sufferers in the fan-cooled hospital corridors.

The tour wrapped up with a walk through the basic but well-used teaching rooms, some of which had been turned into makeshift wards to cope with the dengue rush.

And then, to Aaron's intense annoyance, his focus snapped straight back to Ella.

Tina and Brand would expect him to check on her, right?

And, okay, *he* wanted to make sure for himself that she was going to recover as quickly and easily as Dr Seng seemed to think.

One visit to ease his conscience, and he would put Ella Reynolds into his mental lockbox of almost-mistakes and double-padlock the thing.

And so, forty minutes after leaving the hospital, with
Kiri safely in Jenny's care at the hotel, he found himself
outside Ella's guesthouse, coercing her room number from
one of the other boarders, and treading up the stairs.

CHAPTER FOUR

AARON FELT SUDDENLY guilty as he knocked. Ella would have to drag herself out of bed to open the door.

Well, why not add another layer of guilt to go with his jumble of feelings about that night at the bar?

The boorish way he'd behaved—when he was *never* boorish.

The way he'd assumed her headache was the result of booze, when she'd actually been coming down with dengue fever.

The door opened abruptly. A pretty brunette, wearing a nurse's uniform, stood there.

'Sorry, I thought this was Ella Reynolds's room,' Aaron said.

'It is.' She gave him the appreciative look he was used to receiving from women—women who weren't Ella Reynolds, anyway. 'She's in bed. Ill.'

'Yes, I know. I'm Aaron James. A...a friend. Of the family.'

'I'm Helen. I'm in the room next door, so I'm keeping an eye on her.'

'Nice to meet you.'

She gave him a curious look and he smiled at her, hoping he looked harmless.

'Hang on, and I'll check if she's up to a visit,' Helen said.

The door closed in his face, and he was left wondering whether it would open again.

What on earth was he doing here?

Within a minute Helen was back. 'She's just giving herself a tourniquet test, but come in. I'm heading to the hospital, so she's all yours.'

It was gloomy in the room. And quiet—which was why he could hear his heart racing, even though his heart had no business racing.

His eyes went first to the bed—small, with a mosquito net hanging from a hook in the ceiling, which had been shoved aside. Ella was very focused, staring at her arm, ignoring him. So Aaron looked around the room. Bedside table with a lamp, a framed photo. White walls. Small wardrobe. Suitcase against a wall. A door that he guessed opened to a bathroom, probably the size of a shoebox.

He heard a sound at the bed. Like a magnet, it drew him.

She was taking a blood-pressure cuff off her arm.

'I heard you were ill,' he said, as he reached the bedside. 'I'm sorry. That you're sick, I mean.'

'I'm not too happy about it myself.' She sounded both grim and amused, and Aaron had to admire the way she achieved that.

'Who told you I was sick?' she asked.

'The hospital. I'm filming there for the next week.'

She looked appalled at that news. 'Just one week, right?'

'Looks like it.'

She nodded. He imagined she was calculating the odds of having to see him at work. Flattering—not.

He cleared his throat. 'So what's a tourniquet test?'

'You use the blood-pressure machine—'

'Sphygmomanometer.'

'Well, aren't you clever, Dr *Triage*! Yes. Take your BP, keep the cuff blown up to halfway between the diastolic and systolic—the minimum and maximum pressure—wait a few minutes and check for petechiae—blood points in the skin.'

'And do you have them? Um…it? Petechiae?'

'Not enough. Less than ten per square inch.'

'Is that…is that bad?'

'It's good, actually.'

'Why?'

Audible sigh. 'It means I have classic dengue—not haemorrhagic. As good as it gets when every bone and joint in your body is aching and your head feels like it might explode through your eyeballs.'

'Is that how it feels?'

'Yes.'

Silence.

Aaron racked his brain. 'I thought you might want me to get a message to Tina.'

Her lips tightened. Which he took as a no.

'That would be no,' she confirmed.

A sheet covered the lower half of her body. She was wearing a red T-shirt. Her hair was piled on top of her head, held in place by a rubber band. Her face was flushed, a light sheen of sweat covering it. And despite the distinct lack of glamour, despite the tightened lips and warning eyes, she was the most beautiful woman he'd ever seen.

'Shouldn't you keep the net closed?' he asked, standing rigid beside the bed. Yep—just the sort of thing a man asked a nurse who specialised in tropical illnesses.

'Happy to, if you want to talk to me through it. Or you can swat the mosquitoes before they get to me.'

'Okay—I'll swat.'

She regarded him suspiciously. 'Why are you really here? To warn me I'll be seeing you at the hospital?'

'No, because it looks like you won't be. I just wanted to make sure you were all right. See if you needed anything.'

'Well, I'm all right, and I don't need anything. So thank you for coming but…' Her strength seemed to desert her then and she rolled flat onto her back in the bed, staring at the ceiling, saying nothing.

'I heard it was your birthday. That night.'

An eye roll, but otherwise no answer.

He came a half-step closer. 'If I'd known…'

Aaron mentally winced as she rolled her eyes again.

'What would you have done?' she asked. 'Baked me a cake?'

'Point taken.'

Trawling for a new topic of conversation, he picked up the photo from her bedside table. 'Funny—you and Tina sound nothing alike, and you look nothing alike.'

Silence, and then, grudgingly, 'I take after my father's side of the family. Tina's a genetic throwback.' She smiled suddenly, and Aaron felt his breath jam in his throat. She really was gorgeous when she smiled like that, with her eyes as well as her mouth—even if it was aimed into space and not at him.

He gestured to the photo. 'I wouldn't have picked you for a Disneyland kind of girl.'

'Who doesn't like Disneyland? As long as you remember it's not real, it's a blast.'

Aaron looked at her, disturbed by the harshness in her voice. Did she have to practise that cynicism or did it come naturally?

Ella raised herself on her elbow again. 'Look, forget Disneyland, and my birthday. I *do* need something from you. Only one thing.' She fixed him with a gimlet eye. 'Silence. You can't talk about that night, or about me being sick. Don't tell Tina. Don't tell Brand. My life here has nothing to do with them. In fact, don't talk to anyone about me.'

'Someone should know you've got dengue fever.'

'*You* know. That will have to do. But don't worry, it won't affect you unless I don't make it. And my advice then would be to head for the hills and forget you were ever in Cambodia, because my mother will probably kill you.' That glorious smile again—and, again, not directed at him, just at the thought. 'She never did like a bearer of bad tidings—quite medieval.'

'All the more reason to tell them now.'

Back to the eye roll. 'Except she's not really going to kill you and I'm not going to drop dead. Look...' Ella seemed to be finding the right words. 'They'll worry, and I don't want them worrying about something that can't be changed.'

'You shouldn't be on your own when you're ill.'

'I'm not. I'm surrounded by experts. I feel like I'm in an episode of your TV show, there are so many medical personnel traipsing in and out of this room.'

Aaron looked down at her.

'Don't look at me like that,' Ella said.

'Like what?' Aaron asked. But he was wincing internally because he kind of knew how he must be looking at her. And it was really inappropriate, given her state of health.

With an effort, she pushed herself back into a sitting position. 'Let me make this easy for you, Aaron. I am not, ever, going to have sex with you.'

Yep, she'd pegged the look all right.

'You have a child,' she continued. 'And a wife, ex-wife, whatever. And it's very clear that your...encumbrances... are important to you. And that's the way it *should* be. I understand it. I respect it. I even admire it. So let's just leave it. I was interested for one night, and now I'm not. You were interested, but not enough. Moment officially over. You can take a nice clear conscience home to Sydney, along with the film.'

'Ella—'

'I don't want to hear any more. And I really, truly, do not want to see you again. I don't want— Look, I don't want to get mixed up with a friend of my sister's. Especially a man with a kid.'

Okay, sentiments Aaron agreed with wholeheartedly.

So he should just leave it at that. Run—don't walk—to the nearest exit. Good riddance. So he was kind of surprised to find his mouth opening and 'What's Kiri got to do with it?' coming out of it.

'It's just a…a thing with children. I get attached to them, and it can be painful when the inevitable goodbyes come around—there, something about me you didn't need to know.'

'But you're working at a children's hospital.'

'That's my business. But the bottom line is—I don't want to see Kiri. Ergo, I don't want to see you.' She stopped and her breath hitched painfully. 'Now, please…' Her voice had risen in tone and volume and she stopped. As he watched, she seemed to gather her emotions together. 'Please go,' she continued quietly. 'I'm sick and I'm tired and I— Just please go. All right?'

'All right. Message received loud and clear. Sex officially off the agenda. And have a nice life.'

'Thank you,' she said, and tugged the mosquito net closed.

Aaron left the room, closed the door and stood there.

Duty discharged. He was free to go. *Happy* to go.

But there was some weird dynamic at work, because he couldn't seem to make his feet move. His overgrown sense of responsibility, he told himself.

He'd taken two steps when he heard the sob. Just one, as though it had been cut off. He could picture her holding her hands against her mouth to stop herself from making any tell-tale sound. He hovered, waiting.

But there was only silence.

Aaron waited another long moment.

There was something about her. Something that made him wonder if she was really as prickly as she seemed…

He shook his head. No, he wasn't going to wonder about Ella Reynolds. He'd done the decent thing and checked on her.

He was not interested in her further than that. Not. Interested.

He forced himself to walk away.

Ella had only been away from the hospital for eight lousy days.

How did one mortal male cause such a disturbance in so short a time? she wondered as she batted away what felt like the millionth question about Aaron James. The doctors and nurses, male and female, Khmer and the small sprinkling of Westerners, were uniformly goggle-eyed over him.

Knock yourselves out, would have been Ella's attitude; except that while she'd been laid low by the dengue, Aaron had let it slip to Helen—and therefore everyone!—that he was a close friend of Ella's film director brother-in-law. Which part of 'Don't talk to anyone about me' didn't he understand?

As a result, the whole, intrigued hospital expected her to be breathless with anticipation to learn what Aaron said, what Aaron did, where Aaron went. They expected Ella to marvel at the way he dropped in, no airs or graces, to talk to the staff; how he spoke to patients and their families with real interest and compassion, even when the cameras weren't rolling; the way he was always laughing at himself for getting ahead of his long-suffering translator.

He'd taken someone's temperature. Whoop-de-doo!

And had volunteered as a guinea pig when they'd been demonstrating the use of the rapid diagnostic test for malaria—yeah, so one tiny pinprick on his finger made him a hero?

And had cooked alongside a Cambodian father in the specially built facility attached to the hospital. Yee-ha!

And, and, and, *and*—give her a break.

All Ella wanted to do was work, without hearing his name. They'd had their moment, and it had passed. Thankfully he'd got the message and left her in peace once she'd laid out the situation. She allowed herself a quick stretch before moving onto the next child—a two-year-old darling named Maly. *Heart rate. Respiration rate. Blood pressure. Urine output. Adjust the drip.*

The small hospital was crowded now that the dengue fever outbreak was peaking. They were admitting twenty additional children a day, and she was run off her still-wobbly legs. In the midst of everything she should have been too busy to sense she was being watched...and yet she knew.

She turned. And saw him. Aaron's son, Kiri, beside him.

Wasn't the hospital filming supposed to be over? Why was he here?

'Ella,' Aaron said. No surprise. Just acknowledgement.

She ignored the slight flush she could feel creeping up from her throat. With a swallowed sigh she fixed on a smile and walked over to him. She would be cool. Professional. Civilised. She held out her hand. 'Hello, Aaron.'

He took it, but released it quickly.

'And *sua s'day*, Kiri,' she said, crouching in front of him. 'Do you know what that means?'

Kiri shook his head. Blinked.

'It means hello in Khmer. Do you remember me?'

Kiri nodded. '*Sua s'day*, Ella. Can I go and see her?' he asked, looking over, wide-eyed, at the little girl Ella had been with.

'Yes, you can. But she's not feeling very well. Do you think you can be careful and quiet?'

Kiri nodded solemnly and Ella gave him a confirming nod before standing again. She watched him walk over to Maly's bed before turning to reassure Aaron. 'She's not contagious. It's dengue fever and there's never been a case of person-to-person transmission.'

'Dr Seng said it deserved its own documentary. The symptoms can be like malaria, right? But it's a virus, not a parasite, and the mosquitoes aren't the same.'

Ella nodded. 'The dengue mosquito—' She broke off. 'You're really interested?'

'Why wouldn't I be?'

'I just…' She shrugged. 'Nothing. People can get bored with the medical lingo.'

'I won't be bored. So—the mosquitoes?'

'They're called *Aedes aegypti*, and they bite during the day. Malaria mosquitoes—*Anopheles*, but I'm sure you know that—get you at night, and I'm sure you know that too. It kind of sucks that the people here don't get a break! Anyway, *Aedes aegypti* like urban areas, and they breed in stagnant water—vases, old tyres, buckets, that kind of thing. If a mosquito bites someone with dengue, the virus will replicate inside it, and then the mosquito can transmit the virus to other people when it bites them.' Her gaze sharpened. 'You're taking precautions for Kiri, aren't you?'

'Oh, yes. It's been beaten it into me. Long sleeves, long pants. Insect repellent with DEET. And so on and so forth.'

'You too—long sleeves, I mean. Enough already with the T-shirts.'

'Yes, I know. I'm tempting fate.'

Silence.

He was looking at her in that weird way.

'So, the filming,' she said, uncomfortable. 'Is it going well?'

'We're behind schedule, but I don't mind because it's given me a chance to take Kiri to see Angkor Wat. And the place with the riverbed carvings. You know, the carvings of the genitalia.' He stopped suddenly. 'I—I mean, the…um…Hindu gods…you know…and the—the…ah… Kal…? Kab…?'

Ella bit the inside of her cheek. It surprised her that she could think he was cute. But he sort of was, in his sudden embarrassment over the word genitalia. 'Yes, I know all about genitalia. And it's Kbal Spean, you're talking about, and the Hindu God is Shiva. It's also called The River of a

Thousand Lingas—which means a thousand stylised phalluses,' she said, and had to bite her cheek again as he ran a harassed hand into his hair.

'So, the filming?' she reminded him.

'Oh. Yeah. A few more days here and then the final bit involves visiting some of the villages near the Thai border and seeing how the malaria outreach programme works, with the volunteers screening, diagnosing and treating people in their communities.'

'I was out there a few years ago,' Ella said. 'Volunteers were acting as human mosquito bait. The mosquitoes would bite them, and the guys would scoop them into test tubes to be sent down to the lab in Phnom Penh for testing.'

'But wasn't that dangerous? I mean...*trying* to get bitten?'

'Well, certainly drastic. But all the volunteers were given a combination drug cocktail, which meant they didn't actually develop malaria.'

'So what was the point?'

'To verify whether the rapid treatment malaria programme that had been established there was managing to break the pathways of transmission between insects, parasites and humans. But you don't need to worry. That was then, this is now. And they won't be asking you to roll up your jeans and grab a test tube.'

'Would you have rolled up your jeans, Ella?'

'Yes.'

'And risked malaria?'

'I've had it. Twice, actually. Once in Somalia, once here.'

'Somalia?'

Uh-oh. She was not going there. 'Obviously, it didn't kill me, either time. But I've *seen* it kill. It kills one child every thirty seconds.' She could hear her voice tremble so she paused for a moment. When she could trust herself, she added, 'And I would do anything to help stop that.'

Aaron was frowning. Watching her. Making her feel uncomfortable. Again. 'But you're not— Sorry, it's none of my business, but Kiri isn't going with you there, right?'

'No.' Aaron frowned. Opened his mouth. Closed it. Opened. Closed.

'Problem?' she prompted.

'No. But… Just…' Sigh.

'Just…?' she prompted again.

'Just—do you think I made a mistake, bringing him to Cambodia?' he asked. 'There were reasons I couldn't leave him at home. And I thought it would be good for him to stay connected to his birth country. But, like you, he's had malaria. Before the adoption.'

'Yes, I gathered that.'

'I'd never forgive myself if he got it again because I brought him with me.'

Ella blinked at him. She was surprised he would share that fear with her—they weren't exactly friends, after all— and felt a sudden emotional connection that was as undeniable as it was unsettling.

She wanted to touch him. Just his hand. She folded her arms so she couldn't. 'I agree that children adopted from overseas should connect with their heritage,' she said, ultra-professional. And then she couldn't help herself. She unfolded her arms, touched his shoulder. Very briefly. 'But, yes, we're a long way from Sydney, and the health risks are real.'

'So I shouldn't have brought him?'

'You said there were reasons for not leaving him behind—so how can I answer that? But, you know, these are diseases of poverty we're talking about. That's a horrible thing to acknowledge, but at least it can be a comfort to you. Because you know your son would have immediate attention, the *best* attention—and therefore the best outcome.'

He sighed. 'Yes, I see what you mean. It is horrible, and also comforting.'

'And it won't be long until you're back home. Meanwhile, keep taking those precautions, and if he exhibits any symptoms, at least you know what they are—just don't wait to get him to the hospital.'

She swayed slightly, and Aaron reached out to steady her.

'Sorry. Tired,' she said.

'You're still not fully recovered, are you?' he asked.

'I'm fine. And my shift has finished so I'm off home in a moment.'

Ella nodded in Kiri's direction. The little boy was gently stroking the back of Maly's hand. 'He's sweet.'

'Yes. He's an angel.'

'You're lucky,' Ella said. She heard the...thing in her voice. The wistfulness. She blinked hard. Cleared her throat. 'Excuse me, I need to— Excuse me.'

Ella felt Aaron's eyes on her as she left the ward.

Ella was doing that too-slow walk. Very controlled.

She'd lost her curves since the wedding. She'd been thin when he'd visited her a week ago, but after the dengue she was like a whippet.

But still almost painfully beautiful. Despite the messy ponytail. And the sexless pants and top combo that constituted her uniform.

And he still wanted her.

He'd been furious at how he'd strained for a sight of her every time he'd been at the hospital, even though he'd known she was out of action. Seriously, how pathetic could a man be?

He'd tried and tried to get her out of his head. No joy. There was just something...something under the prickly exterior.

Like the way she looked at Kiri when he'd repeated her Cambodian greeting. The expression on her face when she'd spoken about diseases of the poor. It was just so hard to reconcile all the pieces. To figure out that *something* about her.

He caught himself. Blocked the thought. Reminded himself that if there *was* something there, he didn't want it. One more week, and he would never have to see or think of her again. He could have his peace of mind back. His libido back under control.

He called Kiri over and they left the ward.

And she was there—up the corridor, crouching beside a little boy who was on one of the mattresses on the floor, her slender fingers on the pulse point of his wrist.

Arrrggghhh. This was *torture*. Why wasn't she on her way home like she was supposed to be, so he didn't have to see her smile into that little boy's eyes? Didn't have to see her sit back on her heels and close her eyes, exhausted?

And wonder just who she really was, this woman who was prickly and dismissive. Knowledgeable and professional. Who wouldn't think twice about letting mosquitoes bite her legs for research. Who looked at sick children with a tenderness that caused his chest to ache. Who made him feel gauche and insignificant.

Who made him suddenly and horribly aware of what it was like to crave something. Someone. It was so much more, so much *worse*, than purely physical need.

'Ow,' Kiri protested, and Aaron loosened his hold on Kiri's hand.

Ella looked up, saw them. Froze. Nodding briefly, she got to her feet and did that slow walk out.

This was not good, Aaron thought.

A few days and he would be out of her life.

Ella felt that if only she didn't have to converse with Aaron again, she would cope with those days.

But she hadn't banked on the *sight* of him being such a distraction. Sauntering around like a doctor on regular rounds, poking his nose in everywhere without even the excuse of a camera. Not really coming near her, but always *there*.

It was somehow worse that he was keeping his distance, because it meant there was no purpose to the way she was perpetually waiting for him to show up.

Him and the boy, who reminded her so much of Sann.

It was painful to see Kiri, even from a distance. So painful she shouldn't want to see him, shouldn't want the ache it caused. Except that alongside the pain was this drenching, drowning need. She didn't bother asking why, accepting that it was a connection she couldn't explain, the way it had been with Sann.

On her fourth day back at work, after broken sleep full of wrenching nightmares, the last thing she needed was Aaron James, trailed by his cameraman, coming into the outpatient department just as a comatose, convulsing two-year-old boy was rushed up to her by his mother.

The look in Ella's eyes as she reached for the child must have been terrible because Aaron actually ran at her. He plucked the boy from his mother's arms. 'Come,' he said, and hurried through the hospital as though he'd worked there all his life, Ella and the little boy's mother hurrying after him.

This was a child. Maybe with malaria. And Aaron was helping her.

How was she supposed to keep her distance now?

CHAPTER FIVE

AARON SIGNALLED FOR the cameraman to start filming as what looked like a swarm of medical people converged on the tiny little boy in the ICU.

Ella was rattling off details as he was positioned in the bed—name Bourey, two years old, brought in by his mother after suffering intermittent fever and chills for two days. Unable to eat. Seizure on the way to the hospital. Unable to be roused. Severe pallor. Second seizure followed.

Hands, stethoscopes were all over the boy—pulling open his eyelids, taking his temperature. Checking heart rate, pulse and blood pressure. *Rash? No.* Feeling his abdomen.

I want a blood glucose now.

Into Bourey's tiny arm went a canula.

Blood was taken, and whisked away.

Intravenous diazepam as a slow bolus to control the seizures.

The doctor was listening intently to Bourey's breathing, which was deep and slow. The next moment the boy was intubated and hooked up to a respirator.

Every instruction was rapid-fire.

'Intravenous paracetamol for the fever.'

'Intravenous artesunate, stat, we won't wait for the blood films—we'll treat for falciparum malaria. Don't think it's menigococcus but let's give IV benzylpenicillin. We'll hold

off on the lumbar puncture. I want no evidence of focal
neuro signs. What was his glucose?'

'Intravenous dextrose five per cent and normal saline
point nine per cent for the dehydration—but monitor his
urine output carefully; we don't want to overdo it and end
up with pulmonary oedema, and we need to check renal
function. And watch for haemoglobinuria. If the urine is
dark we'll need to cross-match.'

Overhead an assortment of bags; tubes drip, drip, dripping.

How much stuff could the little guy's veins take?

A urinary catheter was added to Bourey's overloaded
body. Empty plastic bag draped over the side of the bed.

A plastic tube was measured, from the boy's nose to
his ear to his chest, lubricated, threaded up Bourey's nose,
taped in place.

'Aspirate the stomach contents.'

'Monitor temp, respiratory rate, pulse, blood pressure,
neuro obs every fifteen minutes.'

*Hypoglycaemia, metabolic acidosis, pulmonary oedema,
hypotensive shock. Watch the signs. Monitor. Check. Observe.*

Aaron's head was spinning. His cameraman silent and
focused as he filmed.

And Ella—so calm, except for her eyes.

Aaron was willing her to look at him. And every time
she did, she seemed to relax. Just a slight breath, a soften-
ing in her face so subtle he could be imagining it, a lessen-
ing of tension in her shoulders. Then her focus was back
to the boy.

The manic pace around Bourey finally eased and Aaron
saw Ella slip out of the ICU. Aaron signalled to his cameraman to stop filming and left the room.

They had enough to tell the story but they needed a
face on camera.

He went in search of Dr Seng, wanting to check the

sensitivity of the case and get suggestions for the best interviewee.

Dr Seng listened, nodded, contemplated. Undertook to talk to Bourey's family to ascertain their willingness to have the case featured. 'For the interview, I recommend Ella,' he said. 'She knows enough about malaria to write a textbook, and she is highly articulate.'

Aaron suspected the ultra-private Ella would rather eat a plate of tarantulas and was on the verge of suggesting perhaps a doctor when Ella walked past.

Dr Seng beckoned her over, asked for her participation and smiled genially at them before hurrying away.

Ella looked at Aaron coolly. 'Happy to help, of course,' she said.

They found a spot where they were out of the way of traffic but with a view through the ICU windows. The cameraman opted for handheld, to give a sense of intimacy.

Great—intimacy.

'Well?' she asked, clearly anxious to get it done.

'Don't you want to…?' He waved a hand at his hair. At his face.

'What's wrong with the way I look?'

'Nothing. It's just that most people—'

'What's more important, how my hair looks or that little boy?'

'Fine,' Aaron said. 'Tell me about the case.'

'This is a two-year-old child, suffering from cerebral falciparum malaria. Blood films showed parasitaemia—'

'Parasitaemia?'

'It means the number of parasites in his blood. His level is twenty-two per cent. That is high and very serious. Hence the IV artesunate—a particular drug we use for this strain—which we'll administer for twenty-four hours. After that, we'll switch to oral artemisinin-based combination therapy—ACT for short. It's the current drug regime for falciparum. We'll be monitoring his parasitaemia, and we'd expect to see the levels drop relatively quickly.'

She sounded smart and competent and in control.

'And if they don't drop?' Aaron asked.

Her forehead creased. 'Then we've got a problem. It will indicate drug resistance. This region is the first in the world to show signs of resistance to ACTs, which used to kill the parasites in forty-eight hours and now take up to ninety-six hours. It was the same for previous treatments like cloroquine, which is now practically useless—we're like the epicentre for drug resistance here.'

'How does it happen, the resistance?'

'People take just enough of the course to feel better. Or the medicines they buy over the counter are substandard, or counterfeit, with only a tiny fraction of the effective drug in it. Or they are sold only a fraction of the course. Often the writing on the packet is in a different language, so people don't know what they're selling, or buying. And here we have highly mobile workers crossing the borders— in and out of Thailand, for example. So resistant strains are carried in and out with them. The problem is there's no new miracle drug on the horizon, so if we don't address the resistance issue...' She held out her hands, shrugged. Perfection for the camera. 'Trouble. And if the resistance eventually gets exported to Africa—as history suggests it will—it will be catastrophic. Around three thousand children die of malaria every day in sub-Saharan Africa, which is why this is a critical issue.'

He waited. Letting the camera stay on her face, letting the statistic sink in. 'Back to this particular case. What happens now?'

'Continuous clinical observation and measuring what's happening with his blood, his electrolytes. I could give you a range of medical jargon but basically this is a critically ill child. We hope his organs won't fail. We hope he doesn't suffer any lifelong mental disabilities from the pressure on his brain. But, first, we hope he survives.'

A forlorn hope, as it turned out.

One minute they had been working to save Bourey's life, preparing for a whole-blood transfusion to lower the concentration of parasites in Bourey's blood and treat his anaemia. The next, Ella was unhooking him from the medical paraphernalia that had defined his last hours.

She left the ICU and her eyes started to sting. She stopped, wiped a finger under one eye, looked down at it. Wet. She was crying. And what was left of the numbness—one year's worth of carefully manufactured numbness—simply fell away.

She heard something and looked up. She saw Aaron, and tried to pull herself together. But her body had started to shake, and she simply had no reserves of strength left to pretend everything was all right.

A sobbing sort of gasp escaped her, a millisecond before she could put her hand over her mouth to stop it. Her brain and her heart and her body seemed to be out of synch. Her limbs couldn't seem to do what she was urging them to do. So the horrible gasp was followed by a stumble as she tried to turn away. She didn't want Aaron to see her like this. Didn't want anybody to see her, but especially not Aaron. He knew her sister. He might tell her sister. Her sister couldn't know that she was utterly, utterly desolate.

'I'm fine,' she said, as she felt his hand on her shoulder, steadying her.

Aaron withdrew his hand. 'You don't look fine,' he said.

Ella shook her head, unable to speak. She took one unsteady step. Two. Stopped. The unreleased sobs were aching in her chest. Crushing and awful. She had to get out of the hospital.

She felt Aaron's hand on her shoulder again and found

she couldn't move. Just couldn't force her feet in the direction she wanted to go.

Aaron put his arm around her, guiding her with quick, purposeful strides out of the hospital, into the suffocating heat, steering her towards and then behind a clump of thick foliage so they were out of sight.

Ella opened her mouth to tell him, again, that she was fine, but… 'I'm sorry,' she gasped instead. 'I can't— Like Sann. My Sann. Help me, help me.'

He pulled her into his arms and held on. 'I will. I will, Ella. Tell me how. Just tell me.'

'He died. He died. I c-c-couldn't stop it.'

Aaron hugged her close. Silence. He seemed to know there was nothing to say.

Ella didn't know how long she stood there, in Aaron James's arms, as the tears gradually slowed. It was comforting, to be held like this. No words. Just touch. She didn't move, even when the crying stopped.

Until he turned her face up to his. And there was something in his eyes, something serious and concerned.

A look that reminded her Aaron James could not be a shoulder to cry on. He was too…close, somehow. She didn't want anyone to be close to her. Couldn't risk it.

Ella wrenched herself out of his arms. Gave a small, self-conscious hunch of one shoulder. 'It shouldn't upset me any more, I know. But sometimes…' She shoved a lank lock of hair behind her ear. 'Usually you think if they had just got to us faster…they are so poor, you see, that they wait, and hope, and maybe try other things. Because it is expensive for them, the trip to the hospital, even though the treatment is free. But in this case I think…I think nothing would have made any difference… And I…I hate it when I can't make a difference.'

She rubbed her tired hands over her face. 'Usually when I feel like this I donate blood. It reminds me that things that cost me nothing can help someone. And because the hospital always needs so much blood. But I can't even do that now because it's too soon after the dengue. So I've got nothing. Useless.'

'I'll donate blood for you,' Aaron said immediately.

She tried to smile. 'You're doing something important already—the documentary. And I didn't mind doing that interview, you know. I'd do anything.'

She started to move away, but he put his hand on her arm, stopping her.

'So, Ella. Who's Sann?'

Ella felt her eyes start to fill again. Through sheer will power she stopped the tears from spilling out. He touched her, very gently, his hand on her hair, her cheek, and it melted something. 'He was the child I wanted to adopt,' she said. And somehow it was a relief to share this. 'Here in Cambodia. A patient, an orphan, two years old. I went home to find out what I had to do, and while I was gone he…he died. Malaria.'

'And you blame yourself,' he said softly. 'Because you weren't there. Because you couldn't save him. And I suppose you're working with children in Cambodia, which must torture you, as a kind of penance.'

'I don't know.' She covered her face in her hands for one long moment. Shuddered out a breath. 'Sorry—it's not something I talk about.' Her hands dropped and she looked at him, drained of all emotion. 'I'm asking you not to mention it to Tina. She never knew about Sann. And there's no point telling her. She doesn't need to know about this episode today either. Can I trust you not to say anything?'

'You can trust me. But, Ella, you're making a mistake. This is not the way to—'

'Thank you,' she said abruptly, not wanting to hear advice she couldn't bear to take. 'The rain…it's that time of the day. And I can feel it coming. Smell it.'

'So? What's new?'

'I'd better get back.'

'Wait,' he called.

But Ella was running for the hospital.

She reached the roof overhang as the heavens opened. Looked back at Aaron, who hadn't moved, hadn't taken even one step towards shelter. He didn't seem to care that the gushing water was plastering his clothes to his skin.

He was watching her with an intensity that scared her.

Ella shivered in the damp heat and then forced her eyes away.

The next day Helen told Ella that Aaron James had been in and donated blood.

For her. He'd done it for her.

But she looked at Helen as though she couldn't care less. The following day, when Helen reported that Aaron had left for his visit to the villages, same deal. But she was relieved.

She hoped Aaron would be so busy that any thought of her little breakdown would be wiped out of his mind.

Meanwhile, she would be trying to forget the way Aaron had looked at her—like he understood her, like he knew how broken she was. Trying to forget *him*.

There was only one problem with that: Kiri.

Because Kiri and Aaron came as a set.

And Ella couldn't stop thinking, worrying, about Kiri. Knowing that the cause was her distress over Bourey's death didn't change the fact that she had a sense of dread about Kiri's health that seemed tied to Aaron's absence.

Which just went to prove she was unhinged!

Kiri has a nanny to look after him. It's none of your business, Ella.

She repeated this mantra to herself over and over.

But the nagging fear kept tap-tapping at her nerves as she willed the time to pass quickly until Aaron could whisk his son home to safety.

When she heard Helen calling her name frantically two days after Aaron had left, her heart started jackhammering.

'What?' Ella asked, hurrying towards Helen. But she knew. *Knew*.

'It's Aaron James. Or rather his son. He's been taken to the Khmer International Hospital. Abdominal pains. Persistent fever. Retro-orbital pain. Vomiting. They suspect dengue fever.'

Ella felt the rush in her veins, the panic.

'They can't get hold of Aaron,' Helen said. 'So the nanny asked them to call us because she knows he's been filming here. I thought you should know straight away, because— Well, the family connection. Ella, what if something goes wrong and we can't reach Aaron?'

Ella didn't bother to answer. She simply ran.

Aaron had been unsettled during his time in the monsoonal rainforest.

Not that it hadn't been intriguing—the medical challenges the people faced.

And confronting—the history of the area, which had been a Khmer Rouge stronghold, with regular sightings of people with missing limbs, courtesy of landmines, to prove it.

And humbling—that people so poor, so constantly ill, should face life with such stoic grace.

And beautiful, even with the daily downpours—with the lush, virgin forest moist enough to suck at you, and vegetation so thick you had the feeling that if you stood still for half an hour, vines would start growing over you, anchoring you to the boggy earth.

But!

His mobile phone was bothering him. He'd never been out of contact with Kiri before, but since day two, when they'd headed for the most remote villages that were nothing more than smatterings of bamboo huts on rickety stilts, he'd had trouble with his phone.

He found himself wishing he'd told Jenny to contact

Ella if anything went wrong. But Jenny, not being psychic, would never guess that was what Aaron would want her to do—not when she'd never heard Ella's name come out of his mouth. Because he'd been so stupidly determined *not* to talk about Ella, in a misguided attempt to banish her from his head. And what an epic fail *that* had been, because she was still in his head. Worse than ever.

He'd hoped being away from the hospital would cure it. Not looking likely, though.

Every time he saw someone with a blown-off limb, or watched a health worker touch a malnourished child or check an HIV patient, he remembered Ella's words at the wedding reception. *I've seen the damage landmines can do. Had children with AIDS, with malnutrition, die in my arms.* He hadn't understood how she could sound so prosaic but now, seeing the endless stream of injuries, illness, poverty, he did.

And anything to do with malaria—well, how could he not think of her, and that searing grief?

The malaria screening process in the villages was simple, effective. Each person was registered in a book. *Ella, in the outpatient department, recording patient details.*

They were checked for symptoms—simple things like temperature, spleen enlargement. *Ella's hands touching children on the ward.*

Symptomatic people went on to the rapid diagnostic test. Fingertip wiped, dried. Squeeze the finger gently, jab quickly with a lancet. Wipe the first drop, collect another drop with a pipette. Drop it into the tiny well on the test strip. Add buffer in the designated spot. Wait fifteen minutes for the stripes to appear. *Ella, soothing children as their blood was siphoned off at the hospital.*

Aaron helped distribute insecticide-impregnated mosquito nets—a wonderfully simple method of protecting against malaria and given out free. *Ella, blocking him out so easily just by tugging her bed net closed.*

Arrrggghhh.

But relief was almost at hand. One last interview for the documentary and he would be heading back to Kiri. Jenny would have already packed for the trip home to Sydney. Ella would be out of his sight, out of his reach, out of his life once they left Cambodia.

Just one interview to go.

He listened closely as the village volunteer's comments were translated into English. There were three thousand volunteers throughout Cambodia, covering every village more than five kilometres from a health centre, with people's homes doubling as pop-up clinics. Medication was given free, and would be swallowed in front of the volunteers to make sure the entire course was taken. People diagnosed with malaria would not only have blood tested on day one but also on day three to assess the effectiveness of the drug treatment. *Ella, explaining drug resistance. Mentioning so casually that she'd had malaria twice.*

Half an hour later, with the filming wrapped up, they were in the jeep.

Twenty minutes after that his phone beeped. Beeped, beeped, beeped. Beeped.

He listened with the phone tight to one ear, fingers jammed in the other to block other sounds.

Felt the cold sweat of terror.

If he hadn't been sitting, his legs would have collapsed beneath him.

Kiri. Dengue haemorrhagic fever. His small, gentle, loving son was in pain and he wasn't there to look after him.

His fault. All his. He'd brought Kiri to Cambodia in the middle of an outbreak. Left him while he'd traipsed off to film in the boondocks, thinking that was the safer option.

He listened to the messages again. One after the other. Progress reports from the hospital—calm, matter-of-fact, professional, reassuring. Jenny—at first panicked, tearful. And then calmer each time, reassured by one of the nurses.

Rebecca frantic but then, somehow, also calmer, mentioning an excellent nurse.

Three times he'd started to call the Children's Community Friendship Hospital to talk to Ella, wanting her advice, her reassurance, her skills to be focused on Kiri. Three times he'd stopped himself—he *had* expert advice, from Kiri's doctor and a tropical diseases specialist in Sydney he'd called.

And Ella had made it clear she wanted nothing to do with him.

And his son wasn't Ella's problem. Couldn't be her problem.

He wouldn't, couldn't let her mean that much.

The hospital where Kiri had been taken was like a five-star hotel compared with where Ella worked, and Kiri had his own room.

Ella knew the hospital had an excellent reputation; once she'd satisfied herself that Kiri was getting the care and attention he needed, she intended to slide into the background and leave everyone to it.

There was no reason for her to be the one palpating Kiri's abdomen to see if his liver was enlarged, while waiting to see if Kiri's blood test results supported the dengue diagnosis. Hmm, it was a little tender. But that wasn't a crisis and she didn't need to do anything *else* herself.

The blood tests came back, with the dengue virus detected. Plus a low white cell count, low platelets and high haematocrit—the measurement of the percentage of red blood cells to the total blood volume—which could indicate potential plasma leakage. Serious, but, as long as you knew what you were dealing with, treatable. He was still drinking, there were no signs of respiratory distress. So far, so good.

Hands off, Ella, leave it to the staff.

But… There was no problem in asking for a truckle to

be set up for her in Kiri's room, was there? At her hospital, the kids' families always stayed with them for the duration.

So all right, she wasn't family, but his family wasn't here. And kids liked to have people they knew with them. And Ella knew Kiri. Plus, she was making it easier for his nanny to take a break.

She'd got Aaron's cell number from Jenny, and was constantly on the verge of calling him. Only the thought of how many panicked messages he already had waiting for him stopped her. And the tiny suspicion that Aaron would tell her she wasn't needed, which she didn't want to hear—and she hoped that didn't mean she was becoming obsessive about his son.

By the time she'd started haranguing the doctors for updated blood test results, double-checking the nurses' perfect records of Kiri's urine output, heart and respiratory rates, and blood pressure, taking over the task of sponging Kiri down to lower his fever and cajoling him into drinking water and juice to ensure he didn't get dehydrated, she realised she was a step *beyond* obsessive.

It wasn't like she didn't have enough to do at her own place of work, but she couldn't seem to stop herself standing watch over Kiri James like some kind of sentinel—even though dashing between two hospitals was running her ragged.

Kiri's fever subsided on his third day in hospital—but Ella knew better than to assume that meant he was better because often that heralded a critical period. The blood tests with the dropping platelet levels, sharply rising white cells and decreasing haematocrit certainly weren't indicating recovery.

And, suddenly, everything started to go wrong.

Kiri grew increasingly restless and stopped drinking, and Ella went into hyper-vigilant mode.

His breathing became too rapid. His pulse too fast. Even

more worryingly, his urine output dropped down to practically nothing.

Ella checked his capillary refill time, pressing on the underside of Kiri's heel and timing how long it took to go from blanched to normal: more than six seconds, when it should only take three.

His abdomen was distended, which indicated ascites— an accumulation of fluid in the abdominal cavity. 'I'm just going to feel your tummy, Kiri,' she said, and pressed as gently as she could.

He cried out. 'Hurts, Ella.'

'I'm so sorry, darling,' she said, knowing they needed to quickly determine the severity of plasma leakage. 'You need some tests, I'm afraid, so I'm going to call your nurse.'

Ella spoke to the nurse, who raced for the doctor, who ordered an abdominal ultrasound to confirm the degree of ascites and a chest X-ray to determine pleural effusion, which would lead to respiratory distress.

'As you know, Ella,' the doctor explained, drawing her outside, 'a critical amount of plasma leakage will indicate he's going into shock, so we're moving Kiri to the ICU, where we can monitor him. We'll be starting him on intravenous rehydration. We'd expect a fairly rapid improvement, in which case we'll progressively reduce the IV fluids, or they could make the situation worse. No improvement and a significant decrease in haematocrit could suggest internal bleeding, and at that stage we'd look at a blood transfusion. But we're nowhere near that stage so no need to worry. I'll call his father now.'

'Aaron's phone's not working,' Ella said mechanically.

'It is now. He called to tell us he's on his way. I know you're a close friend of the family, so…'

But Ella had stopped listening. She nodded. Murmured a word here and there. Took nothing in.

The doctor patted her arm and left. The orderly would be arriving to take Kiri to ICU. This was it. Over. She wasn't needed any more. And she knew, really, that she had never been needed—the hospital had always had everything under control.

Ella braced herself and went to Kiri's bedside. 'Well, young man,' she said cheerfully, 'you're going somewhere special—ICU.'

'I see you too.'

Ella felt such a rush of love, it almost choked her. 'Hmm. In a way that's exactly what it is. It's where the doctors can see you every minute, until nobody has to poke you in the tummy any more. Okay?'

'Are you coming?'

'No, darling. Someone better is coming. The best surprise. Can you guess who?'

Kiri's eyes lit up. 'Dad?'

'Yep,' she said, and leaned over to kiss him.

The door opened. The orderly. 'And they'll be putting a special tube into you here,' she said, touching his wrist. 'It's superhero juice, so you're going to look like Superman soon. Lucky you!'

A moment later Ella was alone, gathering her few possessions.

Back to reality, she told herself. Devoting her time to where it was really needed, rather than wasting it playing out some mother fantasy.

Ella felt the tears on her cheeks. Wiped them away. Pulled herself together.

Walked super-slowly out of the room.

Ella was the first person he saw.

Aaron was sweaty, frantic. Racing into the hospital. And there she was, exiting. Cool. Remote.

He stopped.

If Ella is here, Kiri will be all right. The thought darted into his head without permission. The relief was immediate, almost overwhelming.

A split second later it all fell into place: Ella was the nurse who had spoken to Rebecca. His two worlds colliding. Ex-wife and mother of his child connecting with the woman he wanted to sleep with.

No-go zone.

He reached Ella in three, unthinking strides. 'It was you, wasn't it?'

His sudden appearance before her startled her. But she looked at him steadily enough, with her wedding face on. 'What was me?'

'You spoke to Rebecca.'

'Yes. Jenny handed me the phone. I wasn't going to hang up on a worried parent. I had no *reason* to hang up on her.'

'What did you tell her?'

She raised an eyebrow at him. 'That you and I were having a torrid affair.'

She looked at him, waiting for something.

He looked back—blank.

'Seriously?' she demanded. '*Seriously?*' She shook her head in disgust. 'I told her what I knew about dengue fever, you idiot. That it was a complex illness, and things did go wrong—but that it was relatively simple to treat. I shared my own experience so that she understood. I said that early detection followed by admission to a good hospital almost guaranteed a positive outcome. I explained that, more than anything else, it was a matter of getting the fluid intake right and treating complications as they arose.'

'Oh. I—I don't—'

'I told her Kiri was handling everything bravely enough to break your heart, and that Jenny and I were taking shifts to make sure he had someone familiar with him at all times. I didn't ask her why she wasn't hotfooting it out here, despite the fact that her son was in a lot of pain, with his joints aching and his muscles screaming, and asking for her, for you, constantly.'

'I—'

'Not interested, Aaron.'

'But just—he's all right, isn't he? In ICU, right?'

A look. Dismissive. And then she did that slow walk away.

'Wait a minute!' he exploded.

But Ella only waved an imperious hand—not even bothering to turn around to do it—and kept to her path.

CHAPTER SIX

WELL...IT BOTHERED Aaron.

Ella's saunter off as though he wasn't even worth talking to.

Followed by Jenny's report of Ella's tireless care: that Ella had begged and badgered the staff and hadn't cared about anyone but his son; the fact that she of all people had been the only one capable of reassuring Rebecca.

He had to keep things simple.

But how simple could it be, when he *knew* Ella would be visiting Kiri—and that when she did, he would have to tell her that, all things considered, she would have to stay away from his son.

Two days. The day Kiri got out of ICU. That's how long it took her.

Aaron had left Kiri for fifteen minutes to grab something to eat, and she was there when he got back to Kiri's room, as though she'd timed it to coincide with his absence.

It wrenched him to see the look on Ella's face as she smoothed Kiri's spiky black hair back from his forehead. To experience again that strange combination of joy and terror that had hit him when he'd seen her coming out of the hospital.

He would *not* want her. He had enough on his plate. And if Ella thought she got to pick and choose when their lives could intersect and when they couldn't—well, no! That was all. No.

She looked up. Defensive. Defiant. *Anxious?*

And he felt like he was being unfair.

And he was *never* unfair.

No wonder she made him so mad. She was changing his entire personality, and not for the better.

After a long, staring moment Ella turned back to Kiri. 'I'll see you a little later, Kiri. Okay?' And then she walked slowly away.

Kiri blinked at his father sleepily, then smiled. 'Where's Ella gone?'

'Back to her hospital. They need her there now. And you've got me.'

Kiri nodded.

He was out of danger, but he looked so tired. 'Are you okay, Kiri? What do you need?'

'Nothing. My head was hurting. And my tummy. And my legs. But Ella fixed me.'

'That's good. But I'm here now.'

'And I was hot. Ella cooled me down.'

'How did she do that?'

'With water and a towel.'

'I can do that for you, sport.'

'I'm not hot any more.' Kiri closed his eyes for a long moment, then blinked them open again and held out his skinny forearm, showing off the small sticking plaster. 'Look,' he said.

'You were on a drip, I know.'

'Superhero juice, Ella said.'

'To get you better.'

A few minutes more passed. 'Dad?'

'What is it, sport?'

'Where's Ella?'

Aaron bit back a sigh. 'She has a lot of people to look after. I'm back now. And Mum will be coming soon.'

'Mum's coming?'

'Yes, she'll be here soon.'

Kiri's eyes drifted shut.

The elation at knowing Kiri was out of danger was still with him. Even the prospect of calling Rebecca again to reinforce his demand that she get her butt on a plane didn't daunt him—although he hoped that, this time, Rebecca wouldn't be off her face.

Of course, breaking the other news to her—that he and Kiri would be heading to LA for his audition after Kiri's convalescence, and then straight on to London—might set off a whole new word of pain. He knew Rebecca was going to hate the confirmation that Aaron had landed both the audition and a plum role in Brand's film, because she resented every bit of career success that came his way.

He suspected she would try to guilt him into leaving Kiri in Sydney with her, just to punish him—for Kiri's illness and for the role in Brand's film—but that wasn't going to happen. Until Rebecca got herself clean, where he went, Kiri went.

So he would call Rebecca, get her travel arrangements under way so she could spend time with Kiri while he got his strength back, and tell her that London was all systems go.

Then he would have only two things to worry about: Kiri's convalescence; and figuring out how to forget Ella Reynolds and the way she had looked at his son.

Rebecca wasn't coming.

It was a shock that she would forego spending time with Kiri, knowing she wouldn't see him for months.

Aaron was trying to find the right words to say to Kiri and had been tiptoeing around the subject for a while.

The last thing he needed was Ella breezing in—triggering that aggravating, inexplicable and entirely inappropriate sense of relief.

Not that she spared Aaron as much as a look.

'You don't need to tell me how you are today,' she said to Kiri, leaning down to kiss his forehead. 'Because you look like a superhero. I guess you ate your dinner last night! And are you weeing? Oops—am I allowed to say that in front of Dad?'

Kiri giggled, and said, 'Yes,' and Ella gave his son that blinding smile that was so gut-churningly amazing.

She looked beautiful. Wearing a plain, white cotton dress and flat leather tie-up sandals, toting an oversized canvas bag—nothing special about any of it. But she was so…lovely.

She presented Kiri with a delicately carved wooden dragonfly she'd bought for him at the local market and showed him how to balance it on a fingertip.

Then Kiri asked her about the chicken game she'd told him about on a previous visit.

'Ah—you mean Chab Kon Kleng. Okay. Well they start by picking the strongest one—that would be you, Kiri—to be the hen.'

'But I'm a boy.'

'The rooster, then. And you're like your dad—you're going to defend your kids. And all your little chickens are hiding behind you, and the person who is the crow has to try and catch them, while everyone sings a special song. And, no, I'm not singing it. I'm a terrible singer, and my Khmer is not so good.'

'You asked me something about *ch'heu*. That's Khmer.'

'Yes—I was asking if you were in pain and forgot you were a little Aussie boy.'

'I'm Cambodian too.'

'Yes, you are. Lucky you,' Ella said softly.

Aaron was intrigued at this side of Ella. Sweet, animated, fun.

She glanced at him—finally—and he was surprised to see a faint blush creep into her cheeks.

She grabbed the chart from the end of Kiri's bed, scanning quickly. 'You will be out of here in no time if you keep this up.' Another one of those smiles. 'Anyway, I just wanted to call in and say hello today, but I'll stay longer next time.'

'Next time,' Kiri piped up, 'you'll see Mum. She's coming.'

'Hey—that's great,' she replied.

Aaron sucked in a quick, silent breath. Okay, this was the moment to tell Kiri that Rebecca wasn't coming, and to tell Ella that she wasn't welcome. 'Er...' *Brilliant start.*

Two pairs of eyes focused on him. Curious. Waiting.

Aaron perched on the side of Kiri's bed. 'Mate,' he said, 'I'm afraid Mum still can't leave home, so we're going to have to do without her.'

Kiri stared at him, taking in the news in his calm way.

'But she knows you're almost better, and so you'll forgive her,' Aaron continued. 'And I have to give you a kiss and hug from her—yuckerama.'

Kiri giggled then. 'You always kiss and hug me.'

'Then I guess I can squeeze in an extra when nobody's looking.'

'Okay.'

'Right,' Ella said cheerily. 'You'd better get yourself out of here, young man, so you can get home to Mom. You know what that means—eat, drink, do what the doctor tells you. Now, I'm sure you and Dad have lots to plan so I'll see you later.'

That smile at Kiri.

The usual smile—the one minus the eye glow—for him.

And she was gone before Aaron could gather his thoughts.

See you later? No, she would *not*.

With a quick 'Back soon' to Kiri, Aaron ran after her.

'Ella, wait.'

Ella stopped, stiffened, turned.

'Can we grab a coffee?'

Ella thought about saying no. She didn't want to feel that uncomfortable mix of guilt and attraction he seemed to bring out in her. But a 'no' would be an admission that he had some kind of power over her, and that would never do. So she nodded and walked beside him to the hospital café, and sat in silence until their coffee was on the table in front of them.

'I wanted to explain. About Rebecca.' He was stirring one sugar into his coffee about ten times longer than he needed to.

'No need,' she said.

'It's just she had an audition, and because Kiri was out of danger...'

She nodded. 'And he'd probably be ready to go home by the time she arrived anyway...'

Aaron looked morosely at the contents in his cup, and Ella felt an unwelcome stab of sympathy.

'Actually, the audition wasn't the main issue,' he said. 'I know the director. He would have held off for her.'

Ella waited while he gave his coffee another unnecessary stir.

'Has Tina told you about Rebecca?' he asked, looking across at her.

'Told me what?'

'About her drug problem?'

'Ah. No. I didn't know. I'm sorry.' That explained the not-really-divorced divorce; Sir Galahad wasn't the type to cut and run in an untenable situation.

'Things are...complicated,' he said. 'Very.'

'I'm sure.'

'It doesn't mean Rebecca isn't anxious about Kiri. I mean, she's his mother, and she loves him.'

'I understand. But he should recover quickly now. At this stage—the recovery phase—all those fluids that leaked out of his capillaries are simply being reabsorbed by his body. Like a wave—flooding, receding, balancing. But he'll be tired for a while. And there may be a rash. Red and itchy, with white centres. Don't freak out about it. Okay?'

Silence. Another stir of the coffee.

'Are you going to drink that, or are you just going to stir it to death?' Ella asked, and then it hit her: this was not really about Rebecca. 'Or...do you want to just tell me what this all has to do with me?'

Aaron looked at her. Kind of determined and apologetic at the same time. 'It's just...he's very attached to you. *Too* attached to you. I don't know how, in such a short time, but he is.'

'It's an occupational hazard for doctors and nurses.'

'No, Ella. It's you. And that makes things more complicated, given he won't be seeing you again once we leave the hospital. I—I don't want him to miss you.'

'Ahhh,' she said, and pushed her cup away. 'I see. Things are complicated, and he already has a mother, so stay away, Ella.'

'It's just the flip side of what you said to me—that you don't like saying goodbye to a child when a relationship goes south.'

'We don't have a relationship. And the fact you're a father didn't seem to bother you when you were kissing me, as long as we weren't *in* a "relationship".'

'Don't be naïve, Ella. It's one thing for us to have sex. It's another when there are two of us sitting together at my son's bedside.'

The hurt took her by surprise. 'So let me get this straight—you're happy to sleep with me, but you don't want me anywhere near your son?'

'We haven't slept together.'

'That's right—we haven't. And calm yourself, we won't. But the principle is still there: it would be *okay* for you to have sex with me, but because you *want* to have sex with me, it's *not* okay for me to be anywhere near your son. And don't throw back at me what I said about not wanting to get mixed up with a man with a kid—which would be my problem to deal with, not yours. Or tell me it's to protect him from the pain of missing me either. Because this is about *you*. This is because *you're* not comfortable around me. I'd go so far as to say you disapprove of me.'

'I don't know what to think of you.' He dragged a hand through his hair. 'One minute you're letting a drunk guy in a bar paw you and the next you're hovering like a guardian angel over sick kids. One minute you're a sarcastic pain in the butt, and the next you're crying like your heart's breaking. Do I approve of you? I don't even know. It's too hard to know you, Ella. Too hard.'

'And you're a saint by comparison, are you? No little flaws or contradictions in your character? So how do you explain your attraction to someone like me?'

'I don't explain it. I can't. That's the problem.' He stopped, closed his eyes for a fraught moment. 'Look, I've got Rebecca to worry about. And Kiri to shield from all that's going on with her. That's why I told you I couldn't develop a relationship with you. To make it cl—'

'I told *you* I didn't want one. Or are you too arrogant to believe that?'

'Wake up, Ella. If Kiri has developed an affection for you, that means we're *in* a relationship. Which would be fine if I didn't—'

'Oh, shut up and stir your coffee! This is no grand passion we're having.' Ella was almost throbbing with rage, made worse by having to keep her voice low. A nice yelling match would have suited her right now but you didn't yell at people in Cambodia.

She leaned across the table. 'Understand this: I'm not interested in you. I'm not here, after having worked a very long day, to see you. I'm here to see Kiri, who was in this hospital parentless. No father. No mother. Just a nanny. And me. Holding his hand while they drew his blood for tests. Coaxing him to drink. Trying to calm him when he vomited, when his stomach was hurting and there was no relief for the pain. Knowing his head was splitting and that paracetamol couldn't help enough. So scared he'd start bleeding that I was beside myself because what the hell were we going to do if he needed a transfusion and you weren't here? How dare you tell me after that to stay away from him, like I'm out to seduce you and spoil your peace and wreck your family?'

She could feel the tears ready to burst, and dashed a hand across her eyes.

He opened his mouth.

'Just shut *up*,' she said furiously. 'You know, I'm not overly modest about my assets, but I somehow think a fine upstanding man like you could resist making mad passionate love to a bottom feeder like me in front of Kiri, so I suggest you just get over yourself and stop projecting.'

'Projecting?'

'Yes—your guilty feelings on me! I have enough guilt of my own to contend with without you adding a chunky piece of antique furniture to the bonfire. It's not my fault your wife is a drug addict. It's not my fault you got a divorce. It's not my fault your son got dengue fever. It's not my fault you find me attractive, or a distraction, or whatever. I am not the cause or the catalyst or the star of your documentary, and I didn't ask you to lurk around hospital corners, watching me.'

She stood, pushing her chair back violently. 'I'm no saint, but I'm not a monster either.'

She headed for the door at a cracking pace, Aaron scrambling to catch up with her.

He didn't reach her until she was outside, around the corner from the hospital entrance.

'Wait just a minute,' he said, and spun her to face him.

'This conversation is over. Leave me *alone*,' she said, and jerked free, turned to walk off.

His hand shot out, grabbed her arm, spun her back. 'Oh, no, you don't,' he said, and looked as furious as she felt. 'You are not running off and pretending I'm the only one with a problem. Go on, lie to me—tell me you don't want me to touch you.'

He wrenched her up onto her toes and smacked her into his chest. Looked at her for one fierce, burning moment, and then kissed her as though he couldn't help himself.

In a desperate kind of scramble, her back ended up against the wall and he was plastered against her. He took her face between his hands, kissed her, long and hard. 'Ella,' he whispered against her lips. 'Ella. I know it's insane but when you're near me I can't help myself. Can't.'

Ella was tugging his shirt from his jeans, her hands sliding up his chest. 'Just touch me. Touch me!'

His thighs nudged hers apart and he was there, hard against her. She strained against him, ready, so ready, so—

Phone. Ringing. His.

They pulled apart, breathing hard. Looked at each other. Aaron wrenched the phone from his pocket. Rebecca.

The phone rang. Rang. Rang. Rang. Stopped.

And still Ella and Aaron stared at each other.

Ella swallowed. 'No matter what you think of me—or what I think of myself right now, which isn't much—I don't want to make things difficult. For you, for Kiri. Or for me.' She smoothed her hands down her dress, making sure everything was in order. 'So you win. I'll stay away.'

'Maybe there's another way to—'

Ella cut him off. 'No. We've both got enough drama in our lives without making a fleeting attraction into a Shakespearean tragedy. I just…' Pause. Another swallow.

'I don't want him to think I don't care about him. Because he might think that, when I don't come back.'

Aaron pushed a lock of her hair behind her ear. It was a gentle gesture that had her ducking away. 'That's not helping,' she said.

'Don't think I don't know how lucky I am to have had you watching over Kiri. He knows and I know that you care about him. And I know how much, after Sann—'

'Don't you dare,' she hissed. 'I should never have told you. I regret it more than I can say. So we'll make a deal, shall we? I'll stay away and you don't ever, *ever* mention Sann again, not to anyone. I don't need or want you to feel sorry for me. I don't need or want *you*. So let's focus on a win-win. You go home. I'll go…wherever. And we'll forget we ever met.'

Ella walked away, but it was harder than it had ever been to slow her steps.

The sooner Aaron James was back in Sydney the better.

She was putting Sydney at number three thousand and one on her list of holiday destinations—right after Afghanistan.

CHAPTER SEVEN

'ELLA!'

Tina was staring at her. Surprised, delighted. 'Oh, come in. Come in! I'm so glad you're here. I was wondering when you'd use that ticket. Brand,' she called over her shoulder.

Ella cast appreciative eyes over the grand tiled entrance hall of her sister's Georgian townhouse. 'Nice one, Mrs. McIntyre,' she said.

Tina laughed. 'Yes, "nice".'

'So I'm thinking space isn't a problem.'

'We have *oodles* of it. In fact, we have other g—. Oh, here's Brand. Brand, Ella's here.'

'Yes, so I see. Welcome,' Brand said, pulling Tina backwards against his chest and circling her with his arms.

Ella looked at Brand's possessive hands on Tina's swollen belly. In about a month she would be an aunt. She was happy for her sister, happy she'd found such profound love. But looking at this burgeoning family made her heart ache with the memory of what she'd lost, what she might never have.

Not that Ella remembered the love between her and Javier being the deep, absorbing glow that Tina and Brand shared. It had been giddier. A rush of feeling captured in a handful of memories. That first dazzling sight of him outside a makeshift hospital tent in Somalia. Their first tentative kiss. The sticky clumsiness of the first and only time they'd made love—the night before the malaria had hit her; two nights before he was taken.

Would it have grown into the special bond Tina and Brand had? Or burned itself out?

Standing in this hallway, she had never felt so unsure, so…empty. And so envious she was ashamed of herself. Maybe it had been a mistake to come. 'If you'll show me where to dump my stuff, I'll get out of your hair for a couple of hours.'

Tina looked dismayed. 'But I *want* you in my hair.'

'I'm catching up with someone.'

'Who? And where?'

Ella raised her eyebrows.

Tina made an exasperated sound. 'Oh, don't get all frosty.'

Ella rolled her eyes. 'She's a nurse, living in Hammersmith. We're meeting at a pub called the Hare and something. Harp? Carp? Does it matter? Can I go? Please, please, pretty please?'

Tina disentangled herself from her laughing husband's arms. 'All right, you two, give it a rest,' she said. 'Brand—show Ella her room. Then, Ella, go ahead and run away. But I don't expect to have to ambush you every time I want to talk to you.'

Ella kissed Tina's cheek. 'I promise to bore you rigid with tales of saline drips and bandage supplies and oxygen masks. By the time I get to the bedpan stories, you'll be begging me to go out.'

London in summer, what was there not to like? Aaron thought as he bounded up the stairs to Brand's house with Kiri on his back.

He went in search of Brand and Tina and found them in the kitchen, sitting at the table they used for informal family dining.

'Good news! We've found an apartment to rent,' he announced, swinging Kiri down to the floor.

Tina swooped on Kiri to kiss and tickle him, then settled him on the chair beside her with a glass of milk and a cookie. She bent an unhappy look on her husband. 'Why do all our house guests want to run away the minute they step foot in the place?'

'We've been underfoot for two weeks!' Aaron protested. 'And we're only moving down the street.'

'It's her sister,' Brand explained. 'Ella arrived today, stayed just long enough to drop her bag and ran off to some ill-named pub. Princess Tina is *not* amused.'

Aaron's heart stopped—at least that's what it felt like—and then jump-started violently. He imagined himself pale with shock, his eyes bugging out. He felt his hair follicles tingle. What had they said while he'd been sitting there stunned? What had he missed? He forced himself to take a breath, clear his mind, concentrate. Because the only coalescing thought in his head was that she was here. In London. In this house.

He'd thought he would never see her again. Hadn't wanted to see her again.

But she was here.

'…when we weren't really expecting her,' Tina said.

Huh? What? What had he missed while his brain had turned to mush?

'You know what she's like,' Brand said.

What? What's she like? Aaron demanded silently.

'What do you mean, what she's like?' Tina asked, sounding affronted.

Bless you, Tina.

'Independent. Very,' Brand supplied. 'She's used to looking after herself. And she's been in scarier places. Somehow I think she'll make it home tonight just fine.'

'Yes, but what time? And she hasn't even told me how long she's staying. Mum and Dad are going to want a report. How can I get the goss if she runs away when she should be talking to me?'

Brand gave her a warning look. 'If you fuss, she *will* go.' He turned to Aaron, changing the subject. 'So, Aaron, when do you move in?'

'A week,' Aaron said, racking his brain for a way to get the conversation casually back to Ella. 'Is that all right? I mean, if your sister is here…' he looked back at Tina '…maybe Kiri and I should leave earlier.' He'd lost it, obviously, because as the words left his mouth he wanted to recall them. 'We can easily move to a hotel.' Nope. That wasn't working for him either.

He caught himself rubbing his chest, over his heart. Realised it wasn't the first time he'd thought of Ella and done that.

'No way—you're not going any earlier than you have to,' Tina said immediately, and Aaron did the mental equivalent of swooning with relief.

And that really hit home.

The problem wasn't that he didn't want to see Ella—it was that he did.

On his third trip downstairs that night, Aaron faced the fact that he was hovering. He hadn't really come down for a glass of water. Or a book. Or a midnight snack.

Barefoot, rumpled, and edgy, he had come down looking for Ella.

On his fourth trip he gave up any pretence and took a seat in the room that opened off the dimly lit hall—a library-cum-family room. From there he could hear the front door open and yet be hidden. He turned on only one lamp; she wouldn't even know he was there, if he chose the sensible option and stayed hidden when the moment came.

He was, quite simply, beside himself.

Aaron helped himself to a Scotch, neat, while he waited.

His blood pressure must have been skyrocketing, because his heart had been thumping away at double speed all day.

And he had *excellent* blood pressure that *never* skyrocketed.

He knew precisely how long he'd been waiting—an hour and thirteen minutes—when he heard it.

Key hitting the lock. Lock clicking. Door opening.

A step on the tiled floor. He took a deep breath. Tried—failed—to steady his nerves. Heard the door close. Then nothing. No footsteps. A long moment passed. And then another sound. Something slumping against the wall or the door or the floor.

Was she hurt? Had she fallen?

Another sound. A sort of hiccup that wasn't a hiccup. A hitched breath.

He got to his feet and walked slowly to the door. Pushed it open silently. How had he ever thought he might sit in here and *not* go to her? And then he saw her and almost gasped! He was so monumentally unprepared for the punch of lust that hit him as he peered out like a thief.

She was sitting on the floor. Back against the door, knees up with elbows on them, hands jammed against her mouth. He could have sworn she was crying but there were no tears.

He saw the complete stillness that came into her as she realised someone was there.

And then she looked up.

CHAPTER EIGHT

AARON WALKED SLOWLY towards Ella. She was wearing a dark green skirt that had fallen up her thighs. A crumpled white top with a drawstring neckline. Leather slide-on sandals. Her hair was in loose waves, long, hanging over her shoulders—he'd never seen it loose before.

He felt a tense throb of some emotion he couldn't name, didn't want to name, as he reached her. He stood looking down at her, dry-mouthed. 'Where have you been?' he asked.

'Why are you here?' she countered, the remembered huskiness of her voice scattering his thoughts for a moment.

The way her skirt was draping at the top of her thighs was driving him insane. *Concentrate.* 'Here? I've been staying here. I'm working here. In London, I mean. Brand's film.' He couldn't even swallow. 'Didn't they tell you?'

'No,' Ella said, sighing, and easily, gracefully, got to her feet. 'Well, that's just great. I guess you're going to expect me to move out now, so I don't corrupt Kiri—or you.'

'No. I don't want you to move out. We'll be leaving in a week, anyway.'

'Oh, that makes me feel *so* much better. I'm sure I can avoid doing anything too immoral for one lousy week.'

Her silky skirt had settled back where it was supposed to be. It was short, so he could still see too much of her thighs. He jerked his gaze upwards and it collided with her breasts. He could make out the lace of her bra, some indistinguishable pale colour, under the white cotton of her top.

His skin had started to tighten and tingle, so he forced his eyes upwards again. Jammed his hands in his pockets as he caught the amused patience in her purple eyes.

'Why are you waiting up for me?' she asked.

He had no answer.

She sighed again—an exaggerated, world-weary sigh. 'What do you want, Aaron?'

'I want you,' he said. He couldn't quite believe he'd said it after everything that had gone on between them, but once it was out it seemed so easy. So clear. As though he hadn't spent agonising weeks telling himself she was the *last* thing he needed in his life and he'd been right to put the brakes on in Cambodia. 'I haven't stopped wanting you. Not for a second.'

Her eyebrows arched upwards. Even her eyebrows were sexy.

'I think we've been through this already, haven't we?' she asked softly, and started to move past him. 'One week— I'm sure you can resist me for that long, Sir Galahad.'

His hand shot out. He saw it move, faster than his brain was working. Watched his fingers grip her upper arm.

She turned to face him.

He didn't know what he intended to do next—but at least she wasn't looking amused any more.

She looked hard at him for a moment. And then she took his face between her hands and kissed him, fusing her mouth to his with forceful passion. She finished the kiss with one long lick against his mouth. Pulled back a tiny fraction, then seemed to change her mind and kissed him again. Pulled back. Stepped back. Looked him in the eye.

'Now what?' she asked, her breathing unsteady but her voice controlled. 'This is where you run away, isn't it? Because of Rebecca. Or Kiri. Or just because it's me.'

That strange other being still had control of him. It

was the only explanation for the way he jerked her close, crushed his arms around her and kissed her. He broke the contact only for a second at a time. To breathe. He wished he didn't even have to stop for that. His hands were everywhere, couldn't settle. In her hair, on her back, gripping her bottom, running up her sides. And through it all he couldn't seem to stop kissing her.

He could hear her breathing labouring, like his. When his hands reached her breasts, felt the nipples jutting into his palms through two layers of clothing, he shuddered. He finally stopped kissing her, but kept his mouth on hers, still, reaching for control. 'Now what?' He repeated her question without moving his mouth from hers, after a brief struggle to remember what she'd asked. Kissed her again.

Ella wrapped her arms around his waist and he groaned. He looked down into her face. 'There doesn't seem to be much point in running away, because you're always there. So now, Ella, I get to have you.'

One long, fraught moment of limbo.

He didn't know what he'd do if she said no, he was so on fire for her.

But she didn't say no. She said, 'Okay. Let's be stupid, then, and get it done.'

Not exactly a passionate acquiescence, but he'd take it. Take her, any way he could get her.

He kissed her again, pulling her close, letting her feel how hard he was for her, wanting her to know. Both of his hands slipped into her hair. It was heavy, silky. Another time he would like to stroke his fingers through it, but not now. Now he was too desperate. He dragged fistfuls of it, using it to tilt her head back, anchoring her so he could kiss her harder still. 'Come upstairs,' he breathed against her mouth. 'Come with me.'

'All yours,' Ella said in that mocking way she had— but Aaron didn't care. He grabbed her hand and walked quickly to the staircase, pulling her up it at a furious pace.

'Which way to your room?' he asked.

Silently, she guided him to it.

The room next to his.

Fate.

The moment they were inside he was yanking her top up and over her head, fumbling with her skirt until it lay pool-like at her feet. The bedside lamp was on and he said a silent prayer of thanks because it meant he could see her. She stood before him in pale pink underwear so worn it was almost transparent, tossing her hair back over her shoulders. He swallowed. He wanted to rip her underwear to shreds to get to her. It was like a madness. Blood pounding through his veins, he stripped off his T-shirt and shoved his jeans and underwear off roughly.

She was watching him, following what he was doing as she kicked off her sandals. Aaron forced himself to stand still and let her see him. He hoped she liked what he saw.

Ella came towards him and circled his biceps with her hands—at least, partly; his biceps were too big for her to reach even halfway around. Aaron remembered that she liked tattoos. His tattooed armbands were broad and dark and intricately patterned—and, yes, she clearly did like what she saw. The tattoos had taken painful hours to complete and, watching her eyes light up as she touched them, he'd never been happier to have them. He hoped during the night she would see the more impressive tattoo on his back, but he couldn't imagine taking his eyes off her long enough to turn around.

He couldn't wait any longer to see her naked. He reached for her hips, and she obligingly released his arms and stepped closer. She let him push her panties down, stepped free of them when they hit the floor. Then she let him work the back fastening of her bra as she rested against him, compliant. As he wrestled with the bra, he could feel her against him, thigh to thigh, hip to hip. The tangle of soft hair against his erection had his heart bashing so hard and fast in his chest he thought he might have a coronary. Oh, he liked the feel of it. She was perfect. Natural and perfect. His hands were shaking so badly as he tried to undo her bra he thought he was going to have to tear it off, but it gave at last. Her breasts, the areoles swollen, nipples sharply erect, pressed into his chest as he wrenched the bra off. He was scared to look at her in case he couldn't stop himself falling on her like a ravening beast...but at the same time he was desperate to see her.

'Ella,' he said, his voice rough as he stepped back just enough to look. With one hand he touched her face. The other moved lower to the dark blonde hair at the apex of her thighs. He combed through it with trembling fingers. Lush and beautiful. He could feel the moisture seeping into it. Longed to taste it. Taste her. He dropped to his knees, kissed her there.

Aaron loved the hitch in her voice as his fingers and tongue continued to explore. 'I do want you, Aaron. Just so you know. Tonight, I do want you,' Ella said, and it was like a flare went off in his head. He got to his feet, dragged her into his arms, holding her close while his mouth dived on hers. He moved the few steps that would enable him to tumble her backwards onto the bed and come down on her.

The moment they hit the bed he had his hands on her thighs and was pushing her legs apart.

'Wait,' she said in his ear. 'Condoms. Bedside table. In the drawer.'

Somehow, Aaron managed to keep kissing her as he fumbled with the drawer, pulled it open and reached inside. His fingers mercifully closed on one quickly—thankfully they were loose in there.

He kissed her once more, long and luscious, before breaking to free the condom from its packaging. Kneeling between her thighs, he smoothed it on, and Ella raised herself on her elbows to watch. She looked irresistibly wicked, and as he finished the job he leaned forward to take one of her nipples in his mouth. She arched forward and gasped and he decided penetration could wait. She tasted divine. Exquisite. The texture of her was maddeningly good, the feel of her breasts as he held them in his hands heavy and firm. He could keep his mouth on her for hours, he thought, just to hear the sounds coming from her as his tongue circled, licked.

But Ella was shifting urgently beneath him, trying to position him with hands and thighs and the rest of her shuddering body. 'Inside,' she said, gasping. 'Come inside me. Now.'

With one thrust he buried himself in her, and then he couldn't seem to help himself. He pulled back and thrust deeply into her again. And again and again. He was kissing her mouth, her eyes, her neck as he drove into her over and over. The sound of her gasping cries urged him on until he felt her clench around him. She sucked in a breath, whooshed it out. Again. Once more. She was coming, tense and beautiful around him, and he'd never been so turned on in his life. He slid his arms under her on the bed, dragged her up against him and thrust his tongue inside her mouth. And with one last, hard push of his hips he came, hard and strong.

As the last waves of his climax receded, the fog of pure lust cleared from Aaron's head and he was suddenly and completely appalled.

Had he hurt her? Something primal had overtaken him, and he hadn't felt in control of himself. And he was *never, ever* out of control.

He kissed her, trying for gentleness but seemingly unable to achieve it even now, because the moment his mouth touched hers he was out of control again.

Aaron couldn't seem to steady his breathing. It was somehow beautiful to Ella to know that.

He sure liked kissing. Even now, after he'd exhausted

both of them and could reasonably be expected to roll over and go to sleep, he was kissing her. In between those unsteady breaths of his. He seemed to have an obsession with her mouth. Nobody had ever kissed her quite like this before. It was sweet, and sexy as hell, to be kissed like he couldn't stop. It was getting her aroused again. She'd sneered at herself as she'd put those condoms in the drawer, but now all she could think was: did she have enough?

He shifted at last, rolling onto his back beside her. 'Sorry, I know I'm heavy. And you're so slender,' he said.

'It's just the—' She stopped. How did you describe quickly the way long hours, fatigue and illness sapped the calories out of you at breakneck speed? 'Nothing, really. I'm already gaining weight. It happens fast when I'm not working.'

'So you can lose it all over again the next time,' Aaron said, and Ella realised she didn't have to explain after all.

His eyes closed as he reached for her hand.

Okay, so now he'll go to sleep, Ella thought, and was annoyed with herself for bringing him to her room. If they'd gone to his room she could have left whenever she wanted; but what did a woman say, do, to get a man to leave?

But Aaron, far from showing any signs of sleep, brought her hand to his mouth and rolled onto his side, facing her. He released her hand but then pulled her close so that her side was fitted against his front, and nuzzled his nose into the side of her neck. He slid one of his hands down over her belly and between her legs. 'Did I hurt you, Ella?'

Huh? 'Hurt me?'

'Yes. I was rough. I'm sorry.'

As he spoke his fingers were slipping gently against the delicate folds of her sex. It was like he was trying to soothe her. Her heart stumbled, just a little, as she realised what he was doing. And he was looking at her so seriously while he did it. He had the most remarkably beautiful eyes. And, of course, he was ridiculously well endowed, but she'd been so hot and ready for him it hadn't hurt. It had been more erotic than anything she could have dreamed.

How did she tell him that his fingers, now, weren't soothing? That what he was doing to her was gloriously *good*, but not soothing?

'No, Aaron, you— Ah...' She had to pause for a moment as the touch of his fingers became almost unbearable. 'I mean, no. I mean, you didn't hurt me.' She paused again. 'Aaron,' she said, almost breathless with desire, 'I suggest you go and get rid of that condom. And then hurry back and get another one.'

He frowned, understanding but wary. 'You're sure? I mean— Oh,' as her hands found him. 'I guess you're sure.' He swung his legs off the side of the bed and was about to stand but Ella, on her knees in an instant, embraced him from behind. Her mouth touched between his shoulder blades then he felt her tongue trace the pattern of the dragon inked across his back.

'I don't want to leave you,' he said huskily. 'Come with me.'

Ella, needing no second invitation, was out of the bed and heading for the en suite bathroom half a step behind him.

Ella trailed the fingers of one hand along his spine and snapped on the light with the fingers of her other. 'Oh, my, it's even better in the full light.'

Aaron discarded the condom and started to turn around. She imagined he thought he was going to take her in his arms.

'No, you don't. It's my turn,' Ella said.

She turned on the shower, drew Aaron in beside her, and as he reached for her again she shook her head, laughing, and dodged out of the way. 'I'm glad this is such a small shower cubicle,' she said throatily. 'Close. Tight.' She spun Aaron roughly to face the tiled wall, slammed him up against it and grabbed the cake of soap from its holder.

Lathering her hands, his skin, she plastered herself against his back, moving her breasts sensually against his beautiful tattoo as she reached around to fondle him. 'I love the size of you,' she said, as his already impressive erection grew in her hands. 'I want to take you like this, from behind.'

'I think I'd take you any way I could get you,' Aaron said, groaning as she moved her hands between his legs. He was almost panting and Ella had never felt so beautiful, so powerful.

At last.

She could have this, at last.

As her hands slid, slipped, squeezed, Aaron rested his forehead against the shower wall and submitted.

Aaron watched as Ella slept. She'd fallen into sleep like a stone into the ocean.

No wonder. Aaron had been all over her from the moment they'd left the shower. Inexhaustible. He didn't think he'd understood the word lust until tonight. If he could have breathed her into his lungs, he would have.

He didn't know why he wanted her so badly. But even having had her three times, he couldn't get her close enough. She was in his blood. What a pathetic cliché. But true.

The bedside light was still on, so he could see her face. She looked serious in her sleep. Fretful. Aaron pulled her closer, kissed one of her wickedly arched eyebrows. He breathed in the scent of her hair. Looking at her was almost painful. The outrageous loveliness of her.

Sighing, he turned off the bedside light. It was past five in the morning and he should go back to his room, but he wanted to hold her.

He thought about their last meeting, in Cambodia. The horrible things they'd said to each other. They'd made a pact to forget they'd ever met. How had they gone from that to being here in bed now?

What had he been thinking when he'd left the library, when he'd seen her slumped against the front door with her fists jammed against her mouth?

On a mundane level, he'd thought she must have been drinking. Or maybe he'd hoped that, so he could pigeon-hole her back where he'd wanted to.

Oh, he had no doubt she regularly drank to excess—it fitted with the general wildness he sensed in her. But to-night she'd smelled only like that tantalising perfume. And her mouth had tasted like lime, not booze. It was obvious, really, when he pieced together what he knew about her, what he'd seen of her: she wouldn't let Tina see her out of control. She would be sober and serene and together in this house. The way her family expected her to be. The way she'd been described to him before he'd ever met her.

He thought about the day he'd held her as she'd cried over Bourey's death. And the other boy, Sann, whose death had been infinitely painful for her. Things she didn't want anyone to know.

She was so alone. She chose to be, so her fears and sorrows wouldn't hurt anyone else.

Aaron pulled her closer. She roused, smiled sleepily at him. 'You should go,' she said, but then she settled herself against him and closed her eyes, so he stayed exactly where he was.

Wondering how he could both have her and keep things simple.

CHAPTER NINE

ELLA ROLLED RESTLESSLY, absent-mindedly pulling Aaron's pillow close and breathing in the scent of him, wondering what time he'd left.

She didn't know what had come over her. She'd finally managed to get past second base—way past it, with a blistering home run. And it had been with her brother-in-law's friend under her sister's roof. Not that there had seemed to be much choice about it. It had felt like…well, like fate.

And Aaron wouldn't tell, she reassured herself.

She got out of bed, reached for her robe, and then just sat on the edge of the bed with the robe in her lap. She didn't want to go downstairs. Because downstairs meant reality. It meant Tina and Brand. And Aaron—not Lover Aaron but Friend-of-her-sister Aaron. Daddy Aaron.

She stood slowly and winced a little. It had been a very active night. A fabulous night. But she would have been relieved even if it had been the worst sex of her life instead of the best. Because she had needed it.

Yesterday she'd forced herself to think about Sann. Tina's pregnancy was an immutable fact, and Ella knew she had to come to terms with it; she couldn't run away every time a pang of envy hit her. So she had deliberately taken the memories out of mothballs and examined them one by one. A kind of desensitisation therapy.

But forcing the memories had been difficult. So when

she'd come home to find Aaron there, sex with him had offered an escape. A talisman to keep her sad thoughts at bay, hopefully ward off the bad dreams.

She had been prepared to make a bargain with herself—sex and a nightmare-free night, in exchange for guilt and shame today.

And she did feel the guilt.

Just not the shame.

What did that mean?

Get it together, Ella. It was just a one-night stand. People do it all the time. Simple.

Except it was *not* simple. Because she hadn't managed it before. And she recalled—too vividly—Aaron walking towards her in the hallway, and how much she'd wanted him as their eyes had met. She was deluding herself if she thought she'd only been interested in a nightmare-free night. Oh, he had certainly materialised at a point when she'd been at her lowest ebb and open to temptation, but she had wanted him, wanted the spark, the flash of almost unbearable attraction that had been there in Cambodia.

But now what?

Nothing had really changed. All the reasons not to be together in Cambodia were still there. Kiri. Rebecca. Javier.

Definitely time to return to reality.

Ella tossed the robe aside and strode into the bathroom.

She looked at herself in the mirror. Her mouth looked swollen. Nothing she could do to hide that, except maybe dab a bit of foundation on it to minimise the rawness. She could see small bruises on her upper arms—easily covered. There were more bruises on her hips, but nobody would be seeing those. She sucked in a breath as more memories of the night filled her head. Aaron had been insatiable—and she had loved it. She had more than a few sore spots. And, no doubt, so did he. Like the teeth marks she'd left on his inner thigh.

Ella caught herself smiling. Aaron had called her a vampire, but he hadn't minded. He hadn't minded at all, if the passionate lovemaking that had followed had been any indication.

The smile slipped.

He would have come to his senses by now. Remembered that he didn't like her. Didn't want her near his son.

Time to store the memory and move on.

Tina checked the clock on the kitchen wall as Ella walked in. 'So lunch, not breakfast.'

'Oh, dear, am I going to have to punch a time clock whenever I come and go?'

'Oh, for heaven's sake!'

'Well, sorry, Tina, but really you're as bad as Mom. Just sit down and tell me stories about Brand as a doting father while I make us both something to eat.'

Ella forced herself to look at Tina's stomach as she edged past her sister. Bearable. She could do this.

Tina groaned as she levered herself onto a stool at the kitchen counter. 'I am so over the doting father thing. We've done the practice drive to the hospital seven times. And he's having food cravings. It's not funny, Ella!'

But Ella laughed anyway as she laid a variety of salad vegetables on a chopping board. 'Where is he now?'

'On the set, thank goodness. Which reminds me—I didn't tell you we have other guests.'

Ah. Control time. Ella busied herself pulling out drawers.

'What are you looking for?' Tina asked.

Ella kept her head down and pulled open another drawer. 'Knife.'

'Behind you, knife block on the counter,' Tina said, and Ella turned her back on her sister and took her time selecting a knife.

'Where was I?' Tina asked. 'Oh yes, Aaron. Aaron James and his son. You know them, of course.'

Indistinct mumble.

'Aaron is in Brand's movie,' Tina continued. 'That's why he's in London. They've been staying with us, but they're only here for another week.'

'Why's that?' Ella asked, desperately nonchalant, and started chopping as though her life depended on the precision of her knife action.

'Aaron was always intending to find a place of his own, and yesterday he did.'

'So...would it be easier if I moved out for the week? Because I have friends I was going to see and I—'

'What is wrong with you people? Everyone wants to move out. We've got enough room to house a baseball team! And, anyway, I need you to help me look after Kiri.'

Uh-oh. 'What? Why?'

'Kiri's nanny had some crisis and can't get here until next week. Aaron's due on set tomorrow so I volunteered. I told him it would be good practice. And Kiri is adorable.'

Ella's hand was a little unsteady so she put down the knife. Kiri. She would be looking after Kiri. Aaron wouldn't want that. 'But what about—? I mean, shouldn't he have stayed in Sydney? With his mother?' *Drugs, Ella, drugs.* 'Or—or...someone?'

Tina looked like she was weighing something up. 'The thing is—oh, I don't know if... Okay, look, this is completely confidential, Ella.'

Tina put up her hands at the look on Ella's face. 'Yes, I know you're a glued-shut clam. Aaron is just sensitive about it. Or Rebecca is, and he's respecting that. Rebecca is in rehab. Drugs. Apparently, she auditioned for a role in a new TV show while Aaron was in Cambodia, but didn't get it. The director told her if she didn't get things under control, she'd never work again.'

'That's...tough. How—how's Kiri coping with the separation?'

'Aaron does all the parenting, so it's not as big a deal as you'd think. He has sole custody. But that's not to say

Rebecca doesn't see Kiri whenever she wants. It's just that the drugs have been a problem for some time.'

'Oh. *Sole* custody. Huh.' Ella scooped the chopped salad vegetables into a large bowl. 'But should he...Aaron... should he be here while she's there?'

'Well, they *are* divorced, although sometimes I wonder if Rebecca really believes that. But in any case, it's not a case of him shirking responsibility. Aaron found the clinic—in California, while he was over there auditioning for a new crime show—because Rebecca wanted to do it away from her home city where it might have leaked to the press. And he got her settled in over there, which pushed back filming here so it's all over the place, but what can you do? And of course he's paying, despite having settled a fortune on her during the divorce. He'll be back and forth with Kiri, who thinks it's a spa! But there are strict rules about visiting. Anyway, I hope it works, because Aaron needs to move on, and he won't until Rebecca gets her act together.' She slanted an uncomfortably speculative look at Ella.

'Don't even!' Ella said, interpreting without difficulty.

'Come on, Ella. He's totally, completely hot.'

Ella concentrated on drizzling dressing over the salad.

'Hot as Hades,' Tina said, tightening the thumbscrews. 'But also sweet as heaven. He is amazingly gentle with Kiri. And with me, too. He took me for an ultrasound last week. I had a fall down the stairs and I was petrified.'

Ella hurried to her sister's side, hugged her. 'But everything's all right. You're fine, the baby's fine, right?'

'Yes, but Brand was filming, and I couldn't bring myself to call him. Because I'd already had one fall on the stairs, and he was furious because I was hurrying.'

'Well *stop* hurrying, Tina.' Tentatively, Ella reached and placed a hand on Tina's stomach. The baby kicked suddenly and Ella's hand jerked away—or would have, if Tina hadn't stopped it, flattened it where it was, kept it there.

Tina looked at her sister, wonder and joy in her eyes, and Ella felt her painful envy do a quantum shift.

'So anyway, Aaron,' Tina said. 'He was home. Actually, he saw it happen. I don't know which of us was more upset. He must have cajoled and threatened and who knows what else to get the ultrasound arranged so quickly. He knew it was the only way I'd believe everything was all right. And he let me talk him into not calling Brand until we got the all clear and I was back home.' Tina smiled broadly. 'Unbelievably brave! Brand exploded about being kept in the dark, as Aaron knew he would, but Aaron took it all in his stride. He just let Brand wear himself out, and then took him out for a beer.'

Ella tried not to be charmed, but there was something lovely about the story. 'Well I'm here now to take care of you,' she said, navigating the lump in her throat.

'And I'm very glad.' Tina took Ella's left hand and placed it alongside the right one that was already pressed to her stomach. 'It really scared me, Ella. But I'm not telling you all this to worry you—and don't, whatever you do, tell Mum and Dad.'

'I wouldn't dream of it.'

'I just wanted you to know. I mean, you're my sister! And a nurse. And...well, you're my sister. And I wanted to explain about Aaron. Don't disapprove of him because of Rebecca. He takes his responsibilities very seriously. He practically raised his three young sisters, you know, after his parents died, and he was only eighteen. They idolise him. So does Kiri. And so do I, now. He'll do the right thing by Rebecca, divorced or not, and—more importantly—the right thing by Kiri.'

Ella moved her hands as Tina reached past her to dig into the salad bowl and extract a sliver of carrot.

'You're going to need more than salad, Ella,' Tina said. 'You're like a twig.'

'Yes, yes, yes, I know.' Ella moved back into the food preparation area. 'I'll make some sandwiches.'

'Better make enough for Aaron and Kiri—they should be back any minute.'

For the barest moment Ella paused. Then she opened the fridge and rummaged inside it. 'Where are they?'

'The park. Aaron's teaching Kiri how to play cricket.'

'Ah,' Ella said meaninglessly, and started slapping various things between slices of bread like she was in a trance.

'Yeah, I think that's enough for the entire Australian and English cricket teams,' Tina said eventually.

'Oh. Sorry. Got carried away.'

Breathe, Ella ordered herself when she heard Aaron calling out to Tina from somewhere in the house as she was positioning the platter of sandwiches on the table.

'In the kitchen,' Tina called back.

Tina turned to Ella. 'And I guess you'll tell me later about last night. Probably not fit for children's ears, anyway.'

Ella froze, appalled. Tina *knew*?

'I mean, come on, your mouth,' Tina teased. 'Or are you going to tell me you got stung by a bee?'

'Who got stung by a bee?' Aaron asked, walking in.

CHAPTER TEN

'OH, NOBODY,' TINA said airily.

But Aaron wasn't looking at Tina. He was looking at Ella.

And from the heat in his eyes Ella figured he was remembering last night in Technicolor detail. Ella felt her pulse kick in response. *Insane.*

'Nice to see you again, Ella,' he said.

Could Tina hear that caress in his voice? Ella frowned fiercely at him.

He winked at her. Winked!

'Kiri can't wait to see you,' he continued. 'He's got a present for you—he's just getting it.'

'Oh, that's— Oh.' She gave up the effort of conversation. She was out of her depth. Shouldn't Aaron be keeping Kiri *away* from her? Ella wondered if Aaron had taken a cricket ball to the head. They were deadly, cricket balls.

Ella was aware a phone was ringing. She noted, dimly, Tina speaking. Sensed Tina leaving the room.

And then Aaron was beside her, taking her hand, lifting it to his mouth, kissing it. The back, the palm. His tongue on her fingers.

'Stop,' she whispered, but the air seemed to have been sucked out of the room and she wasn't really sure the word had left her mouth.

Aaron touched one finger to her swollen bottom lip. 'I'm sorry. Is it sore?'

Ella knocked his hand away. 'What's gotten into you?'

The next moment she found herself pulled into Aaron's arms. 'I've got a solution,' he said, as though she would have *any* idea what he was talking about! Yep, cricket ball to the head.

'A solution for what?'

'You and me. It's based on the KISS principle.'

'The what?'

'KISS: keep it simple, stupid.'

'*Simple* would be to forget last night happened.'

Ella started to pull away, but he tightened his arms.

He rested his forehead on hers. 'Let me. Just for a moment.'

Somehow she found her arms around his waist, and she was just standing there, letting him hold her as though it were any everyday occurrence. *Uh-oh. Dangerous.*

'There's no solution needed for a one-night stand,' she said.

He released her, stepped back. 'I don't want a one-night stand.'

'Um—I think you're a little late to that party.'

'Why?'

'Because we've already had one.'

'So tonight will make it a two-night stand. And tomorrow night a three-night stand, and so on.'

'We agreed, in Cambodia—'

'Cambodia-shmodia.'

'Huh?'

'That was then. This is now.'

'Did you get hit in the head with a cricket ball?'

'What?'

'You're talking like you've got a head injury.'

'It's relief. It's making me light-headed. Because for the

first time since Tina and Brand's wedding I know what I'm doing.'

'Well, I don't know what you're doing. I don't think I want to know. I mean, the *KISS* principle?'

'I want you. You want me. We get to have each other. Simple.'

'Um, *not* simple. Kiri? Rebecca? The fact you don't like me? That you don't even know me?'

'Kiri and Rebecca—they're for me to worry about, not you.'

'You're wrong. Tina wants me to help her look after Kiri. Surely you don't want that? Aren't you scared I'll corrupt him or something?'

'Ella, if I know one thing, it's that you would never do anything to hurt Kiri. I've always known it. What I said, in Cambodia...' He shrugged. 'I was being a moron. Projecting, you called it, and you were right. There. I'm denouncing myself.'

'I don't want to play happy families.'

'Neither do I. That's why your relationship with Kiri is separate from my relationship with Kiri, which is separate from my relationship with you. And before you throw Rebecca at me—it's the same deal. You don't even have a relationship with her, so that's purely my issue, not yours.'

'You said the R word. I don't want a relationship—and neither do you.'

Aaron took her hand and lifted it so that it rested on his chest, over his heart. 'Our relationship is going to be purely sexual. Casual sex, that's what you said you wanted. All you were interested in. Well, I can do casual sex.'

'You're not a casual kind of guy, Aaron,' she said.

He smiled, shrugged. 'I'll *make* myself that kind of guy. I said last night I would take you any way I could get you. We're two adults seeking mutual satisfaction and nothing more. An emotion-free zone, which means we can keep it strictly between us—Tina and Brand don't need to know, it's none of Rebecca's business, and Kiri is…well, protected, because your relationship with him is nothing to do with your relationship with me. Simple. Agreed?'

Ella hesitated—not saying yes, but not the automatic 'no' she should be rapping out either. Before she could get her brain into gear, the kitchen door opened.

As Ella pulled her hand free from where, she'd just realised, it was still being held against Aaron's heart, Kiri ran in, saw her, stopped, ran again. Straight at her.

'Kiri, my darling,' she said, and picked him up.

She kissed his forehead. He hugged her, his arms tight around her neck, and didn't seem to want to let go. So she simply moved backwards, with him in her arms, until she felt a chair behind her legs and sat with him on her lap.

Kiri kissed her cheek and Ella's chest tightened dangerously. Kiri removed one arm from around Ella's neck and held out his hand to her. His fist was closed around something.

'What's this?' Ella asked.

Kiri opened his fingers to reveal an unremarkable rock. 'From the beach where you live,' he said. 'Monica.'

Ella smiled at him. 'You remembered?'

Kiri nodded and Ella hugged him close. Santa Monica. He'd been to Santa Monica, and remembered it was where she lived.

She felt a hand on her shoulder and looked up. Aaron was beside her, looking down at her, and she couldn't breathe.

The door opened and Tina breezed in. She paused—an infinitesimal pause—as she took in Aaron's hand on Ella's shoulder, Kiri on her lap.

Aaron slowly removed his hand, but stayed where he was.

'So,' Tina said brightly, 'let's eat.'

* * *

Lunch was dreadful.

Kiri was at least normal, chattering away about Cambodia, about Disneyland, about Sydney, completely at ease.

But Tina was giving off enough gobsmacked vibes to freak Ella out completely.

And Aaron was high-beaming Ella across the table as though he could get her on board with the force of his eyes alone—and if they were really going to carry on a secret affair, he'd have to find his poker face pretty damned fast.

If? Was she really going the 'if' route? Not the 'no way' route?

Casual sex.

Could she do it? She'd liked having someone close to her last night. She'd felt alive in a way she hadn't for such a long time. And she hadn't had the dreaded nightmares with Aaron beside her. So. A chance to feel alive again. With no strings attached. No emotions, which she couldn't offer him anyway.

But, ironic though it was, Aaron James seemed to have the ability to make her want to clean up her act. Maybe it was the way he was with Kiri, or that he cared so much about an ex-wife who clearly made his life a misery, or his general tendency to turn into Sir Galahad at regular intervals and save damsels in distress—his sisters, ex-wife, Tina, her.

Whatever the reason, if she wanted to rehabilitate her self-image, was an affair the way to start? Every time she'd let a guy pick her up, determined to do it, just do it and move on, she'd hated herself. Now that she'd gone the whole nine yards, wouldn't she end up hating herself even more? Especially if it became a regular arrangement?

'I'll clear up,' Tina said, when lunch couldn't be stretched out any more.

'Ella and I can manage,' Aaron said quickly.

'No, *Ella and I* can manage,' Tina insisted. She stood and arched her back, grimaced.

Ella got to her feet. 'You should rest,' she told her sister. 'And you…' with an almost fierce look at Aaron '…should get Kiri into bed for a nap. He's sleepy.' She started gathering empty plates.

Aaron looked like he was about to argue so Ella simply turned her back on him and took an armload of plates to the sink. She stayed there, clattering away, refusing to look up, willing him to leave.

And then, at last, Tina spoke. 'The coast is clear. You can come up for air.'

Ella raised her head cautiously and waited for the inevitable.

'What's going on?' Tina asked simply.

'If you mean between me and Aaron, nothing.'

'Of course I mean you and Aaron. He's gaga. It's so obvious.'

'He's not *gaga*.'

'Oh, I beg to differ.'

'We just… We just got to know each other in Cambodia. I called in to check on Kiri a few times when he was ill with dengue fever and Aaron was out in the field, so he's…grateful. I guess.'

Tina snorted out a laugh. 'If that's gratitude, I'd like to get me a piece of it. I'm going to remind Brand tonight just how grateful he is that he met me.'

Ella had stayed out as long as public transport allowed but Aaron was nevertheless waiting for her when she got back, leaning against the library door.

No reprieve.

She'd three-quarters expected this, though, so she had a plan.

She would be *that* Ella—the cool, calm, untouchable one—so he knew exactly what he'd get if he pursued this insanity that she couldn't quite bring herself to reject. With luck, he would run a mile away from her, the way he'd run in Cambodia, and spare them both the heartache she feared would be inevitable if they went down this path.

If not…well, they'd see.

'Are you going to wait up for me every night?' she asked, in the amused tone that had infuriated him in the past.

'I can wait in your bed if you prefer.'

The wind having effectively been taken out of her sails, Ella headed slowly up the stairs without another word. Aaron followed her into her room, reached for her.

'Wait,' she said, stepping back. 'You really want to do this?'

'Yes.'

'One hundred per cent sure?'

'Yes.'

She sighed. 'It's going to end in tears, you know.'

'I'll take my chances.'

Another sigh. 'Okay, then—but, first, ground rules.'

He nodded, deadly serious.

'No PDAs,' she said. 'If this is casual sex, it stays in my bedroom—or your bedroom. No touchy-feely stuff beyond bed. And *absolutely* nothing in front of Tina or Brand or Kiri.'

'Agreed.'

'When one or the other of us decides the arrangement is over there will be no questions, no comments, no recriminations, no clinging. I will let you go as easily as that…' she clicked her fingers '…if you're the one ending things. And I expect you to do the same.'

He narrowed his eyes. 'Agreed.'

'No prying into my private life.'

He looked at her.

'Agreed?' she asked impatiently.

'I don't know what "prying" means to you—you're su-persensitive about things other people consider normal conversation, and I don't want you taking a machete to my head if I ask what any reasonable person would think is an innocuous question.'

'If you think I'm unreasonable, why do you want to go down this path?'

He smiled, a smile that held the promise of hot, steamy sex. 'Oh, I think you know why, Ella.'

She was blushing again.

'What about if I agree that you are under no obligation to tell me anything that makes you uncomfortable?' he asked.

She digested that. 'Fair enough. Agreed. And ditto for you.'

'No need. You can ask me anything you want, and I'll answer you.'

That threw her, but she nodded. 'But I won't ask. Any conditions from your side?'

'One. Monogamy. Nobody else, while you're sleeping with me.'

'Agreed,' she said, but she tinkled out a little laugh to suggest she thought that was quaint. 'Anything else?'

'No. So take off your clothes.'

CHAPTER ELEVEN

'I DO LIKE a masterful man,' Ella said. And then she reached for the hem of her dress.

But Aaron stopped her. 'I've changed my mind,' he said. 'Come here.'

Ella stepped towards him, her eyebrows raised in that practised, disdainful way that seemed to aggravate him.

When she reached him, he took the neckline of her cotton dress in his hands, and ripped the dress down the front.

A surprised 'Oh...' whooshed out of her. There went the practised disdain.

She looked up at him. His face was stark as he dragged her bra down her arms, imprisoning her with the straps, and bent his head to her breasts. He sucked one nipple, hard, into his mouth, and she gasped. Moved to the other. He eased back to look into her eyes as he pushed her tattered dress almost casually over her hips until it dropped to the floor. 'I'll buy you another,' he said.

She couldn't speak, couldn't raise her defensive shield of indifference. Could only wait and watch. Her arms were still trapped, and he made no move to free them. Instead, he brought his hands up to cup her breasts, thumbs smoothing across her nipples, and then lowered his mouth again.

How much time had passed—a minute? Ten? Longer? He wouldn't let her move, just kept up that steady pressure, hands and lips, until she was almost weeping with pleasure. Ella was desperate to touch him, but every time she tried to reach around to unhook her bra and free herself, he stymied her.

At last he stepped back, examined her with one long, lascivious look from her head to her toes. Then his hands went to the front of her panties and she felt, heard, the fine cotton tear. 'I'll replace those too,' he said softly, and then her breath shuddered out, rough and choppy, as one of his hands reached between her legs. Within moments she was shuddering as the pleasure tore through her like a monsoon. Hot, wet, wild.

He spun her, unhooking her bra with a swift efficiency that seemed to scorn his earlier languorous attention to her body. With the same speed, he stripped off his own clothes. Then his hands were on her again, arousing her, preparing her, as he backed the two of them towards the bed.

He fell onto the bed, on his back, and dragged her on top of him. 'Here, let me.' His voice was hoarse and urgent as he positioned her over him, moving her legs so that they fell on either side of his and thrusting blindly towards her centre.

'Wait,' she said.

It took only moments for her to raise herself, straddling him with her knees on each side of his straining body. She reached over him, grabbed a condom from the drawer. She ripped the package open with her teeth, slid the sheath onto him with slow, steady movements. Smoothing it as he jumped against her hand. And then she took him inside her with one undulating swirl of her hips. Stilled, keeping him there, not letting him move, deep inside her.

'No,' she said, as he started to buck upwards against her. 'Let me.' And, rising and falling in smooth, steady waves, she tightened herself around him until he gasped her name. Clutching her hips, he jammed her down on top of him and exploded.

Ella, following him into ecstasy, collapsed on top of him.

She stayed there, spent, as his hands threaded through her hair, stroking and sliding.

She wanted to stay like that all night, with Aaron inside her, his hands in her hair, his mouth close enough to kiss.

Except that he hadn't kissed her. Not once.

For some reason, she didn't like that.

It's just casual sex, she reminded herself.

On that thought, she disengaged herself from his body and got off the bed. Pulling her hair back over her shoulders, she smiled serenely down at him. 'Excellent, thank you,' she said. 'But there's no need for you to stay. I'll see you tomorrow night.'

Tina had assorted chores to do the next day, so she left Kiri in Ella's sole company.

Ella had taken him to the park to practise catching the cricket ball. Was that the hardest, unkindest ball in international sport? Ella thought so, as she looked at her bruised shin.

So for the afternoon she'd chosen a more intellectual pursuit—painting. It was a challenge to keep Kiri's paint set in the vicinity of the special child-sized activity table Tina had moved into the library for him, but they'd accomplished it.

As assorted paintings, laid out across every available surface, were drying, she and Kiri curled up together in one of the massive leather chairs, where she entertained him by letting him play with her cellphone.

She was laughing at Kiri's attempt at an emoticon-only text message when Aaron walked in.

'Shouldn't you be on set?' she asked, sitting up straighter.

'I'm on a break so thought I'd come back to the house. What happened to your leg?'

'Cricket-ball injury. That's a sport I am never going to figure out.' She gestured around the room. 'Check out Kiri's paintings while you're here. Which one's for Dad, Kiri?'

Kiri scrambled out of the chair. 'Two of them. Here's Mum…' He was pointing out a painting of a black-haired woman in an orange dress. 'And here's Ella.' In her nursing uniform.

Ella felt her stomach drop with a heavy thud. Just what the man needed; his ex-wife and his current lover, as depicted by his son, who knew nothing of the tension in either relationship.

But Aaron was smiling like it was the most wonderful gift in the world. 'Fabbo. One day, when you're famous, these are going to be worth a fortune.'

Kiri giggled, and then went to perch back with Ella. 'Ella's teaching me the phone,' he confided. 'I called Tina.'

'You're not international roaming, are you?' Aaron asked. 'That will cost you a fortune.'

Ella shrugged, not having the heart to deny Kiri. 'They're only short calls.' She smiled at Kiri as she scrolled through her contact list.

'See, Kiri, there's Dad's number. If you hit this, it will call him. Yes, perfect.'

Aaron's phone rang, and he dutifully answered it and had a moment's conversation with Kiri.

And then Aaron tossed metaphorical hands in the air. He asked Ella for her phone number, punched it into his contact list, then handed his phone to Kiri, showed him the entry and let him call her.

She and Kiri chatted for a while, as though they were on opposite sides of the world instead of sitting together.

Then Kiri looked pleadingly at his father. 'Dad, can I have a phone?'

Aaron laughed. 'Who do you need to call, mate?' he asked.

'You. Mum. Tina. Jenny. And Ella.'

'Well, calling Ella might be tricky,' Aaron explained,

and lifted Kiri into his arms. 'Because we'll never know where in the world she is. And we don't want to wake her up at midnight!'

An excellent reminder, Ella thought, of the transience of their current arrangement—because at some point in the near future she would indeed be somewhere else in the world, far away from Aaron and Kiri.

When Aaron took his leave a short while later, she felt ill at ease.

It had been a strange interlude. Why had he even come? Maybe he didn't trust her with Kiri after all, and was checking up on her.

But it hadn't felt like that. In fact, he'd seemed delighted at her obviously close relationship with Kiri. And not at all freaked out at having a painting of her presented to him as a gift, which must have been awkward.

Knowing how much Aaron adored Kiri, and how keen he'd been to keep the two parts of this London life separate, well, it didn't make sense.

And Ella didn't like it.

Ella spent the next three days in a kind of hellish heaven.

Taking care of Kiri during the day and spending her nights with Aaron.

She adored her time with Kiri. She took him to Madame Tussaud's and to see the changing of the guard at Buckingham Palace, toy shopping for the baby, and for him. In the process, falling a little more in love with him every day.

She longed for her nights with Aaron. The pleasure that made her want to sigh and scream, the roughness and gentleness, the speed and languor, and everything in between.

But the arrangement was playing havoc with her emotions. Kiri's innocent stories about his father were making her feel altogether too soppy about a casual sex partner. And there were moments during the steamy nights when she and Aaron seemed to forget their agreed roles, becoming almost like real parents having the whole family chat.

Minus the kissing.

An omission that should have reassured her that this was just sex...but didn't.

And then, after five consecutive nights of lovemaking, Ella opened the morning paper and the sordidness of her current situation was thrown into sudden, sharp relief.

Only one half-column of words, not even a photo. But, still, the wreck of her life came crashing back.

It was an article about Javier, full of platitudes from various authorities with no actual news of his fate. But it felt like an omen, and it savaged Ella's conscience. Because she realised that since being with Aaron, not only had she been free of nightmares but she hadn't had any thoughts about Javier either.

So when Aaron came to her room that night, carrying a bag, she pleaded a migraine, knowing she looked ill enough for him to believe her.

'Can I get you anything?' he asked, concern creasing his forehead as he dumped the bag carelessly on her bed.

She forced a strained smile. 'Hey, I'm a nurse, remember?'

He nodded, and then completely disarmed her by drawing her against him and just holding her. 'Sleep well, angel,' he said, and left her.

Angel?

That was going to have to be nipped in the bud.

She approached the bag with some trepidation. Pulled out a raspberry-coloured dress that even she could see was something special, and a bra and panties set in a matching shade that was really too beautiful to wear. The replacements for the things Aaron had ripped off her, obviously—although, strictly speaking, he didn't owe her a bra.

She stared at them, spread on the bed, and tried to shrug off the sense of doom that gripped her.

* * *

Aaron was dragged out of a deep slumber by a kind of screeching wail, abruptly cut off.

He sat up, perfectly still, perfectly silent, and listened. Nothing.

He shook his head to clear it.

Nothing. Imagination.

So—back to sleep. He gave his pillow a thump and lay back down.

Sat back up. Nope—something was wrong. He could feel it.

He got out of bed, padded out of the room, shirtless and in his shorts.

He opened the door to Kiri's room opposite and peered in. He was sleeping soundly.

So…Ella? He opened the door to her room quietly.

She was lying perfectly still, her eyes wide and staring, her hands jammed against her mouth.

He didn't think. Just slid into bed beside her, took her in his arms and arranged her limbs for maximum sleeping comfort.

She said nothing, but she didn't kick him away, which had to be a good sign.

'Just to be clear,' he said, 'I'm not asking questions. So don't even think of telling me to leave.'

She looked at him for one heartbeat, two, three. Then she closed her eyes, and eventually he felt her ease into sleep.

It wasn't going to be easy to not ask at some point. He'd better wear his thermal underwear to ward off the frostbite during that moment. Hmm. Oddly enough, it didn't daunt him. He snuggled her a little closer, kissed the top of her head. *One day, Ella, I'll know it all.*

Damn Aaron James.

It was his fault she was in a dingy hotel room that wasn't big enough to swing a rodent in, let alone a cat.

Not that she hadn't slept in an array of substandard places over the years, though none had ever cost her a staggering hundred and twenty pounds per night.

He'd had to come into her room last night when she'd been at her most vulnerable. And sneaked out this morning without waking her, without having the decency to talk about it so she could slap him down.

So here she was. Hiding out. Staying away until she could find the best way to end things with him. Because things were just not quite casual enough to make this arrangement work.

Aaron was moving house tomorrow. That should signal the end of their liaison. She shouldn't have let Aaron persuade her in the first place. Because look where it had landed her. She was confused about Aaron, guilt-stricken about Javier, miserable about everything—and in a shoebox-sized room that was costing her a bomb.

Ella sighed heavily, and sat dispiritedly on the bed. It was kind of slippery, as if the mattress protector was plastic. She popped into the bathroom to splash some water on her face and the *eau de* public toilet aroma jammed into her nostrils.

Well, that settled one thing: she might have to sleep here, but she wasn't going to breathe in that smell until she had to. She was going out for the evening.

In fact, for this one night she was going to rediscover the excesses she'd left behind in Cambodia. And when she was sozzled enough, she would return to face the room.

She would *not* run headlong to Tina's and one last night with Aaron.

Which was how Ella found herself playing pool with Harry, Neal and Jerome; three gorgeous, safely gay guys.

She was hot. Sweaty. Dishevelled. A little bit drunk.

Just how you wanted to look for a surprise visit from your lover.

Because that was definitely Aaron James, entering the

pub just as she hit the white ball so awkwardly it jumped off the table.

Aaron James, who was standing there, glaring at her. Fate. It really wasn't working for her.

CHAPTER TWELVE

HE'D BEEN WORKING his way through the pubs in the vicinity of Tina and Brand's because he'd known Ella wasn't staying with friends, as she'd told Tina, and he suspected she wouldn't stray too far, given Tina's advanced pregnancy. So it wasn't exactly fate that he'd found her, because this was the seventh pub he'd tried. But it sure felt like it.

He should go, leave her to it. She didn't *have* to see him every night. Didn't have to get his permission to stay out all night. Didn't have to explain why she was laughing over a pool table with three handsome men.

Except that she kind of *did* have to.

And it would have been stupid to search through the pubs of Mayfair for her and then turn tail the moment he found her.

She was wearing a skin-tight black skirt that would give a corpse a wet dream. A clingy silver singlet top just covering those perfect breasts. Black high heels—that was a first, and a very sexy one. Her hair was piled on her head, who knew how it was staying up there? In fact, not all of it was. Her messy hair made him think of having her in bed.

Aaron watched as she bounced the white ball off the table. As all four of them chortled. He seethed as the blond guy kissed her. Felt murderous as the other two hugged her, one each side.

She knew he was here. He'd seen the flare in her eyes,

the infinitesimal toss of her head as she'd directed her eyes away.

Oh no you don't, Ella. Oh, no. You. Don't.

Ella decided the best thing to do was carry on with her evening as though she hadn't seen Aaron standing on the other side of the pub with his hands fisted at his sides like he was trying not to punch something. She was not going to be made to feel guilty about this.

The guys started hunting in their pockets for beer money. Ella dug into her handbag. 'Don't think so,' she said mournfully, as she scrabbled around inside. And then her eyes widened. 'Hang on,' she said, and triumphantly drew a ten-pound note from the depths, along with one old mint and a paper clip.

'Hooray!' Jerome exclaimed with great enthusiasm. 'Off you go, my girl—to the bar.'

'Or maybe not.'

The voice came from behind Ella but she knew to whom it belonged. That accent.

She'd known he would come to her. Had expected it. Was she happy about it? Yes, unbelievably, given she'd intended to avoid him tonight, she was happy. *A bad sign.*

She looked over her shoulder at him. 'Hello, Aaron.'

'You and pool tables, what's up with that?' Aaron asked mildly. He tucked a strand of loose hair behind one of Ella's ears. 'Run out of money, sweetheart?'

'Yes,' she said, looking at him carefully as she turned fully towards him. He wasn't giving off *sweetheart* vibes. Aaron dug into his jeans pocket, pulled out a fifty-pound note and handed it to her.

'Are you going to introduce me to your friends?' he asked, as she stared at the cash as though she couldn't believe she was holding it.

'Huh?' she said eloquently.

'Your friends?' he prompted.

Ella looked around as though she'd forgotten their existence. Pulled herself together as she noted her three new drinking buddies gazing at her with avid interest.

'Oh. Yes,' she said, and hastily performed the introductions.

'And do you really want another drink, or shall we hand that money over to the guys and head off?'

Ella was torn.

'Ella? Are we staying or going?' Aaron asked, steel in his voice.

She *should* tell him to go to hell. But she found she didn't want to fight with Aaron. Not here. Didn't want to fight with him, period.

'I guess we're going,' she said. 'So here you go, boys, thanks for buying my drinks all night and I hope this covers it.' She smiled at them. 'I had a brilliant time. And remember what I said about LA. If you're ever there...'

Assorted hugs and kisses later, Ella did her slow walk out of the pub.

'You're not fooling me with the slow walk, Ella,' Aaron said as they reached the footpath.

She stopped. Turned to him. 'I don't know what you m—'

He pulled her into his arms sharply, shocking that sentence right out of her head.

He moved to kiss her but Ella put her hands up, pushing against his chest. 'You don't kiss me any more.'

'Is that so?' Aaron asked. Purely rhetorical—she had no time to answer as he planted his mouth on hers like a heat-seeking missile hitting its target. His hands went to her bottom and he pulled her against him, pelvis to pelvis.

Ella gasped as he released her, and her fingers came up to touch her mouth. 'Why are you so angry with me?'

Aaron looked down at her, unapologetic. 'Because you left me.'

Ella couldn't help herself—she touched his cheek.

She went to pull her hand away but Aaron caught it, held it against his face. 'And because I'm jealous,' he said.

'Jealous?'

Aaron nodded towards the pub.

Ella was stunned. 'But they're gay.'

He didn't miss a beat. 'I don't care if they're eunuchs. Because it's not sex I'm talking about. We're monogamous, you and I, and I trust you with that.'

That certainty shook her. She swallowed hard. 'Then what?'

'It's the whole deal. Being with you. In the moment. In public. *That* smile. That's what I'm talking about.'

That smile? Huh? 'We're in the moment in public now,' she said. 'Which I hope you don't regret.' She tilted her head towards a small group of women as she tugged her hand free. They were staring at Aaron as they walked past. 'I think they know you. I keep forgetting you're a celebrity.'

'I don't care.'

'You're *supposed* to care. Just sex, on the quiet—no scandal. Look, let's be honest. It's not working out, this casual sex thing.'

'No, it's not.'

She couldn't think straight for a moment. Because he'd agreed with her. Which meant it was over. Just what she'd wanted.

'Right,' she said. And then, because she still couldn't think straight, 'Right.'

'We're going to have to renegotiate.'

'There doesn't seem to be much point to that, or much to negotiate *with*,' Ella said, as her brain finally engaged. 'Given you're moving out tomorrow, let's just call it quits.'

Aaron pursed his lips. 'Um—no.'

'No?'

'No.'

'Remember our agreement? No questions, no—'

'I don't give a toss about our agreement. We are not

going to go our separate ways because you decided to click your fingers on a public street.'

'See? I told you it's not working. The casual sex deal meant no messy endings. And you're making it messy.'

'But it's not casual, is it, Ella? And I don't want to let you go.'

Her heart did that stuttering thing. She forced herself to ignore it. 'You knew there couldn't be anything except sex. And it will be too hard to keep even that going once we're living in different places.' Swallow. 'And I—I have an extra complication.'

'Which is?' he asked flatly.

'I have—I have...someone.'

'Look at me, Ella.'

She faced him squarely, threw back her head, eyes glittering with defiance.

'No, you don't,' Aaron said.

'Oh, for goodness' sake, I do! I do, I do!'

'If you had someone, you couldn't be with me the way you have been.'

She gasped. He couldn't have hurt her more if he'd stabbed her.

Because he was right.

How could she love Javier if she could pour herself into sex with Aaron in the no-holds-barred way that had become their signature? It had never happened before—only drunken fumbling that she'd run away from every single time. The antithesis of what she did with Aaron.

Aaron was looking at her with almost savage intensity. 'We need to settle this, and not here. Come with me.'

'Where are we going?'

'I don't know—a hotel.'

She laughed, but there was no softness in it. 'I have a hotel room. It stinks like a public toilet and has a plastic mattress protector. That sounds about right. Let's go there. And don't flinch like that.'

'I think we can do better than that, Ella.'

Ella wanted to scream. But she also wanted to cry. And instead of doing either, she was goading him, making everything ugly and tawdry, turning it into the one-night stand it should have always been. 'All right, then. Let's "settle" this,' she said. 'One last time. I'm up for it. You can use my body any way you want, and I will show you there is nothing romantic about an orgasm—it's just technique.'

'Is that so?'

'Let's find out. But if I'm going to play the mistress, I warn you now that I'm going to want access to the mini-bar.'

'Any way I can get you, Ella,' he said, unperturbed. 'You can devour everything in the mini-bar, order everything off the room-service menu, steal the fluffy robe, take the towels—anything you want.'

'I've always wanted to steal the fluffy robe,' Ella said, and took his arm.

CHAPTER THIRTEEN

AARON HAILED A cab and asked to be taken to the closest five-star hotel. On the way, he called to check on Kiri and let Jenny, who'd arrived in the early evening, know he wouldn't be home that night.

Ella waited through the call, clearly still furious with him. Well, too damned bad.

Aaron hastily secured them a room for the night and as they headed for the hotel elevator, he drew Ella close to him, holding her rigid hand. He breathed in the slightly stale pub scent of her. But he couldn't have cared less whether she came to him straight from the shower or after running a marathon through the city sewers.

The elevator doors opened and then they were inside. Alone. The second the doors closed, he was kissing her, sliding his hands under her top. One hand moved up to cover her breast, moulding it to his palm, teasing the nipple to maddening hardness with unsteady fingers. He'd thought she might push him away but, no, she kissed him back, straining against him. He broke the kiss, his breath coming fast and hard now, and bent his mouth to her shoulder, biting her there.

The elevator stopped and they broke apart, staring at each other. Without a word, Aaron grabbed her hand and pulled her quickly out and along the corridor. His hands were shaking so much he almost couldn't work the door mechanism to their suite. And then they were inside and Aaron reached for her again. Wordless. Driven. Desperate.

But so was Ella.

She yanked his T-shirt up his chest and over his head. 'Ah,' she breathed, as her hands went to his hips and she pulled him toward her. She put her mouth on one of his nipples and held tight to his hips as he bucked against her.

'Ella,' he groaned, hands moving restlessly to try to hold onto her as her tongue flicked out. 'Let me touch you.'

'Not yet,' she said, and moved her mouth to his other nipple. As she did so, she started to undo the button fly of his jeans.

He groaned again but couldn't speak as her hands slid inside his underwear.

'Do you like me to touch you like this?' she asked.

'You know I— Ahh, Ella, you're killing me.'

Laughing throatily, Ella stepped back, started to undress.

'Hurry up,' she said, as he stood watching as she wriggled out of her skirt.

It was all the encouragement Aaron needed. In record time, he'd stripped.

Ella, naked except for her high heels, turned to drape her clothes over the back of a handily positioned chair. Aaron came up behind her and caught her against his chest. His arms circled her, hands reaching for her breasts.

She dropped her clothes and leaned back against him, thrusting her breasts into his hands. She moaned as he kissed the side of her neck, gasped as one questing hand dived between her thighs.

'Oh, you're good at this,' Ella said, as she felt her orgasm start to build.

'You can still talk,' Aaron said against her ear. 'So not good enough.'

With that, he bent her forward at the waist until she was clinging to the chair, and thrust inside her. His hands were on her hips as he continued to move inside her, pulling all the way out after each thrust before slamming into her again.

The feel of her bottom against him, the intoxicating sounds of her pleasure as she orgasmed, clenching around him until he thought he'd faint from desire, the exquisite friction of his movements in and out of her built together until the blood was roaring in his head and demanding he take her harder, harder, harder.

Ella. This was Ella.

His.

Ella slumped against Aaron. After that explosive orgasm, he'd turned her around to face him, kissed her for the longest time, and now he was holding her with every bit of gentleness his lovemaking had lacked.

What she'd meant to do was give him a clinical experience. Instead, she'd drenched herself in soul-deep, emotionally fraught lust. Her anger was gone. And the bitterness. She felt purged, almost. Which wasn't the way it was supposed to be.

Nothing had changed. Nothing that could open the way for her to have what she wanted with a clear conscience. Sex couldn't cure things. Even phenomenal sex. Life couldn't be that simple.

Javier was still out there, the uncertainty of his fate tying her to him. Aaron still had a problematic ex-wife and a little boy whose inevitable loss, when they went their separate ways, would devastate her.

'Did I hurt you?' he asked, kissing the top of her head.

'This really is a regular post-coital question of yours, isn't it?'

'No. It's just that I've only ever lost control with you.'

There was a lump in her throat. 'Well, stop asking,' she said, when she trusted herself to speak. 'You didn't hurt me.' *Not in that way.*

'I didn't even think about a condom,' Aaron said.

Ella shrugged restlessly, eased out of his arms. 'I know. I wasn't thinking straight either. And me a nurse.'

'I'm sorry.'

'Me too, but it's done. Not that it's really the point, but I'm on the Pill. So if that worries you, at least—'

'No. No—I'm not worried about that. At least, not for myself. I wish I *could* have a child with you, Ella. Not to replace Sann but for you.'

That lump was in her throat again. She turned away. 'Complicating as all hell, though, pregnancy, for casual sex partners,' she said, trying for light and airy and not quite making it. She remembered ordering him to never say Sann's name again. But it didn't hurt to hear the name now. Not from him.

Aaron—what an unlikely confidant. The only one who knew her pain.

She cleared her throat, 'But now, do you think we could actually move out of this hallway? And where are those fluffy robes?'

Aaron obligingly guided Ella into the lounge area of the suite. He fetched a robe for each of them, and watched as Ella belted hers on, then sat on the sofa to remove her shoes.

He came to sit beside her, slipped an arm around her shoulders and drew her back against him so that her head was against his shoulder.

'You know, don't you, that I'm not a nice person?' she said.

'No, I don't know that. I've watched you work. Seen how much you care. The way you are with Kiri. I know how protective you are of your family. I know you wanted to adopt an orphan from Cambodia, and I've seen what the grief of that did to you. These things don't add up to "not nice".'

'I've been jealous of my sister, of the baby. That's not nice.'

'It doesn't look to me like Tina's had her eyes scratched out,' Aaron said calmly.

'Well, I'm over it now,' she admitted. 'But it took some soul searching.'

'I'm thinking soul searching is a bit of a hobby of yours.'

'And I— Over the past year I've done things. Things I'm not proud of.'

'You've had a lot to deal with. Cut yourself some slack, Ella.'

'You stopped kissing me.'

'And you think that was some kind of judgement?' He broke off, laughed softly. 'That was a defence mechanism. That's all.'

'What?'

'Casual sex? Just sex—no kissing, because kissing is not casual.'

'Oh.'

They stayed sitting in silence, his arm around her, for a long moment.

Now what? Ella wondered.

But then Aaron broke the silence. 'So tell me, Ella, about the "someone". The someone I know you don't have. The someone I think you once *had*. Past tense. Right?'

'Had *and* have.'

'Hmm, I'm going to need a little more.'

'His name is Javier. He's a doctor. Spanish. He was kidnapped in Somalia.' *Whew.* 'There was an article in the paper this morning.' She looked up at him briefly. 'Hence my need to go a little off the rails tonight.'

Aaron nodded, saying nothing. And somehow it was easy to relax against him and continue. Aaron, her confidant. 'We were in love. Very newly in love, so new that nobody else knew about it, which was a blessing the way things turned out, because I couldn't have borne the questions, the sympathy.' Pause. 'I should have been with him that day. It was my twenty-fifth birthday, two years ago. I was supposed to be in the jeep with him.'

Long pause. She could almost hear her own pulse. 'You've got no idea how awful it was. The conditions. The soul-sapping struggle to provide healthcare to people who desperately needed it. Because even before you think about treating illnesses like malaria and TB and pneumonia and HIV, you know that the drought, the violence, the poverty, the poor harvests have made malnutrition a force that simply can't be reckoned with. The kids are starving. Sometimes walking hundreds of kilometres just to drop dead in front of you. And ten thousand people a day are dying.

'And your colleagues are being kidnapped or even murdered, and armed opposition groups make it almost impossible to reach people in need, even though everyone *knows* the suffering, and even hiring a vehicle to get to people is a tense negotiation with clans in constant conflict, and the very people who are providing the tiny bit of security you can get are okay with the deaths and the kidnappings.'

She stopped again. 'Sorry I'm so emotional.' She shook her head. 'No, I'm not sorry. It needs emotion. When you're resuscitating a one-year-old girl, and there is a tiny boy next to her so frail that only a stethoscope over his heart tells you he's alive, and two more critically ill children are waiting behind you, why *not* get emotional?'

His hand was in her hair, stroking, soothing. 'Go on, Ella. I'm here.'

'Anyway. Javier and I were heading to one of the refugee camps in Kenya. But I got malaria and I couldn't go. So I'm here and he's somewhere. Alive, dead, injured, safe? I don't know.' Ella drew in a shuddering breath. 'And I feel guilty, about having a normal life while he's lost. And guilty that I can be with you like this when I should be waiting for him. And just plain guilty. I'm a wreck.'

'Ah, Ella.' He eased her out from under his arm and turned her to face him. 'I'd tell you it's not your fault, that you have a right to go on with your life, that anyone who loved you would want that for you, that you wouldn't want Javier to be trapped in the past if your situations were reversed; but that's not going to set you free, is it?' He ran his fingers down her cheek. 'You have to be ready to let it go.'

'The thing is I don't know what he'd want me to do, or what he'd do in my place.'

'That says something, doesn't it? You were only twenty-five, and in a very new relationship. If you're really going to keep a candle burning in the window for the rest of your life, I'm going to have to find the guy and make sure he's worth it, and I don't really want to do that. Somalia is scary!'

Ella smiled. 'You really do have that heroic thing going on, don't you? I think you *would* go there if you thought it would help me.'

'Nah. It's not heroic, it's self-interest. Memories can bring on rose-tinted-glasses syndrome. Which, in this case, makes it really hard for a mere actor to measure up to a Spanish doctor kidnapped while saving lives in Africa. Even with the malaria documentary under my belt, I'm coming in a poor second.' He kissed her forehead. 'But it's just possible, in a real flesh-and-blood contest, I could edge past him. Unless he happens to be devastatingly attractive as well.'

'As a matter of fact...' Ella trailed off with a laugh.

'Well, that sucks. Maybe I *won't* go and find him after all.'

'Yeah, well, Somalia really *is* scary, so I wouldn't let you go. I wouldn't like to lose you too.' Ella resettled her head on his shoulder. 'Okay—now you know all the salient bits about my past. So, let's talk about you. You said I could ask you anything, and you'd answer.'

'Ask away.'

'I'll start with something easy. Tina told me you raised your sisters after your parents died.'

'Easy? Ha! It was like a brother-sister version of *The Taming of the Shrew*, but in triplicate.'

Ella smiled. 'And you love them very much.'

'Oh, yes. Lucinda, Gabriella and Nicola. My parents were killed in a boating accident when I was eighteen. The girls were fifteen, twelve and ten. I was old enough to look after them, so I did. End of story, really. Two of them are married with kids now, one is married to her job—she's an actuary but she looks like a fashion designer—and all of them are happy.'

'It can't have been easy.'

'We had some nail-biting moments over the years, no doubt about it. But I won't go into the scary boyfriend stories or the fights over schoolwork and curfews. We just belonged together. Simple.'

Pause. And then, 'Is it okay to ask about Rebecca? Like, how you met?'

'Sure. I met her through Brand. The way I meet all my women.'

Ella pinched his thigh.

'All right, not *all* of them,' he amended, laughing. 'Let me give you the abridged version. We met at one of Brand's parties. He was living in Los Angeles back then and I was over there, trying to make the big time— unsuccessfully. Rebecca was doing the same, equally unsuccessfully.'

'So you drowned your sorrows together?'

'Something like that. We were an item in pretty short order. Happily ever after. For a while at least.'

'What went wrong?'

'Nothing. That's what I thought, anyway.' He sighed. 'But looking back, it was all about work. When we returned to Australia I started getting steady jobs. We adopted Kiri and everything seemed fine. But I got more work. Better work. And more work. Making a fortune, no worries. But Rebecca's career stalled. She wasn't happy, and I was too busy to notice. Until it was too late. She started doing a few outrageous things to get publicity in the mistaken belief it would help things along. And before I knew it, it was party, party, party. Drugs. Booze. More drugs. I know Tina told you about the rehab. Well, Rebecca's been to rehab before. Twice.' He shrugged. 'I'm praying this time it will work. This place, it's called Trust, it really seems good.'

'Oh, Trust—I know it, and it is good. She's in safe hands there.'

'Thanks, Ella.'

Ella brought his hand to her lips and kissed it. 'So I guess you've been trying to make up for being too busy to notice when things started to go wrong.'

'That's about the sum of it.'

'Am I going to do the "not your fault" routine?'

Aaron touched her hair. 'No. I'm as bad as you are when it comes to guilt, I think.'

'And Kiri? Why adopt? And why do you have full custody?'

'The adoption? We'd always planned to adopt a child in need and that just happened to come before trying for our own. The custody thing? Well, no matter what's between Rebecca and me, she wants only the best for Kiri, and she recognised that that was living with me, because although she likes to pretend she's in control, she knows she's not.'

She touched his hand. 'You love her. Rebecca.'

'Yes, I do,' Aaron said. 'But it's no longer *that* love. I care about her, as a friend and as the mother of my son.'

'It sounds very mature.'

'Hmm, well, don't be thinking it's all sugar plums and fairy cakes, far from it. She likes to get what she wants.' He laughed. 'I suppose we all do, if it comes to that. But when she needs something, she tends to forget we're divorced and she's not above a bit of manipulation. That can make it hard for us to move on.'

'She wouldn't like it? The fact that I'm here with you.'

'Probably not,' he admitted. 'Unless she had someone first.'

'So you won't tell her.'

'That depends, Ella. On whether we're sticking to our initial arrangement.'

Silence.

Ella wasn't ready to face that.

She got to her feet, headed for the mini-bar and started looking through the contents. 'So,' she said, moving various bottles around without any real interest, 'getting back to the important stuff. Condoms. Or the lack of them. Pregnancy we've covered. But I can also reassure you that I was checked before I left Cambodia and am disease-free. It's something I do regularly, because of my work with AIDS patients.'

'Me too, disease-free, I mean. I've been an avid fan of the condom for a long, long time.'

She turned. 'But weren't you and Rebecca starting to try for…?'

'Trying for a baby? No. For the last year we weren't trying *anything*. You see, along with the drugs came other problems—new experiences Rebecca wanted, such as sex with a variety of men. Including two of my friends. *Ex*-friends,' he clarified. 'I could forgive her for that. I *did* forgive her, knowing what was going on with her. But I couldn't…well, I just couldn't after that.'

'I don't know what to say to that.'

'Not much *to* say. I did try to keep my marriage together, because commitments are important to me. But some things just…change.'

Ella thought about that. What a lovely thing to accept. *Some things just change.*

'Anyway, enough gloom.' He walked over to her, gave her a quick, hard kiss. 'Come and have a bath with me.'

Aaron grabbed the scented crystals beside the deep bath and threw them in as the tub filled. Then he lifted her in his arms and kissed her as he stepped into the water, settled. Kept kissing her until the bath was full. He took the soap from her and washed her, kissing, touching, until she was gasping for air. But he wouldn't take her. Not this time. 'Condoms, so you don't have to wonder,' he said, by way of explanation.

'I have some in my bag,' she said, shivering with desire.

'Monogamy, remember?' Aaron said. 'I don't think roaming around London with a bag full of condoms fits the principle.'

'Just handbag history—like the expired bus tickets in there. I wasn't going to use them.'

'It's okay, Ella. I know that. Somehow, I really do know that.' He got to his feet, streaming water, but before he could leave the tub Ella got to her knees. 'Not yet,' she said, and looked up at him as she took him in her mouth.

The next morning Aaron ordered a veritable banquet for breakfast.

He was whistling as he opened the door, as the food was laid out in the living room. The robe he'd purchased for Ella was in its neat drawstring bag, positioned on one of the chairs.

He'd left Ella in bed with the television remote control, and was halfway to the bedroom to fetch her for their lovers' feast, mid-whistle, when he heard it. A sound between a choke and a gasp.

'Ella, what is it?' he asked, hurrying into the room.

She was pale. Deathly so. Like the life had drained out of her. She looked up at him, and then, like she couldn't help herself, back at the television.

There was a man being interviewed. A gaunt man. Beautiful—not handsome, beautiful.

'It's him,' Ella said.

CHAPTER FOURTEEN

'HIM?' AARON ASKED. But he knew.

The news moved onto the next item and it was like a signal had been transmitted directly to Ella's brain.

She got out of bed. 'I have to go,' she said. But then she simply stood there, shivering.

'Go where?'

'Africa.'

'You can't go anywhere in that state, and certainly not Africa.'

'Don't tell me what to do,' she said, and started dressing. It took her less than a minute.

'Ella, you have to talk to me.'

'I did enough talking last night.'

'For God's sake Ella, I—'

'No,' she cried, and then raced to her bag. She looked up, wild-eyed. 'Money. I don't have money for a cab.'

'Calm down, Ella. I'll take you where you need to go.'

'I don't want you to take me anywhere. I want—I want—' She stopped, looked at him, then burst into tears.

Aaron tried to take her in his arms but she wrenched away from him, turned aside to hide her face and walked to the window. She cried as she looked out at the world. Cried as though her soul was shattering.

And just watching her, helpless, Aaron felt his life start to disintegrate.

Gradually, her sobs subsided. She stood leaning her forehead against the window.

Aaron came up behind her, touched her gently on the shoulder. She stiffened but didn't pull away.

'You're going to him,' he said.

'Of course.'

'You're still in love with him, then.'

Pause. And then, 'I have to be. And I have to go.' She turned to face him. 'I know I already owe you money but will you lend me enough for a cab?'

'You don't owe me anything, Ella.'

Aaron grabbed her by her upper arms and drew her forward. 'I'll wait for you to sort this out, Ella. I'll be here, waiting.'

'I don't deserve for anyone to wait for me,' she said, and her voice was colourless. 'Because *I* didn't wait. I *should* have been waiting for him. I *intended* to wait for him. But I didn't. Instead I—I was…' A breath shuddered in. Out. 'I can't stand it. I have to go. Now. I have to go.'

'All right.' Aaron grabbed his jeans and pulled out a handful of notes. 'Take this. And here…' He grabbed the hotel notepad and pen from beside the phone and scribbled a few lines. 'It's my address in London. We'll be there from today. And this…' he dashed another line on the paper '…is the phone number for the house. You've already got my mobile number. Whatever you need, Ella, whenever.'

'Thank you,' Ella said, and raced from the room without another word or glance.

Aaron looked at the sumptuous breakfast, at the robe he'd bought for Ella just because she'd joked about wanting to steal one. She hadn't seen it, wouldn't have taken it if she had.

Javier was back. And that was that.

And then, two days later, Rebecca disappeared from rehab in the company of a fellow addict, a film producer, and he knew he was going to have to fly to LA at some point to bail her out of some heinous situation.

Yep. That really was that.

Ella felt weird, being with Javier, even after a week together.

He was the same and yet not the same.

Every time she broached the subject of the past two years he closed the discussion down. He simply thought they would pick up exactly where they'd left off, as though those two years had never happened, but Ella couldn't get her head into the same space.

She couldn't bear to sleep with him, for one thing.

She told *him* it was to give them a chance to get to know each other again. She told *herself* it was because she'd been stupid enough to forget the condom with Aaron— that meant she had to wait and see, because things *did* go wrong with the Pill.

But, really, she just didn't want to.

She tried, desperately, to remember what it had been like, that one time with Javier, but the only images that formed were of Aaron.

So it would have been disloyal somehow. To Javier, who didn't deserve for her to be thinking about another man. And, bizarrely, to Aaron, who was now effectively out of her life.

Ella sighed and got out of bed in her tiny hotel room. Padded into the bathroom and looked in the cabinet mirror. What did Aaron see that made him fall on her like he was starving for the taste of her? She was beautiful, she'd been told that often enough to believe it, but had never thought it important. Until now. Because maybe Aaron wouldn't have wanted her so much if she'd looked different.

Was it shallow to be glad that something as insignificant as the shape of her mouth made Aaron kiss her as though it was the only thing in the world he needed?

Ella gave herself a mental shake. She had to stop thinking about Aaron. Javier was her future. Javier, who'd been
returned to her, like a miracle.

Today, they would fly to London so she could introduce
Javier to Tina, who'd had the Javier story thrown at her like
a dart as Ella had packed her bags. He would be there with
her for the baby's birth. Even her parents would be coming
in a month, to meet their grandchild…and the strange man
who'd been kept a secret from them. And wouldn't *that* be
interesting, after her mother's blistering phone soliloquy
on the subject of Ella keeping her in the dark?

Out of control, the whole thing. A runaway train, speed-
ing her into an alien future.

Ella closed her eyes.

Did I hurt you? Aaron's voice whispered through her
memory.

Yes, she answered silently. *Yes, you did.*

Heathrow was bedlam, but Ella almost dreaded exiting
the airport.

She was so nervous.

About introducing Javier to Tina and Brand.

And about the inevitable meeting between Javier and
Aaron.

Javier, she'd discovered, was the jealous type. Not the
cute, huggable kind of jealous Aaron had been that night
outside the pub in Mayfair. Sort of *scary* jealous. The prospect of him and Aaron in the same room was enough to
make her break into a cold sweat.

She welcomed the flash of cameras as they emerged
from Customs. Javier was whisked away for a quick photo
op, and she was glad. It meant she would have a moment
to herself.

Or not.

Because, groan-inducingly, Aaron was there, waiting for her. In his T-shirt and jeans. Looking desperately unhappy.

He strode forward. 'Tina sent me instead of a limo. Sorry. I tried to get out of it, but nobody's allowed to say no to her at the moment, she's been so worried about you.'

'Everyone must hate me.'

'Nobody hates you, Ella. Everyone just wants things to work out.'

Ella could feel one of those awful blushes racing up her neck. 'I'm sorry. For running out like that, I mean. I should have explained, I should have—'

'Ella, don't. I know you. I know what you went through. I know why you had to go. I should have just stood aside. Please don't cry.'

Ella blinked hard, managed to gain her composure. 'You always seem to know. I wish… Oh, he's coming.'

Javier, unsmiling, put his arm around Ella the moment he reached them.

Aaron held out his hand, just as unsmiling.

It was like an old cowboy movie, trigger fingers at the ready, Ella thought, a little hysterically.

'Javier,' Aaron said. His hand was still out, ignored.

Ella took Javier's elbow. 'Javier, this is a friend of Tina and Brand's. And mine. Aaron James. He's very kindly giving us a ride.' Ugh, was that a *wheedle* in her voice? Disgusting.

'I'm pleased to meet you,' Javier said solemnly, at last taking Aaron's proffered hand for a single jerking shake.

Aaron gave him a narrow-eyed look. There was a small uncomfortable pause and then, taking their baggage cart, Aaron said, 'Follow me.'

Javier held Ella back for a moment. 'I don't like the way he looks at you,' he said.

Ella gritted her teeth. This was the fifth time in a week Javier had taken exception to the way a man had looked at her. She would have loved to tell him to get over it, but this particular time he had a right to be suspicious.

Aaron looked over his shoulder, no doubt wondering what was keeping them.

Looking straight ahead, Ella took Javier's arm and followed Aaron.

It was always going to be an uncomfortable drive, but this was ridiculous.

Aaron was fuming, relegated to the role of chauffer.

Javier spoke only to Ella, and only in Spanish.

Charming!

Ella answered him in English, but the agonised looks he was catching in the rear-view mirror told Aaron she knew her Spaniard was behaving like a jackass.

Okay—so maybe jackass was his word, not Ella's, but he stood by it. *Nice choice, Ella.*

It was a relief to pull up at the house. After he helped hoist their luggage out of the boot, Aaron drew Ella a little aside. 'Ella, so you know, Tina's insisting I come to dinner tonight,' he said softly.

'That…that's fine,' Ella said, glancing nervously at Javier, who was giving her a very dark look as he picked up their bags. With a poor attempt at a smile Ella hurried back to Javier, took his arm and ushered him quickly into the house.

Aaron sighed, wondered why he'd even bothered warning her about him being at dinner. However prepared any of them were, when you parcelled it all up—Ella's uncharacteristically submissive demeanour, Javier's haughty unfriendliness, the prospect of witnessing the reunited lovebirds cooing at each other all evening, and his own desire to do some kind of violence to Javier that would ruin at least one perfect cheekbone—dinner was going to be a fiasco of epic proportions.

* * *

Aaron had been braced ever since he'd got to Tina's, but he still couldn't help the way his eyes darted to the door of the living room when it opened for the final two guests.

Ella looked like a deer caught in the headlights. She was wearing a dress. Dark grey. Silky. Simple. Classy. She was wearing her black high heels. He wanted to run his hands up her legs. He could drool at any moment.

Their eyes met for one sharp, tense moment and she blushed.

Javier said something and Aaron shifted his gaze.

Javier was everything Aaron wasn't. It was more pronounced tonight than it had been at the airport. Javier was elegant and sophisticated. Stylish in that way Europeans seemed to manage so effortlessly. Javier's hair was jet black, lying against his perfect skull in well-behaved waves. His eyes were equally black—dramatically moody. He was dressed in black pants and a pale pinkish-purple shirt that not many men could carry off.

And since when had Aaron ever noticed, let alone cared about, what other men were wearing?

He tore his eyes away, took a bracing sip of his Scotch.

Hellos were said. A drink pressed into Javier's hand, another into Ella's. Tina kissed Javier on the cheek. Javier touched Tina's ringlets as though entranced.

Tina laughed. 'A curse, this hair. Only Brand likes it.'

Javier smiled. 'Not only Brand. I like it too. Lively hair.'

Tina laughed again, shaking her head until her curls danced a little.

Great, Aaron thought. Javier was going to be adored by Ella's sister. Just great.

Brand, who was standing beside him, made a disgusted sound and rolled his eyes. He'd always known Brand was an excellent judge of character.

Tina was saying something about the need to fatten Ella up.

'It's her work,' Javier said, pulling Ella very close. 'She worked too hard in Cambodia.'

'Getting any information out of Ella about her work is like pulling teeth, but Aaron told us a little about the conditions there.'

Javier looked straight at Aaron. Hostile.

Not that he could work out the whole backstory of Aaron's obsession with Ella from one glancing look.

Could he?

'And what were *you* doing, Aaron? In Cambodia?' Javier's voice was perfectly polite, and chilling.

'I was filming a documentary on malaria.' *And fantasising about your girlfriend.*

Tina was starting to take on a little of Ella's deer-in-the-headlights look. Sensing the undercurrents, no doubt. 'So, Javier,' Tina said, 'are you able to share with us a little about…about…your experience?'

Javier smiled at her, but to Aaron it looked almost dismissive.

'I was not badly treated,' Javier said. 'Just not free. But not, perhaps, a subject for tonight. Tonight is a celebration, you see. Ella and I…' He stopped, smiled again, drew Ella nearer.

How much closer could he *get* her, anyway? Aaron wondered furiously as he watched Ella. But she wouldn't meet his eyes. Wouldn't meet anyone's eyes.

'Ella and I would like to share our news,' Javier said, and raised Ella's hand to kiss the palm. 'Ella has done me the honour of accepting my proposal of marriage.'

Aaron caught the sparkle on Ella's finger, and turning away, swallowed the rest of his Scotch in one swig.

Aaron hadn't come looking for Ella.

Didn't want to be alone with her. Not now. When he felt so raw.

And yet there she was, in the kitchen, straightening up after putting something in the fridge.

And there he was. In the kitchen. Forgetting why.

He must have made some sound because she straightened. Turned. The fridge door swung closed behind her.

For a moment Aaron couldn't breathe.

'How are you, Aaron?' she asked quietly.

'Fine.' The word sounded as though it had been bounced into an airless room.

'And Kiri?'

'Fine. He misses you.'

He saw her swallow. She said nothing. Well, what did he expect her to say?

Aaron took a step closer to her. 'There were no consequences? I mean as a...a result of—'

'I know what you mean. I told you I was on the Pill. But just in case, I'm waiting...' Stop. Another swallow. 'I mean, I'm not doing anything... I'm not...with...' She drew an audible breath. 'Until I know.'

'That's good,' Aaron said, miraculously understanding. 'I mean, is it good? Yes, I guess it's good. I guess it's...' Nope. He couldn't finish that.

Silence.

Ella was turning the engagement ring round and round on her finger. 'How's Rebecca? Rehab? How's it going?'

'It's not. She left early; with a drug-addicted film producer. Never anything mundane for Rebecca.'

'Oh, I'm so sorry.'

He rubbed a hand behind his neck. 'Just one thing. I told her about you, about us. In case...'

Ella was fidgeting—which he'd never seen her do. Playing with the damned ring. 'Does that mean...? Does everyone know about us?' she asked.

'No. Nobody else. And Rebecca isn't talking—except to her publicist, who's working out how to go public with the film producer.'

'It's just…Javier's the jealous type. I don't want him to… You know what I mean.'

'I'll fix it so nothing rebounds on you, I promise. And I guess there's nothing to say, anyway. You're engaged.'

Another awful silence.

Aaron took one step closer. 'Have you picked a date? For the wedding?'

'No. Not yet.'

'Why are you doing it, Ella?'

She held out her hands. Imploring. 'How could I say no? How could I refuse him anything after what he's been through?'

He had a few pithy answers for that—but found he couldn't voice them, not when she looked so tormented. 'I'm glad you're not sleeping with him,' he said instead.

He took one more step, close enough now to take her hands, hold them. 'And I know that's unworthy, Ella, but I've discovered I'm not good at giving in gracefully.'

'This is not doing us any good, Aaron.' Ella tried to pull her hands free, but Aaron held on. 'Let me go. If you don't, I don't know how I'll bear it.'

He pulled her hands against his chest, held them there. 'Ella, we need to talk.'

'We are talking.'

'Not here, not like this.'

'I can't. I need to get back in there.' She pulled her hands free. '*Please*, Aaron. It's very difficult just now. Please.'

'*Porque estas tardano tanto?*'

Both Aaron and Ella turned towards the doorway, where a frowning Javier was standing.

'I'm coming now,' she said in English, and walked out of the room, pausing just outside the kitchen door to wait for Javier to join her.

'*Andante, te seguire pronto,*' he said.

Ella looked at Aaron quickly, nervously, then as quickly away. 'All right,' she said.

Javier moved further into the kitchen. He looked Aaron over and seemed to find nothing there to worry about if his slight sneer was anything to go by.

'You know Ella well.' Statement, not question.

'Yes. I do.'

'You watch her.'

The comment surprised Aaron; he'd been conscious of *not* looking at her all night. 'Do I?'

'I can understand. She is beautiful.'

Aaron was silent.

Javier smiled, but it wasn't a friendly smile. 'She is beautiful, and she is mine.'

'If she's yours, what's your problem?'

'I just want it to be clear. So, I think you were bringing the cheese? I'm here to help.'

Cheese. Of course. He had offered to go to the kitchen and get the cheese.

When the two men returned to the dining room, Ella smiled blindingly at her fiancé—the mouth-only version, ha!—put her hand over Javier's when he paused by her chair and touched her shoulder, then moved her chair a smidgeon closer to his when he sat beside her.

Ella's hand kept disappearing under the table and Aaron guessed she was giving Javier's thigh an intermittent pat. Probably reassuring him that she was not remotely attracted to the brooding thug at the other end of the table who now, perversely, couldn't seem to keep his eyes off her.

Which word was stronger—disaster or catastrophe?

Because he was designating this dinner party a catastrophic disaster or a disastrous catastrophe—whichever was worse.

CHAPTER FIFTEEN

WHEN ELLA'S CELLPHONE trilled the next morning and Aaron's name flashed, she felt a wash of emotion that was a weird hybrid of joy and anxiety.

'Hello? Ella?'

Ella gasped. *Not* Aaron. 'Kiri! Is everything all right?'

'Where are you, Ella?'

'I'm at Tina's darling, why?'

'We're going to see Mum, and I want to say goodbye. But Dad says you're too busy.'

'Where's Dad?'

'Filming.' Giggle. 'He forgot his phone.'

Her heart swelled with longing. 'When do you leave, Kiri?'

'Soon.'

Which was kid-speak for any time. Tomorrow. Next week. An hour.

Ella bit her lip, thinking. Aaron was on set so the coast was clear. Javier was out, and he didn't have to know. The apartment was within walking distance. Could she do this? See Kiri once more? 'What about if I come over now?' Ella found herself asking.

'Yes!' Kiri said, excited. 'I painted you a picture. Of you and me.'

'Well, I have to see that!' she exclaimed. 'I'll be there soon.'

* * *

It didn't take long for Aaron to realise he'd left his phone at home. He felt guilty that he'd be late to the set, because Brand had to head to York in the afternoon to check out locations for an evening shoot, and the schedule was already tight, but he just had to turn back for it. After Kiri's dengue fever episode Aaron liked to be instantly contactable at all times.

Aaron raced into the apartment. 'Jenny?' He called out, and hurried into the living room. 'I forgot my phone, so—' He broke off, and his heart leapt so savagely he couldn't catch his breath.

Ella. Here.

She was sitting with Jenny and Kiri, one of Kiri's paintings in her hands, but she seemed to be holding her breath as her beautiful violet eyes rose to his and stuck there.

Jenny, looking from one to the other of them, murmured something about Kiri needing something. She took Kiri by the hand, led him from the room.

Ella shrugged awkwardly. 'Sorry,' she said, putting down the painting and getting to her feet. 'But he called and I… He said you were leaving?'

'We are—in a few days. Rebecca overdosed. I've got to make sure she's okay.'

'Oh, Aaron.'

'But there's a bright side. It scared her. She's heading back to Trust.'

'That's good. Great.'

'And I'm going to meet Scott too.'

'Scott?'

'The film producer. He's with her. Thank heavens he seems to be on track. She says it's serious between them, and I need to think about what that means for Kiri.'

He could smell her. His heart was aching. He couldn't seem to stop his hand moving up to rub his chest, not that it ever made a difference to the pain.

'We're going to move to LA once the film is done,' he said. 'To support her. I had an audition there a while back, and I've got a callback, so hopefully…'

'That's great.' Ella smiled—that infuriating smile that didn't reach her eyes. She picked up her bag, preparing to leave. 'I'll be moving, too. Spain.'

'Not LA?'

She shook her head vehemently. 'Not LA. So maybe this time fate will do the right thing and keep us out of each other's way, huh?'

She laughed, but Aaron had never felt less like laughing, and her own dwindled away until she was staring at him, equally silent.

Aaron watched her closely. 'So, we're going to stand here, are we, Ella, and smile and laugh and pretend we don't mean anything to each other? Because I don't think I can do it.'

Her eyes widened. 'Don't,' she said. 'You and Rebecca and Kiri have a long path ahead of you. You need to concentrate on that.'

'And you have to concentrate on martyring yourself, is that it?'

'Stop it, Aaron. Loyalty is not martyrdom. I *owe* Javier this.'

'Two years apart, and then suddenly you get engaged? What do we even know about him?'

'*We* don't need to know anything. Only I do.'

'I told you I'd be waiting for you. And then—'

'Waiting for what? Don't throw Rebecca's new man in my teeth as though that's supposed to make a difference. You've just told me you're following her to America. Where does that leave me? Where?'

He crossed the floor to her. 'I *hoped* in LA. Close to me. Where we could work it out.'

'Oh, spare me. I'd just be carrying two loads of guilt—leaving Javier when he needs me, and being your bit on the side. Well, I'm not doing it.' She paced. One step. Two. Three. Back. 'I knew this would happen. Keep it simple, you said. Casual. And then you proceeded to make it anything but. I tried to make you leave me alone. Sydney, Cambodia, London—every time. Why couldn't you? Why?'

'Because.' *Oh, great answer. Who wouldn't buy that?*

She looked, rightly, incredulous. 'That's an answer?' She turned away, tearing her hands through her hair as though her head was aching.

'All right, I'll tell you why. Because I'm in love with you.'

She spun back to face him. Her mouth formed a silent 'O'. She seemed incapable of speech.

'It's true,' Aaron said, and felt a sense of wonder himself. 'I couldn't leave you alone, because I loved you. I *love* you.'

'I don't want you to.'

'You don't get to dictate to me on this, Ella. If I could have dictated *myself* out of it, I would have. Because, I can assure you, it's not something I wanted either.'

She backed away a step. 'It's just proximity. Because I'm here. And I threw myself at you.'

He laughed harshly. 'Except that I've been lugging it around since Cambodia.' It was true. True! Since *Cambodia*. Why hadn't he realised it before? 'And I'm the one who was doing the throwing,' he continued. 'Always, always me. You were the one running. And I'll tell you this: it's a pain in the butt. *You're* a pain in the butt most of the time, with your bad-girl routine and your secrets. But...' he shook his head '...I love you.'

'Well, stop it. This is a mess. We're a mess. Just as predicted.' Her breath hitched. 'And I—' She broke off, rubbed her hands over her face again. 'This is so frustrating. Why do we do this to each other? Why can't we ever have a normal discussion?'

'I think it's because I love you, Ella.'

'Stop saying that.'

'And I think it's because you don't want to hear it, so you prefer to fight.'

She did that thing where she got herself together, visibly changing from distraught to pale and blank and cool. 'Remember what I said about Disneyland? That it's a blast as long as you remember it isn't real? Let's just say we've had too many turns on the teacups. Your head will stop spinning soon.'

'No, it won't, Ella. My head will still be spinning. My heart will still be aching. And I will still be in love with you.'

She looked at him coldly. 'Then just be happy I'm refusing to help you mess up your life.'

CHAPTER SIXTEEN

ELLA HAD AN uncomfortable night.

Aaron loved her. *Loved* her.

But it didn't change anything. Because with Brand stuck in York and Tina needing a distraction from her constant back pains, it was *Javier* who took her and her sister out for dinner. It was *Javier* stopping outside Ella's bedroom door when they got home, kissing her, urging her with that sharp, impatient edge to his voice, *'Let me in, Ella. It's time, Ella. Why not, Ella?'*

Why not, Ella? Because Aaron loved her. How was she supposed to sleep with anyone else, knowing that?

It was a relief when Javier left the house after breakfast the next morning, so she didn't have to feel the heavy weight of his dark eyes on her, silently accusing her, questioning her, beseeching her.

Tina was restless, and irritable, and uncomfortable. Demanding a cappuccino from a particular café, which Ella took herself off to buy and bring back so Tina didn't have to get out of her nightgown. Ella hoped Brand's train was on time. She had a nervous feeling Tina's persistent backache meant the baby was preparing to introduce itself to its parents, and Tina would make Brand's life hell if he missed even a second of her labour.

The thought made her laugh as she walked into the house, takeaway coffee in hand. It always amused her to think of Brand—for whom the term alpha male could have been coined—as putty in her sister's hands. Because that's what—

The coffee cup slipped through Ella's fingers. 'Tina!' she cried, and ran towards her sister's crumpled form at the foot of the stairs.

Tina groaned.

Ella closed her eyes, silently thanking every deity she could think of. And then she crouched beside her sister. 'How many times do you have to fall down the stairs before you learn that you do *not* hurry when you're about to give birth?' Ella demanded. 'Brand is going to maim everyone in sight if anything happens to you.'

'It was only the last couple of stairs. I was feeling so awful, and I'm having those horrible Braxton-Hicks things, and I thought I'd go back to bed. So shut up, Ella, and just help me up.'

'Let me check you out first,' Ella said, but Tina was already struggling to her feet—only to slump back down again with a sharp cry.

'I can't get up, Ella. I think I sprained my ankle. And I…' She stopped, and her eyes widened as she looked down at herself, at the floor beneath her. 'Ella!'

She sounded scared. And Ella, seeing the puddle pooling around her sister, understood. Tina's waters had broken.

'But Brand's not here,' Tina wailed, and then she gasped and grabbed Ella's hand. A long, keening moan slipped out between her clenched teeth. 'Oh, no, oh, no,' she whimpered, as her hand loosened after a long moment. 'Ella, I can't do this without Brand. I promised him I wouldn't. He's going to kill me.'

Ella gave a shaky laugh. 'Tina, my darling, the only way he's going to kill you is by kissing you to death. Now, there will be ages to go, but if you're okay to stay there for a moment, I'll go and call the hospital and tell them we're coming in. And I'll call Aaron—he's on standby to drive you to the hospital, right?'

'Okay. Good. No!' Tina grabbed Ella's hand again and held on so tightly Ella wondered if her phalanges were about to snapped in two. Instinctively, she timed the hold. Counting down, counting, counting.

Seventy seconds. The contractions were coming close together. *Uh-oh.*

Tina let go, took a shaky breath.

'Right,' Ella said again, super-calm despite a finger of unease trailing a line down her spine. 'I have to let you go, okay? Just for a moment, to call the hospital.'

Tina, white-faced, nodded. 'And Brand. You have to call Brand. Oh, what's the time? He told me this morning he was trying for an earlier train.'

'I'll try. Just wait, okay?'

Ella raced for the phone and let the private hospital where Ella and Brand had chosen to deliver their baby know they were on their way in. She tried to call Brand but got his voicemail. Assuming he was out of range, she opted not to leave a message; if he got a message about Tina going into labour the moment he switched on his phone, he'd likely hijack the train and make the driver go faster!

She came haring back to Tina, who was in the throes of another contraction—*way* too soon. She allowed both her hands to be grabbed, the knuckles crunched, for the duration, but said, 'Try not to hold your breath, Tina. Just breathe, nice and deep and slow.'

Tina gave her a look that promised her a slow death, but she gave it a gasping try. At the end of the contraction Tina looked up at her. 'Did you get Brand?'

'He must be out of range, Tina. But I'm sure he'll be here soon.'

Tina started to cry, and Ella hugged her. 'Shh,' she said, kissing the top of Tina's head. 'Everything's going to be fine. But we need to get you off these hard tiles and clean you up, and I still need to call Aaron— Oh, hang on, someone's at the door.'

Praying it would be someone useful, Ella raced to the door, tugged it open. Aaron—in the process of knocking again—almost fell inside, and slipped on the spilled coffee. 'Whoa,' he said.

'Thank goodness!' Ella said, and dragged him further into the hall.

'Before you say anything, Ella, I'm not stalking you. I promised Brand I'd look in on Tina, so—' He broke off. 'What's happening?'

'It's Tina, she's in full-on labour!' Ella whispered.

At the same time Tina threw out a wobbly, wailing, 'I know, it *suuuucks*,' from the floor at the base of the stairs.

Ella gave Aaron a warning look. 'It does not suck,' she said, all brisk and professional. 'Because the hospital is expecting us and Aaron is going to get the car and Brand is going to arrive, and everything is going to go according to plan.' She smiled brightly at Tina as she hurried back to her—just in time to take her sister's hands as a scream, followed by a string of graphic curses, tore from Tina's throat.

When the contraction finally stopped, Tina was incoherent, so Ella quickly pulled Aaron aside. 'We're not going to make it to the hospital,' she told him.

'What's wrong?' he asked, sharp and serious.

'Her contractions are too close together, they're too intense, and they're lasting too long. I'm thinking precipitous labour.'

'That sounds bad! *Is* that bad?'

'Well, it's fast, and it's going to be very painful.'

'But if we get her into the car straight away?'

Ella was shaking her head before he'd finished. 'No, the way things are heading, we'll be delivering the baby by the side of the road, and that's *not* happening with this baby. I'm calling an ambulance, but childbirth isn't the highest condition on the triage list. So I'm going to get ready here, just in case. And I'm going to need you to help me.'

Aaron looked completely appalled, but he nodded. 'Just tell me what to do.'

'She's twisted her ankle so—'

A scream from Tina interrupted her. Another contraction.

Ella hurried back to her sister, Aaron beside her. Ella gripped her sister's hand, uttering useless, placating nothings, until the contraction passed. Then she brushed Tina's sweat-damp hair off her face. 'Right, darling, we're not taking any chances with an Aussie driving in London. I'm calling an ambulance instead, and then we're going to make you comfortable while we wait for it to get here, okay?'

Tina nodded, white with stress and pain and terror.

'Aaron's going to stay with you while I'm gone—just for a minute, okay?'

'Okay,' Tina said, sounding pitiful.

Ella drew Aaron aside again. 'Just keep her calm. Encourage her to breathe, deep and slow, deep and slow, but get ready for some screaming.'

'I can take it,' he said.

Tina, eyes glazed, wasted no time in grabbing Aaron's hand as he dropped beside her, squeezing tightly through another fierce contraction. Ella waited, roughly timing through a scream, scream, scream, to the whimper and slump. Ninety seconds.

'Hello, Hercules!' Aaron said admiringly. 'I need to get me some of whatever it is you're eating, bruiser.'

As Ella raced for the phone, she heard Tina give a strangled laugh. She gave another silent prayer of thanks, for Aaron's arrival. Aaron would look after her sister in every way possible—her health, her spirits, her dignity. What more could you ask for at a time like this?

Three calls later, the ambulance, Tina's private obstetrician and another fruitless try for Brand, and she raced up the stairs as another agonising contraction ripped through her sister, with Aaron encouraging her to scream her lungs out if that's what she felt like doing. Not exactly keeping her calm, but Ella had the felling Aaron had the right of it. If Tina wanted to scream her way through, let her!

Ella grabbed an armload of sheets, towels and blankets. She added a fresh nightgown. She then picked up several pairs of sterile surgical gloves from her ever-ready supply, a bandage for Tina's ankle, scissors, rubbing alcohol and an assortment of cotton wool and gauze pads. She winced as she heard Tina's wailing cry as another contraction hit her.

She juggled the goods into a semi-manageable pile in her arms and descended the stairs again. Halfway down, when Tina was silent again, she heard Aaron say, 'You know, Tina, women have been giving birth for thousands of years—and *you're* the one who gets to have Ella personally presiding over the action. How cool is that?'

'Very cool,' Tina gasped out, and met Ella's eyes as she arrived at the bottom of the stairs. 'Very, very cool.' She mouthed, 'I love you,' at Ella, and Ella almost cried.

'Love you too,' she mouthed back. And then she took a deep breath and hurried into the library. She shifted the couch so she had room to stand at the end of it, then quickly put down a thick layer of towels, covered them with a sheet, spread more towels where Tina's hips and thighs would go. She propped cushions, stacking more towels close by, and prepared blankets for when they'd be needed. Over the sounds of her sister screaming, she quickly used the rubbing alcohol to clean the surface of Kiri's activity table, then laid out on it everything else she'd brought from upstairs.

By the time she was back at the stairs, Tina was lying on her side, half on Aaron, abusing him for not massaging her in the right spot.

Aaron, accepting the abuse with equanimity, merely looked up at Ella and asked, 'Ready?'

'Ready,' Ella said.

'Tina,' he said, 'I'm going to lift you now, okay?'

Tina, distressed and almost incoherent, shook her head. 'I'm too messy. Look! I can walk. Or hop. Arm. Just your arm.'

'Tina, when did you start being such a girl?' he asked. 'Get over it and put your arms around my neck.' And then he effortlessly gathered Tina close and lifted her. He carried her into the library, oblivious to the amniotic fluid soaking his T-shirt and jeans.

'Can you balance her while I get her changed?' Ella asked.

'Sure, if you promise not to tell Brand I saw her naked,' Aaron said, and that gave Tina a much-needed laugh—quickly choked off as another contraction hit her.

Somehow, Ella and Aaron managed to get her stripped, freshly nightgowned and settled on the couch.

Ella stroked Tina's sodden hair off her face again. 'Shall I tie your hair back?' she asked,

'Yes, it's really annoying me.'

Ella whipped the elastic from her own hair and bundled Tina's heavy mass of ringlets into a ponytail high on her head. 'And now,' she said, 'I'm going to go and wash my hands, while Aaron waits with you.'

Five minutes later she was back. 'Tina, I need to check how dilated you are, okay?'

Tina cast a look in Aaron's direction.

Ella smiled, understanding. 'While I do that, Aaron is going to go and get me an ice pack for your ankle.' She looked quickly at Aaron. 'And I need some string or twine—I think I saw some in the kitchen drawer. And I need bowls and a plastic bag. Oh, and warm water, but you can get that next trip.'

'On it,' he said, and bolted from the room as Tina went mindless with another contraction, her painful, guttural cries making Ella wish she could take the pain for her.

'Ella. Ambulance. Not…going…to get…here,' Tina gasped as the contraction eased.

'I don't think so, darling,' Ella said 'My niece or nephew seems particularly impatient. Like you, always in a damned hurry.'

'Okay, so let's get onto the important question,' Tina panted out. 'Do you…th-think Brand…is going to be upset…when he finds out I'm in love…with Aaron?'

Ella forced a laugh as she snapped on her sterile gloves, marvelling that her sister could crack a joke at such a time—her precious, amazing sister! 'I think Brand is going to be in love with Aaron himself once all this is over,' Ella said, and searched her head for a distraction. 'So, names. I'm thinking Boadicea, Thorberta and Nathene for a girl. Burford, Lindberg and Ogelsby for a boy. Nice, huh?'

But Tina's strained chuckle was cut off by another moaning scream. 'Ella, Ella, I need to push.'

'Just hang on, hang on, darling. Try to breathe through it.'

'Breathe? Don't be so stupid, Ella. I need to push!'

Tina was sprawled, spread-eagled, with one leg off the couch. Ella positioned herself between her sister's thighs as Tina pushed, pushed hard. She lifted the sheet she'd draped over her sister's legs and, as soon as the contraction eased, inserted her fingers to find—

Oh, no. 'Tina, darling, I can feel the baby's head,' she said.

'What? What?' Tina panted.

'The baby's well and truly on the way. I think we can assume all those back pains you had yesterday weren't back pains, they were labour pains, so…'

But Tina was having another contraction, so Ella shut up, caught her sister as she surged up off the couch, held her and let her yell.

'You were saying?' Tina asked weakly, as she sagged back limply. But almost immediately another contraction hit her, and Ella held onto her again and simply breathed, hoping to calm her.

'I'm going to kill Brand. Kill him!' Tina screamed.

Aaron, coming back into the room loaded up with everything Ella had asked for, said, 'Let me do it for you.'

Tina's laugh turned into another screech, and then it was roller-coaster time.

The contractions had Tina in their vicious grip and wouldn't let her go. She was sweating gallons, and Aaron stayed by her side, hanging onto her hand when she needed it, wiping her brow, occasionally leaning over to wipe Ella's too.

Ella had gloved up again, and this time when Tina said she had to push she told Tina to go ahead, because nothing was going to slow this baby down.

All modesty had fled. Tina just wanted the baby out, even if Aaron had to reach in and yank it through the birth canal—which Aaron pronounced himself ready to do, only to be punched and to be told not to be such an idiot.

Ella was staring between her sister's legs. 'The head is crowning,' she said, very calmly. 'Not long now.'

The house phone was ringing. Then Ella's. Then Aaron's. All were ignored.

More contractions. 'Now push, Tina, push now.'

Phones ringing again. One after the other. Once again ignored.

Another contraction. Pushing, pushing, panting, pushing. Tina was shaking. 'Here comes the baby's head,' Ella said. 'Try to stop pushing now, Tina. Stop, the head is here. It's here, Tina.' Ella checked quickly to ensure there was no cord wrapped around the baby's neck. Breathed a sigh of relief. 'Beautiful. Oh, Tina, so beautiful.'

Aaron was holding a weeping Tina's hand, whispering encouragement, kissing her forehead, tears in his eyes, while Ella was supporting the baby's head.

Phones. Ignored.

'One more push and it will all be over,' Ella said, as the baby's head rotated to one side as though it knew what it was doing. And then one shoulder emerged, and the other, and the baby shot into Ella's hands like a bullet. Ella was crying, Tina was crying, Aaron was crying.

'It's a girl,' Ella announced, and, supporting the tiny baby's head and neck carefully, she tilted her to enable any fluids to drain from her nose and mouth.

The baby, eyes wide open like she was completely outraged, gave a strong, angry cry, and Ella quickly checked that she was pink right down to her extremities, her limbs were strong and flexed and that basically she was alert and perfect and gorgeous. Tina held out her arms, and Ella laid the baby on her mother's chest.

Ella checked the wall clock as she took off her gloves. Forty-five minutes from the time she'd spilled that coffee in the hall to the birth of her niece. Incredible! 'Aaron, just pull Tina's nightgown down a little, off her shoulders. Tina, that will let you be skin to skin with the baby. It will help release oxytocin in your body, which will make the placenta slip out faster.'

Judging by the delirious look on Tina's face, Aaron could have done anything just then and she wouldn't have known it. As Aaron adjusted Tina's nightdress, Ella drew a blanket up over the baby's back, making sure Tina, who was shivering, was covered too.

'What can I do next?' Aaron asked, looking at the blood soaking the towels underneath Tina.

'The blood's nothing to worry about, Aaron.'

He passed a shaking hand over his eyes. 'Thank goodness.'

'There is just the placenta to go, if you can pass me that bowl,' she said.

'And then do we get to cut the cord?' Aaron asked.

We. Such a little word, but it made Ella want to kiss him. 'When it's stopped pulsing, if the ambulance isn't here.'

She ran a tired hand across her forehead. 'But first—the phones, Aaron. I'll bet it was Brand. Can you—?'

But Aaron didn't have to do anything, because Brand erupted into the room, wild-eyed, followed by two paramedics. 'What the hell—?' he started, and then came to a dead stop. His mouth dropped open as he stared at Tina. Then he rushed forward, fell to his knees on the floor beside the couch. 'Tina?' He sounded awed and shaken. 'How did this happen?'

Teary, exhausted, but smiling, Tina reached out a hand, and touched his cheek. Ella and Aaron shared a look as Brand grabbed Tina's hand, pressed a kiss to the palm—just a simple kiss and yet it was so intimate.

One of the paramedics came over to confer with Ella, who quickly provided details of the morning's drama.

And then Ella realised she and Aaron were *de trop*.

The baby was being checked; the placenta would be delivered and bagged; Tina would be taken care of. Brand was cooing at his wife and daughter.

With a smile at Aaron Ella inclined her head towards the door, and the two of them left the library. The stood in the hall, looking at each other. And then Aaron said, 'I never did get the warm water.'

Ella started to laugh.

'And where the hell did I put the ice pack?' he asked.

And then they were both laughing. They laughed, laughed, laughed, as Aaron—covered in dried amniotic fluid—pulled Ella—covered in blood—into his arms. He buried his face in her loose hair. They clung together for a long moment, before drawing apart slowly.

Euphoric, shaken, exhausted, they stared at each other. Ella's heart was aching, her breath jammed in her throat with a lurching, desperate need to touch him. To huddle against him and weep and sigh and just *have*.

Brand broke the spell, exploding out of the library with

the same energy with which he'd entered it. 'I cut the cord,' he announced proudly.

Next moment, he was grabbing Ella, hugging her. Ella could feel him shaking. 'I love you,' he whispered in her ear.

'I love you too, Brand,' Ella whispered back, and kissed his cheek. 'And your beautiful wife, and your adorable baby girl.'

'Audrey Ella McIntyre—that's her name,' he said. And then he freed one arm and reached for Aaron, dragged him in. 'Mate,' he said. Just one word, but it said everything, because in it was joy and love and excitement and gratitude.

'Do we get to smoke a cigar now?' Aaron joked, and was dragged closer still.

'You're an uncle now—no smoking,' Brand said, in a suspiciously husky voice.

Then Tina and the baby were being wheeled out of the library, and Brand, laughing maniacally, was off like an arrow as he followed his wife and daughter out of the house.

Aaron cocked an eyebrow at Ella. 'So, can I clean up that spilled coffee over there and make you a new one?' he asked.

He was very conscious of the butterflies swooping in his gut, now he was alone with her.

Butterflies? Did a grown man even *get* butterflies?

He *never* got butterflies.

Ella looked at him, biting her bottom lip. Was she going to say no?

'It wasn't my coffee. It was Tina's.'

'So I *can't* make you one?'

'Yes, yes, of course you can,' she said, but she looked nervous. 'I'll clean the spill later, though.' She took a deep breath. 'Right now, I really, really do need coffee. Just as soon as I wash myself up.'

Aaron did what he could to clean himself up, then made

his way to the kitchen. He wondered what kind of conversation they could have after delivering a baby together. And after yesterday's conversation, when he'd told her he loved her.

So, Ella, how's it going? Decided you love me yet?

His smile twisted. Maybe not.

Aaron realised he was standing there in a trance, looking at her while he rubbed his hand over his heart. He hated it that he did that when he looked at her, whenever he even *thought* of her. His T-shirts were all going to start showing wear and tear in that one spot.

He busied himself with boiling water, setting out cups, spooning instant coffee. Ella came in and took a seat at the kitchen counter.

Aaron handed her a mug. 'So, Ella, do you need…do you need…anything? From me? Now? Do you need…' *Me? Me, me, me? Do you need me, Ella?* 'Um…anything?'

'No. It's just…'

Just her voice. Her husky Yankee voice was enough to make him melt. 'Just?'

'I can't believe I was jealous—of my own sister, of this baby. Because now…' She stopped, shook her head. 'It's just so perfect. Isn't it? Perfect!'

'Yes it's perfect, so take off the hair shirt for a while, Ella, hmm?' He reached over, touched her hair, just once. 'Funny, isn't it? Brand had every specialist in Europe on speed dial, and all it took was you.'

'I was so scared,' she said, and he heard the steadying breath she dragged in. 'I don't know what I would have done if you weren't here.'

'Nobody would have known you were scared. You're just amazing, Ella. But, hey, if you want to fall apart now it's all over, here I am,' he said. 'You can cry all over me.'

Ella looked at him and smiled—that glorious smile, with her mouth and her eyes and her heart and her soul.

That smile.

It told him that, regardless of what they wanted or didn't want, they were connected.

It was fate.

'Oh, Aaron,' she said.

He thought she would say more, but then, outside the room, there was a quick burst of Spanish.

'I'd better go,' Ella said, and leaving her coffee, untouched, on the counter, she rushed from the kitchen.

Hmm. Fate had a lousy sense of timing, all things considered.

When Aaron and Kiri walked into Tina's hospital room that night, Ella was there, holding the sleeping baby.

Her eyes lit up when she saw him and his heart felt like it was doing a triple back somersault with a full twist. He caught himself doing that hand-rubbing thing over it again and had a bad feeling it wasn't a habit he was going to kick any time soon.

'Hello, Kiri,' she said. 'Aaron.' She looked kind of shy. It was entrancing. 'Recovered from today's high drama, then?'

'Yes,' he said. Not exactly a scintillating conversationalist tonight, but after the intimacy they'd shared at Audrey's birth—even though they'd been so focused on Tina they'd barely spoken to each other through the experience—he found himself tongue-tied. He was just so in love with her. He wondered how he hadn't seen his obsession with her for what it was sooner.

Love. If he'd admitted it to himself in Cambodia, they'd be married and she'd be pregnant by now; although, after today, how he'd actually *live* through Ella in labour he didn't know, and nobody would have the power to keep her from him—not even her.

'Ah, Kiri, my favourite boy,' Tina said. 'Did you come to see me or Audrey?'

'You *and* Audrey,' Kiri said, approaching the bed. His eyes were huge, staring at the baby.

'Smooth talker,' Tina said, laughing. 'Ella, let Kiri see her properly.'

Ella settled herself in the chair next to Tina's bed and beckoned Kiri closer.

When Kiri was beside her he asked, 'Can I touch her?'

'Yes,' Ella said. 'In fact…' She shot Tina a questioning look and waited for Tina to nod. 'You can hold her. But you'll have to sit very still in this chair. Can you do that?'

'Give Tina the picture first, mate,' Aaron told him, and Kiri handed it to his father without taking his eyes off the baby.

Aaron laughed as he presented it to Tina. 'I think we know where his priorities lie, Tina, and they're not with you or me—or even Ella, who used to be his favourite up until two minutes ago.'

Ella settled Audrey on Kiri's lap and positioned his arm so that it was firmly under her head. 'She doesn't have a strong neck yet, so you need to be careful that you hold her head like this. All right?'

Kiri nodded. Audrey didn't fret, just accepted this little boy who was holding her as though it was the biggest adventure of his life. Then Kiri leaned his face down to the baby and softly kissed her forehead.

Ella looked at Aaron. Aaron looked at Ella. Aaron reckoned an outsider could have mistaken them for the parents of both children.

Tina cleared her throat. 'Ella,' Tina said, 'why don't you take those flowers from Aaron?'

'Sure,' Ella said, and there was relief in her voice. 'I'll go and cajole another vase out of the nursing staff.'

Aaron perched on the edge of Tina's bed, watching Kiri with the baby.

'I'm so grateful, Aaron, for what you did today,' Tina said.

'I didn't do anything.'

'You kept me calm, you rubbed my aching back, you let me squeeze your fingers, you took more verbal abuse than any man should have to.' Slight pause. 'And you gave my sister strength, just by being there.'

Aaron shook his head. 'Ella didn't need me, Tina.'

Tina looked at him, like he was a puzzle. 'Men really are stupid, aren't they?' she asked. 'Look, Aaron, now that you've seen my lady bits being stretched to oblivion, I feel I know you well enough to be blunt with you. So I'm just going to come right out and ask you: what are you going to do about Ella?'

Aaron jerked so suddenly his leg slipped off the bed. 'I—I— She—'

'Yes, you're as articulate on the subject as she is. Look— you're divorced. Can you make like you really, really mean that, Aaron? And then get my sister away from that man.'

'I thought you liked him?'

'And that's what's stopping you, is it? The way you think I feel?'

'Ella doesn't feel that way about me.'

She fixed him with an incredulous stare. 'Don't be an imbecile. She won't *admit* to feeling that way about you while you've got a wounded animal to look after. Apologies to Rebecca, but you get the picture.'

'She won't leave Javier.'

Tina gave an exaggerated sigh. 'Stupid and so damned *aggravating*. All right, then, forget Ella. Stay in your rut, juggling all your balls and making sure none of them accidentally hits another while they're in the air, and let Javier have her. Because she will marry him, you know. She has a greater capacity for pity than Mother Teresa ever did. Oh, well, at least they'll have good-looking kids.' She turned to Kiri. 'Kiri, sweetheart, I think Daddy wants a turn. You come and tell me about this lovely painting.'

Aaron took that to mean she couldn't bear to speak to him.

He lifted Audrey out of Kiri's arms and stood there, staring down at the newborn and rocking her in his arms. And wondering...

Ella smiled at him as she came back into the room. 'Got a vase,' she announced, and positioned it, flowers already arranged, on the window ledge.

'I think Audrey's smiling at me,' Aaron said.

'If she is, Brand will beat you to a pulp,' Tina said, sounding like she was relishing the thought.

Ouch. 'All right, maybe she's not smiling,' he said. Her tiny mouth opened and closed a few times. 'Is that what you'd call gurgling, maybe?'

Ella laughed. 'No,' she said.

'Hmm. Man, she smells good,' he said after a moment.

'Yes. Babies always smell delicious.' She made a last adjustment to the flowers and then held out her arms for Audrey. 'Time for her to go back to bed,' she said. Aaron gently laid the baby in her arms so she could place her in her bassinette.

Oh, Lord, he thought as that mesmerising scent of Ella's hit his nostrils. She smelled more delicious than a thousand babies.

'Where's Javier tonight?' Tina asked, all innocence.

'He's out with some of his friends. There's a new medical mission in Ethiopia and...' She shrugged.

Tina raised her eyebrows. The picture of disapproval. 'So he's going back to Africa. Would that be before or after you're married, Ella?'

'I don't know, Tina. I guess he'll tell me when he tells me.'

A snort from the bed. 'Very wifely of you, waiting to be told. But not very Ella.'

'It's not like that.'

Another snort.

Aaron judged it time to step into the breach. 'I have

something to talk to Ella about.' he said to Tina. 'Can we leave Kiri with you for a few minutes?'

Tina gave him a beaming smile. 'Go. Please. Go.'

'I guess we'll go, then,' Ella said dryly.

Ella and Aaron paused outside the room. And then Ella burst out laughing. 'Is it hormones, or did I miss something?'

'You missed something. I don't know how to break this to you, but I don't think she's crazy about your fiancé.'

'Oh, I know that. Subtle, she isn't.'

'What happened?'

'Just a vibe, I think.' She looked hesitant. 'Do you think we can grab that coffee, without launching World War Three across the table?'

'I'm game if you are. I'll try to keep it at skirmish level rather than a heavy mortar attack.'

'Then I'll keep my grenade pins just half-pulled. Cafeteria, then? The coffee will be awful, but—'

'Cafeteria,' he agreed.

Ella wondered what the hell she was doing.

In a cafeteria, with Aaron, on purpose. Aaron, whose last attempt at drinking a cup of coffee with her had ended with her running to Javier. Aaron, whom she'd basically ordered not to love her.

'So what's the vibe?' Aaron asked, sliding a cup of coffee across the table to her.

Her mind went momentarily blank.

'Javier, Tina?' Aaron prompted. 'The vibe?'

'Oh. Well.' She stalled, taking a sip of coffee. 'She says he's too controlling.'

'Is she right?'

'He...' Another sip of coffee.

'What's wrong, Ella?'

'Huh?'

'If you can take two sips of that coffee and not make an

icky face, then you're not tasting it. Which means you're distracted. So, what's wrong?'

What was *wrong* was having this conversation with Aaron. But somehow, bizarrely, it was *right* too.

'Javier is...different,' she started, hesitantly. 'From what I remember, I mean.'

Aaron leaned back in his chair. 'And we're not talking good different.'

It wasn't a question, but Ella answered anyway. 'I think, no. But I don't really know yet. He won't talk about what happened. It makes it...hard.'

She watched as he absorbed that. His fists had clenched. And there was something in his eyes that urged caution.

'Go on,' he said.

She shook her head. 'This is a bad idea, talking to you about this. After...well, after—'

'After I declared my undying love and you threw it back in my face?'

'Yes, definitely a mistake.' She started to get to her feet.

He reached across the table, gripped her wrist. 'Sorry, Ella. If I promise to not let my skyrocketing testosterone get in the way, will you tell me?'

She relaxed into her seat. Nodded. Then she licked her lips, nervous. 'I told you he's the jealous type. Well, he *really* is.'

'You mean, of me?'

'Oh, yes. Even the thought of you helping me today with the baby? Well, let's just say it didn't go down well.'

'But that's insane.'

'And it's not just that. Not just you. He's jealous of everyone. Every man I talk to. Every man who looks at me.'

'Frankly, he's an insecure dirtbag.'

That surprised a laugh out of her. 'That's your testosterone not getting in the way, is it?'

'But he really *is* a dirtbag. Jealous of me? I get it. Because I want you. You know it. I know it. Tina and Brand know it. Tinkerbelle the neighbour's Chihuahua knows it. But, Ella, he does realise you're Hollywood-gorgeous, doesn't he? Every heterosexual man on the planet would take a second look at you. Come on! He's going to be living in hell if he can't cope with that—or he's going to make *you* live in hell because you won't be able to stop it. If he knew you, he'd trust you. So you're basically telling me he doesn't know you.'

Coffee. Sip. Ghastly. Okay, tasting the coffee was a good sign. 'You're so sure you know me that well?'

'I know that much about you. In fact, I'm wishing you were a little *less* faithful the way things are panning out. So, we're back to him being a dirtbag.'

'I haven't exactly been the poster girl for virtue, though, have I?'

'People do all kinds of things to get through tough times. They drink. They play pool with strange men.' Smile. 'They have sex with hunky Australian television stars.' Bigger smile. 'So what? Last time I looked, it wasn't the twelfth century. Nobody expects a twenty-seven-year-old woman to be a virgin, or to enter a convent to wait until her man rises from the dead.' He took her hand. 'Here's the sales pitch for me, just in case you ever end up interested: I wouldn't care if you'd had sex with a thousand men before me, Ella.'

She wanted to both smile and cry, but did neither. 'It wasn't like that, ever. In fact—'

He cut her off with a sharp, 'Hey, stop.'

'Stop?'

'Yes, stop. Don't tell me. And it's not because I'm squeamish either. Or *jealou*s. It's just none of my business. As long as it was *before*. Now, after? Well, that's another story.'

'But it wasn't before, was it?' she said. 'It was after. I had the option of waiting for him and I didn't. I was with you.'

'You are *not* serious, Ella! He was missing for two years; maybe dead. And in my book you *were* waiting. You certainly weren't living.' He squeezed her hand. 'You're not really going all hair shirt on me, are you?'

'I don't think you're the right person to be lecturing me on excessive conscience, Mr Married-Not-Married.' Her shoulders slumped. 'I wish he was more like…' She cleared her throat. 'Nothing.'

'It's "not married". *Not* married. Just to be clear, in case that's what's stopping you from leaving him and throwing yourself at me.' Pause. 'And it's not nothing, I think.'

She smiled. 'It's just…well, you're very different from Javier. And I think he *would* care that I'd been with you. And I think…' Pause, swallow. 'I think I have to tell him. Don't you?'

He let go of her hand, sat back abruptly. 'How did we end up here? One minute we're talking about your sister's excellent intuition when it comes to fiancés and the next you're getting ready to throw yourself on your sword and confess something that's *none of his business*. Shall I say that again? *None of his business.*'

'But what if he finds out? *After* we're married?'

'Who's going to tell him?' Then Aaron seemed to catch himself. He shook his head, bemused. 'I can't believe I'm saying this! If it sounds like I'm talking you into marrying him, don't listen to me.'

'It just seems dishonest. Knowing how he feels about other men even looking at me, telling him is the honourable thing to do.' She looked Aaron straight in the eye. 'It's what you would do, isn't it?'

'I'd break up with him. That's what I'd do.'

'Be serious.'

'I am. Serious as a sudden home birth.'

'You told Rebecca about us.'

'Rebecca and I are divorced, remember?'

'And when you found out about Rebecca being unfaithful, you forgave her.'

He sighed. 'It's not the same, Ella. It's not as simple as

admitting you've been unfaithful—although in your case I'll dispute that to my dying day—and getting a blessing in return for being honest.'

'*You'd* forgive me.'

'As far as I'm concerned, there's nothing to forgive. But that's me. If he's the jealous type, and controlling...' He paused, seemed to be weighing his words. 'Who knows how he'll react?'

She looked at her watch. 'Anyway, we'd better get back to Tina. It's late and you need to get Kiri home.'

They left the cafeteria and walked in silence back to Tina's room.

'Thank you for listening,' she said, stopping him just outside. 'You know, don't you, that I've never been able to talk to anyone the way I talk to you? I *don't* talk to anyone like this. Only you. Do you know how much it means to me to have this?'

She reached up, cupped his cheek, and he pressed his hand over hers.

'You don't need to do this, Ella,' he said.

She removed her hand. 'I do,' she insisted. 'And I have to believe he'll forgive me.'

He blew out a breath. 'He will, if he's not a complete idiot. And, for the record, I'd forgive you anything shy of genocide.' He pursed his lips. 'Nah—I'd forgive you that as well.' He frowned down at her. 'And if he *is* a complete idiot, you've got my number. I told you I loved you and I meant it. And I told you I'd wait for you. I will, Ella.'

His hand was over his heart, rubbing. Ella, noticing it, frowned. 'Are you all right?'

'What?' He looked down, stopped the movement straight away. She was surprised to see a slight flush stain his cheekbones. 'Oh, yes,' he said.

Long pause. 'It's hopeless for us, you know that, Aaron.'

'No, I don't,' he answered. 'And I hope you realise I'm

in deep trouble with your sister. She thinks I'm out here convincing you to run away with me.'

'You don't want that, Aaron. Not really. Rebecca needs you. Kiri needs Rebecca. And Javier needs me. That's our lives.'

'You left out who you need, Ella. And who I need. I don't accept that our lives are about what everyone *except* us needs. If you could be a little less martyr-like about it—'

'I am not a martyr.'

'Maybe not all the time, but you're in training. Inconveniently, right after meeting me.' He took her hands in his, forestalling any more protestations. 'Anyway, just don't get married too soon. Make sure you get to know the man a little better first.'

'Ella?'

They broke apart and Ella whirled in the direction of Javier's voice.

Ella hurried towards Javier. 'I'm glad you made it.'

He made no move to touch her. 'Are you?' he asked, keeping his flashing black eyes trained on Aaron, who nodded at him and stayed exactly where he was.

Like he was on sentry duty.

Ella was torn between wanting to thump Aaron and wanting to kiss him. Here he was, protecting her from her fiancé in case Javier didn't like what he'd seen—when, really, what was there to like about it? Seeing your future wife holding another man's hands and gazing at him.

There was going to be an argument. And it wasn't going to be pleasant. But not here.

'Yes, I am,' Ella said, determinedly cheerful. 'Visiting hours are over but they're not too strict. Let's go and see Audrey. She looks just like Tina.' She looked at Aaron. 'Doesn't she?'

'Yes,' Aaron agreed. 'It was good to see you, Ella. I'll just pop in for a moment to say goodbye and collect Kiri, then leave you to it.' With what Ella could only describe as a warning look at Javier, Aaron walked into Tina's room, saying, 'Kiri, time to make tracks.'

Ella started to follow Aaron in but Javier stopped her with a hard grip on her arm. 'First, I think you had better tell me what is going on with you and him,' he said.

'Not in a hospital corridor.' Ella eased her arm free. 'Now, come in and see my sister. See the baby. Then we'll go home. And we'll talk.'

Javier didn't touch her on the way home. Didn't speak to her. Didn't look at her.

Ella dreaded the impending argument. But she longed for it too. Because they had to deal with everything—their pasts, their fears, their insecurities, their hopes—before they took another step towards marriage.

Having Aaron to talk to had made her realise she should never have kept her grief locked in for so long. Being able to talk to someone, confide in someone would have eased two long years of heartache.

So now she was going to talk to *this* man. She was preparing to share her life with him, and she couldn't do that without sharing how the past two years had changed her. And if Javier wouldn't confide in her in return, tell her how he'd stayed sane during two years of captivity…well, she didn't know what she'd do. Because she needed that knowledge. The insight. The trust.

They entered the house, went to Javier's room.

'So talk,' he said, and closed the door.

'I—I guess I should start with—'

'Start with what is going on with Aaron James. Why was he holding your hands?'

Ella stayed calm. 'He was comforting me. That's all.'

'Comforting you *why*?'

Still calm. But she licked her lips. 'Because I had just made a difficult decision.'

'What decision? And why were you with him when you made it? Why not me?'

Okay, not so calm. 'I was with him because the decision concerns you.'

His eyes narrowed. He said nothing. Just waited.

'To explain, I need to go back. To when you were kidnapped, and I tried so hard to find out what happened to you, and nobody could—or would—tell me anything. I wasn't a wife, I wasn't a sister. Nobody knew I was even a girlfriend. I'm not sure anyone would have helped me anyway. Because nobody knew anything. All I could do was wait. And wait. And…wait.'

He hadn't moved a muscle.

'It does something to you, the waiting,' she said, drowning. 'And I know you must know what I mean, because you were waiting too.'

'This is about you, Ella, not me.'

'But you never talk about it. You never—'

'You. Not me,' he rapped out.

She jumped. 'Right. Yes. Well…I—I—'

'Waited for me,' he finished for her, and it was more of a taunt than a statement.

'Yes, I did.'

'And you kept waiting, and waiting, and waiting.'

'Y-yes.'

'Until Aaron James came along.'

She sucked in a breath. Sudden. 'No. At least, yes but… no.'

He looked at her. Utterly, utterly cold. 'Yes but no?'

The snap in his voice had her stomach rioting.

'You slept with Aaron James. Just say it.'

She jumped, jolted. 'I thought you were dead.'

He had started pacing the room. 'You wished I was.'

'No!' she cried. 'Never, ever, ever.' She felt like she was running at a brick wall. It wouldn't yield; only she could.

Or try, at least. 'It's over between me and Aaron. He is no threat to you.'

Javier stopped, looked at her, incredulous. 'No threat to me? No *threat*?'

'I will be living in Barcelona, with you. He will be on the other side of the world.'

He shoved her against the wall. 'He is your sister's friend. He will be there, always.' He punched his fist into the wall beside her head. 'You have been denying me what you gave *him*. You introduced him to me. You made a fool of me.'

Ella stayed ultra-still, scared to move. 'I wanted to tell you. I am telling you. Now.'

'Now!' He looked into her face. He was only just holding his fury in check. 'Two years I survived, to come back and learn that you have slept around.'

'Don't say that,' Ella said.

'How do I know that you weren't sleeping with who knows how many men from the moment I was gone? We'd only known each other a few weeks when you slept with me. A woman like you would sleep with anyone. That's what I think you have spent the last two years doing. Now, just admit it, Ella.'

Ella thought of all the things she had planned to tell him tonight. The confession about Aaron, yes, but also about Sann, about her life in despairing limbo. And this is what it had come down to. 'No,' she said quietly. 'I will not admit to that.'

He raised his hand as if to hit her.

Her eyes blazed. 'If you touch me, I will make you sorry you're not still in Somalia,' she said.

'No, I won't hit you,' he said. 'You're not worth it, Ella.'

It took all of Ella's courage to turn from Javier. To walk slowly out of the room, not run, as his curses continued to rain on her.

She sat in her bedroom, shaking. She could hear drawers and cupboard doors slamming. Curses. Wheels on the floor—his bag. There was a pause outside her door. She imagined him coming in...

She held her breath, realised she was trembling like a leaf.

Then another inarticulate curse. Footsteps going down the stairs.

Out of her life.

Even three floors up she heard the front door slam.

'Some things just change,' she whispered to herself, and remembered Aaron saying exactly that to her.

She'd thought it would be comforting to accept that.

Instead, it made her cry.

CHAPTER SEVENTEEN

ELLA? ELLA PICK up. It's me.

Hellooo? Ella? Why didn't you return my call?

Ella, pick up! Come on, pick up!

Yeah, three messages were probably enough, Aaron decided, catching himself before he could leave a fourth.

He contemplated calling Brand to do some back-door sleuthing—but pictured his lifeless body sporting a variety of blunt and sharp force injuries should Ella get wind of that, and opted to spend the night tossing and turning instead as he wondered how the confession had gone. Whether Javier and Ella were in bed, burying the infidelity hatchet in a lusty bout of lovemaking.

No!

He would *not* imagine that.

He would, instead, plan what he would say, how he would act, tomorrow, when he made a last-ditch effort to woo Ella, regardless of what had happened between her sheets tonight.

And screw the best-buddy routine the two of them had enacted at the hospital; he should have whisked her off into the night instead of letting her saunter off with the darkly brooding doctor.

Anyway, enough dwelling on what he should have done. More important was the future.

So, back to what he was going to say to Ella.

And it was suddenly so clear! Why did it have to be three o'clock in the morning when he realised that keeping things simple was not about compartmentalising things to death? Ella in one corner, Rebecca in another, Kiri in a third. Him in the fourth, sashaying back and forth between them. Tina had put it best—he was juggling balls to make sure they didn't ever connect.

Dumb, dumb, dumb.

Because who wanted to juggle for eternity? It was exhausting. You had to stop some time and hold all the balls together in your hands, if you didn't want your arms to fall off.

Yep, it was crystal clear at three o'clock.

He was getting quite poetic.

And perhaps a little maudlin. Because he couldn't help revisiting every stupid argument he and Ella had ever had, wishing he could go back and fix every single one of them to get the right ending.

How arrogant he'd been, to insist they couldn't have a relationship because of his complicated life. Who *didn't* have a complicated life? Ella's was worthy of its own miniseries! All he'd managed to do was give Ella every argument she'd ever need to keep him at arm's length for the rest of their natural lives.

And she knew how to use them.

One. What was good for Rebecca. Well, if Rebecca knew she was the main obstacle to his relationship with Ella, she'd laugh herself sick.

Two. What was good for Kiri. As if being around Ella could ever be bad for him!

Three. His own initial disapproval of her. Short-lived it may have been, but Ella had turned out to be an expert at hurling that at his head.

He wanted to slap himself in the head when he thought back to how he'd made Ella feel like she wasn't good enough to be near his son. Except that he couldn't hit himself hard enough; he'd need some kind of mediaeval mace with all the spiky protuberances to do his self-disgust justice.

Just how was he going to fix the situation?

He could do better. He *would* do better. He would be sane, articulate, charming, passionate, clever. He would convince her that she belonged with him.

Tomorrow he would prove that love was really simple. Just being in it and grabbing it when it hits you and making your life fit around it, not it fit around your life. *Very* simple.

What time was a decent time to arrive at Brand's, given Tina and Audrey were coming home from the hospital? Just after lunch? That seemed good timing. For a sane, reasonable man who was insanely, unreasonably in love with a woman who held all the cards.

He found that he was rubbing his chest over his heart again.

Man, he hated that.

One look in the mirror the next day had Ella raiding Tina's store of make-up.

She couldn't look like one of the undead for Tina's return from the hospital.

And she would have to handle the news of her break-up with Javier carefully, with no mention of last night's awful showdown, if she didn't want Tina packing the electrical wires and blowtorch in a backpack and going off to hunt Javier down.

But she would, at last, tell her sister everything about the past two years, including what had happened with Sann. She would let her into her pain and grief the way she should have done all along.

And then she would go back to Los Angeles. And she would tell her parents.

And then it would be time for her to move on, and make new memories.

No guilt, no shame.

'She's not here, Aaron.'

Aaron heard the words come out of Brand's mouth but couldn't quite compute.

'Not here?' His eyes widened. 'Then where is she? *How* is she?'

'If it's the break-up with Javier you're talking about, she's fine. I'd go so far as to say she's relieved.'

Aaron felt a wave of intense happiness, until the look on Brand's face registered. 'So when will she be back?' he asked.

And then Brand put his arm around Aaron's shoulder, steered him into the library.

Not promising.

Brand poured Scotch into a glass, held it out for Aaron. 'Her flight home took off about half an hour ago,' he said.

Aaron took the glass, almost mechanically sipped.

Brand walked over to his desk, plucked a small envelope off it, handed it to Aaron.

Aaron.
I think we've all had enough upheavals for a while so let's not add any more drama. Good luck with Rebecca. And hug Kiri for me.
Ella

He looked up and caught Brand's eye.

'That's it?' he demanded.

'That's it.'

He reread the note.

'Yeah, screw that,' he said. 'When do we wrap up filming?'

'Four weeks.'

'Then that's how long she's got before I go after her.'

'Princess Tina will be pleased,' Brand said, and slapped him on the shoulder.

CHAPTER EIGHTEEN

ELLA WASN'T HOME.

Aaron almost laughed as he recalled the way he'd played this scene out in his head. He would knock on the door of her apartment. She would open the door, stare at him, smile that dazzling smile—the one that had her heart and soul in it—and then she would leap into his arms and kiss him. She would tell him she loved him, that she couldn't live without him. That she'd been waiting for him.

Very satisfactory.

Except that she wasn't home.

The only romance he'd had so far had involved charming Ella's young gay doorman into letting him into the building.

Well, he'd told Ella more than once he would wait for her. And here he was, waiting.

It had been four weeks. Enough time for Ella to miss him desperately. Enough time for him to get all the elements in place to counteract Ella's martyrish inclinations: Rebecca was doing brilliantly at Trust; her new love affair was steaming ahead and Aaron liked the guy; custody arrangements had been sorted; and Aaron had even managed to nab that lead role in the LA-based detective series he'd auditioned for.

Fate was lining up for him at last.

Now he just had to pray that Ella wasn't about to head

off to the Congo or float herself down the Amazon, and life would be perfect.

If he could just get her to say three little words.

He didn't really know if she could say those words. Or feel them.

He heard the elevator, and scrambled to his feet. He'd done this four times already—all false alarms—but, hey, he wasn't about to be found by the love of his life sitting on the floor.

Then he saw her. She was wearing the dress he'd bought her in London. That *had* to be a sign.

He felt those blasted butterflies again. Actually, forget butterflies; these were more like bats. Humongous bats.

He knew the moment she saw him. The hitch in her stride. Then the slow, gliding tread towards him.

'Well,' Ella said inadequately, with the smile that didn't reach her eyes.

All Aaron's optimism dropped through his gut to the floor. 'Don't,' he said. 'Don't smile like that. Not like that. Not now.'

'I don't—'

'And don't say you don't know what I mean. Because you do. Aren't you happy to see me, Ella?'

He heard her suck in a breath. And then she said, 'Is everything...? Is everything okay? Rebecca...'

'In rehab. Taking control. Doing great. But even if her life were off the rails, I'd still be here, Ella. What I would have told you, if you hadn't left London when you did, was that I was going to make things work for us come hell or high water. No matter what was happening with anyone else. Rebecca, Kiri, your family, even Javier—I'd still want you with me. All right, to be honest, I still want to damage one of Javier's cheekbones, so having him in our lives might take a little work.'

'Javier just couldn't forgive. Couldn't even accept. And I realised either he'd changed or I never really knew him.

But if you'd seen him, so heroic and caring and brilliant in Somalia, you—'

'Yeah, yeah, don't expect me to get all misty-eyed over his good doctor deeds, Ella. And he had nothing to forgive. I don't want to talk about him. I don't care about him. I only care about you.'

He stepped closer to her. 'I don't know what I'll do if I can't have you. You and I, we're supposed to be together. Can't you feel it? We've learned, both of us, that life isn't about hanging on the sidelines, waiting for things to get better. Or worse. Waiting for fate to come and toss a grenade or a bouquet or a wet fish. I'll catch every grenade, Ella, and I'll still love you. I'll navigate any difficulty to have you.'

She blinked hard. Again. 'Oh.'

'I'll follow you to Sierra Leone or Chad or Somalia or Laos.'

She shook her head. 'It's good old America for a long time to come, so you'll have to think of something else.'

'Hmm. So, what about…?' He held up his hands. They were shaking. 'What about this? Nobody else has ever made me shake just because they were near me, Ella.'

'Are you sure? Are you really sure, Aaron?'

He waved his hands at her. 'Look at them! Like a leaf in a gale.'

'I don't mean— I mean I don't want you to regret me. I don't want to become one more responsibility to bear. And you know, better than most, I've hardly been a saint, so I'd understand—'

'Stop talking like that!' He started undoing his shirt.

'What about Kiri? How will Rebecca take it?'

'Kiri loves you, and as for Rebecca—was I just talking about not caring? But if it will get you over the line, I swear I'll get her blessing in writing. My sisters—they've posted an embarrassing video on YouTube begging you to take me—wait until you see it. And I've already gone and—'

'What are you doing?' she asked, seeming to notice at last that he was removing his shirt. 'I'm not— I don't— I— Oh!'

'Do you like it?'

Ella came forward, put her hands on his chest. He'd had her name tattooed across his chest. Her name. Bold and beautiful.

And something else.

Dropping from the A over his left pectoral muscle was a gold ring that looked like it was entering his skin where his heart was, anchoring her name there. Her fingers traced it. 'Oh, Aaron. Yes, I like it.'

'I'll ink my whole body for you Ella, if you want.'

'No, just this,' she said. 'It looks…permanent.' She put her head on one side, querying him. 'Is it?'

'The things I'll do to get a green card,' Aaron quipped, and then gathered her in, held her against his chest, tilted her face up to his. 'Yes, it's permanent. And so are you. Are you ready, Ella, my darling? You know I want you. You know I'm obsessed, besotted, madly and wildly in love with you. Tell me you feel the same. Tell me you're ready. Come on, Ella. Say it. Say it.'

'I love you. And, yes,' she breathed. And then she smiled and her face lit up like the sun. Bright and gold and glowing. His smile. Just for him. 'I'm ready.'

He closed his eyes. Breathed in. Out. Opened his eyes. 'Then let's get inside. I want to have my way with you— No, wait! I want you to have your way with me. Hang on, I want— Oh, Ella, just open the door.'

* * * * *

THE DOCTOR'S
REDEMPTION

SUSAN CARLISLE

To Kathy Cooksey and Jeanie Brantley.
Thanks for sharing Mardi Gras with me.

CHAPTER ONE

THE PARADES WERE what Laura Jo Akins enjoyed most about the Mardi Gras season in Mobile, Alabama. This year was no different. She placed a hand on the thin shoulder of her eight-year-old daughter, Allie.

Her daughter smiled up at her. "When does the parade start?"

"It should already be moving our way. Listen. You can hear the band."

The faint sound of a ragtime tune floated from the distance.

Allie looked up at Laura Jo. "Can we stay for the next one too?"

The sure thing about Mardi Gras was that the parades kept coming. The closer the calendar got to Fat Tuesday the more heavily the days were filled with parades. Sometimes as many as four a day on the weekends.

"No, honey. They're expecting me at the hospital. We'll watch this one and then we have to go."

"Okay, but we get to see one another day, don't we?"

"Maybe on Wednesday. Next Monday and Tuesday you'll be out of school for a long weekend. We'll be sure to watch more then."

"Why can't I be in one?" Allie asked, turning to look at Laura Jo.

It had been a constant question during last year's Mardi Gras season and had become more demanding during this one. "Maybe when you get older. For now we'll just have to watch."

As the banner holders at the head of the parade came into sight the crowd pushed forward, forcing her and Allie against the metal barriers. A bicycling medical first responder or mobile EMT circled in front of them then rode up the street. He looked familiar for some reason but, then, most of the medical help during the carnival season were employed at the hospital where she worked. Dressed in red biking shorts and wearing a pack on his back, he turned again and pedaled back in their direction. Laura Jo squinted, trying to make out his features, but his helmet obscured her view.

Members of the medical community volunteered to work during Mardi Gras to help out with the crowds. Most of the nurses and doctors gave up their days off during the season to work the parades. It wasn't required but many enjoyed being a part of the celebration. Laura Jo knew most of the employees at Mobile General, at least by face. Although she couldn't place the rider, he looked just fine in his form-fitting pants. He must bike regularly.

"Look, Mommy." Allie pointed to a group of people who had come through the barriers and were entertaining the crowd standing on both sides of the street. They were dressed in clown-type outfits and were riding three-wheeled bikes with bright-colored fish attached to the side.

Laura Jo smiled down at her daughter. "That's the Mystic Fish."

They made a circle or two in the open parade area and then disappeared into the crowd across the street from her and Allie. Laura Jo knew from years of watching parades that they would appear somewhere else along the parade route.

"What's a mystic fish?" Allie asked.

"You know what a fish is. In this case it's a club or group of people. It's also called a krewe. Because they meet in secret they are mystic or mysterious. It's all just fun."

"Are you in a queue?"

"It's krewe. Like a crew member. And, no, I'm not." She placed a hand on her daughter's head. "I have you to take care of, work at the shelter and at the hospital. No time."

Laura Jo understood being a member of a krewe. Her family had been participants all her life. In fact, they had been a part of the largest and most prestigious krewe in Mobile. She'd been one of the Mobile society that had celebrated her coming of age at carnival time. But no more.

The noise level increased as the first high-school band approached. She positioned Allie between her and the barrier so Allie could see. As the first ostentatiously decorated float rolled by the spectators pressed closer to them. The float was designed in a dragon motif and painted green, purple and gold with piles of beads hanging off pegs. Members of the krewe were dressed in costumes and wore masks.

She and Allie joined those around them in yelling, "Throw me something, mister."

Raising their hands along with everyone else, she and Allie tried to catch the beads, plastic cups with the krewe name printed on them or stuffed animals that were being thrown from the float. Bands playing and music blaring from large speakers mounted on the floats made it difficult to hear.

One krewe member made eye contact with Laura Jo and pointed at Allie. He threw a small stuffed gorilla to

Laura Jo, which she handed to Allie, who hugged it to her and smiled up at the grinning man. The float moved on.

When a strand of brightly colored beads flew through the air in Allie's direction from the next float, Laura Jo reached to catch them. She couldn't and they were snatched by the man standing behind her. He handed them to Allie. She smiled brightly at him. That was one of the special things about Mardi Gras in Mobile. It was a family affair. Any age was welcome and everyone saw that the children had a good time. Twenty minutes later a fire truck that signaled the end of the parade rolled by.

The man standing next to them shifted the barrier, creating an opening. A few people rushed through in an effort to snatch up any of the goodies that had fallen on the pavement.

"Mama, can I get those?" Allie pointed out into the street, now virtually empty except for a few children.

Laura Jo searched for what Allie was asking about. On the road lay a couple of plastic doubloons. "Sure, honey. There won't be another parade for an hour."

Allie ran through the opening and ran in the direction of the strand of gold and silver disks. In her exuberance to reach her target she stumbled and fell, stopping herself with her hands. Laura Jo gasped and rushed to her. Allie had already pushed herself up to a sitting position. Tears welled in her eyes but she'd not burst into sobs yet. There was an L-shaped hole in the thin material of her pants and a trickle of blood ran off the side of her knee.

"Oh, honey," Laura Jo said.

"My hands hurt." Allie showed Laura Jo her palms. The meaty part looked much like her knee.

"Friction burns." Laura Jo took one of Allie's wrists and raised her hand, blowing across it. Here she was a registered nurse with not a bandage to her name. Allie's injuries were going to require far more than what Laura Jo was doing.

"Can I help here?" a deep male voice said from above them.

Laura Jo glanced up to see the bike medic she'd admired earlier. She'd been so adsorbed with Allie she'd not noticed him ride up.

"Do you have any four-by-fours? Some antibiotic cream?" Laura Jo asked.

The man gave her a curious look then stepped off the bike. He slung the red pack off his back and crouched down on his haunches. "Let me see what I can do."

Laura Jo looked at him through moisture in her eyes. She knew him. Or more accurately knew who he was. Mark Clayborn. She'd had no idea he was back in town. But, then, why would she? "If you'll just share your supplies I can handle it. I'm her mother and a nurse."

"I appreciate that but I need to treat your daughter since it happened at the parade. I'll have to make a report anyway."

She gave him room. Years ago she'd been very enamored of Mark Clayborn. Just young enough to hero worship him, she'd often dreamed of "what if" when he'd glanced her way. Which he never had, unless it had been to smile at the gaggle of young maids in his queen's court. He'd had it all. Good looks, social status, education and a bright future. And to top it off he'd been Mardi Gras King that year. Every girl had dreamed of being on his arm and she'd been no different. She had watched him so closely back then no wonder he seemed familiar.

Allie winced when he touched the angry skin of her knee.

Laura Jo's hands shook. As an emergency room nurse she'd seen much worse, but when it came to her own child it was difficult to remain emotionally detached. Still, she should be the one caring for Allie. She'd been her sole caretaker and provider since her daughter's father had left Laura Jo when she was three months pregnant. Having been pushed aside before, she didn't like it any better now than she had then. No matter how irrational the reaction.

"So what's your name, young lady?" Mark asked Allie. She told him.

"So, Allie, what have you liked best about Mardi Gras this year?"

Allie didn't hesitate to answer. "King Cake."

He nodded like a sage monk giving thought to the answer. "I like King Cake, too. What's your favorite? Cinnamon or cream cheese?"

"Cinnamon."

"I'm a fan of cream cheese. So have you ever found the baby?"

"Yeah, once. I had to take a cake to school the next week."

"So you baked one?"

"No, my mother did." She pointed at Laura Jo.

Mark glanced at her with a look of respect but there was no sign of recognition. Even though their families had known each other for years he didn't remember her. The last she'd really heard, he'd been in a bad car accident and had later left for medical school.

"You mom didn't get it from a bakery?"

"No. She likes to make them." Allie smiled up at Laura Jo. "She lets me put the baby inside."

Allie continued, telling him how she liked to stand beside Laura Jo as she rolled the pastry out. She would wait patiently until it was time to put the miniature plastic baby into one of the rolls before Laura Jo braided them into a cake. When it came out of the oven Allie begged to be the one to shake the green, purple and gold sugar on top.

"Well, that sounds like fun. Are you ready to stand?"

Laura Jo couldn't help but be impressed. Mark had cleaned up Allie with little more than a wince from her.

He placed a hand below Allie's elbow and helped her to stand then said to Laura Jo, "Keep the area clean. If you see any infection, call a doctor right away or take her to the ER."

Laura Jo rolled her eyes. "I'm a nurse, remember?"

"I remember, but sometimes when it's someone we love our emotions get in the way."

That was something close to what her father had said when she'd announced that she was marrying Phil. "He's only interested in your last name and money." Her father had gone on to say that Phil certainly wasn't worth giving up her education for. When she'd asked how her father knew so much about Phil he admitted to having had someone check into his background. That Phil had already been married once and couldn't seem to hold down a job. "He's not good enough for you. Not welcome in our home," had been her father's parting words.

She'd chosen Phil. Even though she'd soon learned that her father had been right, the situation had created a rift between Laura Jo and her parents that was just as wide today as it had been nine years earlier. She had sworn then never to ask her parents for help. She had her pride.

Taking Allie's hand, Laura Jo said, "Let's go, honey. I'm sure we have taken enough of the medic's time."

"Bye," Allie said.

Mark bent and picked up the doubloons off the pavement and placed them carefully in Allie's hand. "I hope you find a baby in your next cake. Maybe it'll bring you luck."

Allie grinned back at him with obvious hero worship.

"Thank you." She led Allie through the barrier. "Bye."

That would be it for the reappearing Mark Clayborn. He had been a part of her life that was now long gone. She wouldn't be seeing him again.

Mark had never planned to return to Mobile to live permanently, but that had changed. He'd worked hard to make LA home. Even the few times he'd come back to Alabama he'd only stayed a few days and then gone again. When his father's houseman had phoned to say Mark Clayborn, Sr. had suffered a stroke, Mark could no longer refuse not to make southern Alabama his home again. His mother was gone and his brother was in the military with no control over where he was stationed. Mark was left no choice. Someone needed to live close enough to take care of his father.

Pulling up the circular drive framed by a well-manicured yard in the center of the oldest section of homes in Mobile, Mark stopped in front of the antebellum mansion. This house had been his home for the twenty-five years before he had moved to LA. Now just his father lived here. Mark had chosen to take up residence forty-five minutes across the bay in the Clayborn summer house in Fairhope, Alabama. He had joined a general practice group made up of five doctors. The clinic was located in the town of Spanish Fort, which was halfway between Mobile and Fairhope. He lived and worked close enough to take care of his father and far enough away that memories of the past would remain murky instead of vivid.

It had been carnival season when he'd left for LA. He'd been riding high on being the king. His queen had been his girlfriend for the last two years and one of the most beautiful girls in Mobile society. He'd gotten his pick of medical fellowships that had allowed him to only be a few hours away in Birmingham. Gossips had it that he and his queen would ride off into the happily-ever-after as soon as he finished his fellowship. Mark had not planned to disappoint them. That was until he and Mike had decided they needed to drive to the beach after the krewe dance on Fat Tuesday night.

How many times since he'd been back had he picked up the phone to call and see how Mike was doing? How many times had he not followed through? He'd seen Mike a few times over the years. Those had been brief and uncomfortable meetings. Mark had always left with another wheelbarrow of guilt piled on top of the mountain that was already there.

He and Mike had made big plans. They had both been on their way to Birmingham, Mark to complete his fellowship and Mike to earn his Master's in Business. They would return to town to set up a clinic practice, Mark handling the medical end and Mike overseeing the business side. They'd even talked about their families building homes next door to each other. But after the accident Mike's longtime girlfriend had left him. Those dreams vanished. Because of Mark.

As time had gone by it had become easier to satisfy his need to know how Mike was doing by asking others about him. Often when Mark had spoken to his father he'd ask about Mike. His father had always encouraged him to call and talk to Mike if he wanted to know how he was doing. Mark hadn't. That way the guilt didn't become a throbbing, breathing thing.

Mark pushed the front doorbell of his father's house then opened the door. He was met in the high-ceilinged hall by John, the man who had worked for Mark, Sr. since Mark, Jr. had been a boy.

"Hi. How's he doing today?"

"Your dad has had a good day. He's out by the pool."

Mark headed down the all-too-familiar hall that led

through the middle of the house and out onto the brick patio with the pool beyond. His father sat in a wheelchair in the sun, with his nurse nearby, reading a book. Mark winced at the sight. It hurt his heart to see the strong, commanding man brought to this by a stroke. Only with time and patience and massive amounts of physical therapy would he regain enough strength to walk again. At least his father had a chance of getting out of the chair, unlike Mike, who had no choice.

Mark circled his father so he faced him. "Hi, Dad."

His white-haired father gave him a lopsided smile. "Hello, son."

Fortunately his mind was still strong. His nurse closed her book and after a nod to Mark made her way toward the house.

Mark pulled a metal pool chair close so he could sit where his father could see him. "How are you doing today?"

"Fine. Emmett has been by to tell me what went on at the board meeting. He said you didn't make it."

"No, I had patients to see. We've talked about this already. You've put good people in place to handle the company. Let them do it."

"It's not the same. We need a Clayborn there."

"I know, Dad."

His father continued. "I'm glad you stopped by. I wanted to talk to you about attending the krewe dance next week. I can't go and our family needs to be represented. You're the only one to do it."

Mark had always enjoyed the fanfare and glamour of The Mystical Order of Orion dance, the visit from the king and queen and their court. But after what had happened twelve years ago he was hesitant to attend. He took a deep breath. "It's not really my thing anymore but I know it's important to you to keep up appearances."

"You were king. That is and was a high honor. You owe it to the krewe, to the Clayborn name to attend."

"I know, Dad. I'll do my duty."

"This used to be your favorite time of the year. You need to let yourself off the hook, son. It wasn't your fault."

Maybe everyone thought that but Mark sure didn't. He carried the horror of what had happened to Mike with him daily. Now that he was back in Mobile it was more alive than it had ever been. Time hadn't healed the wound, only covered it over.

Mark had dinner with his father then headed across the bay to Fairhope, a small township where the family summer home was located. When he'd arrived in Alabama he'd needed a place to live. Staying in Fairhope gave him a house of his own, a safe haven. Since he was working at a clinic in Spanish Fort, a city just north of Fairhope, living there was convenient.

Entering the large dark room with hardwood paneling, Mark walked through to the family-style kitchen. There he pulled a drink out of the refrigerator and went out to the deck. Mobile Bay stretched far and wide before him. He could see the tall buildings of the city in the distance. The wind had picked up, rustling the shrubbery around the deck. A seagull swooped down and plucked a fish out of the water near the end of the pier. No, this wasn't LA anymore.

Mark had agreed to pitch in and work the parades as a first responder when one of his new partners had said that they did that as a public service during Mardi Gras season. He'd agreed to do his part but had expected that it would be in some of the surrounding smaller towns. When he'd been assigned the parade in downtown Mobile he hadn't felt like he could say no. He needed to be a team player since he'd only joined the medical group a few months earlier. Despite the parade location, Mark had enjoyed the assignment. Especially helping the young girl. Her mother had been attractive. More than once since then he'd wondered where she worked.

He'd spent the rest of the parade scanning the crowd. His chest still contracted at the thought he might see Mike. He'd spent years making a point of not thinking about the automobile accident. Now that he was back it seemed the only thing on his mind.

His cell phone rang. He pulled it out of his pocket. "This is Dr. Clayborn."

"Hey, Mark, it's Ralph. We need you again the day after tomorrow if you can help us out. Afternoon parade in Dauphine."

He didn't mind working a parade in Dauphine. It was on his side of the bay. As long as it wasn't in Mobile. There the chance of facing his past became greater. "Yeah, I'm only seeing patients in the morning. Will I be on a bike again?"

"Not this time. I just need you at the med tent. It'll be set up in the First Baptist Church parking lot."

"I'll be there."

"Marsha?" Laura Jo called as she and Allie opened the door of her best friend's apartment Wednesday afternoon.

"Hey, we're back here," a voice came from the direction of the kitchen area located in the back of the apartment.

She followed Allie down the short hallway to find Marsha and her son, Jeremy, decorating a wagon with purple, green and gold ribbons.

Marsha looked up as they entered. "You know Mardi Gras almost kills me every year. I say I'm not going to do anything next year then here I am, doing even more."

Allie had already joined in to help Jeremy with the decorations.

"I know what you mean. It makes working in the ER

interesting. I've enjoyed my day off but I'll pay for it, no doubt, by being on the night shift. I appreciate you letting Allie spend the night."

"It's not a problem. I love her like my own." She ruffled Allie's hair.

Laura Jo had met Marsha at the Mothers Without Partners clinic. Phil had lived up to all her father's predictions and more when he'd left her pregnant and cleaned out their bank account to never be seen again. Even after all these years he hadn't even checked to see if he had a son or daughter. Marsha's husband had died in a fishing accident. She and Marsha had hit it off right away. Circumstances had brought them together but friendship had seen to it that they still depended on each other.

They'd shared an apartment for a few months and had traded off their time watching the kids while the other had worked or gone to school. They had their own apartments now but in the same complex and Marsha was more like family than the one Laura Jo had left behind.

They had joined forces to help other mothers who didn't have anyone to fall back on. They had convinced the city to sell them an old home so these women would have a place to live and receive help while they were getting their lives in order. The deadline to pay for the house was looming. Finding the funding had become more difficult than Laura Jo had anticipated.

Marsha announced, "I heard from the city contact. He said we had to move soon on the house or the city will have to announce it's for sale. They can't hold it forever."

Laura Jo groaned. That wasn't what she wanted to hear. "How much time do we have?"

"Week or two. At least until things settle down after Mardi Gras. We've got to come up with a good way to raise a lot of money. Fast. I know you don't want to do it but you do have the contacts. Maybe you could put on a party dress and go pick the pockets of all those society friends you used to hang around with."

Laura Jo shook her head. "That's not going to happen. We'll have to find another way."

What if she had to face her mother and father? Worse, have them see her asking for money. That's what they had thought she'd be doing if she married Phil. That's what he'd wanted her to do, but she'd refused. After her fight with her parents she and Phil had gone to Las Vegas that night to get married.

When they'd returned Phil had left to work on an oil rig. Three weeks later he'd come home. A week later all his pay had gone and he'd admitted he'd been fired. He'd made noises about looking for a job but in hindsight she didn't think he'd ever really tried. Things had got worse between them. The issue that finally snapped them had been Laura Jo telling him she was pregnant. Phil's snarling parting words were, "I didn't sign on for no kid. You can't put that on me. Having you is bad enough."

Marsha gave her questioning look. "You know I'm kidding but…"

"I'll come up with something." She checked her watch. "Now, I have to get to the hospital." Stepping toward Allie, Laura Jo said to Marsha, "I'll meet you at the parade tomorrow evening."

"Sounds like a plan."

Laura Jo leaned down and kissed Allie on the head. "See ya. Be good for Marsha."

"I will," Allie replied, then returned to what she was doing.

"Thanks, Marsha." Laura Jo called as she went up the hall.

Six hours later, Laura Jo was longing for her dinner and a moment to put her feet up. She wasn't going to get either anytime soon. Working in a trauma one level hospital meant a constant influx of patients, not only the regular cases but Mardi Gras's as well, which brought out the revelers and daredevils. Weekend nights were the worst and the place resembled a circus with not enough clowns to go around. Everyone had their hands full. The doors were swishing open regularly with people coming in. The constant ringing of the phone filled the area, blending with the piercing scream of ambulance sirens.

As she stepped back into the nursing station the phone rang again. Seconds later the clerk called out, "Incoming. Sixty-seven-year-old male. Heart attack. Resuscitating in transit. Child with head trauma behind that. ETA ten."

"I'll take the heart. Trauma six." Laura Jo hurried to set up what was needed before the patient arrived.

Minutes later the high-pitched sound of the ambulance arriving filled the air and Laura Jo rushed outside. The double rear doors of the vehicle stood wide open. Usually by this time the EMTs would be unloading the patient.

Looking inside, she immediately recognized the EMT working over the patient but not the other man. Then she did. *Mark Clayborn.* Again he was wearing red biking shorts and a yellow shirt of a first responder.

Mark held the portable oxygen bubble away from the patient as the EMT placed the defibrillator paddles on the patient's chest. The body jerked. The beep of the machine monitoring the heart rate started and grew steadier. Putting the earpieces of the stethoscope that had been around his neck into place, Mark listened to the man's heart. "Let's get him inside," he said with a sharp tone of authority. He then made an agile jump to the ground, turned toward the interior of the ambulance and helped bring out the patient on the stretcher.

Although confused by why he had been allowed in the

emergency vehicle, she still followed his lead. It was against policy to ride in the back unless you were part of the EMT staff. But now wasn't the time for questions. She stood aside while the two men lifted out the stretcher. The wheels dropped to the pavement and Laura Jo wrapped her hand around the yellow metal frame and pulled. Mark kept his fingers on the pulse point of the patient's wrist while the EMT pushed.

They had reached the doors when Mark said, "We're losing him again."

Tall enough to lean over and push on the patient's chest, he began compressions. Another nurse met them and gave oxygen. Laura Jo kept moving ahead, her arm burning. To her relief, they got the patient into the trauma room. There Mark and the EMT used the defibrillator once again. Seconds later the monitor made a beep and the line went from straight to having peaks and valleys. After they gained a steady pulse, she worked to place leads to the monitors on the patient. The ER doctor rushed in.

Mark and the EMT backed away with exhausted sighs, giving the ER doctor, Laura Jo and the other staff members space to work. For the next twenty intensive minutes, Laura Jo followed the ER doctor's instructions to the letter. Finally they managed to stabilize the patient enough to send him to surgery.

Laura Jo had to talk to the family. They must be scared. When she asked the admission clerk where they were she was told exam room five.

"Why are they in an exam room?"

"The man's granddaughter is being evaluated."

Laura Jo headed for the exam room. It shouldn't have surprised her that Mark was there, too. He came out as she was preparing to go in.

"Well, fancy meeting you here," he drawled in a deep voice that made her think of a dark velvet night.

"It's not that amazing really. I work here."

"I figured that out. So how's your daughter? Healing nicely?"

"She's fine. A little tender but fine."

"Good. By the way, I'm Dr. Mark Clayborn."

"Yes, I know who you are. As in the Clayborn Building, Clayborn Bank, Clayborn Shipping.

He gave her a studying look. "Do I know you?"

"I'm Laura Jo Akins. Used to be Laura Jo Herron."

"Herron? My parents used to talk about the Herrons. Robert Herron. Real estate."

She looked away. "Yes, that's my father."

He had pursed his lips. "Well, that's a surprise. Isn't it a small world?"

Too small for Laura Jo's comfort. It was time to change the subject. "Thanks for helping out. Now I need to talk to the family." She gave the door to the exam room a quick knock and pushed it open.

It turned out that she was wasting her time. "The nice Dr. Clayborn" had updated them and also seen to Lucy, their little girl, but they appreciated Laura Jo coming in. By the time she'd returned to the nursing station things seemed to be under control in the ER. All the exam and trauma rooms were full. The critical cases were being cared for. Those waiting were not serious.

"Why don't you take your supper break while you can?" the lead nurse said.

"Are you sure?"

"It's now or never. You know the closer we get to Fat Tuesday the merrier it gets around here."

Laura Jo laughed. "If merry is what you want to call it. Okay, I'll go."

"I'd rather call it merry otherwise I think I might cry," the lead nurse said with a grin.

Laura Jo grabbed her lunch box. It had become a habit to pack a lunch when money had been so tight even before Phil had left. Reaching the cafeteria, she scanned the room for an empty table. The busy ER translated to a full room. As soon as a table opened up she headed for it. Before she could get to it Mark slid into one of the two seats available. Disappointed, she stopped and looked around for another spot.

He waved her toward him. "You can join me, if you like."

Laura Jo looked at him. Did she really have a choice? She was expected back in the ER soon. "Thank you."

He grinned at her. "You don't sound too excited about it."

What was he expecting her to say? *You're right, I'm not?* "I have to eat. The ER won't stay calm for long."

"It did look a little wild in there. I've certainly had more than my share this evening. I haven't done this much emergency work since I was on my med school rotation. Don't see many head trauma and heart attacks in family practice."

Laura Jo pulled her sandwich out of the plastic bag. "I understand that the girl was sitting on top of her father's shoulders and toppled off. When the grandfather saw what had happened he had a heart attack."

"Yeah. Thank goodness it all happened within running distance of the med tent. For a few minutes there wasn't enough of us medical personal around to handle all that was going on. I'm just glad the girl has regained consciousness and the grandfather is stable."

"The girl will be here for observation for at least one night and the grandfather for much longer, I'm afraid."

He took a large bite of his hamburger and they ate in silence for a while before he asked, "So you knew who I was the other day. Why didn't you say something?"

"There just didn't seem a right moment."

"So you've seen a lot of Mardi Gras."

She straightened her back and looked directly at him. "I'm not that old."

He grinned. "I'm sorry, I didn't mean to imply that."

Laura Jo had to admit he had a nice smile. She grinned. "That's not what it sounded like to me."

"I was just trying to make pleasant conversation and didn't mean—"

"I know you didn't." Still, it would have been nice if he'd at least thought she looked familiar. She'd been invisible to her parents, unimportant to her husband and just this once it would have been nice to have been memorable. But, then, it had been a long time ago.

"So do you attend any of the krewe festivities?" He chewed slowly, as if waiting patiently for her answer.

"No. I don't travel in that social circle anymore." She took a bite of her sandwich.

"Why not? As I remember, the Herrons were a member of the same krewe as my family."

"I'm an Akins now."

"So Mr. Akins isn't a member either, I gather."

"No, and Mr. Akins, as you put it, isn't around to be a member."

"I'm sorry."

"I'm not. He left years ago."

"Oh, I thought…"

"I know. For all I know, he's alive and well somewhere."

Having finished his meal, Mark leaned back in his chair and crossed his arms over his chest. "Well, it has been a pleasure running into you, Ms. Atkins."

Laura Jo stood to leave. "You, too, Dr. Clayborn. We do seem to keep running into each other."

"Why, Ms. Akins, you don't believe in serendipity?"

"If I ever did believe in serendipity, that would've been a long time ago. Now, if you'll excuse me, I need to get back to work."

CHAPTER TWO

ON SATURDAY AFTERNOON Mark made his way through the side streets of Mobile, working around the parade route, which was already blocked off. It was one more week before Mardi Gras weekend and there would be a large parade that afternoon and another that night in downtown Mobile.

Throughout the week in the surrounding towns parades were planned, culminating in three or four per day until the final one on Fat Tuesday. Then Ash Wednesday would arrive and end all the revelry.

He'd been assigned to work in the med tent set up just off Government Street at a fire station. He'd wanted to say no, had even suggested that he work one or two of the parades in a nearby town, but he'd been told that he was needed there. His gut clenched each time he crossed the bay but his partners wouldn't like him not being a team player during this time of the year. Plus, Mark had no desire to admit why going into Mobile bothered him.

All he hoped for now was a slow day, but he didn't expect it. He wanted less drama than the last time he'd worked a med tent a few days earlier. Still, there had been some interesting points.

Dinner with Laura Jo Akins had been the highlight. He had at least found out she wasn't married. And she seemed to be anti-krewe for some reason. He had no doubt that she'd grown up on the social club festivities of a krewe, just like him. Why would she have such a negative view now? Or was her pessimistic attitude directed toward him? Did she know about the accident? His part in it?

Laura Jo Akins also appeared to be one of those women who knew her mind and stood her ground, but it also seemed there was a venerable spot to her, too. As if she hid something from the world. What was that all about?

Mark looked over the crowd again. At least she took his thoughts off worrying that he might see Mike at a parade. He looked forward to seeing her pixie face if they ever met again. People were creatures of habit and usually showed up in the same places to watch the parades. He wasn't sure why she interested him so, but she'd popped into his head a number of times over the past few days.

He had been at the med tent long enough to introduce himself to some of the other volunteers when he looked up to see none other than Laura Jo walking toward the tent. She caught sight of him about the same time. He didn't miss her moment of hesitation before she continued in his direction. He smiled and nodded at her. She returned his smile.

A few minutes later he was asked to help with a woman who was having an asthma attack in the unseasonably warm weather. It was some time later before he had a chance to speak to Laura Jo.

"I believe we might be caught in some Mardi Gras mystical mojo," he said, low enough that the others around them couldn't hear.

"I don't believe any sort of thing. I'm more of the dumb luck kind of person," she responded, as she continued to sort supplies.

He chuckled. "Didn't expect to see me again so soon, did you?"

She spun around, her hands going to her hips. "Did you plan this?"

"I did not," he said with complete innocence. "I was told when and where to be."

"I thought maybe with the Clayborn name…"

What did she have against the Clayborns? Did she know what he'd done? If she did, he couldn't blame her for not wanting to have anything to do with him. "Excuse me?"

"Nothing."

"Dr. Clayborn, we need you," one of the other volunteers called.

Mark had no choice but to go to work.

Half an hour later, the sound of a jazz band rolled down the street. Because the med tent was set up at the fire station, no one could park or stand in front of it. Mark and the others had an unobstructed view of the parade. Thankfully there was no one requiring help so they all stepped out toward the street curb to watch. Laura Jo seemed to appreciate the parade. She even swayed to the music of "Let the good times roll."

He wandered over to stand just behind her. "You enjoy a good parade as much as your daughter does, I see." Mark couldn't help but needle her. She reacted so prettily to it.

"Yes, I love a good parade. You make it sound like it should be a crime."

"And you make it sound like it's a crime that I noticed," he shot back.

"No crime. Just not used to someone taking that much notice."

"That's hard to believe. You mean there's no man who pays attention to you?"

"Getting a little personal, aren't you, Doctor?" She glanced back at him.

"No, just making conversation."

"Hey, Mom."

They both turned at the sound of Laura Jo's daughter's voice. She was with another woman about Laura Jo's age and there was a boy with them about the same height as the daughter.

Before her mother could respond the girl said to Mark, "I know you. You're that man who helped me the other day. Look, my hands are all better." She put out her hands palms up. "My knee still hurts a little." She lifted her denim-covered knee.

"And I know you." He smiled down at her. "But forgive me, I've forgotten your name."

"Allie."

He squatted down to her level. "I'm glad you're feeling better, Allie." Standing again, he glanced in the direction of the woman he didn't know. Laura Jo must have gotten the hint because she said, "This is Marsha Gilstrap. A friend of mine." She looked toward the boy. "And Jeremy, her son. I thought ya'll were going to watch the parade over on Washington."

"We wanted to come by and say hi to you," Allie said.

Laura Jo gave her daughter a hug then looked down at her with what Mark recognized as unbounded love. He liked it when he saw parents who really cared about their children. Her actions hadn't just been for show when her daughter had been hurt at the parade. She truly cared about her child. He recognized that love because his parents had had the same for him. That's why his father had insisted Mark not get involved with Mike's case after the accident. His father had feared what it might do to Mark's future. He been young enough and scared enough that he'd agreed, despite the guilt he'd felt over leaving the way he had. Now he didn't trust himself to get close enough to care about someone. If he did, he might fail them, just as he had Mike. He hadn't stood beside Mike, whom he'd loved like a brother, so why would he have what it took to stand by a wife and family?

A float coming by drew Allie's attention. Mark put a hand on her shoulder. "Come on. This is a great spot to watch a parade."

Allie looked at her mother in question. Laura Jo took a second before she gave an agreeable nod but he got the sense that she didn't want to.

Allie glanced at the boy. "Can Jeremy come, too?"

"Sure."

Jeremy's mother, in contrast to Laura Jo, was all smiles about the boy joining them.

"We'll just be right up here if you need us." Mark made an effort to give Laura Jo his most charming smile.

He nudged one of the volunteers out of the way so that the children had a front-row place to stand. A couple of times he had to remind them not to step out beyond the curve. Because they were standing in front of the fire station, there were no barriers in place. After a few minutes Laura Jo and her friend joined them.

"Thanks, we'll take these two off your hands," Laura Jo said, as if she was helping him out. What she was really doing was trying to get rid of him.

"Look at the dog. How funny." Allie squealed. The dog was wearing a vest and a hat. "I wish I had a dog to dress up. Then we could be in a parade."

Laura Jo placed her hand on top of Allie's shoulder. "Maybe one day, honey."

There was something in the wispy tone in the girl's voice that got to him. It reminded him of how he'd sounded the first time he'd asked if he could be in a dog parade. When he and his brother had participated in a parade it had been one of the greatest pleasures of his childhood. He could surely give that to Allie without becoming too involved in her and her mother's lives. "You could borrow my dog. Gus would be glad to let you dress him up," Mark offered.

"Could I, Mom?" Allie looked at Laura Jo as if her life depended on a positive answer.

"I don't know."

"I think Allie and Gus would make a great pair." He had no doubt Laura Jo hated to say no to something her daughter so obviously wanted to do. But why was he making it his job to see that Allie had a chance to be in a parade? Was it because Laura Jo was a hard-working mother who couldn't do this for her daughter and it was easy enough for him to do? It would be a great memory for Allie, just as it had been for him.

"Please, Mom."

"Fairhope has a parade on Sunday evening that I believe dogs are allowed in. Why don't you and Allie come and meet Gus that afternoon? You could bring some clothes for him and see how he likes them."

Laura Jo gave him a piercing look that said she wasn't pleased with the turn of events.

In a perverse way he liked the idea he was able to nettle her.

"Allie, I don't think we should take advantage of Dr. Clayborn's time."

"Please, call me Mark. And I don't mind." He really didn't. Since he'd been back in town he had kept to himself. It would be nice to spend the afternoon with someone. "I'm sure Gus will be glad to have the company. I've not been around much the past few days. Marsha, you and Jeremy are welcome, too."

"Thanks. It sounds like fun but I can't. Jeremy can if Laura Jo doesn't mind," Marsha said, smiling.

Laura Jo shot Marsha a look as if there would be more to say about this when they were alone.

"Mom, please," Allie pleaded. "Please."

"Won't your wife mind us barging in? Won't your children be dressing him up?"

"No wife. No children. So there's no reason you can't."

"Then I guess we could come by for a little while but I'm not making any promises about the parade." Laura Jo looked down at Allie.

"Great. I'll expect you about two. Here's my address." He pulled out a calling card, turned it over and, removing a pen from his pocket, wrote on it. "I'll have Gus all bathed and waiting on you."

Allie giggled. "Okay."

Mark looked at Laura Jo. "See you tomorrow."

She gave him a weak smile and he grinned. He was already looking forward to the afternoon.

Laura Jo wasn't sure how she'd managed to be coerced into agreeing to go to Mark's. Maybe it was because of the look of anticipation on Allie's face or the maternal guilt she felt whenever Allie asked to do something and she had to say no because she had to go to work or school. Now that she was in a position to give her child some fun in her life, she couldn't bring herself to say no. But going to Mark Clayborn's house had to be one for the record. She didn't really know the man. She'd admired him with a young girl's hero worship. But she knew little about the man he had become. He'd been nice enough so far but she hadn't always been the best judge of character.

She'd searched for a sound reason why they couldn't do it. Marsha certainly hadn't been any help. It was as if she had pushed her into going. For once Laura Jo wished she had to work on Sunday. But no such luck.

Allie was up earlier than usual in her excitement over the possibility of being in the dog parade. Jeremy had been almost as bad, Marsha said, when he ran to meet them at the car later that day.

"So are you looking forward to an afternoon with the handsome, debonair and rich Dr. Mark Clayborn?" Marsha asked with a grin.

They'd had a lively and heated discussion over a cup of coffee late the night before about Mark. Marsha seemed to think she should develop him as an ally in funding the single mothers' house. Laura Jo wasn't so sure. That was a road she'd promised herself she'd never go down again. She wasn't ever going to ask her parents or her society friends for anything ever again. That certainly included Mark Clayborn.

After today she didn't plan to see him again. This afternoon was about Allie and seeing a smile on her face. That only. Allie had been begging for a dog for the past year but they didn't have a lifestyle that was good for taking care of a dog.

Laura Jo pulled her aging compact car off the winding, tree-shaded road into the well-groomed, riverbed-pebbled drive of the address she'd been given. The crunch made a familiar sound. Her own family's place just a few miles down the road had the same type of drive, or at least it had the last time she'd been there.

The foliage of the large trees with moss hanging from them gave the area a cozy feel. Soon she entered an open space where a sweeping, single-story beach house sat with a wide expanse of yard between it and the bay beyond.

"Do you see Gus?" Allie strained at her seat belt as she peered out the window.

"Now, honey, I don't want you to get your hopes up too

high. Gus may not like being dressed up." Laura Jo didn't want to say "or you." Some owners thought their dogs loved everyone when they often didn't.

"He'll like it, I know he will."

"I think he will, too," Jeremy said from the backseat.

Laura Jo looked at him in the rearview mirror and smiled. "We'll see."

She pulled to a stop behind a navy blue high-end European car. To Mark's credit, it wasn't a sports car but it was finer than Laura Jo had ever ridden in, even when she'd still been living with her parents.

Her door had hardly opened before Allie ran toward a basset hound, whose ears dragged along the ground. Not far behind him strolled Mark. For a second her breath caught. He had all the markers of an eye-catching man. Tall, blond wavy hair and an air about him that said he could take care of himself and anyone else he cared about. It was a dazzling combination.

She'd been asked out a number of times by one of the men at the hospital, but she'd never had a man both irritate her and draw her to him at the same time. That was exactly what Mark Clayborn did.

He looked down with a smile at Allie, with her arms wrapped around Gus, and Jeremy, patting him, then at Laura Jo.

Her middle fluttered. If it wasn't for all the baggage she carried, her inability to trust her judgment of men, maybe she might be interested. She'd let Allie have her day and make a concerted effort not to see Mark again.

"Hey. Did you have any trouble finding it?"

"No trouble. I knew which one it was when you told me you lived in Fairhope."

"Really?"

"I remember passing it when I was a kid." She'd been aware all her life where the Clayborn summer home was located.

He glanced back to where the children played with the dog. "I think they're hitting it off."

Laura Jo couldn't help but agree.

"Allie, did you bring some clothes for Gus? I got a few things just in case you didn't," Mark said, strolling toward the kids and dog.

"They're in the car."

"I'll get them, honey," Laura Jo called, as the kids headed toward the large open yard between the house and bay. "Don't go near the water and stay where I can see you."

She walked to the car and Mark followed her. "You're a good mother."

Laura Jo glanced at him. "I try to be."

"So when did Allie's father leave?"

Laura Jo opened the passenger door then looked at him. "When I was three months pregnant."

Mark whistled. "That explains some of your standoffishness."

She pulled a large brown sack out of the car and closed the door with more force than necessary. "I'm not."

"Yeah, you are. For some reason, you don't want to like me, even when you do."

She was afraid he might be right. Thankfully, squealing in the front yard drew their attention to the two children running around as a dog almost as wide as he was tall chased them.

Mark checked his watch and called, "Allie and Jeremy, we need to get started on what Gus will wear because the parade starts in a couple of hours."

The kids ran toward them and Gus followed.

"Why don't we go around to the deck where it's cooler? We can dress Gus there," Mark said to the kids.

Mark led the way with the kids and Gus circled them. Laura Jo hung back behind them. Mark was good with children. Why didn't he have a wife and kids of his own? She imagined she was the only one of many who didn't fall at his charming feet.

The deck was amazing. It was open at one end. Chairs and a lounge group were arranged into comfortable conversation areas. At the other end was an arbor with a brown vine that must be wisteria on it. Laura Jo could only envision what it would look like in the spring and summer, with its green leaves creating a roof of protection from the sun. She'd love to sit in a comfortable chair under it but that wasn't going to happen.

"Allie, why don't you and Jeremy pull the things you brought out of the bag while I go get what I bought? Then you can decide how to dress Gus."

Allie took the bag from Laura Jo. With the children busy pulling feather boas, old hair bows, purple, green and gold ribbon from the bag, Laura Jo took a seat on the end of a lounge chair and watched.

Mark quickly returned with an armload of stuff.

"I thought you only got a few things," Laura Jo said.

He grinned. Her heart skipped a beat.

"I might have gotten a little carried away." He looked directly at her. "I do that occasionally."

For some reason, she had the impression he might be talking about sex. She hadn't had a thought like that in forever. Not since Phil had left. He'd made it clear that she hadn't been wanted and neither had their child.

Mark added his armload to the growing pile on the deck.

"Okay, Allie, I want you and Jeremy to pick out a winning combination. They give prizes for the funniest dog, best dressed, most spirited and some more I don't remember. Let's try to win a prize," Mark said, as he joined them on the planks of the wooden deck and held Gus. "I'll hold him while you dress him."

Laura Jo scooted back in the lounge to watch. It was a February day but the sun was shining. It wasn't long until her eyes closed.

She didn't know how long she'd been out before Mark's voice above her said, "You'd better be careful or you'll get burned. Even the winter sun in the south can get you."

"Thanks. I'm well aware of that. Remember, I've lived here all my life."

"That's right, a Herron."

"Who is a Herron, Mommy?"

"They're a family I used to know."

Mark's brows rose.

"Now, let me see what ya'll have done to Gus while I was napping," Laura Jo said quickly, before he could ask any more questions in front of Allie.

Mark didn't question further, seeing that Laura Jo didn't want to talk about her family in front of Allie. But he would be asking later. Allie didn't even know who her grandparents were? There was a deep, dark secret there that he was very interested in finding out about. Why hadn't he recognized Laura Jo? Probably because she had been too young to take his notice. His mouth drew into a line. More likely, he had been so focused on his world he hadn't looked outside it.

"My, doesn't Gus look, uh…festive?"

Mark couldn't help but grin at Laura Jo's description. Festive was a good word for it, along with silly. His dog wore a purple, gold and green feather boa wrapped around his neck. A dog vest of the same colors was on his body, bands on his ankles and a bow on the end of his tail. This being the one thing Allie had insisted he needed. Mark was amazed the Gus was as agreeable as he was about that.

Allie pronounced him "Perfect."

"I think we should be going if we want to make the start time."

"Start time?" Laura Jo asked.

"For the Mystic Mutts parade."

"I don't think—"

"We can't miss it. Isn't that right, Allie and Jeremy?"

"Right," both children said in unison.

Great. Now she was being ganged up on.

"Come on, Mommy. We have to take Gus," Allie pleaded.

Laura Jo glared at Mark. "I guess I don't have much of a choice."

Allie and Jeremy danced around her. "Yay."

"Let me get Gus's leash and we'll be all set." Mark went inside and returned with a lead.

As they rounded the house and headed toward the cars he looked at Laura Jo's. It was too small for all of them.

"I don't think we can all get in my car," Laura Jo said from beside him.

Mark stopped and looked at hers again. "I guess I should drive."

"You don't sound like you really want to do that. We could take two cars but I'm sure parking will be tight."

Mark's lips drew into a tight line. The thought of being responsible for Laura Jo and the kids gave him a sick feeling. Children had never ridden in his car. Since the accident he'd made it a practice not to drive with others in the car if he could help it. Often he hired a driver when he went out on a date. Unable to come up with another plan, he said,

"Then we'll go in my car. Please make sure the children are securely buckled in."

Laura Jo gave him an odd look before she secured Allie and Jeremy in the backseat. Gus found a spot between them and Allie placed an arm around him. Laura Jo joined him in the front. Mark looked back to check if the children were buckled in.

"Is there a problem?" Laura Jo asked.

If he kept this up he would make them all think he was crazy. He eased his grip on the steering wheel and let the blood flow back into his knuckles. "No. I was just double-checking they were okay."

Laura Jo shook her head as she ran a hand across the leather of the seat. "Worried about having kids in your fancy car?"

"No."

"Nice," she murmured.

"Like my car?"

"Yes," she said, more primly than the situation warranted, as she placed her hand in her lap.

He grinned. At least this subject took his mind off having a carload of passengers. "It's okay to say what you think."

"I wouldn't think it's very practical. The cost of a car like this could help a lot of people in need."

"I help people in need all the time. I also give to charities so I don't feel guilty about owning this car." Taking a fortify breath, he started it and pulled away from the house. At the end of the drive, he turned onto the road leading into town.

"I'm just not impressed by fancy cars and houses. People with those think they can tell you what to do, how you need to live. Even look down on others."

He glanced at her. "That's an interesting statement. Care to give me some background?"

"No, not really."

"Well, you just insulted me and my family and yours as well, and you won't even do me the courtesy of telling me why?"

"I'm sorry I insulted you. Sometimes my mouth gets ahead of my brain." She looked out the side window.

Yes, he was definitely going to find out what gave her such a sour view of people with money. He'd always prided himself on the amount he gave to charities. He had nothing to be ashamed of where that was concerned. Standing beside someone he loved when there was a disaster was where he failed.

A few minutes later he pulled the car into a tight space a couple of blocks from the parade route. It was the only spot he could find after circling the area. How had he gotten through the short drive without breaking into a sweat? Amazingly, talking to Laura Jo had made him forget his anxiety over driving. "This is the best I can do. We'll have to walk some."

Laura Jo saw to getting the children out. He leashed Gus and then gave him over to Allie. The girl beamed.

"I checked the paper this morning and the start of the parade is at the corner of Section and Third Street."

They weaved their way through the already growing crowd. As the number of people increased, Mark took Gus's leash from Allie and made sure that space was made for the dog, children and Laura Jo. A few times he touched her waist to direct her through a gap in the crowd. At the first occurrence she stiffened and glanced back at him. When he did it again she seemed to take it in her stride.

Mark was pleased when his little party arrived at the starting line without a loss of personnel. He looked at Laura Jo. "Why don't you wait here with the kids while I check in?"

"We'll be right over here near the brick wall." She took Gus's lead and led Allie and Jeremy to the spot she'd indicated.

"I'll be right back."

"You hope." She smiled.

It was the first genuine one he'd seen her give. It caught him off guard. It took him a second to respond. "Yeah."

Fifteen minutes later he had Gus, Allie and Jeremy signed in for the parade. He found Laura Jo and the kids waiting right where she'd said they would be. She had her head down, listening to something that Jeremy was saying. The angle of her head indicated she was keeping an eye on her daughter at the same time. Once again he was impressed by her mothering skills. The women he'd gone out with had never shown any interest in being mothers. He'd always thought he'd like to be a father, but he wouldn't let that happen. What if he ran out on them, like he had Mike, when the going got tough? He couldn't take that chance.

There was nothing flashy or pretentious about Laura Jo. More like what you saw was what you got. He'd grown up within the finely drawn lines of what was expected by the tight-knit Mobile society. He hadn't met many women who'd seemed to live life on their own terms. Even in California the women he'd dated had always worn a false front, literally and physically.

Laura Jo's face was devoid of makeup and she wore a simple blouse and jeans with flats. She reminded him of a girl just out of high school. That was until she opened her mouth, then she left no doubt she was a grown woman who could defend herself and her child. Nothing about her indicated she had been raised in one of local society's finest families.

Allie said something and Laura Jo turned her head. Both

mother and child had similar coloring. Pretty in an early-spring-leaves-unfolding sort of way. Easy on the eye. Why would any man leave the two of them?

If he ever had a chance to have something as good in his life as they were, he'd hold on to them and never let them out of his sight. He sighed. What he saw between Laura Jo and Allie wasn't meant for him. It wasn't his to have. He'd taken that chance from Mike and he had no right to have it himself. What they had he couldn't be trusted with.

"Hey, there's Dr. Clayborn," Allie called.

Mark grinned as he joined them. He ruffled Allie's hair. "That's Mark to you. Dr. Clayborn sounds like a mouthful for such a little girl."

Allie drew herself up straight. "I'm a big girl."

Mark went down on one knee, bringing himself to eye level with Allie. "I apologize. Yes, you are a big girl. Big enough to walk with Gus in the parade?"

"Really, you're going to let me take Gus in the parade?"

"Yes, and Jeremy, too. But I have to come along with you."

She turned to Laura Jo. "Mommy, I'm going to get to be in the parade."

"I heard, honey, but I don't know."

"I'll be right there with them the entire time." Mark reassured Laura Jo.

The look of hesitation on her face gave him the idea that she didn't often trust Allie's care to anyone but her friend Marsha.

He reached for Gus's leash and she handed it to him. The nylon was warm from her clasp. "She'll be perfectly safe. We'll meet you and Jeremy at the car when it's over. The parade route isn't long."

"I guess it'll be okay." She looked at Allie. "You and Jeremy do just what Mark tells you to do." Laura Jo pinned

Mark with a look. "And you turn up with my daughter and Jeremy at the end of the parade."

"Yes, ma'am." He gave her a smile and a little salute. "I'll take good care of them, I promise. Let's go, kids. We need to get in line."

Laura Jo watched as Mark took her daughter's much smaller hand in his larger one and Jeremy's in his other one. Gus walked at Allie's heels as they were swallowed up by the crowd.

What was it about Mark that made her trust him with the most precious person in her life? She'd never allowed anyone but Marsha that privilege. Maybe it was the way he'd care for Allie's knee, or his devotion to the grandfather and later the girl he'd cared for. Somehow Mark had convinced her in a few short meetings that he could be trusted. Now that she was a mother she better understood how her parents had felt when she had insisted on going off with someone they hadn't trusted.

Alone, she made her way through the crowd to the curb of a street about halfway along the parade route. Taking a seat on the curb, she waited until the parade approached. For this parade there would be no bands involved. All the music would come from music boxes pulled in carts by children. The floats would be decorated wagons and dogs of all shapes and sizes.

Twenty minutes later the first of the parade members came into view. Not far behind them were Allie, Jeremy and Mark. Laura Jo stood as they approached. She'd never seen a larger smile on Allie's face. Mark and Jeremy were grinning also. Gus was lumbering behind them, looking bored but festive. Allie held his leash proudly.

She screamed and waved as they came by. Allie and Jeremy waved enthusiastically back at her. Mark acknowledged her also. As they came closer he stepped over to Laura Jo and said, "The kids are having a blast."

Laura Jo smiled.

An hour later Laura Jo stood waiting outside Mark's car. Anxiousness was building with every minute that passed. Something had to have gone wrong. Mark and the children should have been there by now. Had something happened to one of the kids? She shouldn't have let them out of her sight. Was this how her parents had felt when she'd run off with Phil?

He had been a master of manipulation. Before they'd got married he'd made her believe he had a good job and he would take care of her. "Don't worry about what your parents think, I'll take care of you," he would say. The worst thing was that he'd made her believe he'd loved her.

Had she let Mark do the same thing? Persuade her to let the kids be in the parade. Had she made a poor character judgment call again? This time with her daughter? Her palms dampened. She'd promised herself to be careful. Now look what was happening. She headed in the direction of where the parade had ended, and soon recognized Mark's tall figure coming in her way. He pulled a wagon on which Gus, Allie and Jeremy rode. With relief filling her chest, she ran toward them.

Mark was red-faced. Jeremy wore a smile. Allie looked pleased with herself as she held Gus's head in her lap. The dog was wearing a crown.

"Where have ya'll been? I was getting worried." Laura Jo stopped beside them.

"Mommy, we won first place for the slowest dog in the parade." Allie beamed.

Laura Jo gave her a hug. "That's wonderful, honey."

"Sorry we made you worry. I should have given you my

cell number. Gus also got slower after the parade. I carried him halfway here until I saw a kid with a wagon. I had to give him fifty dollars for it so I could haul Gus back."

At the sound of disgust in Mark's voice Laura Jo couldn't help but laugh. His look of complete exasperation and her sense of relief made the situation even more humorous.

"I'm glad someone thinks it's funny." Mark chuckled.

Laura Jo had to admit he was a good sport and he'd certainly made her daughter happy. Every time she tried to stop laughing she'd think of Mark begging a boy for his wagon and she'd burst out in laughter again. It had been a long time since she'd laughed hard enough to bring tears to her eyes.

"If you think you can stop laughing at me for a few minutes, we can load up this freeloader…" he gave the dog a revolted look "…and get him home."

"Had a workout, did you?" Laura Jo asked, trying to suppress the giggles that kept bubbling up.

"Yeah. No good deed goes unpunished."

"Whose idea was it to be in the parade?"

"Okay, it was mine."

Laura Jo burst into another round of snickers.

"Mommy, are you all right?" Allie looked at her in wonder.

"Oh, honey. I'm fine. I'm just glad you had a good time." She looked over the top of her head and grinned at Mark. Had it really been that long since Allie had seen her laugh?

Mark scooped Gus up in his arms. "If you'll get the door, I'll get this prima donna in the car."

Laura Jo's snort escaped as she opened the door. Allie climbed in next to the dog then Jeremy clambered in. Laura Jo saw they were buckled in. Mark put the wagon in the trunk and slapped the lid down harder than necessary.

"So you plan on being in another parade anytime soon?" she asked him, as she took her place in the front seat.

Mark sneered at her as he started the car. Laura Jo's smile grew. Before they left the parking spot, he twisted to study the children. As he turned the first corner, she looked back to find both of the children asleep. Most of the people at their end of the parade had left already, which made it easy for him to maneuver out of town and back to his home.

As they drove down the drive, Laura Jo said, "Thanks for going to so much trouble for Allie. She had the time of her life."

"You're welcome. Despite Gus being in slow motion, I enjoyed it. I've been a part of a number of parades in my time but never one like today's."

Laura Jo grinned. Something she seemed to have been doing more of lately. "Well, I appreciate it. I'll get the kids loaded up and we'll get out of your hair."

"Mommy, I'm hungry."

Laura Jo sighed and looked back at her daughter. "I thought you were asleep."

"I bet they are hungry. They've had a busy day. I've got some hot dogs I could put on the grill," Mark suggested, as he pulled the car to a stop.

"You've already done enough. I think we had better go." Laura Jo didn't want to like him any more than she already did, and she was afraid she might if she stayed around Mark much longer. The picture of him pulling the dog and Allie and Jeremy put a warm spot in her heart. He wasn't the self-centered man she'd believed he might be.

"Can't I play with Gus a little while longer?" Allie pleaded.

"Face it, you're not going to win this one." Mark grinned.

"You're sure about this?" Laura Jo realized she'd lost again.

"Yeah. It'll be nice to have company for a meal."

"Okay," she said to Mark, then turned and looked at Allie. "We'll stay for a little while longer but when I say it's time to go, we go without any argument, understood?"

"Yes, ma'am," Allie said, and Jeremy, who had awoken, nodded in agreement.

Laura Jo opened the door for Allie while Mark did the same for Jeremy and Gus.

"If you both give your mom and me just a few minutes, we'll have the hot dogs ready. Why don't you guys watch the parade on TV? Look for us."

"Do you think they'll have it running already?" Laura Jo asked.

"They should. When I told friends on the West Coast that we had Mardi Gras parades on TV they were amazed." Mark turned to the kids again. "I'll turn the TV on and we'll give it a look."

They all followed Mark through the front door of the house. Laura Jo studied the interior. The foyer had an easy, casual feel to it but every piece of furniture was placed so that it reminded her of a home decorating magazine. From the entrance, it opened into a large space with an exterior glass wall that gave the room a one-hundred-and-eighty-degree view of the deck area and the bay. Full ceiling-to-floor green-checked curtains were pushed back to either side of the windowed area. The late-afternoon sunlight streamed into the room, giving it an inviting glow.

Overstuffed cream-colored couches faced each other. A table with a chess set on it sat to one side of the room. Opposite it there was a large-screen TV built into the wall, with bookshelves surrounding it. Comfortable-looking armchairs were placed throughout the room. The house gave her the feeling that a family had lived and loved here.

"What a wonderful room," Laura Jo whispered.

"Thanks. It's my favorite space."

She turned, startled, to find Mark standing close. She had been so caught up in the room she hadn't noticed him approach.

"I'll turn the TV on for the kids then get started on those dogs. You don't need to help. You're welcome to stay with them."

"No, I said I would help and I will. After all, I haven't carried a dog around town all afternoon," she said with a grin.

"You're not going to let that go, are you?" He gave her a pained look.

She shook her head. "The visual is just too good to let go of."

He picked up a remote and pushed a button. The TV came on. The kids had already found themselves a place on a sofa. After a few changes of channels he stopped. "I do believe this is ours."

"You guys stay right here. Don't go outside," Laura Jo said.

Mark headed toward the open kitchen Laura Jo could see off to the left. She followed. It was a modern and up-to-date space that was almost as large as her entire apartment. She ran a hand across the granite of the large counter in the middle of the room with a sigh of pleasure. "I wish I had a place like this to cook. I bet you could make a perfect king cake on this top," she murmured, more to herself than Mark.

"You're welcome to come over anytime and use it. I get nowhere near the use out of it that I should." Mark put his head in the refrigerator and came out with a package of hot dogs.

"Thanks for the offer. But I don't really have time to do a lot of cooking." She wished she did have. Even if she did, she wouldn't be coming here to do it.

"That's not what Allie led me to believe." He picked through a drawer and found some tongs.

"I'd like to but I don't think we'll be getting that friendly."

He came to stand across the counter from her. "Why not? You might find you like me if you'd give me a chance."

"We're from two different worlds now and I don't see us going any further than we did today."

"What do you mean by two different worlds? Our parents have been acquaintances for years. I don't see that we are that different."

Had she hurt his feelings? No, she couldn't imagine that what she thought or felt mattered that much to him. But he had been nice to Allie and he deserved the truth. "I have nothing to do with that society stuff anymore."

"I had no idea you were such a snob, or is it narrow-mindedness?"

"I'm not a snob and it has nothing to do with being narrow-minded and everything to do with knowing who the Clayborn family is and what they represent. I want no part of that world again."

"Once again, I think I have been insulted. Do you know me or my family well enough to have that opinion? What have we done to you?" His tone had roughened with each sentence. "I think I deserve to hear you expound on that statement."

"Well, you're going to be disappointed."

Mark's brows came together over his nose.

"Instead, why don't you tell me what has you living on this side of the bay when I know the other side is thought to be the correct one?"

He placed some hot dog buns on the counter. "I needed a place to stay when I moved back and no one was staying in the summer house. It's no big mystery."

"That's right. I remember hearing talk that you were in a bad accident and left town afterwards."

He winced. "Yeah, I left to do my fellowship in California."

"Well, do tell. I am surprised. I would have never thought a Clayborn would live anywhere but Mobile."

"And for your information, my brother and I both moved away. I came back because my father had a stroke and needs someone close."

"I'm sorry to hear about your father." And she was. It was tough to see someone suffer that way. She remembered Mr. Clayborn, Sr. being a larger-than-life man whom everyone noticed when he came into the room. Much like Mark. She admired Mark for giving up his life in California to return home to care for his father. In comparison, she lived in the same town and didn't even speak to her parents.

"He had a bad stroke but he is recovering. Working every day is over for him but at least he's alive."

"Mommy," Allie called. "I'm hungry."

Mark shrugged. "I guess we'd better save this conversation for later. If you really want to help, why don't you get the plates and things together while I get these hot dogs on the grill? The plates are in that cabinet—" he pointed to one to the right of the stove "—and the silverware is in that drawer." He indicated the one right in front of her. "Condiments in the refrigerator. What few there are." He went out the side door of the kitchen without another word.

What Mark didn't realize was that she was through having any type of conversation about her past. Why she'd told him so much she had no idea.

CHAPTER THREE

MARK STARTED THE gas grill and adjusted the flame, before placing the hot dogs on the wire rack above it. He glanced back into the house through the window of the door. He could just see Laura Jo moving around.

She had a real chip on her shoulder about the world in which they had been raised. For a moment there he'd thought she might open up and tell him why but then she'd shut down. Why did it matter to him anyway?

Maybe it was because for some reason he liked the brash, independent and absolutely beautiful woman, especially when she laughed. He couldn't get enough of that uninhibited embracing of life. Would she act that way in bed?

Whoa, that was not where he was headed. He didn't really know her and what he did know about her was that she'd sooner sink her teeth into him than allow him to kiss her.

Just what was going on between her and her family? He knew of the Herrons. They were good people but Laura Jo had certainly had a falling out with them. She hadn't even told Allie she had grandparents living in town. Who did that? It just didn't make sense.

He'd enjoyed his afternoon with the children. It had been tough to drive with them in the car but he'd done it. He'd had a taste of what it would be like to have a child in his life and he rather liked it. In fact, he liked it too much.

Laura Jo made another trip by the door. He jerked around when she called from the doorway, "Hey, do you need a platter for those?"

"Yeah." Why did he feel like he'd just been caught in someone else's business? What was going on between her and her family wasn't his problem.

"Where do I find it? I'll bring it to you."

She looked so appealing, framed by the door with the afternoon sun highlighting one side of her face. The urge to kiss her almost overwhelmed him. He'd like to prove that they weren't different in the areas that mattered. He had to say something to get rid of her until he regained his equilibrium. "Cabinet below the plates."

Laura Jo disappeared into the house again. A few minutes later she came out and stood beside him. Her head reached his shoulders. She was close enough that he smelled a hint of her floral shampoo but not near enough that they touched. He was aware of the fact that all he had to do was take a half step and her body would be next to his.

"You might want to turn those. They look like they're burning."

Great. He had been so focussed on her that he wasn't thinking about what he was doing. "So now you're going to come out here and start telling me how to cook my hot dogs. Do you like to be bossed?"

She took a step back. Her eyes turned serious. "No. I don't. I'm sorry." She moved to leave.

He caught her wrist. "Hey, I was just kidding. They're just hot dogs."

Laura Jo pulled her arm out of his grip. "I know. But I need to get us some drinks. I saw the glasses when I was looking for a bowl." With that she was gone.

This was a woman better left alone. She had more hang-ups than he did and, heaven knew, he had plenty.

Twenty minutes later, Allie and Jeremy were picnicking, as they called it, in front of the TV so they could watch another parade. Mark had persuaded Laura Jo to join him on the deck. This was what he remembered it being like when he'd been a kid. He liked having people around. Being part of a family. Could he ever have that again?

He and Laura Jo ate in silence for a while, but not a comfortable one. Mark worked to come up with a subject they could discuss. Finally, he asked, "So you remembered me from years ago, so why don't I remember you?"

She grinned. "Oh, I don't know. Maybe because the only person you saw was Ann Maria Clark."

He had the good grace to turn red. "Yeah, we were a hot item back then."

"That you were. There was no reason you'd see a simple lady-in-waiting."

His gaze met hers. Something about her tone made him think she might have liked him to notice her. "You were in her court?"

She nodded. "I was."

"I can't believe it."

"Well, it's true."

"We were that close all those years ago and it took a skinned knee at a parade for us to get to know each other."

She fingered the hot dog. "Life can be strange like that."

"That it can."

"I thought you two would get married," Laura Jo said, more as a statement of fact than someone fishing for information.

"That had been the plan but things changed."

"That happens. Especially where people are concerned."

She sounded as if she was speaking about herself more than him.

It was time to change the subject. "Have you and Jeremy's mom been friends for a long time?"

"No. We only met a few years ago."

Well, at least he was getting more than a one-word answer.

"She works at the hospital?"

Laura Jo gave him a speculative look. "Are you interested in her?"

"I'm just trying to make conversation. Maybe learn a little more about you."

Laura Jo placed her half-eaten hot dog on the plate in front of her. She looked at him from across the table for a second before saying, "We met at a group for mothers without partners. Her husband had died. We became friends, at first because we needed each other, then we found we liked each other."

"So she was there when you needed someone." He knew well what it was like to be alone and need someone to talk to. There had been no one when he'd arrived in LA. He had been lonely then and, come to think of it, he'd been lonely in Mobile at least up until the last week.

"Your parents weren't around?"

"No. Hers had died. Mine...well, that's another story. That's why Marsha and I are trying to open a house for mothers who are on their own."

"So how's that going?"

"The city has agreed to sell us a house at a good price that would be perfect but we're running out of time to raise the money."

"Maybe I could be of some help. Atone for my car."

"A check for three hundred thousand would be great."

She grinned at him as if she was making a joke but he could see hope in her eyes.

He winced. "That would be my car and at least one or two more."

"I've seen you ride a bike." She grinned.

He threw back his head and laughed. "You'd make me resort to that to get your house?'

"I'd do almost anything. This chance might not come again."

She took a swallow of her drink as if her mouth had suddenly gone dry.

Why did that thought of her in bed, beneath him, pop into his head? He raised a brow.

Her eyes widened. A stricken look covered her face. "You know what I mean."

"I have an idea. We could go to the Krewe of Orion dance together. See some of our old friends. There should be plenty of people there willing to donate. All you'd have to do is get one to agree to support you and then the others would line up to help out."

"I don't think so."

"To going with me or that others would help?"

"To going."

"Do you mind if I ask why?" He caught her gaze.

"That's not my idea of a good time anymore."

What had brought on that remark? He pushed his plate away. "Well, this is a first. A woman who doesn't want to get dressed up and go to a party."

"Not all women like that sort of stuff."

"It's just one night. Attending with me isn't like going to the gallows." He chuckled. "I promise."

"It's still no, thank you." She pushed half of her leftover hot dog bun across the plate.

"Well, I guess you have other plans for the way you're

going to get the money for the house. I'm sorry, I need my car. However, I'll make a donation to the cause."

As if she was all of a sudden concerned about sounding rude, she said, "I do appreciate you trying to help. I'll take you up on that." She stood with plate in hand. "I guess I better get the kids home to bed. They have school tomorrow."

Mark also gathered his plate and joined her as she walked into the house. They found Allie and Jeremy on the couch, Gus snoring between them.

"I'll write that check and help you get them loaded," Mark said as he took her plate and walked into the kitchen. While there he wrote a check. When he returned, Laura Jo already had Allie in her arms. He scooped Jeremy up and followed her out of the house. They worked together to get each child in and secured.

Digging in his front pocket, he pulled out the check and handed it to Laura Jo.

Laura Jo read it. Her eyes widened. She looked at him. "Thank you. This is very generous."

"You're welcome."

"Also thanks for giving Allie today. I don't have much of a chance to do things like this for her."

"I didn't just do it for Allie." They walked around to the driver's door and Laura Jo opened it.

"I know Jeremy also had a good time."

"What about you?"

"Me?"

"Yeah. I was hoping you had a nice day, too."

"I did."

She acted as if it was a foreign idea that he might be interested in her having a good time. "Good. Maybe we could do it again sometime. Just you and me."

"I've already told you. We have nothing in common."

"Nonsense. We have a lot in common. Our childhoods,

medicine, parades and laughter. That's more than most people have." When she'd been teasing him about Gus there had been an easiness between them. He wanted to see if she was putting up the front he believed she was. To make her act on her attraction to him. He was tired of being dismissed by her. "I bet if you tried, you could find something you like about me. Maybe this could help."

He wrapped an arm around her waist and pulled her to him. She only had time to gasp before his lips found hers. She didn't react at first, which gave him time to taste her lips. Soft, warm and slightly parted. Then for the briefest of seconds she returned his kiss. His heart thumped against his ribs at the possibilities before her hands spread wide against his chest. She shoved him away, hard.

His hands fell to his sides.

"You had no right to do that," she hissed.

"I can't say that I'm sorry."

She slid behind the steering wheel and before she could close the door he said, "Goodnight, Laura Jo."

"It's more like goodbye." She slammed the door.

Not a chance. Mark watched her taillights disappear up his drive. They'd be seeing each other again if he had anything to say about it. She was the first woman he'd met who had him thinking about the possibilities of tomorrow, even when he shouldn't.

It intrigued him that she put up such a fight not to have anything to do with him. That was except for the moments she'd melted in his arms. Could he get her to linger there long enough to forget whatever stood between them? Long enough to make her appreciate something they might both enjoy?

Laura Jo couldn't remember the last time a man had kissed her, but it sure hadn't been anything near as powerful as the brief one Mark had just given her. Her hands shook on the steering wheel. Why had he done it? Hadn't she made it clear to him that she didn't want to become involved with him? Had she been giving off a different signal?

It didn't matter why. It couldn't, wouldn't happen again. There couldn't be anything real between them anyway. When she did open up again to a man she would know him well. She wanted someone settled, who wouldn't leave town at any moment. Someone who cared nothing for being involved in Mobile society. From what she knew about Mark so far, he had none of those qualities.

The lights of the cars flickered across the water as she traveled over the low bay causeway back to Mobile.

Thinking about and fretting over Mark was a waste of time. Laura Jo fingered the check he had given her. It was literally a raindrop in a pond to what she needed. She had to find some way to raise the money needed to buy the house. There was also Allie to see about and her job to keep. Mark Clayborn hadn't been hers years ago and he wasn't hers now.

Mark, she'd already learned, was a man with a strong sense of who he was. If she let him into her life he might try to control it, like her father and Phil had. She needed a partner, a father for Allie, someone sturdy and dependable. Until that happened it was her job to make decisions about her life and Allie's. She would never again depend on a man or let him dictate to her.

Marsha was there to greet her when she pulled into the parking area of the apartment complex. She had to have been watching for them. Knowing Marsha, she'd want details of the afternoon and evening. When Laura Jo had called her earlier to inform her that they would be staying a little longer at Mark's for supper, her speculative tone had made Laura Jo feel like she needed to justify her decision.

She'd told Marsha, "Don't get any ideas. There's nothing going on here."

"Okay, if you say so." Marsha hadn't sounded convinced before she'd hung up.

Allie and Jeremy woke when she parked. They got out of the car, talking a mile a minute about the parade and Gus. Marsha grinned over their heads at Laura Jo. "Come in and tell me all about your visit to Dr. Clayborn's," Marsha said, as if to the children but Laura Jo had no doubt she meant her.

"There's not much to tell and the kids have school tomorrow." Laura Jo locked her car.

"I know they have school tomorrow but you can come in for a few minutes."

Laura Jo straightened. Marsha wouldn't let it go until she'd heard every detail but Laura Jo wouldn't be telling her about the kiss. The one that had shaken something awake in her. It wouldn't happen again, even if there was an occasion, which there wouldn't be. She doubted that her path and Mark's would cross again. They didn't even live on the same side of the bay.

Allie and Jeremy ran ahead on the way to Marsha's apartment. She and Marsha followed more slowly.

A few minutes later, Marsha set a glass of iced tea in front of Laura Jo and said, "Okay, spill."

"Mark let the kids dress up Gus, his dog."

"So you're on a first-name basis with the good doc now?"

Laura Jo rolled her eyes. It was starting. "He asked me to call him Mark and it seemed foolish not to."

Marsha nodded in a thoughtful way, as if she didn't believe her friend's reasoning. "So what else did you do?"

"We went to the parade. Mark walked with the kids while I watched." She chuckled.

"What's that laugh for?"

"I was just thinking of the look on Mark's face when he showed up pulling a wagon with the kids and the dog in it he'd bought off a boy."

Marsha gave her a long look. "That sounds interesting."

"It was." Laura Jo launched into the story, her smile growing as she told it.

She ended up laughing and Marsha joined her.

"So you went back to his place?"

"I wish you'd stop saying 'so' like that and acting as if it was a date. The only reason I agreed to go was because Allie wanted to dress up the dog and be in the parade so badly."

"So..."

Laura Jo glared at her.

"You didn't enjoy yourself at all?" Marsha continued without paying Laura Jo any attention.

"I don't even like the guy."

"This is the most you've had to do with a man since I've known you. I think you might be a little more interested in him than you want to admit."

"I think you're wrong." Laura Jo was going to see to it that it was the truth. "There's one more thing and I probably shouldn't tell you this, but he did ask me to the krewe dance."

"And you said no." Marsha said the words as a statement of a fact.

"I did. For more than one reason."

Marsha turned serious. "We could use his contacts."

"I've already told you that I'm not going to do that. What if I saw my parents and they found out I was there, asking for money. I couldn't face them like that."

"Even at the cost of losing the house? Laura Jo, you've

been gone so long I can't imagine that your parents would see it as crawling back."

"You don't know my father. It would be his chance to tell me 'I told you so.' I lived though that once. Not again."

Marsha didn't know that Laura Jo hadn't spoken to her parents since before Allie's birth.

"So I guess we'll put all our hope in that grant coming through."

Laura Jo took a sip of her tea then said, "Yes, that and a moneybags willing to help us out."

"You've got a moneybag in Mark Clayborn."

"Oh, I forgot to show you this." Laura Jo pulled the check Mark had given her out of her pocket."

Marsha whistled. "Very generous. He must really like you."

"No. It was more like I made him feel guilty."

"Whatever you did, at least this will help. We just need to get others to be so kind."

"Now I'm not only indebted to him for giving Allie a wonderful afternoon but for helping with the shelter."

"You don't like that, do you, Ms. I-Can-Do-It-Myself?"

"No, I don't. We have nothing in common. He and I don't want the same things out of life anymore."

"Oh, and you know that by spending one afternoon with him?" Marsha picked up both of their glasses and placed them in the sink. "You do know that people with money also care about their families, love them, want the best for them?"

All of what Laura's Jo's father had said to her just before he'd told her that Phil was no good. Had her father felt the same way about her as she did about Allie? Worry that something bad might happen to her? Worry over her happiness?

"Well, it's time for me to get Allie home."

As Laura Jo and Allie made their way to the front door Marsha said, "We've got to find that money for the shelter. There are worse things in life to have to do than dress up and go out with a handsome man to a dance."

"What handsome man, Mama?"

"No one, honey. Aunt Marsha is just trying to be funny."

Mark was handsome. But what Laura Jo was more concerned about was the way his kiss had made her feel. Had made her wish for more.

Mark came out of a deep sleep at the ringing of his cell phone.

What time was it? He checked his bedside clock. 3:00 a.m. This was never good news. Had something happened to his father?

Mark snatched up the phone. "Hello."

"Mark, its Laura Jo."

The relief that he felt that the call wasn't about his father was immediately replaced with concern for her.

"I'm sorry to call…"

He was wide awake now, heart throbbing. "Are you all right? Allie?"

"Yes. Yes. We're fine. It's a child staying at the shelter. The mother has no insurance and is afraid of doctors. I think the child needs to be seen. Fever, sweating, not eating and lethargic. The mother won't agree to go to the hospital. Will you come?"

"Sure, but will she let me examine the child if I do?"

"I'll convince her that it's necessary before you get here. If she wants to stay at the shelter then she'll have to let you."

"Give me directions."

Laura Jo gave him an address in a less-than-desirable area of the city.

"I'll be there in about thirty minutes."

"Thanks, Mark. I really appreciate this."

The longest part of the trip was traveling the two-lane road between his house and the interstate. Even at this early hour it took him more time than he would have liked. Finally, he reached the four-lane, where he could speed across the two-mile causeway that bisected the bay.

The child must really be worrying Laura Jo or she would never have called him. She'd made it clear she didn't plan to see him again when she'd left his house. He'd thought of nothing but their kiss for the rest of the evening. To hear her voice on the other end of the phone had been a surprise. The child's symptoms didn't sound all that unusual but with a small person it wasn't always straightforward.

He drove through the tunnel that went under Mobile River and came up on Governor Street. There were no crowds now, only large oaks and barriers lining the main street. A number of miles down the street he made a left and not long after that he pulled up in front of what looked like a building that had been a business at one time. The glass windows were painted black and there were dark curtains over the door window. One lone light burned above it. It looked nothing like a place for pregnant woman or children. He could clearly see why they needed a house to move to.

Laura Jo's car was parked near the door and he took the slot next to hers. Picking up his cell phone, he pressed Return. Seconds later, Laura Jo's voice came on the line. "I'm outside."

"I'll be right there."

Mark stood at the door for only seconds before the dead bolt clicked back and Laura Jo's face came into view.

After making sure it was him, she opened the door wider. "I appreciate you coming."

He entered and she locked the door behind him. The room he was in resembled a living room with its couches and chairs spread out. There was one small TV in the corner. At least it looked more welcoming from the inside than it did from the outside.

"Anna's family's room is down this way." Laura Jo, dressed in jeans, T-shirt and tennis shoes, led him down a hall toward the back of the building, passing what he guessed had once been offices. Were families living in nothing more than ten-by-ten rooms?

"Has anything changed?" Mark asked.

"No, but I'm really worried. Anna has been so distraught about the loss of her husband I'm not sure she's been as attentive to her children as she should have been."

"I'll have a look and see what we come up with. Don't worry."

They stopped at the last door.

"Anna isn't a fan of doctors."

"I'll be on my best behavior." He gave her a reassuring smile.

Laura Jo nodded and knocked quietly on the door before she opened it. "Anna, someone is here to check on little Marcy."

Laura Jo entered and he followed close behind. A lone light shone, barely giving off enough light for him to see the room. There was a twin bed shoved into the corner and another at a right angle to that one where two children slept feet to feet. There was also a baby bed but it was empty because the child was in her mother's arms. The woman was reed thin, wide-eyed and had wavy hair. She couldn't have been more than twenty-five.

"Hi, Anna, I'm Mark, and I've come to see if I can help little Marcy. Why don't you sit on the bed and hold her while I have a look? I promise not to hurt her."

Anna hesitated then looked a Laura Jo.

"I'll sit beside you." Laura Jo led her over to the bed.

Mark went down on one knee and placed his bag beside him. He pulled out his stethoscope. The heat he felt as he put his hand close to the child's chest indicated she was still running a fever.

"I'm only going to listen to her heart and lungs now. Check her pulse." He gave the mother a reassuring smile and went to work. Done, he asked, "How long has she had this fever?"

"Since yesterday," the mother said in a meek voice.

He looked a Laura Jo.

"I had no idea." She sounded defensive and he hadn't intended to make her feel that.

To Anna he said, "I'm going to need to check Marcy's abdomen."

"Let's lay Marcy on the bed. That way she'll be more comfortable," Laura Jo suggested.

Mark moved his hand over the child's stomach area. It was distended and hard. Something serious was, without a doubt, going on. He glanced at Laura Jo. Their gazes met. The worry in her eyes was obvious.

"Anna, thank you for letting me see Marcy." He looked at Laura Jo again and tilted his head toward the door. As he stood he picked up his bag and walked across the room. Laura joined him. He let her precede him into the hall and closed the door behind him.

Laura Jo looked at him.

"Marcy has to go to the hospital."

"I was afraid of that. What do you think the problem is?"

"The symptoms make me think it might be an obstructive bowel problem. This isn't something that can wait. Marcy must been seen at the hospital."

"I'll talk to her." Laura Jo went back into the room.

Mark pulled out his phone and called the ER. He gave the information about Marcy and they assured him they would be ready when he arrived. Finished, he leaned against the wall to wait.

Soon Laura Jo came out, with Anna holding Marcy in her arms.

"Anna has agreed to go to the hospital as long as you and I stay with her," Laura Jo said. "I need a few minutes to let someone know to see about her other children. Will you drive?"

His stomach tightened. He didn't want to but what was he supposed to say, "No, I might injure you for life"?

"If it's necessary," Mark answered.

Laura Jo looked at him with a question in her eyes before he turned to walk down the hallway to the front.

"The car seat is by the front door," Anna said in a subdued voice.

"I'll get it."

He was still working to latch the child seat into his car when Laura Jo arrived.

"I'll get that."

With efficiency that he envied she had the seat secured and Marcy in it in no time. Laura Jo didn't comment on his ineptness but he was sure she'd made a note of it. She would probably call him on it later.

Anna took the backseat next to Marcy, and Laura Jo joined him in front. Before pulling out of the parking space, he looked back to see that the baby was secure and that Anna was wearing her seat belt. "Are you buckled in, Laura Jo?"

"Yes. You sure are safety conscious."

Yes, he was, and he had a good reason to be. Mark nodded and wasted no time driving to the hospital. He pulled under the emergency awning and stopped.

As they entered the building Laura Jo said to Anna,

"We'll be right here with you until you feel comfortable. They'll take good care of Marcy here."

Anna nodded, her eyes not meeting Laura Jo's.

They were met by a woman dressed in scrubs.

"Lynn, this child needs to be seen," Laura said.

"Is this the girl Dr. Clayborn called in about?"

"Yes," he said. "I'm Dr. Clayborn." Because he wasn't on the staff at the hospital he couldn't give orders. They would have to wait until the ER physician showed up.

"Exam room five is open. Dr. Lawrence will be right in."

Two hours later Marcy was in surgery. Mark's diagnosis had been correct. Thankfully, Laura Jo had called him or the child might have died. They were now sitting in the surgery waiting room with Anna. With Laura Jo's support, Anna had accepted that Marcy needed the surgery. Mark was impressed with the tender understanding Laura Jo had given the terrified mother. He liked this sensitive side of her personally. What would it take for her to turn some of that on him?

Mark approached the two women and handed each one a cup of coffee from the machine. He slipped into the chair beside Laura Jo. Waiting in hospitals wasn't his usual activity. He'd always been on the working end of an emergency.

While Anna was in the restroom Laura Jo said, "I think you can go. She seems to be handling this better than I thought she would."

"No, I said I'd stay and I will."

"You make a good friend."

Mark's chest tightened. No, he didn't. He'd already proved that. Mike certainly wouldn't say that about him. Mark hadn't even gone to the hospital to see Mike before he'd left town. Laura Jo shouldn't start depending on him.

"You might be surprised."

Laura Jo gave him a speculative look but he was saved

from any questions by Anna returning. Soon after that the surgeon came out to speak to them.

The sun was shining when he and Laura Jo stepped outside the hospital. Marcy was doing well in PICU and Anna had insisted that she was fine and no longer needed them there. They left her in the waiting room, dozing. Laura Jo had promised to check on her other children and that she would see to it they were cared for properly.

As he and Laura Jo walked to his car, which he had moved to a parking place earlier, Mark asked, "Where do you get all the energy for all you do?"

"I just do what has to be done."

"You sure have a lot on your plate."

"Maybe so, but some things I can't say no to."

What was it like to feel that type of bond with people? He understood the practical side of doing what needed to be done medically to save a life but it was a completely different concept to support another person emotionally without reservation. Mark understood that well. He hadn't been able to stand beside his best friend when he'd needed him most. He had even ignored his conscience when it had screamed for him to do better. It hadn't gotten quieter when he'd moved back to town but he still couldn't muster the guts to go visit Mike.

"I wish I had your backbone."

"How's that?"

"You face life head-on."

"You don't?"

"What little I have falls short of the amount you have."

"Thank you. That's a nice compliment."

They had reached his car. "How about I buy us some breakfast then take you home? I'm guessing Marsha has Allie."

"Yes. I really need to check on her and Anna's kids. I

need sleep. I'm sure you do also. I have to work this afternoon. Don't you have to be at work this morning?"

"I don't go in until two and you need to eat. I'm hungry so why don't you let me get us some breakfast without disagreeing for once?"

She walked to the passenger door. "I'm already too far in debt to you."

"I don't mind that."

She sighed. "I pick the place."

"Ladies choice, then."

A smile spread across her lips. "I like the sound of that."

Had no one ever let her make a choice of where they went? He liked seeing Laura Jo smile. She didn't do it often enough. She was far too serious.

"Where're we going?"

"I'll show you."

She got in the car and put her seat belt on. When he was ready to pull out he looked over at her.

Laura Jo said, "Yes, I have buckled up."

He had to sound crazy to her, or over-the-top controlling, but he just couldn't face hurting someone with his driving ever again. Somehow it seemed easier when he had her in the car with him; she accepted him for who he was. As he drove she gave him directions into an older and seedier part of downtown Mobile. He had last been to the area when he'd been a teen and trying to live on the wild side some.

"It's just down the street on the right. The Silver Spoon."

Mark pulled into the small parking area in front of a nineteen-fifties-style café that had seen better days.

"You want to eat here?"

"Sure. They have the best pecan waffles in town." Laura Jo was already getting out of the car. She looked back in at him. "You coming?"

Mark had been questioning it. He wasn't sure the place could pass a health inspection.

"Yes, I am." He climbed out of the car. "I wouldn't miss it."

She was already moving up the few steps to the front door.

Because all the booths were full, Laura Jo took an empty stool at the bar. She didn't miss Mark's dubious look at the duct-taped stool next to her before he took a seat.

"You don't frequent places like this, do you?"

"I can say that this is a first."

She grinned. "I thought it might be."

Mark picked up a plastic-covered menu. "So I need to have the pecan waffles."

"They're my favorite." She was going to enjoy watching Mark out of his element.

"Then waffles it is. You do the ordering."

"Charlie," she said to the heavy man wearing what once must have been a white apron, "we'll have pecan waffles, link sausage and iced tea."

"Coming right up, Laura Jo," Charlie said, and turned to give the cook her order.

"I see you're a regular," Mark said.

"I come when I can, which isn't often enough."

Charlie put their glasses of iced tea on the counter with a thump.

"I don't normally have iced tea for breakfast." Mark picked up his glass.

"If you'd rather have coffee…" Laura Jo made it sound like a dare on purpose.

"I said I wanted the same as you and that's what I'm having. So how did you find this place?"

"Charlie gave one of the mothers that came through the shelter a job here after her baby was born."

"That was nice. I'm impressed with what you're doing at the shelter."

"Thanks. But it never seems like enough. You know, I really appreciate you helping me out with Anna and Marcy. I hated to call you but I knew I couldn't get her to the hospital and I was uncomfortable with how Marcy looked."

Mark really had been great with Anna and Marcy. He'd stayed to give moral support even when he hadn't had to. Maybe she had better character radar than she believed.

"I'm glad you thought you could call."

She'd been surprised too that she hadn't hesitated a second before picking up the phone to call him. Somehow she'd just known he would come. "Were you always going to be a doctor?"

"I believe that's the first personal question you have ever asked me. You do want to get to know me better."

Laura Jo opened her mouth to refute that statement but he continued, not giving her a chance to do so.

"Yes, I had always planned to go into medicine. My parents liked the idea and I found I did, too. I've always liked helping people. How about you? Did you always dream of being a nurse?"

"No, I kind of came to that later in life."

"So what was your dream?"

"I don't know. I guess like all the other girls I knew we dreamed of marrying the Mardi Gras king, having two kids and living in a big house."

He looked in her direction but she refused to meet his gaze. "Marrying the Mardi Gras king, was it? So did you dream of marrying me?"

"I don't think your ego needs to be fed by my teenage

dreams. But I'll admit to having a crush on you if that will end this conversation."

"I thought so."

"Now we won't be able to get your head out of the door."

Charlie placed a plateful of food in front of each of them with a clunk on the counter.

"Thanks, Charlie." She picked up her fork and looked at Mark. "You need to eat your waffle while it's hot to get the full effect." She took a bite dripping with syrup.

"Trying to get me to quit asking questions?"

"That and the waffles are better hot."

They ate in silence for a few minutes.

"So I remember something about an accident and then I didn't hear much about you after that. I later heard you'd left town. Did you get hurt?"

Mark's fork halted in midair then he lowered it to the plate.

Had she asked the wrong thing? She looked back at her meal. "You don't have to tell me if you'd rather not."

"I wasn't really hurt. But my friend was. I had to leave a few days later to start my fellowship."

"What happened?"

"It's a long story. Too much of one for this morning."

So the man with all the questions was hiding something. Minutes later she finished her last mouthful. Mark said something. She turned to look at him. "What?"

He touched her face. His gaze caught and held hers as he put his finger between his lips. Her stomach fluttered. She swallowed. Heaven help her, the man held her spellbound.

"You had syrup on your chin."

"Uh?"

"Syrup on your chin." Mark said each word slowly, as if speaking to someone who didn't understand the language.

"Oh." She dabbed at the spot with her napkin. Mark was starting to shatter her protective barriers. "We'd better go."

She climbed off the stool and called, "Thanks, Charlie." She was going out the door as Mark pulled a couple of bills out of his wallet.

Her hand was already on the door handle of his car as Mark pulled into a parking place at the shelter. She needed to get away from him. Find her equilibrium. That look in his eye as he'd licked the syrup on his finger had her thinking of things better left unthought. She stepped out of the car. "Thanks for helping out last night. I don't know how I'll repay you."

"No problem."

"Bye, Mark."

Why did a simple gesture from Mark, of all men, make her run? She had to be attracted to him for that to happen. Surely that wasn't the case.

CHAPTER FOUR

FOUR DAYS LATER, as Laura Jo was busy setting up the med tent on North Broad Street, she was still pondering how to raise the money needed for the single mothers' shelter. The grant they were hoping for had come through, but with a condition that the board match the amount. There were only five more days of Mardi Gras season, then things would settle down. After that the city would place the house on the market. She couldn't let that happen. They had to move out of the too-small building they were in now.

She didn't want anyone to get hurt at the parade but if she was busy tonight it would keep her mind off the issue of money...along with the thoughts of how agreeing to go to the dance with Mark just might solve her problem.

Think of the devil and he shows up. Mark rode over the curb of the street and up onto the grassy lot where the med tent was stationed. His tight bike shorts left little to the imagination and there was nothing small about the man. He unclipped his helmet and set it on the handlebars, before heading in her direction. For a second her heart rate picked up with the thought that he'd come to see her. She wasn't sure if it was relief or disappointment that filled her when he stopped to talk in depth to one of the ER doctors working with her. Mark should mean nothing to her. She shouldn't be feeling anything, one way or another.

Laura Jo returned to unpacking boxes, turning her back to him.

A few minutes later a tenor voice she recognized said, "Hello, Laura Jo."

She twisted, making an effort to act as if she hadn't been aware of where he'd been and what he'd been doing during the past ten minutes. "Hi, Mark. I didn't expect to see you today."

"It would be my guess that if you had you'd have seen to it you were reassigned to another med tent."

"You know me so well," she quipped, returning to what she'd been doing.

"I wish I did know you better. Then maybe I'd understand why I find you so fascinating."

A ripple of pleasure went through her at his statement. She resisted placing a hand on her stomach when it quivered. "It might be that I don't fall at your feet like other women do."

"I don't know about that."

"They used to. I figured now wasn't any different. In fact, I saw and heard the ER nurses swoon when you came in the other day."

"Swoon. That's an old-fashioned word." He leaned in close so that only she could hear. "Did you swoon over me, too, Laura Jo?"

She had but she wasn't going to let him know that. Straightening and squaring her shoulders, she said with authority, "I did not."

He grinned, his voice dropping seductively. "Something about that quick denial makes me think you did."

Her heart skipped a beat. "Would you please go? I have work to do."

He chuckled. "I'm flattered. I had no idea girls swooned over me."

I bet. Laura Jo glared at him.

"I'm going. I wouldn't want to keep you from your work. See you later."

She glanced up to see him disappear through the crowd. Their conversations had been the most thought-provoking, irritating and stimulating ones she'd ever experienced. And that didn't count how he'd made her feel when he'd kissed her. She had to think fast to stay ahead of him. Somehow that made her life more exciting and interesting.

Mark made one more circle around his patrol area along the parade route. He'd not worked patrol in three days and his muscles were telling him they had noticed. Busy at his practice, getting his patient load up, it required late hours to accommodate people coming in after work hours. As the newest man in the six-doctor general practice, it was his duty to cover the clinic for the hours that were least desirable.

He was pulled out of his thoughts by a boy of three or four standing in the middle of the street. The child looked lost. Mark parked his bike and scanned the crowd for some anxious parent. Finding none, he went down on his haunches in front of the boy. "Hello, there, are you looking for someone?"

"My mommy."

"Can I help you find her?"

The boy nodded.

Mark offered his hand and he took it. They started walking along the edge of the crowd, Mark looking for anyone who might claim the boy.

A woman clutching her cell phone stepped out from behind the barriers just ahead of them and hurried toward them. "Lucas, you shouldn't have walked off."

The woman looked at Mark. "I was talking on my phone and then he was gone," she said with a nervous little laugh.

Mark nodded. "I understand. Little ones can get away from you when you aren't paying attention."

The woman's lips tightened. She took her son's hand and left.

He went back to patrolling. Returning to Mobile so close to Mardi Gras season, he had social obligations to consider. He'd been king the year he'd left and now that he was back in town he was expected to attend certain events. He'd once lived for all the fanfare of the season but now it held no real thrill for him. Still, certain things were expected of him. He just wished doing so didn't bring on such heavy guilt.

Mark hadn't expected to find Laura Jo working the same parade as he was but he wasn't disappointed either. He'd missed their sparring. It was always fun to see how she'd react to something he said or did. Especially his kiss. He'd kissed enough women to know when one was enjoying it.

He wasn't disappointed with her reaction today, either. When he'd asked her about swooning over him he'd have to admit her pretty blush had raised his self-esteem. She had been one of those teens who'd wanted to be noticed by him. The sad thing was that he would've crushed her admiration with the self-centered attitude he'd wore like his royal cloak if he'd even noticed her.

Clearly he had noted the woman she'd become. There hadn't been another female who kept him on his toes or stepped on them more than she did. There were so many facets to her. He still didn't understand what made her tick. He couldn't count the number of times she'd been on his mind over the past few days despite his efforts not to let her intervene in his thoughts.

He compared the mother who'd been too busy talking on her phone to show any real concern for her child with

Laura Jo's motherly concern over a skinned knee. She won. Laura Jo had seen the humor when he'd had to carry Gus. He could still hear her boisterous laughter. Under all that anti-society, I-can-do-it-on-my-own attitude, she hid a power to love and enjoy life.

From what he'd heard and read between the lines, she hadn't had much opportunity to take pleasure in life in a number of years. She been busy scrapping and fighting to keep Allie cared for. To go to school, then work and start a shelter. It had to have been hard, doing it all without family support. What was the deal with her family anyway?

No wonder she was so involved with the single mothers' house. She identified with the women, had been one of them. As if she didn't have enough going on in her life now, she was trying to raise funds to buy the house. Was there anything Laura Jo couldn't do?

Mark made another loop through his section of the parade route. He wasn't far from the med tent when he pulled over out of the way to let the parade go by. One girl in a group of dancers he recognized from other parades. She was limping badly. Seconds later, the girl left the line and collapsed to the curb.

To help her, he had to cross the parade route. He raised his hand and the driver of the next float stopped. Mark pushed his bike over to where the teenage girl sat. She was busy removing her tap shoe. Mark noticed that her foot was covered in blood.

He parked his bike and crouched beside her. The girl looked at him with tears in her eyes. "I just couldn't go any further."

It wasn't unusual to see members of the dance groups abusing their feet. Some of the dancers did up to four parades a day when it got closer to Fat Tuesday. More than once Mark had wondered how they kept it up. Almost everyone in the parades rode while these girls danced for miles.

"I don't blame you. That looks painful. How about we get you cleaned up and ease that pain?"

The girl nodded then started to stand. Mark picked up her discarded shoe and placed his hand on her shoulder. "The med tent isn't too far. Do you mind if I carry you? That foot looks too painful to walk on."

The girl nodded. Mark handed her the shoe and scooped her into his arms. The crowd parted so he could get through. "Would someone please follow us with my bike?"

A middle-aged man called, "I'll bring it."

Mark headed for the med tent a block away. As he walked people turned to watch. He was within sight of the tent when he saw Laura Jo look in his direction. It was as if she had radar where he was concerned. She seemed to sense when he was near. He would have to give that more thought later. He hefted the girl closer in his arms. This was turning into a workout.

Laura Jo moved away and when he saw her again she was pushing a wheelchair across the dirt and grass area between them. Mark faltered. The girl's arms tightened around his neck. The blood drained from his face as Mike crossed his mind.

When Laura Jo reached him, he lowered the dancer into the chair.

Laura Jo mouthed over the girl's head, "Are you okay?"

He nodded. But the look on her face had him doubting he'd convinced her.

"What happened?"

"Blisters."

"I'll get things ready." Laura Jo turned and hurried back toward the tent.

Mark let his hands rest on the handles of the chair for

a moment before he started pushing. He wished he could have let Laura Jo do it. Bringing the wheelchair up on its two back wheels, he maneuvered it across the rough ground. When he arrived at the tent Laura Jo was waiting with a square plastic pan filled with what must be saline. He lifted the footrest off the chair. Going on one knee, he removed the girl's other tap shoe. Laura Jo then slipped the pan into position and the girl lowered her feet into the water with a small yelp of pain.

"Do it slowly and it will be less painful. It'll hurt at first but as soon as they are clean we'll bandage them and you'll feel a lot better. Are you allergic to anything?"

"No," the girl said.

Laura Jo then offered her a white pill and a small glass of water that had been waiting on the table beside them. "That should ease the pain." She looked at him. "I'll take care of her from here, Dr. Clayborn."

Had he just been dismissed? He had. Grinning at Laura Jo and then the girl, he said, "I'll leave you in the capable hands of Nurse Akins."

"Thank you," the girl said.

"You're welcome. I hope you get to feeling better. I'll miss seeing you in the parades."

The girl blushed a bright pink then looked away.

Laura Jo gave a dramatic roll of her eyes.

Mark smiled. He looked around to find his bike leaning against a nearby tree. He climbed on and prepared to ride off. He glanced back at Laura Jo. She looked away from caring for the girl's feet to meet his gaze.

He grinned. Maybe he could still make her swoon.

Two hours later, after the last parade of the day, he pulled up beside the med tent. He would leave his reports of the minor injuries he'd handled with them. The city officials liked to keep a record of anything that happened during Mardi Gras season in order to plan for the next year.

Allie came running toward him. "Hey, did you bring Gus with you?"

"No, not today. I couldn't get him to ride the bike."

Allie giggled.

"Had any king cake this week?"

Allie nodded. "I even found the baby."

"Then I guess you're planning to take a cake to school."

"We're out of school today. It's our Mardi Gras break."

"Well, then, how about bringing me one? I haven't even had the chance to find the baby this year."

Laura Jo walked over "I don't think—"

Mark looked at her. "It just so happens that your mother owes me a favor."

"I do?"

"Anna."

Laura Jo's heart fell. She did.

"So how about you and your mother come over to my house tomorrow night and I'll fix sausage gumbo and you bring the king cake. Better yet, your mother can make it at my house." He looked at Laura Jo when he said, "She did say my kitchen was the perfect place to make a cake."

"Can we, Mommy? I want to see Gus. You don't have to work tomorrow."

"Great. Then it's all settled. I'll expect you at four o'clock."

"Do you two think I could say something since you're making plans that involve me?"

Mark looked at her and grinned. "Talk away."

"Allie, I think we need to take it easy while we have a day off. The next few days are going to be busy."

Mark leaned forward, making eye contact. "And I think that you owe me a favor that you are trying to welch on."

Laura Jo shifted from one foot to the other. She did owe him big for helping her with Anna, and the check, and Allie being in the parade. Even so, going to Mark's house again wasn't a good idea. "I thought you might be enough of a gentleman that you wouldn't stoop to calling in a favor."

He gave her a pointed look. "Sometimes you want something badly enough that the social graces don't matter."

She swallowed. The implication was that she might be that "something." When had been the last time she'd felt wanted by a man? It had been so long ago she couldn't remember.

Mark looked at Allie and grinned. "Manners don't matter when you're talking about king cake."

Allie returned the smile and nodded.

Why was she letting Mark talk her into it? Because the least she owed him was a king cake for all that he'd done for her. And she had to admit that deep down inside she'd enjoy cooking in his kitchen and spending time with him.

Mark couldn't remember the last time he'd looked forward to a king cake with such anticipation. He suspected that it had nothing to do with the cake and everything to do with seeing Laura Jo. She and Allie were due any minute. He gave the gumbo a stir. He'd missed the stew-type consistency of the dish while he'd been in California. As hard as he'd tried, he hadn't been able to get the ingredients to make good gumbo. What he had used had never tasted like what he was used to having when he was in Mobile.

He slurped a spoonful of gumbo off the tip of the ladle. It was good.

The doorbell rang. Should a man be so eager to spend time with a woman? For his own self-preservation he'd say no. With a smile on his face, Mark opened the door. To his amazement, Laura Jo smiled in return. He hadn't expected that when he'd given her no choice about coming to his home today. Allie brushed passed his legs.

"Where's Gus?" she asked as she went.

"He was in his bed, sleeping, the last time I saw him."

He liked Allie. He'd never spent much time around children but he found Allie a pleasure. She seemed to like him as much as he did her. What would it be like to be a father to a child like her? Maybe if he had Allie as a daughter he'd have a chance of being a good father.

"I hope Gus is prepared for this," Laura Jo said.

"I wouldn't worry about Gus. Can I take those?" He reached for the grocery bags she carried in either hand.

"Thanks." She handed him one of them. "I guess I'd better get started. It's a long process."

It occurred to him that she'd be anxious to get away as soon as she had met her obligation. He didn't plan to let that happen. "We have plenty of time. I have nowhere to be tonight—do you?"

"Uh, no, but I'd still like to get started."

"Okay, if that's the way you want it." To his astonishment, he said, "I'm going to take Gus and Allie outside to play. Gus needs some exercise." When had he started to think that he was capable of overseeing Allie?

"All right. Just don't let Allie get too close to the water."

"I'll take good care of her." He was confident he would. He headed in the direction of the living room.

Laura Jo watched as Mark left the kitchen after he'd placed the bag on the kitchen counter. He headed out as if he'd given her no more thought. For some reason, she was disappointed he'd not worked harder at encouraging her to join him and Allie. She was even more surprised that she trusted him without question to take care of Allie. Was it because she'd seen him caring for others or that she just innately knew he would see to Allie like she was his own?

Running a hand over the granite counter, she looked around the kitchen. It was truly amazing. If she had this kitchen to cook in every day, she might never leave it. But she didn't. What she had was a small corner one and it was plenty for her and Allie. Mark's kitchen reminded her of her childhood when she'd stood beside Elsie Mae, their cook, and helped prepared meals.

It was time to get busy. She planned to make the most of Mark's kitchen while she had it. Shaking off the nostalgia, Laura Jo pulled the bread flour and eggs out of the bag she'd brought. Over the next twenty minutes she prepared the dough and set it aside to rise.

Going to one of the living-room windows, she looked out. Allie was running with Gus as Mark threw a ball. Laura Jo laughed. Gus showed no interest in going after the ball. Seconds later Mark opened his arms wide and Allie ran into them. He lifted her over his head. Laura Jo could hear her daughter's giggles from where she stood. Her chest tightened.

Allie wrapped her arms around Mark's neck as he brought her back down. They both had huge smiles on their faces. Laura Jo swallowed the lump in her throat. The man had obviously won her daughter over and Laura Jo was worried he was fast doing the same with her.

She pulled open the door and walked out to join them. Allie and Mark were so absorbed in playing that they didn't see her until she had almost reached them. Seeing Allie with Mark brought home how much Allie needed a male figure in her life. Had she done Allie a disservice by not looking for a husband or keeping her away from her grandfather? Had she been so wrapped up in surviving and trying to take care of other mothers that she'd neglected Allie's needs?

"Is something wrong?" Mark asked.

"No, everything is fine."

"You had a funny look on your face. Was there a problem in the kitchen?"

"No, I found what I needed. Now I have to wait for the dough to rise before I do anything more."

"Then why don't we walk down to the dock?" Mark suggested.

"Okay."

"Come on, Allie," Mark called.

"So, do you boat or water-ski?" Laura Jo asked.

Mark stopped and looked at her. "You know, I like you being interested in me."

"Please, don't make more of a friendly question than there is. I was just trying to make conversation. You live on the water, were raised on the water so I just thought..."

"Yes, I have a small sailboat and the family also has a ski boat."

She and Mark walked to the end of the pier and took a seat in the Adirondack chairs stationed there.

"How about you?" he asked.

"I don't sail but I do love to ski." She watched the small waves coming in as the wind picked up.

"Maybe you and Allie can come and spend the day on the water with me when it gets warmer."

Allie ran past them to the edge of the pier.

"Be careful," Mark called. "The water is cold. I don't want you to fall in."

"You sure do sound like a parent."

Mark took on a stricken look that soon turned thoughtful. "I did, didn't I?"

"I don't know why you should act so surprised. You're great with kids."

A few minutes went by before he asked, "I know who your parents are but I can't remember if you have any brothers or sisters."

"Only child." Laura Jo wasn't pleased he'd turned the conversation to her and even less so to her parents. She didn't want to talk about them. The people who had been more interested in their social events than spending time with her. Who hadn't understood the teen who'd believed so strongly in helping the less fortunate. Who had always made her feel like she didn't quite measure up.

"Really? That wouldn't have been my guess."

"Why not?"

"Because you're so strong and self-sufficient. You don't seem spoiled to me."

"You do have a stereotypical view of an only child."

He shrugged. "You could be right."

Laura Jo kept an eye on Allie, who had left the pier and was now playing along the edge of the water as Gus lumbered along nearby.

"So tell me about growing up as a Clayborn with a big silver spoon in your mouth."

"I had no silver spoon that I can remember."

She gave him a sideways look. "I remember enough to know you were the golden boy."

"Well, I do have blond locks." Mark ran his hand through his hair with an attitude.

"And an ego."

They watched the water for a while before she stood and called to Allie, "Do you want to help braid the dough?"

"I want to do the colors," Allie said.

"Okay, I'll save that job for you."

Laura Jo headed back along the pier and Mark followed

a number of paces behind her. As she stepped on the lawn her phone rang. Fishing it out of her jeans pocket, she saw it was Marsha calling and answered.

"Hey, I've just been given tickets to see that new kids' movie. Jeremy wants Allie to go with him. Would you mind if I come and get her?"

"I don't know, Marsha…" If she agreed, it would leave her alone with Mark.

"You mean you'd keep your child from seeing a movie she's been wanting to see because you're too afraid to stay by yourself with Mark Clayborn."

Put that way, it did sound kind of childish. But it was true.

After a sigh Laura Jo said, "Let me speak to Allie. She may rather stay here with the dog."

Laura Jo called to her daughter. Hearing the idea, Allie jumped up and down, squealing that she wanted to go to the movie.

"Okay, Marsha, but you'll have to come and get her. I'm in the middle of making king cakes."

"I'll be there in thirty minutes."

While they waited for Marsha to arrive, Laura Jo punched the dough down and placed it in the refrigerator to rest. She then cleaned Allie up so she'd be ready to go when Marsha arrived.

"Who's going to hide the baby if you leave?" Mark teased Allie.

"I bet Mommy will let you."

He looked over at Laura Jo. "Will you?"

"Yes, you can hide the baby." She made it sound like she was talking to a mischievous boy.

"Mark, will you do the colors for me too?" Allie asked, as she pulled on one of Gus's ears.

"I don't know if I know how to do those." Mark was

sitting in a large chair in the living area with one foot on the ottoman.

"Mommy will show you. She knows how to do it all."

Mark met Laura Jo's gaze over Allie's head. "She knows how to do it all, does she?"

A tingle went down her spine. Leave it to Mark to make baking a king cake sound sexier than it really was.

Five minutes later there was a knock at the door. Allie skipped to it while Laura Jo and Mark followed behind her. Laura Jo stepped around Allie and opened the door.

"Come on, Allie," Marsha said. "We need to hurry if we're going to be there on time." Marsha looked at Laura Jo. "Just let her spend the night since she was coming to me early in the morning anyway. Enjoy your evening. Hi, Mark. Bye, Mark." With that, Marsha whisked Allie away.

"Does she always blow in and blow out with such force?" Mark asked.

Laura Jo closed the door with a heavy awareness of being alone with Mark. "Sometimes. I need to finish the cake and get out of your way."

"I invited you to dinner and I expect you to stay. Are you scared to be here with me, knowing Allie isn't here to protect you?"

"She wasn't protecting me!" Had she been using Allie as a barrier between her and men? No, her first priority was Allie and taking care of her. It had nothing to do with fear.

"Then quit acting as if you're scared I might jump you."

Laura Jo ignored his comment and headed toward the kitchen. She pulled the large bowl of dough out of the refrigerator.

"So what has to be done to it now?" Mark asked.

"Roll it out." She placed the bowl on the corner. "Will you hand me that bag of flour?"

He reached across the wide counter and pulled the bag to him. He then pushed it toward her. Leaning a hip against the cabinet as if he had no place he'd rather be, he asked, "So what happens now?"

"Are you asking for a play-by-play?" She spread flour across the counter.

"Maybe."

"I have to divide the dough." She pulled it apart and set what she wasn't going to use right away back into the bowl.

"Why're you doing that?"

"This recipe makes two cakes. Are you sure there isn't a basketball game on that you want to watch?"

"Nope, I like watching you."

Focusing her attention on her baking again, she dumped the dough onto the granite corner top. She reached into one of the bags and pulled out a rolling pin.

"You didn't think I'd have one of those, did you?" Mark asked from his position beside her.

"Do you?"

"I'm sure I do around here somewhere. I'd have to hunt for it."

"That's why I brought my own." She punched the dough flat with her palms then picked up the pin and started rolling.

"While I roll this out, would you find the cinnamon? It's in one of these bags."

"Sure." He walked to the other side of the room and pulled a bowl out of the cabinet. They each did their jobs in silence."

Heat washed over her. She was far too aware of him being near. All her disquiet went into making the dough thin and wide. "Would you also open the cream cheese? I set it out to soften earlier."

"Will do."

Laura Jo had never had a man help her in the kitchen. Her father had no interest in cooking, not even grilling. Phil had seen it as woman's work and never helped. It was nice to have someone interested in the same thing that she was. To work with her.

"I'm going to need the sugar. I forgot to bring any." Maybe if she kept him busy, he wouldn't stand so close.

"That I do have. Coming right up." Mark reached under the counter and pulled out a plastic container. "Here you go."

"Thanks." Laura Jo brushed her hair away with the back of her hand, sending flour dust into the air.

"Turn around," Mark said.

"Why?"

"Just turn around. For once just trust me."

Behind her there was the sound of a drawer being pulled open then pushed back.

"What are—?"

Mark stepped close enough that she felt his heat from her shoulders to her hips. Strong fingers glided over her scalp and fanned out, gathering her hair.

Her lungs began to hurt and she released the breath she held. Every part of her was aware of how close Mark stood. His body brushed hers as he moved to a different angle. One hand drifted over her temple to capture a stray strand. His warm breath fluttered across the nap of her neck. She quivered.

There was a tug then a pull before he said, "There, that should help."

He moved and the warmth that had had her heart racing disappeared, leaving her with a void that she feared only Mark could fill.

She touched the back of her head. He had tied her hair up with a rag. "Thanks."

"Now you can work without getting flour all in your hair."

He'd been doing something practical and she had been wound up about him being so close. She needed to finish these cakes and go home as soon as possible.

"Would you mind melting a stick of butter?"

"Not at all," Mark said in an all-too-cheerful manner.

Laura Jo continued to roll the dough into a rectangle, while keeping an eye on Mark as he moved around on the other side of the counter. "One more thing."

He raised a brow.

"Would you mix the cinnamon and sugar together?"

"Yeah. How much?" Mark headed again to where the bowls were.

"Like you are making cinnamon toast."

"How do you know I know how to make cinnamon toast?"

"Everyone knows how to do that," she said, as she finished rolling the first half of the dough. "While I roll out the other dough, will you spread butter on this one then put the sugar cinnamon mixture over that?"

"I don't know. All that might be out of my territory."

She chuckled. "I think you can handle it."

Over the next few minutes they each worked at their own projects. Laura Jo was used to making the cakes by herself but found she liked having a partner even in something as simple as a cake. She glanced at Mark. His full attention was on what he was doing. He approached his assignment much as he did giving medical care, with an effort to do the very best, not miss any detail.

She looked over to where he was meticulously shaking

the sugar mixture on the dough from a spoon. "You know you really can't do that wrong."

"Uh?"

He must have been so involved in what he was doing he hadn't heard her. "Enjoy what you're doing a little. It doesn't have to be perfect."

Mark straightened. "This comes from the person who only laughs when my dog gets the best of me."

"I laugh at other times."

"Really?"

Was she truly that uptight? Maybe she was but she could tell that lately she'd been starting to ease up. Ever since she'd started spending time with Mark.

"Speaking of uptight, what's your issue with a wheelchair?"

CHAPTER FIVE

DAMN, SHE'D NOTICED. Mark had thought, hoped, Laura Jo had missed or he'd covered his feelings well enough when he'd seen a wheelchair, but apparently not.

Maybe he could bluff his way out of answering. "I don't know what you mean."

Laura Jo was looking at him. His skin tingled. He glanced at her. She had stopped what she was doing.

"Please, don't insult my intelligence," she said quietly.

He sighed before answering. "My friend who was in the accident is now in a wheelchair."

"I'm sorry to hear that."

"Me, too." He put the empty bowl in the sink.

"What happened?"

"He was thrown from the car."

"Oh, how awful."

"It was." He needed to change the subject. "So what do I need to do now?"

"Roll it into a log, like this." Laura Jo moved close and started working with the dough.

He looked at the honey nape of her neck exposed and waiting for him. Mike went out of his mind and all he could think about was the soft woman so close, the smell of cinnamon and sugar and the need to touch her, kiss her.

The wisps of hair at her neck fluttered as he leaned

closer. He touched the tip of his tongue to her warm skin. He felt a tremor run through her and his manhood responded. His lips found the valley and he pressed. Sweet, so sweet.

She shifted away. "Mark, I don't have time in my life to play games."

"Who said I was playing a game?"

"I have Allie to think about."

He spoke from behind her. "So you're going to put how you feel and your life on hold for Allie? For how long?" He kissed her behind the ear.

Her hands stopped rolling the dough. She stepped to the side so that she could turn to look at him. "What I'm not going to do is get involved with a man I have no intention of marrying."

Mark put some space between them. "Whoa, we're not talking about marriage here. More like harmless fun. A few kisses. Some mutually satisfying petting." He stepped back and studied her. "Are you always this uptight around a man?"

"I'm not uptight."

"The best I can tell is the only time you're not is when I'm kissing you or you're laughing at my dog."

"I wasn't laughing at Gus. I was laughing at you."

He took a step closer, pinning her against the counter. "No one likes to be laughed at. But what I'm really interested in is you showing me how you're not uptight. I want to kiss you, Laura Jo. Just kiss you."

She didn't resist as his lips came down to meet hers. His mouth was firm but undemanding as if he was waiting to see if she would accept him. When had been the last time she had taken a moment's pleasure with a man? What would it hurt if she did? Just to have something that was simple and easy between two adults.

Laura Jo wrapped her hands around his neck, weaved her fingers through his hair and pressed herself against his lean, hard body. With a sigh, she returned his kiss.

Mark encircled her waist and lifted her against him. His mouth took further possession, sending wave after wave of heat through her. He ran the tip of his tongue along the seam of her mouth until she opened for him. The parry and thrust of his tongue had her joining him. He pressed her against the counter, shifted her until his desire stood ridged between them.

Something poked at her bottom just before there was a loud thump on the floor. She broke away. Mark's hand remained at her waist. Her breath was shallow and rapid. She was no longer a maiden but she sure was acting like one. Her heart was thudding against her rib cage. She couldn't look at Mark.

When she did glance at him through lowered lashes, to her great satisfaction he looked rattled, too. He leaned toward her again and she broke the embrace before stepping away. "I need to get these cakes ready to put in the oven." She was relieved that her voice sounded steadier than she felt.

Mark looked for a second as if he might disagree but he didn't move any closer.

"I think I like the sugar you just gave me better than what is on a king cake."

She had to regain her equilibrium. The only way she knew how to do that was to go on the defensive. She placed her hands on her hips. "You haven't tasted one of my cakes."

"No, but I have tasted you," he said in a soft and sultry voice.

Pleasure filled her. Mark had a way of making her feel special.

"Why don't you spread the cream cheese on this cake while I finish braiding the other one?"

"Yes, ma'am."

Minutes later Mark dropped the spatula he had been using in the sink. Laura Jo placed the cake she was working with on a baking pan. She had been aware of every movement he'd made as he'd spread the creamy cheese across the thin pastry.

"While you finish up on this one I'm going to get us each a bowl of gumbo." Mark went to a cabinet and pulled down two bowls.

Laura Jo was both relieved and disappointed when he moved to the other side of the center counter. If Mark was close he made her feel nervous and if he wasn't she missed his nearness.

"We forgot to put the babies in." Laura Jo reached into a bag and brought out a snack-size bag with tiny hard plastic babies in it. Their hands and feet were up in the air as if they were lying in a crib, laughing.

"I'll put those in. I promised Allie I would. I keep my promises."

Mark joined her again and she handed the babies to him. They looked extra-small in his large palm.

"Turn around. And don't peek."

Laura Jo did as he instructed.

"Okay. Done."

Laura Jo started cleaning up the area. "You know, it doesn't have to be such a secret. Mardi Gras will be over in four days and we won't be having another cake until next year."

He met her gaze. "Well, maybe I'll ask for something besides cake if I find the baby inside my piece."

"That's not how it works."

"Then we could just change the rules between us."

Laura Jo wasn't sure she wanted to play that game.

"Are you ready for gumbo?"

"I can eat while these rise." She looked over at the cakes. "I had no idea this much work went into making a king cake."

"They are labor intensive but I enjoy it. Especially when I can make them in a kitchen like this one."

Mark filled the two bowls he'd gotten out earlier. "Do you mind carrying your own bowl to the table?"

"Of course not. I don't expect you to wait on me."

They sat across from each other in the small breakfast nook adjoining the kitchen. From there they had a view of the bay.

"This is delicious." Laura Jo lifted a spoonful of gumbo. "I'm impressed with your culinary skills."

"I think culinary skills is a little strong. It's not hard really."

"Either way, it tastes good." She was glad that they were back to their old banter. She'd been afraid that after their hot kiss, which had her nerves on high alert, they wouldn't be able to have an easy conversation. She rather enjoyed their discussions, even if they didn't always agree.

"How's Marcy doing?"

She looked at him. "Very well, thanks to you. She'll be coming home tomorrow."

"I didn't do anything but provide encouragement. I meant to go by to see them again but I had to work late on the days I wasn't patrolling parades."

"Ann really appreciated the one day you did check in on them. That was nice of you."

"I'm a nice guy."

He really was. She'd done him a disservice when she'd first met him. He'd proven more than once that he was a good person.

"So have you found the funding for the shelter yet?" Mark asked as he pushed his empty bowl away.

"We qualified for the grant I was hoping for but it requires we find matching funds."

"Well, at least you do have some good news." He stood, gathering his bowl. "Do you want any more gumbo while I'm getting some?"

"No, I'm still working on this." Laura Jo watched him walk away. He wore a lightweight long-sleeved sweater and worn jeans. He really had a fine-looking butt.

For a second she'd been afraid he'd ask her about going to the dance. A hint of disappointment touched her when he didn't. He probably had a date with someone else by now. She didn't like that thought any better.

They finished their dinner with small talk about the weather, parades and the coming weekend. Together they carried their bowls to the dishwasher. Mark placed them in it while Laura Jo checked on the rising cake.

"How much longer on those?" Mark asked.

"They need to rise to double their size. Then I'll bake them and be on my way. I can finish the topping when I get home."

"Oh, no, you won't. I want to eat some as soon as you get them done. Besides, I want to do the topping."

"You're acting like Allie."

"Did you think I was kidding when I told you that I liked king cake as much as she did? I haven't had any in a long time and I'm not letting you out of the house without a piece today. While we're waiting, why don't we go out on the deck and have a cup of coffee and watch the sunset?"

She wasn't sure if watching the sunset with Mark was a good idea but she didn't know how to get out of it gracefully. Those darned cakes were taking too long to rise for her comfort. "Make that another glass of tea and I'll agree."

"Done. Why don't you go on out and take your pick of chairs and I'll bring the drinks."

Laura Jo walked through the living area and out one of the glass doors. Gus got up from his bed and ambled out with her. She took one of the lounges, making sure it wasn't near any others. Having Mark so close all the time was making her think of touching him, worse, kissing him again. She needed to put whatever distance she could between them.

Gus lay at the end of the lounge.

"Here you go," Mark said, placing her glass and his mug on the wire mesh table beside her. He then pulled one of the other lounges up on the opposite side of the table. He stretched his long body out and settled in.

"You mind handing me my mug?"

With shaking hands, Laura Jo passed him his drink.

"This is the best part of the day. I miss this when I have to work late."

She had to agree. It was nice to just slow down and be for a few minutes. "Is working here a lot different from your clinic in California?"

"The patients' backgrounds are different but sick people are sick people."

"Do you regret leaving California?"

"I have to admit I like the slower pace here." Mark crossed his ankles and settled more comfortably into the lounge.

"I couldn't leave Mobile and move all the way across the country."

"Sometimes you do things because you don't think you have a choice."

She watched a bird dipping into the water after its evening meal. "I know about not having choices." Maybe in some ways they weren't so different after all.

They both lapsed into silence as the sun slowly sank in the sky.

Laura Jo took a sip of her tea at the same time a breeze came in off the water. She shivered.

Mark put his mug down on the decking and stood. "I'll be back in a sec."

He returned with a jacket in his hand and handed it to her. "Here, you can put this on."

She slipped her arm into one sleeve and Mark held the jacket for her to put the other in. He sat beside her again. She trembled again and pulled the jacket closer around her.

As the wind blew, a scent of spice and musk that could only be Mark tickled her nostrils. She inhaled. For some reason it was a smell she wanted to remember.

Again they lapsed into a relaxed silence.

As the daylight was taken over by the night, Mark reached over and took her hand, weaving his fingers between hers. It was strong, secure and soothing. Laura Jo didn't pull away. Didn't want to.

When the stars came out Mark said, "We need to go and put those cakes in."

Laura Jo started. She'd been so content she'd forgotten about having anything to do. Her hand being surrounded by Mark's added to that feeling. For some reason it made her feel protected, as if she weren't facing the world alone. She hadn't had that in her life for so long it had taken her time to recognize it.

Mark not only made her feel protected but she had seen his security in tangible terms. He was great with Allie. More than once he'd seen to it that she was safe and cared for and that made her happy. She'd also seen him showing that protection to others. He'd been there when she'd called for help with Anna and Marcy. There hadn't been a moment's hesitation on his part about coming. Not once had he acted like her having a daughter was an issue. In fact, he embraced Allie, included her.

Why was Mark the one man who made her feel that way? His background said he wasn't the man for her. She wanted someone who was more interested in her than what her last name had been. But hadn't he proved her background didn't matter? He'd shown his interest well before she had told him her maiden name was Herron.

She might have questioned whether or not he had become a doctor for the money and prestige but the Clayborns already had that. After she'd viewed him seeing to a patient she'd seen his concern was sincere. He was a man interested in caring for people. He had offered to help with the shelter and had proved it with his donation and medical care. How different could he be from Phil, who was the most self-centered man she'd ever known?

She slipped her hand out of his. "I'll bake the cakes. You should stay here. It's a beautiful night."

"I'll help you."

"It won't take me long."

"Do you promise to come back? Not disappear out the front door?"

Laura Jo smiled. "Yes, I'll come back."

"I'll be waiting."

She liked the sound of that. People didn't wait for her, they left her. Mark was starting to mean too much to her. Laura Jo put the cakes in the ovens. Thankfully, Mark had double ovens and she could bake them at the same time.

Still wearing his jacket, she went back outside to join him. If he hadn't stated his fear that she might leave she might have considered going home without telling him. Her attraction to him was growing beyond her control. She didn't trust herself around him.

As she passed him on the way to her lounge he sat up

and snagged her wrist. "Come and sit with me." He pulled her toward him.

She put a hand down next to his thigh to stop herself from falling.

"Mark…" she cautioned.

"I'm not going to jump you. I'd just like to have you close."

"Why?"

The light from inside the house let her see well enough his incredulous look. "Why? Because I'm a man and you're a woman. I like you and I think you like me more than you want to admit. You're as aware of the attraction as I am. You just won't admit it.

She looked down at him for a moment.

"All I want is to sit here with a beautiful woman and watch the stars. Nothing more. But if you don't want to, I'll live with that."

He made it sound like she was acting childishly. "Scoot over."

"If you're going to get bossy then maybe I need to re-consider my invitation."

She snickered and lay on her side next to him. He wrapped an arm around her shoulders and her head naturally went to his chest.

"Now, is this so bad?"

"No. I'm much warmer."

"Good. I'm glad I can be of service." Mark's breath brushed her temple.

"I can't get too comfortable. I don't want to burn the cakes."

"How much longer do they need to cook?" His hand moved up and down her arm.

"Another forty minutes."

He checked his watch. "Then I'll help you remember."

It took her a few minutes to relax and settle into her warm and cozy spot alongside Mark. The lights of Mobile glowed in the distance and the horn of an occasional seagoing freighter sounded. It was a lonesome noise, one that up until this minute she could identify with. Somehow she no longer felt lonely. As they sat in silence her eyelids drooped and closed.

The next thing she knew Mark was shaking her awake. "We need to get the cakes out."

She jerked to a sitting position. "I'm sorry. I went to sleep on you."

"I'm not. It would be my guess you needed to rest after the week you've had."

Laura Jo couldn't argue with that. She struggled to get up.

"Let me climb out first then I'll pull you up," Mark suggested.

As he moved, his big body towered over her. She was tempted to touch him. Before she could stop herself she placed a hand on his chest.

"I'm squishing you?"

"No. I just wanted to touch you," she murmured.

He gave her a predatory glare. "Great. You decide to touch me when the king cakes might be burning. You need to work on your timing."

She nudged him back. "Let me up."

He hesitated a second before he took her hand and pulled her to her feet. "Let's go."

In the kitchen Mark peeked into an oven. He inhaled dramatically. "Smells wonderful."

"If you'll get your nose out of it, I can take it out." Laura Jo handed him a hot pad. "I'll get this one and you can get the other." Laura Jo pulled the golden-brown mound out of the oven and set it on the counter. Mark did the same and placed his beside hers.

Again he leaned over and inhaled deeply. "Perfect."

"I need to mix the icing and then we can put the colors on." Laura Jo found a bowl and added powdered sugar then water. She stirred them into a creamy white mixture. Using a spoon, she drizzled the icing back and forth over the top of the cakes.

Mark dipped a finger through the bowl and put it in his mouth. "Mmm."

She tapped the top of his hand when he started after the cake.

"Ouch."

"I believe you have a sweet tooth."

"I think you are sweet."

"I think you might flatter the cook in order to get your way. It's time for the colored sugar." Laura Jo picked up the food coloring she'd left on the other end of the counter. "We'll need three bowls."

Mark went to a cabinet and brought those to her. Laura Jo put granulated sugar in each of the bowls and added yellow coloring to one, purple to another and green to the last one. She mixed until each granule had turned the color. She sprinkled one color over a third of one cake. In the middle section another and on the last third another.

"Do you know what the colors stand for?" Mark asked.

"No self-respecting citizen of Mobile wouldn't know. Purple is for justice, green is for faith and gold for power."

"You are correct. Can we have a slice now?" Mark asked, sounding much like a child begging at his mother's side.

"You want to eat it while it's hot?"

"Why not?"

"I've just never had it that way. I've always waited until it's cooled."

"Well, there's a first time for everything." Mark pulled a knife out of a drawer and sliced a hunk off the end of one cake. Picking it up, he bit into it. "This is delicious. Allie is right, you do make the best cakes. I've never had one better from a bakery."

His praise made her feel warm inside. She cut a small section and placed it in her mouth. It was good.

"Hey, look what I found." He held up a baby.

"You knew where that was."

"I did not," he said in an indignant tone. "Just good luck."

Laura smiled and placed the items she had brought into bags. She needed to leave before she was tempted to stay longer. Being with Mark had been far more enjoyable than she'd found comfortable. What if he tried to kiss her again? Could she handle that?

"What're you doing?" Mark asked.

"I'm packing up."

"You don't have to go."

"Yes, I do. Do you have something I can wrap one of these cakes in? Allie will be expecting to eat some tomorrow."

Mark opened a drawer and handed her a box of plastic wrap.

She pulled out a length of wrap and started covering the cake. "Do you mind if I take your baking pan? I'll return it."

"I don't mind," he said in an aggravated tone, as if he knew she was dodging the issue.

"Are you running out on me, Laura Jo?"

She refused to look at him. "No, I've been here for hours and I was more worried about wearing out my welcome."

Mark took the wrap from her and put it on the counter. "I don't think that's possible. I believe you're running scared."

"I'm not."

"Then why don't you go to the dance with me on Tuesday night?"

"I've already said I can't." She reached for a bag and put the rest of the items she'd brought in it.

"I think it's 'I won't.'"

"Please, Mark, just leave it alone. I'm not going to change my mind. It's not because of you but for other reasons."

"Care to tell me what those are."

"I'd rather not. I need to be going." She pulled the bags to her.

"I'm a good listener."

"That's not the problem. I just don't want to talk about it. Now, I need to go."

Mark took them from her. "I'll get these. You can get the cake. I'll walk you to your car."

Laura Jo was a little disappointed that he hadn't put up more of an argument to her leaving. Had her refusal to open up about why she didn't want to go to the krewe dance put him off? Wasn't that what she wanted?

"I need to wrap your cake up before I go and clean up this mess."

"Don't worry about doing that. I'll take care of it. Theresa will be in tomorrow."

"Theresa?"

"My housekeeper."

Just another shining example of the fact they lived in two different worlds. "Well, I'm not going to leave anyone, including a housekeeper, this mess."

"I'm not surprised. It's in your nature to see to other people, make it better for them. Who makes things better for you?"

She hadn't ever thought of herself in that context but he might be right. She wouldn't let him know it, though. "I don't need anyone taking care of me."

"We might be perfect for each other because I'm no good at doing so," he said in a dry tone.

What had made him say that? He was always taking care of people.

She went to the sink, picked up the cleaning cloth and started wiping off the counter.

"Leave it." Mark said, taking the cloth and placing it in the sink. "I'll take care of it."

Laura Jo then picked up the cake and headed for the front door. Mark wasn't far behind. When they reached the car, he opened the front passenger-side door and placed the bags on the floor. He then took the cake from her and did the same.

She went to the driver's door and he joined her there. "Thanks for helping me with the cakes."

"Not a problem." Mark reached into his pocket and pulled something out.

Laura Jo could just make out with the help of the light from the porch that he was rotating the baby between his index and thumb.

"We had a deal."

Laura Jo had an uneasy feeling. Where was he going with this? "We did."

"I would like to collect now."

Every nerve in her hummed. Something told her that she might not like his request. "Just what do you want?"

Mark's lips lifted, giving him a wolfish appearance. He took a step closer, coming into her personal space.

Heat washed over her. She looked at him. In the dim light she couldn't see his eyes clearly but she felt their intensity.

"I want you to kiss me."

"What?"

"I want you put your hands on my shoulders, lean up and place your lips on mine."

He said the words in a form of a challenge, as if she would refuse. She'd show him. Placing her hands on his chest, she slowly slid them up and over his shoulders.

His hands went to her waist, tightening around her.

"Remember this is my kiss," she admonished him.

He eased his hold but didn't release her.

Going up on her toes, she took her time, bringing her lips to his. The tension across his shoulders told her Mark was working to restrain himself.

Taking his lower lip between her teeth, she gently tugged.

He groaned.

She let go and smoothed it over with the tip of her tongue. Slowly she moved her lips over his until she almost ended the contact.

At Mark's sound of resistance she grinned and moved her mouth back to press it firmly against his. She didn't have to ask for entrance, he was already offering it. Her tongue met his and danced but he soon took the lead. She'd been caught at her own game. It felt wonderful to have a man touch her. It had been so long. For Mark to be the one made it even more amazing. Wrapping her arms around his neck, she gave herself over to the moment. She wanted more, so much more.

Mark gripped Laura Jo's waist and pulled her closer. He pressed her back against the car. His hand slid under the hem of her shirt and grazed her smooth skin until his fingers rested near the prize. Wanting to touch, taste, tease, he had to remove the barrier. Using the tip of his index finger, he followed the line of her bra around to the clasp. When he hesitated Laura Jo squirmed against him. She wanted this as much as he did. Flicking the clasp open, he moved his hand to the side curve of her breast.

He released her lips and gave a small sound of complaint. Placing small kisses along her neck to reassure her, he skimmed his hand upward to cup her breast. His sigh of pleasure mingled with hers. He tested the weight. Perfect. Using a finger, he circled her nipple then tugged.

Her hips shifted and came into more intimate contact with his ridged manhood. He'd been aware of his desire for Laura Jo for a number of days but it had never been this overwhelming.

He pushed her bra up and off her other breast. Her nipple stood tall, waiting for his attention. That knowledge only fueled his desire.

Laura Jo cupped his face and brought his lips back to hers. She gave him the hottest kiss he'd ever received. Heaven help him, if she could turn him on with just kisses, what could she do to him in bed?

She ran her hands under his shirt and across his back.

When her mouth left his to kiss his cheek, he pushed up her shirt, exposing her breasts. He backed away just far enough to look at her. "Beautiful."

He didn't give her time to speak before his lips found hers again and his fingers caressed her breast. Thankful for her small car, he leaned her back over the hood. Her fingers flexed and released against the muscles of his back as she met him kiss for kiss. Standing between her legs, the heat of her center pressed against his. He pulled his mouth from hers. It went to the top of her right breast, where he placed his lips. Laura Jo shivered.

"Cold?"

"No."

His chest swelled with desire. What he was doing to her had caused the reaction, not the metal of the car. He lowered his mouth to her nipple and took it. Using his tongue, he spun and tugged. Laura Jo bucked beneath him.

Her hand went to the line of his pants and glided just beneath. She ran her hand one way and then the other before it returned to stroking his back.

She wasn't the cold fish she wanted him to believe she was. She was hot and all sensual woman. He smiled as he gave the other nipple the same devotion.

He wanted her here and now. In his driveway. On her car. But that wasn't what Laura Jo deserved. He wasn't that kind of man. She certainly wasn't that type of woman.

"Sweetheart, we need to go inside."

Mark saw her blink once, twice, as if she were coming out of a deep dream. She looked around as if trying to figure out where she was. He saw the moment she came back to reality and his heart dropped.

"Oh, God." She sat up and gave him a shove.

He stepped back and let her slide off the car.

She jerked her shirt down, not bothering to close her bra. "I have to go."

"No, you don't."

He stepped toward her and she stopped him with a hand. "I can't do this."

"Why not?"

"Because it is wrong for me on so many levels." She climbed behind the wheel of the car. "I'm sorry, Mark."

She couldn't have been any more sorry than he was. He stood there with his body as tight as a bike spoke, wanting to reach out to her. Laura Jo didn't even look at him as she started the car and headed out the drive.

It wasn't until the car stopped about halfway down that he knew she hadn't been as unaffected by what had passed between them as she'd acted. She had wanted him, too.

Guilt filled him. He had no business pursuing Laura Jo if he had no intention of the relationship going beyond what they had just experienced. He couldn't let it be more. He'd already proved he would run when the going got tough. Could he trust himself not to let them down, like he had Mike?

As her taillights disappeared, he turned and walked toward the house. All he had waiting for him tonight was a long, cold shower. He needed to stay well out of Laura Jo's life.

Laura Jo opened the door early the next morning to let Allie, Marsha and Jeremy in. Before Laura Jo could say hello, Marsha announced, "We've got a problem."

"Bigger than the one we already have?"

"Yep."

"Come on into the kitchen and tell me what's happened."

Marsha followed her while Jeremy rushed ahead and took the chair next to Allie.

Marsha sat in the other chair while Laura Jo got a bowl from the cabinet and placed it in front of Jeremy. She then sat down. "Okay, let me have it."

"I got an email from the city rep, saying that if we don't get half the asking price in cash to them by the end of next week then there's no deal."

This was worse than Laura Jo had expected. "That only gives us five days, and three of those are holidays," she groaned.

"I know. That's why I'm here. Do you have any ideas?"

Laura Jo propped her elbows on the table and put her head in her hands. "No," she said in a mournful voice.

"I do," Marsha announced emphatically.

Laura Jo looked at her. "You do?"

"You have to go to the knewe dance. It's our only chance."

Laura Jo stood and walked to the sink. After last night, going to the dance had become less about her past and more about her reaction to Mark. She had been so tempted to throw all her responsibilities and concerns into the bay and find paradise in his arms. She'd been lying half-naked on the hood of a car, for heaven's sake. The man made her lose her mind. She'd had to stop at the end of his drive in order to get herself together enough to drive. Her hands had still been shaking when she'd started across the bay.

She couldn't stand the thought of losing the best chance they'd had in years to have a new house. But if she went to the dance she'd have to resist Mark, which she wasn't sure she could do, and face her parents and the social circle she'd left behind. The one she spoke so negatively about. She would be going back with her tail between her legs and begging them to help her. No, she would be asking for help for the shelter. It had nothing to do with her personally.

"I'll call Mark. If he hasn't asked someone else to go, I'll tell him I'll go."

Marsha joined her at the sink. "I wouldn't ask you to do it if I thought there was another way." She put an arm around Laura Jo's shoulders. "The house is too perfect for us not to give it our best shot. I'd go but I don't have the same influence as you or Dr. Clayborn have."

"I know. I just hope it works." Maybe going would not only benefit the house but give her a chance to lay some ghosts to rest.

"Me, too." Marsha squeezed her shoulder.

What if Mark had already found another date? That thought gave Laura Jo a sick feeling. Then she guessed she'd be going to the dance by herself. Not only to face her past alone but to see Mark holding another woman. Neither experience appealed to her.

CHAPTER SIX

It was midmorning and Mark was at his office desk when the woman he'd been planning to ask to the dance informed him that he had a call.

Picking up the phone, he said, "Dr. Clayborn here."

"Mark, its Laura Jo."

Like he wouldn't recognize her voice.

"If you don't already have a date for the dance, I'd like to go after all," she finished on a breathless note.

He'd thought of little else but her since those minutes outside his home. She'd kissed him so thoroughly, leaving him in need of not only one cold shower but two. Laura Jo had completely turned the tables on him with those hot, sexy kisses. He'd only hoped to kiss her one more time but instead he'd been left wanting all of her.

"No, I haven't asked anyone else yet."

After the way she'd left last night, something bad must have happened regarding the shelter for her to agree to go to the dance with him. He didn't care, he wasn't going to question the gift.

"So I'm still invited?"

"If you would like to go."

"I would."

"So what changed your mind?"

"They've moved up the timetable on the shelter house and I've been left no choice."

"Well, it's nice to know it isn't because you might enjoy an evening out with me," he said in his best serious tone.

He had to admit it stung to know that she had no interest in being seen at the most prestigious event of the year with him. The only reason she had agreed to go was because she needed help finding funds for the shelter. She had made it clear on more than one occasion that she didn't want to go, so he could only imagine how desperate she must be to pick up the phone and call him. She wanted that shelter enough to take this bold step. What impressed him most was that it wasn't for her but for someone else.

"I'll pick you up at seven."

"Make it eight. I have to work the parade."

That figured. When did she ever take time for herself? He was going to see to it that she enjoyed the evening out with him if it killed him.

"I'll be there at eight, then. We'll make a grand entrance."

"That's what I'm afraid of. Bye, Mark." With that she rang off.

"Laura Jo, stop fussing, you look beautiful," Marsha nagged as Laura Jo pulled up on the dress that showed far too much cleavage for her comfort.

She'd found the evening dress at the upscale consignment shop downtown. Ironically, it was the same one her mother had taken all the family's outdated clothes to when Laura Jo had been a child. Her mother would say, "Maybe someone less fortunate can use these." Like people who were less fortunate cared whether or not they wore couture clothing.

"I'm only going to this thing to try to drum up funds

for the shelter, not to have men staring at me. I'll have to wear the green dress. Would you get it? It's in my closet."

Laura Jo hadn't had time to look any further for a more appropriate dress. She'd taken the first one that was her size and looked suitable. She hadn't even tried it on and had had no idea this one would be so revealing.

"Isn't the dress formal?" Marsha said, as if she were reassuring a child having a temper tantrum.

"Yes, but I guess I don't have a choice." Laura Jo looked into the full-length mirror one more time. The plunging neckline left the top of her breasts exposed. Each time she breathed she feared more than that might be visible. For a brief second the memory of Mark's lips pressed against her flesh made her sizzle all over. She inhaled sharply.

"Is something wrong?" Marsha asked.

She circled around and faced Marsha. "Don't you have a pink shawl? I could put it around my shoulders and tie it in front. That would fix the problem."

Marsha sighed. "I don't see a problem but I'll go get it. I think you're overreacting. The dress is perfect the way it is."

Laura Jo looked at herself again. Was she overreacting? If so, why? Because she was going to the dance with Mark or because she was afraid she couldn't control herself around him?

She studied the dress. It was midnight blue with the slightest shimmer to it. The material hugged her in all the correct places. Twisting, she turned so that she could see the back. It closed close to her neck so that it formed a diamond-shaped peephole in the middle. It was the loveliest detail of the dress.

"Mommy, you look pretty," Allie said from behind Laura Jo.

"Thank you, honey." She leaned down and kissed the top of Allie's head.

The doorbell rang.

"I'll get it," Allie said, running out of the room.

Laura Jo followed. Surely it was Marsha, returning with the wrap.

Allie opened the door and Mark stood on the other side. Their eyes met and held. Everything that had happened between them the night before flashed through her mind. His gaze slid downward and paused at her breasts.

They tingled and her nipples grew hard. Heat pooled in her middle. What was happening to her? Something as simple as a look from Mark could make her feel alive like no one else could.

Was he remembering, too?

"Doesn't Mommy look pretty?" Allie asked, looking back and forth between them.

Mark's gaze didn't leave her. Seconds later, as if coming out of a stupor, he said, "Uh, yes, she looks wonderful."

Laura Jo swallowed hard. She'd never felt more beautiful than she did right now as Mark admired her. The man was starting to get under her skin and everything about his idea of life was so wrong for her. Or was it? She'd better guard her heart tonight or he might take it.

Allie looked up at Mark. "You look pretty, too."

He did, in the most handsome, debonair and charming way. His blond waves were in place and his eyes shone. Dressed in his formal wear of starched white shirt, black studs and tailcoat, he took her breath away. She'd seen many men wearing their finest but none compared to the man standing before her.

"Thank you, Allie." He was still looking at her when he said, "Do you mind if I come in?"

"Oh, no, do." Laura Jo gave Allie a little nudge back into the hall. She stepped out of the way and let Mark enter.

"Come in and have a seat. I'm waiting for Marsha to bring me a cover-up."

"From where I stand, you look perfect just the way you are." His voice had a grainy sound to it that wasn't normal.

"Thank you." When had she become such a blusher? When Mark had come into her life.

"Have a seat while I get my purse. Marsha should be back by then." Laura Jo indicated a chair in their small living area.

There was a knock on the door and Allie ran to open it. Laura Jo trailed behind her. Her friend breezed in, breathless. "I couldn't find it. I must have given it away at our last clothes drive. Hi, Dr. Clayborn. You look nice." Marsha let the last few words spin out.

"Thank you. I was telling Laura Jo she looks great just as she is."

"I think so, too." Marsha said. She offered a hand to Allie. "Come on. It's time to go. Jeremy will be home in a few minutes."

Laura Jo picked up a small bag and handed it to her daughter. "I'll see you tomorrow afternoon. I'll be picking you and Jeremy up from school." Laura Jo kissed her on the head.

"Okay. Bye, Mark." Allie happily went out the door.

"Have a good time and don't do anything I wouldn't do," Marsha quipped with a wink.

"Marsha!"

Mark's low chuckle didn't help to lessen Laura Jo's mortification.

She turned to him. "You do understand I'm only going to the krewe dance because I need funds for the shelter. Nothing else can happen."

"You more than made it clear that the evening has nothing to do with my company. Are you ready?"

Had she hurt his feelings?

"Mark, I'm sorry. I didn't mean to sound so rude." She looked down. "After the other night I just didn't want you to get the wrong idea. I do appreciate you taking me to the dance. It's just that I have a difficult time with the idea and I seem to be taking it out on you."

"Maybe if you explained, I would understand."

She looked at him again. "It's because...I shunned that world years ago."

"Why?"

"I fell in love, or at least what I thought was love, with a guy who my parents didn't approve of. 'Not of our social status,' my father said. My parents were adamantly against the marriage. They told me Phil was after my name and money, not me. That he was no good. My father was particularly vocal about Phil being the wrong guy. He forced me to make a choice between them or my ex.

"I always felt like I was an afterthought to them. I never quite fit the mold they had imagined for their child. They spent little time with me when I was young and now they wanted to start making parental demands, showing real interest. I had always been more headstrong than they liked, so my father's ultimatum backfired.

"I told my parents if the man I loved wasn't good enough for them then I didn't need them. I chose Phil. Turned out they were right about him. He was everything they said he was and more. I said some ugly things to my parents that I now regret but I couldn't go running back. My pride wouldn't allow that. I had to prove to them and myself I could take care of myself. Live with my mistakes."

Laura Jo would never let Mark know what it took for her to admit her mistakes. No matter how many times or how sweetly Marsha had asked Laura Jo, she had never told her as much as she had just told Mark.

"You haven't spoken to your parents in all that time?"

"I tried to contact them after Phil and I got back from Vegas but the housekeeper told me Mother wouldn't take my call. I phoned a few more times and got the same response. I finally gave up."

"They really hurt you."

Laura Jo fingered a fold in her dress. "Yes. After I had Allie I had a better sense of what it was to have a child's best interests at heart. But after they'd acted the way they did when I called I couldn't take the chance that they would treat Allie the same way as they had me. I'll never let her feel unwanted."

"Maybe they've changed. They might be better grandparents than they were parents. You could try again. At least let them meet Allie."

She shook her head. "I think the hurt is too deep and has gone on for too long."

"You'll never know until you try. I could go with you, if you want."

"I don't know. I'll have to think about that. Let's just get through tonight, then I'll see."

"I'll be there beside you all night. We'll both put in the appearance to get what you need and to also satisfy my father. Then we're out of there."

To her surprise, he didn't sound like he'd been that excited about going to the dance to begin with. Had she made some judgment calls about him that just weren't true? He'd never once looked down on her, her friends or where she lived. Did his status in the area truly not matter to him?

She made a chuckling sound that had nothing to do with humor and more about being resigned. "We sound nothing like two people expecting to enjoy an evening out."

At the car, he opened the door, took her elbow and helped her in. At least if she had to go to the dance she would arrive in a fine car and on the arm of the most handsome man in town.

Mark settled behind the wheel and closed the door but didn't start the engine. Instead, he placed his hand over hers. Squeezing it gently, he said, "I can see by the look on your face that you have no hope of this evening ending well. Why don't you think positive? You might be surprised."

"I'll try."

"Plus you're starting to damage my ego by making me think I no longer know how to show a woman a good time." Mark started the car then checked to see if she was buckled in. She patted her seat belt and he backed out of the parking space.

"This doesn't have anything to do with you personally." She studied his strong profile in the dim light.

"Well, I'm glad to know that. I was starting to think you thought being seen with me was comparable to going to the gallows."

She smiled.

"That's better. At least you haven't lost your sense of humor completely." He pulled out into the street.

They rode down now crowd-free Government Street toward the port. The building where the dance was being held was located on the bay. Mark circled to the elegant glass doors of the historic building.

Mark stopped the car. He handed the keys to the valet then came around to open the door for her. Taking a deep fortifying breath, she placed her hand into Mark's offered one. It was large and steady.

"You're an outstanding nurse, mother of a wonderful daughter and an advocate for mothers, Laura Jo. You're more accomplished than the majority of the people here."

She met his look. His eyes didn't waver. He'd said what he believed. She drew confidence from that. "Thank you."

He pulled her hand into the crook of his arm as they walked toward the door of the building held open by another young man in evening dress. Slowly they ascended one side of the U-shaped staircase to the large room above. Mark paused at the door just long enough for her to survey the space.

People were standing in groups, talking. The room was narrow and long with a black-and-white-tiled floor. Round dining tables were arranged to the right and left, creating an aisle down the middle. The white tablecloths brushed the floor. The Mardi Gras colored decorations centered on each table were elaborate and striking.

The area looked much as it had the last time she'd attended a ball when she'd been nineteen years old and a lady-in-waiting. A month later she'd met Phil and her world had taken a one-eighty-degree turn. Back then she'd been a child of wealthy parents with her life planned out for her. When she'd broken away from her parents, she would never have guessed her life would become what it was now. Still, had she made a mistake by keeping Allie away from them? Her parents had faults but didn't she, too?

Just as eye-catching was the dress of the active men of the krewe. They were all clad in their Louis XVI brocade knee-length satin coats trimmed in gold or silver braid. On their heads were large hats that had one side of the brim pinned up with a plumed feather attached and matched the men's coats. Their pantaloons, white stockings and black buckle shoes added to the mystique. The women who were married to the members of the board wore equally ostentatious dresses, some of them matching their husband's. Otherwise, men and women were dressed in formal wear.

Were her parents here in all their finery?

Mark must have felt her stiffen because he placed his

hand over hers, which was resting on his arm. "Let's go see and be seen."

They hadn't walked far when they were stopped by a man's voice calling, "Mark Clayborn, I heard you were back in town."

Mark brought her around with him. "Mr. Washington, how in the world are you?" Mark shook the man's hand and Laura Jo released his arm but remained beside him.

"I'm doing well."

"I heard about your father. He's recovering, I understand," the older man said.

"Slowly, but retirement is a must," Mark told Mr. Washington with ease.

"I imagine that's difficult for him. I'll make plans to get out to see him."

"I know he would like that."

When she started to move away Mark rested a hand at her waist. It warmed her skin. She was no longer worried about the people they might see. Her focus was on his touch.

Mr. Washington turned his gaze to her. Laura Jo knew who he was but had never met him.

Mark followed his look. "Mr. Washington, I'd like to introduce you to Laura Jo Akins."

Would he recognize her name? No, probably not. There were a number of girls in the south with double first names. Laura Jo wasn't that uncommon.

"Nice to meet you, Ms. Akins."

She forced a smile. "Nice to meet you, too." At least with her married name it wasn't obvious who she was.

"Laura Jo is a nurse at Mobile General and has started a shelter for abandoned mothers." Mark jumped right into helping her look for supporters.

"That sounds like a worthy cause," Mr. Washington said,

as if he was really interested. "What made you decide to do that?"

Laura Jo wasn't going to lie. "I was an abandoned mother. My husband left me when I was pregnant. I have a daughter."

"So you know the need firsthand." He nodded his head thoughtfully.

"I do." Laura Jo lapsed into her planned appeal. Mark offered a few comments and the fact he had made a donation to what he thought was a worthy cause.

"Contact my office tomorrow and I'll have a donation for you," Mr. Washington assured her.

"Thank you. The women I'm helping thank you also."

Mark looked across the room. "Mr. Washington, I think it's time for us to find a place at a table for dinner."

"It does look that way. Good to see you, son. Nice to meet you, young lady."

As Mark led her away she whispered to him, "I never imagined it would be that easy."

"I don't think it will always happen that way. But Mardi Gras season is when people are having fun so they're a little more generous." He took her hand and led her farther into the room.

"You're right about coming tonight. As much as I didn't want to, it was the right thing to do for the shelter."

After they were stopped a couple of times by people Mark knew, he found them a table with two seats left near the front of the room. She still hadn't seen her parents.

Mark remained a gentleman and pulled her chair out for her before he took his own. She could get used to this. As ugly as she had been about coming to the ball, he'd still helped her get a promise of funds from Mr. Washington and was treating her like a lady. She owed him an apology.

He knew a few people sharing their table and introduced her. She recognized a number of other couples by their names but they didn't act as if they knew her. Still, she might run into some of her parents' friends. She looked around.

Mark whispered in her ear, "They might not be here."

Laura Jo knew better. They didn't miss a Mardi Gras ball. One more pass over the crowd and she saw them. They had aged well. There was more gray hair at her father's temples but her mother had a stylish cut and kept it colored. They both looked as elegant as they ever had for one of these events.

"What's wrong?"

"My parents."

Mark looked in the direction she indicated. "Why don't we go and say hello?"

"They won't want to speak to me. I said some horrible things to them."

"I bet that doesn't matter anymore. At least you could give them a chance. They may regret what happened, just like you do. You'll feel better if you do. At least you will know you made the effort. Come on, I'll be right there with you." He stood and offered his hand.

Laura Jo hesitated then placed her hand in Mark's. It was large, warm and strong. A new resolve filled her. No longer the same person she had been nine years ago, she could do this. Mark held her hand tight as they crossed the room. The closer they came to her parents' table the more her gut tightened. The sudden need to run splashed over her. She hesitated.

"You can do this." The small squeeze of her hand told her she wasn't alone.

Her parents looked up at them. Shock registered on their faces.

Mark let go of her hand and cupped her elbow.

"Hello, Mother and Daddy."

"We're surprised to see you here. We had no idea you were coming," her father said in a blunt, boardroom voice.

Well, he was certainly all open arms about seeing her again.

"Hello, I'm Mark Clayborn. Nice to meet you, Mr. and Mrs. Herron."

Her parents looked at Mark as if they weren't sure they had heard correctly. She was just relieved he'd taken the attention off her for a moment.

"Mark Clayborn, junior?" her father asked.

"Yes, sir."

Her father stood and offered his hand. "Pleasure to meet you."

Leaving her seat, her mother came to stand beside her father. "How have you been, Laura Jo?"

She sounded as if she truly cared. "Fine."

"I'm glad to hear that. I understand you've started some type of shelter."

How did they know about that? Was she really interested? "I have."

Mark put an arm around her shoulders. "Laura Jo has helped a lot of women who needed it."

It was nice to have someone sound proud of her. Not till this moment had she realized she'd been missing that in her life.

"Are they unwed mothers?"

At least her mother had asked with what sounded like sincere curiosity. "Some are but most have been abandoned. Those that have no family they can or want to go home to."

Laura Jo didn't miss her mother's flinch.

"That sounds like a worthwhile project," her mother finally said.

"It is," Mark agreed. "She's now trying to buy a larger place for the shelter to move to."

Laura Jo placed her hand on Mark's arm. She didn't want to go into all that with her parents. "I don't think they want to hear all about that."

When Mark started to argue she added, "How have you both been?"

"We've been well," her father said.

They were talking to each other like strangers, which in reality they were.

"I understand you live over in the Calen area."

"I do." Laura Jo was astonished that he knew that. Had they been keeping up with her when she'd had no idea? Did her parents care more than she'd thought or shown?

Her mother stepped toward Laura Jo with an imploring look on her face. "Will you tell us about our granddaughter?"

"You knew?" Laura Jo was thankful for Mark's steady hand steady on her elbow.

"Yes, we've known for a long time." Her mother's look didn't waver.

They had known and they still hadn't helped? Or they'd known that Laura Jo would throw their help back at them if they offered?

"Please, tell us about her," her father pleaded.

Laura Jo spent the next few minutes telling her parents about Allie. They seemed to hang on every word. Had they changed?

"Thank you for telling us," her mother said with a soft sigh when Laura Jo finished.

They were interrupted by the krewe captain getting the attention of the people in the room. He announced the buffet dinner was being served and gave directions about which tables would go first.

"We should return to our table," Laura Jo said.

It was her mother's turn to give her an entreating look. "Laura Jo, may we see Allie sometime?"

Laura Jo stiffened but she forced her voice to remain even. "I'll have to think about that. She knows nothing about you."

Moisture spring to her mother's eyes.

The table next to her parents' rose to get in line for their meal.

"I think it's time that we returned to our table, Laura Jo. It was nice to meet you both, Mr. and Mrs. Herron."

Mr. Herron blinked as if he had forgotten Mark was standing there.

"Thank you for coming over, Laura Jo. It's wonderful to see you."

Her mother sounded like she truly meant it.

"It's nice to see you, too." Laura Jo turned and headed back to their table on shaky knees.

Mark leaned in and asked, "You okay?"

"I'm good." She smiled. "Really good, actually. Thanks for encouraging me to speak to them."

He grinned. "Hey, that's what a good date does. So are you going to introduce Allie to them?"

"I don't know if I'm ready for that but at least I'll think about it."

"Sounds like a plan. Hungry?"

"Much more than I was a few minutes ago."

"Good."

They returned to their table and had to wait until a few tables on the other side of the room lined up and then it was their turn. Mark placed his hand at the small of her back again. As disconcerting as it was to have him touch her, he'd done it enough over the past couple of weeks that she'd grown to not only expect it but to appreciate the simple gesture.

They were almost to the buffet tables in the middle of the room when Mark jerked to a stop. She turned to question him about what was wrong. He stood looking in the direction of a group of people who were obviously together. His face had darkened. All pleasantness of a few minutes ago had washed away. One of the group was in a wheelchair. Did he know the man?

Mark quickly regained his composure and closed the gap between him and her.

"Are you okay?" she whispered when he came to stand next to her.

"I'm fine." He added a smile that for once didn't reach his eyes.

They stood in line for a few minutes, working their way to where the plates were stacked. A large floral arrangement was positioned where the tables intersected. On the four tables were shrimp cocktail, gumbo, salads of all types and prime rib, with a man serving that and desserts.

As they slowly filled their plates, Laura Jo saw Mark glancing toward the end of the line. She noticed the man in the wheelchair. This time Mark seemed even more uncomfortable about the situation.

As they went through the line Mark spoke to people. Thankfully everyone accepted her as his date and nothing more. Maybe she could get through this evening after all. She'd been a teenager when she'd last been at this kind of function. She had matured and changed since then.

During the meal, Mark spoke to the woman to the right of him. Laura Jo had a light conversation with the man in full regalia to her left. Once during the meal Mark gave her knee a reassuring squeeze. That little gesture said, We're in this together. She appreciated it. Except for Marsha, it had been her and Allie against the world.

She had finished her dinner when Mark got her attention and asked her to tell the woman he'd been talking to about the shelter. The woman told Laura Jo that she would like to help and how to contact her.

The conversation was interrupted by the captain announcing that it was time to introduce the krewe directors.

Laura Jo smiled at Mark and mouthed, "Thank you."

He put his arm around her shoulder and gave her a gentle hug and whispered in her ear, "You're welcome. See, it's not as bad as you thought."

"No, it hasn't been. Thanks to you."

He kissed her temple. "You can really thank me later."

Before she could react to that statement the captain started calling names and people were lining up on the dance floor that was acting as a stage.

It was her turn to feel Mark stiffen. She saw the man in the wheelchair Mark had looked at earlier propelling himself across the stage, while an attractive woman walked beside him.

She glanced at Mark. His focus was fixed on the man. "Do you know him?"

"Yes."

"He's your friend from the accident, isn't he?"

"Yes." The word had a remorseful note to it.

The next man was being introduced and she didn't ask Mark any more. With everyone having been presented, the crowd clapped in appreciation for the work the board had done on the dance.

The captain then asked for everyone's attention again. "The king and queen and their court have arrived."

There was a hush over the room as the first lady-in-waiting and her escort were introduced.

The young lady wore an all-white dress made out of satin and adorned with pearls and sparkling stones. Her white train trailed across the floor. It was heavy, Laura Jo knew from experience.

When she had designed her train so many years ago it had had the family crest in the center with a large, pale pink flamingo rising from it. The bird's eye had been an onyx from her grandmother's train when she had been queen. Each pearl and precious stone were sewn on by hand. It had been edged in real white fox fur. She'd worn long white gloves that had reached above her elbows. She'd been told she'd never looked more beautiful.

And this happened every year. The pomp and circumstance of it all still astounded her.

She and her mother had designed and planned her dress and train for months. They had even taken a trip to New York to look for material. A designer there had made the dress then it had been sent back to Mobile, where a seamstress that specialized in embellishments had added them. What she would wear consumed their family life for the entire year before Mardi Gras.

She had no idea what her dress and train had cost but she was sure it would have been enough to run the shelter for two or three months.

"I bet you were a beautiful lady-in-waiting. I'm sorry I didn't pay more attention," Mark whispered close to her ear.

She smiled.

The couple walked to the captain and his wife on the stage and curtsied and bowed, before circling back to the rear of the room. By that time another couple had moved forward. The entire court was dressed in white, with the females having different dress and trains that had their personal design. The escorts wore identical outfits. Each couple paid their respects and this happened eighteen more times.

From the court would come next year's king and queen of Mardi Gras. Since her grandmother had been queen, Laura Jo had been on track to be the queen the year she turned twenty-one. The king would reign the year he turned twenty-five.

She glanced at Mark, who was watching the stage more than the couples parading up the aisle. "I did notice you and you were a handsome king," Laura Jo whispered.

"Thank you, fair maiden."

Laura Jo giggled. She knew well that there was a private and public side to Mardi Gras. It all started around Thanksgiving, with all the coming-out balls for the girls. The society families held the balls and she'd been a part of the process. She'd loved it at the time. Now she looked back on it and saw how spoiled she been and how ignorant of the world. Not until she had gotten away from her parents' house had she realized how many people could have been helped with the money that had gone into just her dresses for Mardi Gras.

As the royalty came into sight, Laura Jo couldn't help but be amazed at the beauty of the couple's attire. No matter how many times she had seen this type of event, she was still left in awe. They wore matching gold outfits trimmed in gold. The king's clothing was adorned as much as the queen's. She had gold beads that came to a peak halfway up the center of her skirt. The bodice had swirls and curls covering it. They carried crowns on their heads that glittered in the lights. The king carried a diamond-headed walking stick while the queen held a scepter that matched her crown.

Laura Jo had forgotten the artistry and how regal their trains were. They were both at least twenty feet long. Theirs, like those of the ladies-in-waiting, told a story of their life. The king's had his family crest with a hunting motif around it, which included an appliqué of a deer head.

The queen's train was also appliquéd but with large magnolias in detail. Around the edge was a five-inch border of crystals that made it shimmer. The neckline had a collar that went from one shoulder to the other in the back. It stood up eight inches high. It bounced gently as the queen walked. It was made from a mass of light and airy bangle beads formed into magnolias and leaves, the centers being made out of pearls.

Their trains alone could buy a room in the house they were looking at for the shelter.

"How did it feel to be the man of the hour?" Laura Jo asked Mark.

"At the time, amazing," he answered in a dry tone.

CHAPTER SEVEN

WITH THE INTRODUCTIONS COMPLETED, everyone returned to their meals and the band struck up a dance tune. Couples moved toward the dance floor.

"Why don't we have a dance before we go and talk to a few more people about the shelter? I think we could both use a few minutes of fun." Mark stood and offered her his hand.

"One dance."

As they entered the dance floor he brought Laura Jo close. She fit perfectly. Wearing high heels, her head came to his shoulder. The band was just beginning the first notes of a slow waltz. Laura Jo put her hand in his and the other on his shoulder. His hand rested on the warm, creamy skin visible on her back.

"You know, I think I like this dress more now than I did when I first saw you in it." The words were for her alone.

She glanced up, giving him a shy smile. Seeing her parents again seemed to have taken some fight out of her. She had to have missed them more than she'd admitted. Leaning in, she put her head into the curve of his shoulder. Mark tightened his hold and slowly moved them around the dance floor.

Other couples surrounded them but for him there was only he and Laura Jo. For once he wished he could hold one woman forever. He'd never allowed himself to dream further but with Laura Jo anything seemed possible.

They were returning to their table when Mr. Washington approached. "I was telling a buddy of mine about the work your young lady is doing. He would like to pledge fifty thousand."

Laura Jo gasped.

"Baba McClure has had a little too much to drink already and he has pledged another fifty."

Laura Jo squeezed his arm.

"The thing is," Mr. Washington went on, "you'd better go over there and get something in writing or they may not remember in the morning."

"Do you have a paper and pen in your purse?" Mark asked Laura Jo.

She picked up the tiny purse she had brought. "I have a small pen. I'll ask at the registration table if they have something we can write on."

Mark watched Laura Jo go. She was soon back. Mr. Washington showed them across the room and introduced them to the two men and let Laura Jo take it from there. Despite wanting to distance herself from her background, she had a way of charming people that had been instilled in her. She soon had a makeshift agreement from both men and had promised she would see them the next day.

Both men groaned and asked her to make it the day after. Before they left the table she gave Mr. Washington a kiss on the cheek. "Thank you."

The eighty-year-old man beamed. "You're welcome, honey."

"Come on, I believe this deserves a victory dance." She pulled Mark to the dance floor. A fast tune was being played.

"I don't fast-dance." Mark pulled to a stop.

"What was it you told me? Uh…let go a little." Laura Jo started moving to the music. She held her hands out, encouraging him to take them.

He wasn't going to turn that invitation down. After a few dances, both fast and slow, he said, "I'm ready to go if you are."

"You're really not any more into this stuff than I am, are you?"

"No, I guess being in California for so long got it out of my system." And what had happened to Mike.

He had glimpsed Mike a couple of times across the room. They had never been near each other and for that Mark was grateful. Once he had thought his onetime friend might have recognized him. Dodging Mike didn't make Mark feel any better. He still couldn't face him. He used having Laura Jo with him as an excuse not to.

"Let's go," Laura Jo agreed. "But I need to stop by the restroom on our way out."

Mark was waiting at the exit when Mike rolled up.

"So was the plan to leave without speaking to me?" he asked, looking directly at Mark. "Running out again?"

He stood dumbstruck. His gut churned. If Laura Jo showed up, would she recognize what a coward he was?

"No," Mark lied boldly. If he could figure out how to leave without having this conversation, he would. "I hadn't realized you were here." Another lie. "It's good to see you." At least that had a small margin of truth.

"I'm not sure that's true." Mike's gaze hadn't wavered.

The ache in Mark's chest increased.

"I hear you're back in town and practicing medicine."

"Yes, I'm in a clinic in Spanish Fort and living in Fairhope." If he could just make it through some small talk, Laura Jo would show up and they could go.

"You always did like it at the summer house," Mike said.

Mark glanced toward the other side of the room. "How have you been? I'm sorry I haven't—"

A blonde woman with twinkling green eyes and a cheery smile approached. "I'd like you to meet my wife." He reached behind him and took the hand of the woman. "This is Tammy."

Mike married? "It's nice to meet you."

"And you, too. Mike has told me a lot about you." Tammy continued to smile but it no longer reached her eyes.

Like how he'd been the cause of Mike being in a wheelchair for life, or the fact he had run out on him when he'd needed him most, or maybe the part where he hadn't bothered to stay in touch, like he should have. Yeah, there was a lot to say about him, but none of it good. Or to be proud of.

Laura Jo walked up beside him. Could she see how uncomfortable he was? He took her hand and drew her forward. "Uh, this is my friend Laura Jo. Laura Jo, Mike and Tammy Egan."

"Hey, I remember a Laura Jo. She was a friend of my kid sister's. I haven't seen her in years." Mike gave her a searching look.

"You're Megan's brother?" Laura Jo studied Mike for a moment.

Great. Mike remembered Laura Jo when he himself hadn't. He truly had been a self-absorbed person in his twenties. Maybe in many ways he still was.

"Yes, and you're Laura Jo Herron."

She smiled at Mike. "Was Herron. Now it's Akins."

"No matter the name, it's good to see you again."

It was time to get out of there. Mark said, "Mike, I'm sorry, we're expected at another dance." Great. He was still running from Mike and lying to do so.

Laura Jo glanced at him but said nothing.

Mike rolled back and forth in his chair with the ease

and agility of someone who had mastered the wheelchair. "I understand."

Somehow Mark was sure he did. All he wanted was to get away, forget, and find some fresh air. "Nice to see you again, Mike." Mark headed for the door. It wasn't until Laura Jo put her hand in his that he realized he had forgotten about her. He was running blind.

Mark didn't say anything on the way to his house. Laura Jo didn't either. They had both had an emotional evening. She let him remain in his thoughts, not even interrupting him to mention that he wasn't going toward her apartment. He didn't even register that he'd driven to his house until he'd pulled to a stop in his drive. "Why didn't you tell me to take you home?"

"Because I thought you needed someone to talk to."

How like her to recognize when someone was having trouble. He was in need, but of all the people he didn't want to look weak in front of it was Laura Jo.

"Let's go in. I'll fix us a cup of coffee." She was already in the process of opening the car door. Inside the house, she dropped her purse on the table beside the door, kicked off her shoes then headed straight for the kitchen. When he started to follow she said, "Why don't you go out to the deck? I'll bring it to you."

"Thanks. I appreciate it." He sounded weary even to his own ears.

"I'm just repaying all the times you've been there for me."

On the deck he sat in one of the chairs, spread his knees wide and braced his elbows on them. Putting his head in his hands, he closed his eyes.

Seeing Mike tonight had been as tough as it had ever been. Mark had prepared himself that he might see him at the dance but that didn't make it any easier. It only added another bag of guilt to the ten thousand he already carried on his shoulders.

Now, with Laura Jo having seen his shame, it made the situation worse.

"Here you go," she said from beside him.

He raised his head to find her holding a mug and looking at him with concern. At least it wasn't pity. He took the cup.

She put the mug she still held on the table nearby and said, "I'll be right back."

Laura Jo returned wearing the jacket he'd offered her the night they'd made the king cakes. Picking up the mug she'd left behind, she took the lounge next to him. They sat in silence for a long time.

Finally Laura Jo said, "Do you want to talk about it?"

"No."

She made no comment, as if she accepted it was a part of him that he wouldn't share. Something about her being willing to do that endeared her even more to him and made him want to have her understand. "You asked me a few days ago about Mike being in an accident, remember?"

He didn't see her nod but somehow he knew she had.

"It was a night like tonight. Clear and warm for the time of the year. I had this great idea that we'd drive to the beach after the dance was over. After all, I'd be leaving in a few days for Birmingham to do my fellowship. My girlfriend, who was the queen that year, was having her last hoorah with her friends, so why not? Mike was going to ride with me and some of the other guys were going to meet us down there."

He swiped his fingers through his hair.

"I'd had a few drinks but I'd been so busy being king I'd had little time to eat, let alone drink. Mike, on the other hand, had had too much. I told him more than once to buckle his seat belt. But he wouldn't listen. I was feeling wild and free that night. I knew I was going too fast for the road... Long story short, I ran off the road, pulled the car back on and went off the other shoulder. And the car rolled. I was hardly injured. Mike was thrown out. It broke his back."

"Oh, Mark."

He jumped up and started pacing. "I don't want your pity. I don't deserve it." Thankfully, Laura Jo said nothing more. "That's not the worst of it." He spun and said the words that he was sure would turn her against him. "I left. The next day I packed my bags, gave up my residency in Birmingham and accepted one in California. I've only seen him a few times since I watched him being put into an ambulance." He all but spat the last sentence.

Mark stopped pacing and placed his back to Laura Jo, not wanting to see the disgust he feared was in her eyes. She made a small sound of anguish. He flinched. His spine stiffened and his hands formed balls at his side. He hung his head.

Laura Jo felt Mark's guilt and pain ripple through her like the sting of a whip. How quickly and effortlessly Mark had worked himself past her emotional barriers. She cared for him. Wanted to help him past the hurt.

No wonder he was so hypervigilant about people buckling up in his car. Now that she thought about it, he'd even hesitated when he'd had to drive someone in his car. He found the responsibility too weighty.

She went to him. Taking one of his fists, she kissed the top of his hand and began gently pulling his fingers open until she could thread her own between his. She leaned her head against his arm. "It wasn't your fault, even if you don't believe it."

Mark snorted. "And it wasn't my fault that I was such a lousy friend that I ran out on him when he needed me most. That was unforgivable. But that wasn't enough, I've compounded it by years of not really having anything to do with him. I was closer to Mike than I was to my own brother. How could I have done that to him? Even tonight I was a coward."

"You know, it's not too late," she said quietly. "You're the one who has been telling me that."

"It's way past too late. How do I tell him I'm sorry I put him in a wheelchair while I still walk around?"

Laura Jo heard his disgust for himself in his voice.

"The same way I have to forgive my parents for the way they treated me. We have to believe people can change and grow."

He took her in his arms and looked down at her. "It's easy for someone with a heart as big as yours to forgive. Not everyone can or will do that."

His lips found hers.

Mark didn't ask for entrance. She greeted him. Welcomed his need. Her hands went to his shoulders. She massaged the tension from them before her fingers moved up his neck into his hair.

His desperation to lose himself in her goodness made him kiss her more deeply. She took all he gave with no complaint. There was a restlessness to his need, as if he was looking for solace. He pulled her closer, gathering her dress as he did so.

For tonight she could be that peaceful place if that was what he needed. Laura Jo tightened her arms around his neck and returned his kiss.

"I need you," he groaned. His lips made a trail down her neck.

Brushing her dress away, he dropped a kiss on the ridge

of her shoulder. His tongue tasted her. The warm damp-
ness he left behind made her quake. His other hand slipped
under the edge of the back of her dress and roamed, leaving a hot path of awareness.

"And I need you," she whispered against his ear.

Mark pushed her dress farther down her arm. His lips
followed the route of the material, leaving hot points along
her skin. Laura Jo furrowed her fingers through his hair,
enjoying the feel of the curl between her fingers.

He released the hook at the back of her neck and her
dress hung at her elbows. Her breasts tingled with anticipation. His head lowered to kiss the top of one breast. He
pushed the edge of her dress away from her nipple and took
it into his mouth and tugged lightly. She shivered from the
sensation. His tongue circled and teased her nipple until
she moaned into the evening air.

When his mouth moved to the other breast he cupped the
first one. The pad of his thumb found the tip of her nipple
and caressed it. He circled her nipple with the end of his
index finger until it stood at attention. He lifted the mound
and placed a kiss on it.

Her heated blood rushed to her center and pooled there.
She wanted to see and feel as much of Mark as he was of
her. Her hands found his lapels and slid beneath them to
his hard chest. There she worked his coat off. She wanted
to touch him. Feel his skin. This had gone beyond giving
comfort to a desire that was building into a powerful animal. It had been feeding and waiting since the first time
Mark had touched her. The more she knew about him, saw
him, felt his kindness, that longing had grown. Now there
was no denying it or fighting it.

Mark's lips came back to hers as he shook himself out
of his tux jacket and let it fall down his arms. Laura Jo's
fingers went to the bow tie and released it, pulling it away

and dropping it beside his jacket. His lips returned to her neck as Laura Jo removed first one stud and then another until she found his skin beneath his shirt.

The tip of her fingers lightly grazed the small patch of hair covering his warm skin. Yes, she'd found what she was looking for.

As Mark's mouth moved to hers for a hot, sinuous kiss, she yanked at his shirt, removing it from his pants. She wrapped her arms around his waist then she ran her hands over his back. She enjoyed the ripple of his muscles as they reacted to her touch. Would she ever get enough of touching him?

Mark gathered her dress, bringing it up until he could put his hand on her thigh. His fingers made circular motions along her bare skin. Slowly, his hand slid higher and higher until he ran his finger over the barrier of her panties at her core.

Laura Jo involuntarily flexed toward him. She'd never wanted a man to touch her more than she did at that moment.

With a growl of frustration, he set her on her feet. "I hope I don't live to regret this." He kissed her on the forehead. "Promise me you'll stay right here."

With heart pounding and body tight with need, Mark hurried into the house and scooped up the bedding in the extra bedroom. He grabbed two pillows, as well. With long strides, he walked back through the house. When he exited he was relieved to find Laura Jo waiting for him right where he'd left her. She had pulled her dress straps up over her shoulders. That was fine. He'd soon be removing her dress completely.

"What?" she murmured, as he came out of the house with his load.

"I want to see you under the stars."

He flipped the heavy spread out, not taking the time to make it neat. He lay down on his side and stretched out a hand in invitation for her to join him. His heart went to drumroll pace when she put her hand in his. This amazing woman was accepting him, even with all she'd learned about him.

She lifted her dress, giving him a tantalizing glimpse of her leg as she came to her knees before him.

Letting go of her hand, he used his finger to run a caressing line down her arm from her shoulder to her elbow. There he circled, then went to her wrist. He was encouraged by the slight tremble of her hand when he took it and eased her closer.

"Kiss me."

She leaned into him, pressing her lips against his. His hand pulled at her dress, bringing it up her leg. Gliding his hand underneath, he ran it along her thigh, moving to the inside then out again.

Laura Jo deepened their kiss.

His finger found the bottom of her panty line and followed it around to the back of her leg then forward again. She placed small kisses across his forehead and then nipped at his ear. He captured her gaze and watched her eyes widen as he slid a finger beneath her underwear at her hip. She gasped as his finger brushed her curls. He moved his finger farther toward her center and found wet, hot heat. His length strained to find release. She moaned against his mouth and bucked against his finger as he entered her.

"Mark." She drew his name out like a sound of adoration as she put her head back and closed her eyes.

When her hand grazed his straining length behind his zipper he jerked. The woman had him aroused to a painful point. The raw need that had built in him sought release.

He feared he might lose his control and be like a teen in the backseat of a car as he fumbled to have all he dreamed of. Laura Jo ran her life with a tight rein and here she was exposing herself completely to him. That knowledge only increased his wish to give her pleasure.

"If you continue that I'm not going to be responsible for what I do," he growled. When had he been more turned on?

Laura Jo felt the same way. It had been a long time for her but she couldn't remember this gnawing hunger for another person that begged for freedom. She wanted to crawl inside Mark, be surrounded by him and find the safety and security she'd been missing for so many years.

He removed his finger.

She made a sound of protest.

"You have too many clothes on."

Could she be so bold as to remove her dress in front of him? She was thankful for the dim light. She was no longer a maiden. She'd had a child, gained a few mature pounds and things on her body had moved around. Would Mark be disappointed?

"Sit up on your knees, Laura Jo," he coached, as he moved to a sitting position.

Laura Jo did as he asked. As he gathered the fabric of her dress she shifted, releasing the long length of material from behind her knees. With it in rolls at her waist, he said, "Raise your arms."

She did so and he slipped the dress off over her head. Braless, she was exposed to Mark and the elements, except for her tiny panties. The cool air of the night licked her body, making her shudder. She was thankful for it because it covered her nervousness. She crossed her arms over her breasts.

"Please, don't hide from me," Mark said in a guttural

tone filled with emotion. "You're beautiful. I want to admire you in the moonlight."

She'd been so absorbed in him she hadn't noticed there was a full moon. Slowly, very slowly, she let her hands fall to her sides. Mark's look started at the apex of her legs and traveled upward. He paused at her breasts. They were already prickly with awareness and had grown heavy. She looked down to see her nipples standing ridged from the cool air and Mark's hot gaze.

He cupped both breasts and she quivered.

"So responsive," he murmured, more to himself than to her. "Lie down. I want to touch all of you."

"But you still have all your clothes on," she protested.

He chuckled dryly. "If I don't remain dressed I might not be able to control myself."

"But I want to—"

"Later. Now I want to give you pleasure."

He nudged her shoulder then supported her until she lay on her back.

Laura Jo felt exposed, a wanton. She shuddered.

"I'm sorry, you must be cold." He leaned behind him and brought a blanket over them. "I hate to cover up all this beauty but maybe next time…"

Would there be a next time? Did she want more?

He rested his hand on the center of her stomach. Her breathing was erratic and shallow. He kissed the hollow of her shoulder. She pushed his open shirt off his shoulders. He finished removing it and threw it over his shoulder to the deck.

Her hand went to the nape of his neck. "I want to feel your skin touching mine."

"Ah, sweetheart…" Mark kissed her gently and brought her against his warm, inviting chest.

Laura Jo went from shivering to feeling warm and sheltered in the harbor of Mark's arms.

Mark lay down, bringing her with him. His mouth found hers. One of his hands went to her waist and shimmered over the curve of her hip and down her thigh and back up to cup her breast.

Her hands found his chest. She took her time discovering the rises and falls as she appreciated the breadth of his muscles as her hand traveled across his skin. Her palm hovered over the meadow of hair, enjoying the springiness of it.

He sucked in a breath.

She let her hand glide downward along his ribs and lower. He groaned when she brushed the tip of his manhood. With that he flipped the blanket off, letting it fall over her. In one smooth, agile movement he stood. He sat in the closest chair and proceeded to remove his socks and shoes. Seconds later his pants found the deck. He looked like a warrior of old as he stood with his feet apart, his shaft straight, with the moonlight gleaming off the water behind him.

Laura Jo bit her lower lip. This piece of masculine beauty was all hers for tonight.

She pushed away the blanket and opened her arms. Mark opened a package and covered his manhood then came down to her. She pulled the cover over them.

His fingers looped into the lace band of her panties and tugged them off. She kicked her feet to finish the process.

"Perfect," Mark murmured, as he kissed the shell of her ear and his fingers traveled over the curve of her hip. "I want you so much."

Desire carried every word. She was wanted. Mark showed her in every way that she was desired by him. It fed her confidence. She arched her neck as his mouth traveled downward to the hollow beneath her chin, to the curve of a breast and out to her nipple. His hand went lower, where it tested and teased until she flexed.

Her core throbbed, waiting, waiting…

He slid a finger inside her, found that spot of pleasure and she bucked.

"So hot for me," he ground out, before placing a kiss on her stomach.

Mark said it as if he didn't think she could want him. Was the guilt he carried that heavy?

Laura Jo pushed him to his back. He made a sound of complaint. She slid on top of him and poured all she felt into making him feel desired. Positioning herself so that his tip was at her entrance, she looked into his eyes. Did he know how special he was to her? She pushed back and slowly took him inside her. His hands ran up and down her sides as his gaze bored into hers. She lifted and went down again.

Before she knew what had happened, Mark rolled her to her back and entered her with one bold thrust. His hold eased. "Did I hurt you?" His question carried an anxiousness that went soul deep.

"No, you would never hurt me."

He wrapped his arms around her as if he never wanted to let her go. When he did let her go he rose on his hands and pulled out of her to push in again.

She moaned with pleasure and his movements became more hurried. Her core tightened, twisted until it sprang her into the heavens.

A couple of thrusts later, Mark groaned his release to the starry night and lay on her.

Just before his weight became too much he rolled to his side and gathered her to him, twining his legs with hers. He adjusted the blanket around them.

"Perfect," he said, worshipful praise, before brushing a kiss over her temple.

* * *

Mark woke to the sound of thunder rolling in the distance. Laura Jo was warm and soft next to him. He shifted. Hard boards weren't his normal sleeping choice but with Laura Jo beside him it wasn't so difficult. He would have some aches in the morning but it would be more than worth it.

He moved to lie on his back. As if she couldn't be parted from him, she rolled in his direction and rested her head on his shoulder. She snuggled close. What would it be like to have Laura Jo in his life all the time?

Lightning flashed in the clouds. Thunder rumbled.

A hand moved over his chest. His body reacted far too quickly for his comfort. Could he ever get enough of her?

"What're you thinking?'

He tightened his hold and then released it. "That if we don't go inside we're going to get wet." The first large drops of rain hit the porch.

"I'll get the pillows. You get the blankets," she said, jumping up. He followed.

They scooped up the bedding and ran to the door, making it inside just before the downpour started. They laughed at their luck. They stood watching the storm for a few seconds.

"Oh, we didn't get our clothes." Laura Jo moved to open the door.

Mark grabbed her hand. "Forget them.

He dropped the blankets on the floor. "Leave the pillows here."

"Where're we going?" Laura Jo asked.

He gave her a meaningful look. "Like you don't know?"

When she only dropped one pillow he raised a questioning brow.

"I'm not used to walking around the house in the nude and certainly not with a man."

Mark chuckled. "I'm glad to hear that. But you have a beautiful body. You shouldn't be so self-conscious."

"Not everyone has thought that."

Her tone told him that she wasn't fishing for a compliment. Had her ex said differently? "Trust me, you're the sexiest woman I've ever seen. Come with me and I'll show you just how much."

She hesitated.

"You can bring the pillow."

Taking her hand, he led her to his bedroom. He was glad that he'd pulled the covers off his guest-room bed instead of his own. Something told him that if he gave Laura Jo more than a couple of seconds to think she'd be dressing and asking to go home.

Mark didn't want that. He made a point not to spend all night with the women he dated because he didn't want them to get any idea that there would ever be anything permanent between them. But he wanted Laura Jo beside him when he woke in the morning. He wanted her close until he had to let her go. For her own good, he would have to let her go.

He clicked on the lamp that was on the table beside his bed. Pulling the covers back, he climbed in, and turned to look at Laura Jo. "You have to let go of that pillow sometime."

There was a moment or two of panic that she wouldn't, before she slowly dropped it.

His breath caught. She'd looked amazing in the moonlight, but in the brighter light she was magnificent. Her husband had really done a number on her to make her believe she wasn't wanted. Mark sure wanted her more than ever.

"Move over."

He grinned. Laura Jo had gained some confidence. She found her place beside him. Where she belonged. But his feeling of ultimate pleasure quickly moved to the deepest depths of despair. He couldn't keep her.

Laura Jo gave him a look of concern that soon turned to one of insecurity. She slid her legs to the side of the bed.

"Oh, no, you don't. I'm not done with you." *Ever.* He rolled her to her back and kissed her.

Over the next minutes he teased, touched and tasted her body until he had her shaking beneath him. When he paused at her entrance she made a noise of disapproval. She wrapped her legs around his waist and urged him closer. He entered her and was lost forever.

Laura Jo woke up snuggled against Mark's hard body. She'd once thought he had none of the qualities in the man that she was looking for. She'd been so wrong. He had them all and more.

He was the opposite of Phil. When she had needed Mark to come help her at the shelter, he hadn't questioned it, just asked directions. He was good with Allie and she loved him. There had never been a question that he supported her cause with the shelter. He'd even been understanding about her relationship with her parents. He had been the support she hadn't had since she'd left her parents' home. Mark had become a person she could depend on, trust.

Her experiences with lovemaking had been about the other person doing all the receiving but Mark's loving had been all about giving, making sure she felt cherished. And she had.

She shifted until she could look at his face. His golden lashes tipped in brown lay unmoving against his skin. She resisted running her finger along the ridge of his nose. His strong, square jaw had a reddish tint of stubble covering it. She'd never seen a more handsome male in her life.

Her breath jerked to a stop. Oh, she couldn't be. But she was in love with Mark Clayborn!

"You're staring at me."

Her gaze jerked to his twinkling eyes. Could he see how she felt? Could she take a chance on trusting another man? She had Allie to consider. Had to act as if nothing had changed between them when everything had. In her best teasing tone she said, "You're so vain."

He moved to face her, propping his head on his hand. "That may be so but I did see you looking at me."

"So what if I was?" she asked in a challenging tone.

"Then..." he leaned into her "...I like it."

Putting an arm around her waist, he pulled her to him. His intention stood rock-hard ready between them. While he kissed her deeply, he positioned her above him and they became one.

CHAPTER EIGHT

AN HOUR LATER they were in the kitchen, working together to make breakfast. Laura Jo wore one of Mark's shirts while her dress hung on a deck chair, dripping, with Mark's jacket on another.

"I can't go home dressed in my evening gown," she mused, more to herself than to Mark.

"I'll find something around here that you can wear. Actually, I kind of like you in my shirt." He gave her a wolfish grin.

Warmth like the beach on a sunny day went through her. It was nice to be desired. It had been so long.

Wearing Mark's clothes and turning up in the morning instead of late at night in her evening gown was more than she wanted to explain to any of her neighbors. Allie deserved a mother who set a good example. More than that, she owed it to her not to become too involved with a man who wasn't planning to stay for the long haul. Mark had once said that marriage wasn't part of their relationship. Had that changed after last night? He'd said he wanted nothing serious. She had major responsibilities, which always meant some level of permanency. Either way, she had other issues to handle in the next few days. She would face that later.

"Butter on your toast?" Mark asked, as he pulled two slices out of the toaster.

"Yes, please." Waking up with Mark, and spending the morning doing something as domestic as making a meal, felt comfortable, right. Did he sense it, too? She liked it that he didn't expect her to prepare their breakfast. Instead, it was a partnership.

A few minutes later they sat across from each other at the table, eating. Mark wore a pair of sport shorts and nothing else. He hadn't shaved yet and the stubble covering his jaw was so sexy she was having trouble concentrating on her food.

"Do you have to work today?" Mark asked.

"No. I work tomorrow morning. But I have to go to the shelter, see Mr. Washington." She couldn't keep from grinning. "And pick up Allie and Jeremy from school."

"I have to work from noon to eight. Could we maybe have a late dinner?"

"Eight is Allie's bedtime. And it's a school night."

He hesitated, stopping his fork halfway to his mouth. Was he thinking about all that was involved in seeing her? She and Allie were a package and she wanted to remind him of that.

"What's your schedule for Thursday night?"

"Work morning then I have to see Mr. Washington's friend then Mr. McClure about their donations."

"That's right. You're supposed to get the house on Friday. We'll make it a celebration. Take Allie to someplace fun."

"That sounds doable. By the way, I don't think I said thank you for all your help with the shelter. We couldn't have done it without you. You're a good man, Mark Clayborn."

A flicker of denial came to his eyes before it changed to

something she couldn't name. He smiled. "Thank you for that, Laura Jo Akins. I think you believe it."

"And I think you should, too."

Mark had picked up his phone to call Laura Jo at least ten times over the course of the day. After returning her home, wearing a beach dress his sister-in-law had left there and one of his sweatshirts that had swallowed her whole, he had headed to work. He couldn't remember a more enjoyable morning. Laura Jo had just looked right in his kitchen. She was right for his life. The simple task of getting ready to leave for work, which turned out to include a very long shared shower, had been nicer when done with Laura Jo. He had it bad for her.

He picked up his phone. This time he texted her: How did it go with Mr. Washington?

Seconds later she returned, Good. Leaving now.

How like Laura Jo to say no more than necessary.

Unable to help himself, he typed, Looking forward to tomorrow evening.

She sent back a smiley face. He grinned. They had come a long way from the snarl that she had given him when they'd first met.

The next day, when he came out of one of the clinic examination rooms, he was told by the receptionist that there was a call for him. Was it Laura Jo? Was something wrong? His heart sank. Had she changed her mind about tonight? Mercy, he was starting to act lovesick.

"This is Dr. Clayborn."

"Hi, this is Marsha Gilstrap. Laura Jo's friend."

"Yes, I know who you are. Jeremy's mother."

"I'm calling because Laura Jo and I are getting ready to meet with the city about the shelter house. They have notified us at the last minute that they expect us to bring in the names of our board members. It has been only Laura Jo and I. Long story short, would you be willing to serve on our board? It would be for two years, with bi-monthly meetings. Would you be willing to serve?" Once again Marsha was talking like a whirlwind.

"Sure. Just let me know when and where I need to be." The shelter was a good cause and he would help Laura Jo in any way he could.

"Thanks, Dr. Clayborn."

"I thought we agreed to Mark."

"Thanks, Mark." With that she hung up.

That evening Mark drove straight from work to Laura Jo's apartment. He was looking forward to the evening far more than he should have been. Getting in too deep with Laura Jo could be disastrous. He wouldn't stay around forever and Laura Jo would expect that. But he couldn't help himself. He was drawn to her like no other woman he'd ever met.

Allie opened the door after he knocked.

"Hi, there." He went in and closed the door behind him. "Now that Mardi Gras is over, what do we need to look forward to next?"

"The Easter bunny bringing a large chocolate egg."

Mark nodded in thought. "Well, that does sound like something worth waiting for. Will you share yours with me?"

"Sure."

Laura Jo came up the hall. She wore nothing but a simple collared shirt that buttoned down the front and slacks but he still couldn't take his eyes off her. "Hello."

"Hi," she said, shyly for her.

He had gotten to her. She must be feeling unsure about them after the amount of time that had passed since they'd been together.

"Allie, would you do me a favor?"

She nodded.

"I'm thirsty. Would you get me a glass of water?"

As soon as she was out of sight Mark pulled Laura Jo to him. "What I'm really thirsty for is you." His mouth found hers.

Laura Jo had to admit that Mark had done well in choosing a place that would suit for a celebration and one Allie would enjoy. The pizza place was perfect. He'd even provided Allie with a handful of tokens so she could play games. Laura Jo was reasonably sure that this wasn't his usual choice of restaurant for a date.

"Thanks for bringing us here. Allie is having a blast." Laura Jo tried to speak loud enough to be heard over the cling and clang of the games being played and the overhead music.

"I love pizza, too," Mark said, as he brought a large slice of pepperoni to his mouth.

She liked his mouth, especially when it was on hers. His kiss at her door had her thinking of calling Marsha to see if Allie could spend the night then pulling Mark into her bedroom.

"So tell me what happened today about the shelter," Mark said, after chewing and swallowing his bite.

"I collected all the donor money." She grinned. "They didn't remember but when I showed them each the promissory note with their signature on it, both men called their accounting departments and told them to cut a check."

Mark chuckled. "Mr. Washington knows his buddies well."

"The only glitch is that the bank keeps throwing these roadblocks in our way. Today's was that we had to show we have a full board. It couldn't just be Marsha and I."

"Did you know she called me?"

"She told me afterward that she had. I would have told her not to if she had asked."

"Why?"

"I didn't want to put you on the spot." After the other night she didn't want him to feel obligated because of their one night of passion.

"It's not a problem. Besides being extremely attracted to one of the board members, I do think the shelter is a worthy cause. I'm more than happy to serve on the board."

Allie came running up. "I need one more token to play a game."

Mark handed her a token. "After you play your game, I want you to play one with me."

"Okay," Allie said, all smiles.

"Stay where you can see me," Laura Jo reminded her, before Allie ran back to a nearby game.

Mark leaned in close so that he was speaking right into Laura Jo's ear. "Is there any chance for you and me to have some alone time?"

"You'll have to wait and see," Laura Jo said with a smile. "There's one more thing about the shelter I wanted to tell you. Just before you picked us up, Marsha called. The city has decided to take bids for the house. They know of no one else who's interested but they want everything to look aboveboard so they have to offer it out for bids."

"Sounds reasonable."

"Yeah, but what if someone comes in and outbids us?"

He looked at her and said in a serious tone, "Then you'll just have to raise the money or find somewhere else. You now have new board members you can depend on to help you make a decision. You and Marsha won't be all on your own anymore."

She smiled at him just as Allie returned. "I'm ready to play."

"Are you ready to lose because I'm the best whack-a-moler you've ever seen," Mark announced as he puffed out his chest.

Laura Jo and Allie laughed.

He really was fun to be around. "Famous last words, the saying goes, I think," Laura Jo remarked. It had just been Allie and herself for so long. Was she ready to share their life with Mark? She smiled. Maybe she was.

"Come on, young lady," Mark said, taking Allie's hand. "Let me show you."

They arrived back at Laura Jo's apartment, laughing at something Mark had done while trying to best Allie at the arcade game. When they had gotten into the car to leave the pizza place, he'd looked back at Allie and then turned to her. Laura Jo had placed her hand on the seat belt and said, "Thank you for seeing to our safety."

He gave her a wry smile before he started the car but he seemed less anxious.

"It's bath- and bedtime," Laura Jo told Allie as they entered her apartment. "Why don't you get your PJs and the water started? I'm going to fix some coffee for Mark and I'll be right in."

Allie left in the direction of her room and she and Mark went to the kitchen. She took the pot out of the coffee-maker and went to the sink.

Mark came up behind her and took the pot from her, setting it on the counter. "I'll fix the coffee while you see to Allie. Right now, I want a kiss." He turned her round and gathered her close, giving her a gentle but passionate kiss.

Laura Jo's knees went weak. Her arms went around him and she pulled him tight.

"Mama, I'm ready," Allie called.

Slowly Mark broke their connection. He brushed his hips against hers and grinned. "I am, too."

Laura Jo snickered and gave him a playful push. "I'll be back in a few minutes. Behave yourself while I'm gone."

Ten minutes later, Mark walked down the hall in the direction of Laura Jo's voice. He stopped and stood in the doorway of the room where the sound was coming from. The lights were off except for one small lamp with a fairy of some sort perched on top. Allie lay in bed and Laura Jo sat on the side, reading a book out loud. He leaned against the wall facing them and continued to listen. Allie's eyes were closed when Laura Jo shut the book and kissed her daughter on the forehead.

His heart constricted. What would it feel like to be a part of their inner circle?

Laura Jo looked at him and gave him a soft smile. She raised her hand and beckoned him to join her.

His heart beat faster. This was his invitation to find out. But if he took that step he'd be lost forever. He couldn't take on the responsibility of protecting them. What if he failed them, like he had Mike? No, as much as it would kill him to do so, he couldn't tangle their lives up in his. He'd let them down. Hurt them, disappoint them at best. They'd both had enough of that in their lives.

Laura Jo's smile faded. He backed out of the door, walked to the kitchen and sat at the small table.

What had just happened? Didn't Mark recognize that she'd just offered her life and heart to him? He'd turned it down. Flat.

Laura Jo could no longer pretend this was a casual thing between them. She couldn't afford to invest any of her life or Allie's in someone who was afraid of their ability to share a relationship. She needed a confident man during the good as well as the tough times. Mark didn't believe he was capable of being that man.

Even if she believed in him and convinced him they could make it, Mark had to believe in himself. She couldn't take the chance of Allie experiencing that loss and devastation, the almost physical pain of believing no one wanted her, if Mark decided he couldn't do it. Allie wouldn't be made to feel as if she were a piece of trash being tossed out the window of a car. No, she wouldn't let it happen. Wouldn't go through that again.

She had to break it off before they became any more involved. Her heartache she would deal with, but her daughter's heart she would protect. Maybe with time, and many tears during the night, she would get over Mark.

Laura Jo found him a few minutes later, looking at his coffee cup as he ran a finger around the edge. She poured herself a cup of coffee she had no intention of drinking and took the chair across the table from him.

"This isn't going to work, Mark."

"Why?"

"Because I need someone who'll be committed to the long haul. I deserve your wholehearted love and loyalty. I won't risk my heart or Allie's for anything less. That is the very least I will agree to."

"You know I won't take the chance. What if I can't do it? I won't hurt you. I'm no better than your ex-husband. When things get too tough to face, I'll be gone. Just like him. I've done it before. I'll do it again."

"You're still punishing yourself for something that isn't your fault. Mike's in a wheelchair because of a choice that he made, not you. Your way of atoning is to remain uninvolved emotionally with anyone you might feel something real for. That translates into a wife and family for you. I can see that you care about Allie and I think you care about me, too. I've spent a long time not trusting my judgment about men. You got past that wall. You're a better man than you give yourself credit for."

He didn't look at her. Her heart ached for him but she had to get through to him. Make him start really living again. He deserved it. She loved him enough to do that and send him away if she had to.

"You can't create someone else's happiness by being unhappy. You can't fix what happened to Mike. Even if you had been wrong. What you can do now is try to be a better friend than you were back then.

"The problem is you have run from and hidden from the issue too long. You've left the subject alone so long that it has grown and festered to a point it's out of control in your mind. Based on what I saw from Mike the other night, he feels no animosity toward you. To me it sounded as if he just misses his friend. Face it, clean the ugliness away then you can see yourself for the person you are. Good, kind, loving, protective and caring. It's time for you to like yourself.

"I hope that one day you realize that and find someone to share your life with. It can't be Allie and I." Those last words almost killed her to say.

His chair scraped across the floor as he pushed it away from the table. He pinned her with a pointed look. His eyes were dark with sadness and something else. Anger? "Are you through?"

She nodded. She was sure she wasn't going to like what came next.

"I have issues, but you do, too. You carry a chip on your shoulder, Laura Jo. In the past nine years you have finished school on your own, raised a wonderful, happy child and started and helped to run a shelter for women, but still you feel you need to prove yourself to the world. You don't need your father and mother's or anyone else's approval. It's time to quit being that girl who had to show everyone she could do it by herself.

"You let your ex overshadow your life to the point it took me using a sledgehammer to get past your barriers. Laura Jo, not every guy is a jerk and doesn't face up to their responsibilities."

"Like you have?"

Mark flinched. She'd cut him to the core. But she had to get through to him somehow.

"I think I'd better go." He stood and started toward the door.

Shocked at his abrupt statement, she said, "I think it's for the best. Goodbye, Mark."

CHAPTER NINE

THE ONLY TIME Laura Jo could remember feeling so miserable had been when she'd taken Allie home from the hospital, knowing the child would have no father or grandparents to greet her. The pain had been heartbreakingly deep. She'd believed the scar had been covered over enough that she would never return to those emotions. But she'd been wrong.

They had rushed in all over again when Mark had walked out the door. The overwhelming despair was back. The problem this time was that it was even more devastating.

Looking back, she could see her goal when she'd been nineteen had been more about breaking away from her parents, standing on her own two feet and discovering what she believed in, instead of following their dictates. Turned out she'd let pride stand in her way all these years. It hadn't been fair to Allie, her parents or herself.

She appreciated Mark's fears, even understood where they came from, but she couldn't accept anything less than full commitment. Allie deserved that, and even she wouldn't settle for anything less.

Experience had shown her what it was like to have a man in her life who didn't stay around. She refused to put Allie through that. If she felt this awful about Mark leaving after they had known each other for such a short time, what would it have been like if they had been together longer?

The past had told her that the only way to survive disappointment and heartache, and in this case heartbreak, was to keep moving. It was Monday morning and Allie had school, she had to work.

Was Mark working the early shift? Moving around his big kitchen dressed only in his shorts? With them hung low on his hips? Bare-chested?

He'd called a couple of times but she had let the answering machine get it. If she spoke to him it would be too easy to open the door wide for him to come into her life. She just couldn't do that.

She groaned, afraid there would be no getting over Mark. She needed to stay busy, spend less time thinking about him. Forcing herself to climb out of bed, Laura Jo dressed for the day, making sure to have Allie to school on time.

Allie asked her during breakfast, "Why're you so sad, Mama?"

Laura Jo put on a bright smile and said in the most convincing voice she could muster, "I'm not sad. Why would I be sad?"

Allie gave her a disbelieving look but said nothing more. For that Laura Jo was grateful. She worried that she'd break down in tears in front of her daughter.

At midmorning, after just releasing a patient home from the ER, Laura's cell phone buzzed. Looking at it, she saw it was Marsha calling. It was unusual for her to call while Laura Jo was working. Something must have happened with the shelter.

"Hello. What's going on?"

"Someone has bid against us for the house. It's far over what we have and I don't see any way for us to come up with that amount of money."

Marsha told Laura Jo the figure. They were doomed. The new house wasn't going to happen this time. "You're right."

"What we'll have to do is use the money we do have to refurbish the place we're in now and start looking for another place to buy. Sorry my call was bad news."

"Me, too, but I was afraid this might happen when the city opened it for bids. I'd prepared myself for it. We'll start making plans this evening when I get home."

Laura Jo hung up. The sting had been taken out of the loss of the house by the loss of Mark. With him no longer in her life, it made everything else feel less important. She and Marsha would deal with this setback somehow.

A week later, her heart was still as heavy as ever over Mark. If she could just stop thinking about him and, worse, dreaming of him, she could start to heal. But nothing she did except working on the shelter, seemed to ease the continuous ache in her chest.

She and Marsha had just finished meeting with a contractor about ideas for changes at the shelter when Laura Jo was called to the front. There a man dressed in a suit waited.

"Can I help you?" she asked.

"Are you Laura Jo Akins?" The man said in an official manner.

"Yes."

"I was instructed to personally deliver this to you."

He handed her an official-looking envelope. Was this some sort of summons?

Laura Jo started opening the letter and before she could finish the man left. What was going on?

Printed on the front was a name of a lawyer's office. Why would a lawyer be contacting her? She opened the envelope and scanned the contents. Her heart soared and her mouth dropped open in disbelief. She thought of telling Mark first, but he wasn't in her life anymore.

"Marsha!" she yelled.

Her friend hurried down the hallway toward Laura Jo. "What's wrong?"

She waved the letter in the air. "You're never going to believe this. My father has bought the house the city was selling and he has deeded it over to me!"

That night Laura Jo wondered about her parents' generosity. Had they had a change of heart years ago but she wouldn't let them close enough to say so? She had been surprised at the krewe dance to discover they knew some of what had been going on in her life. Had they been watching over her? There had been that school scholarship that she'd been awarded that she'd had no idea she'd qualified for, which had covered most of her expenses. Had that been her parents' doing?

She'd told Mark that people had the capacity to change. Had her parents? After speaking to them, she'd certainly seen them in a different light. She'd also told Mark that people could forgive. Maybe it was past time she did.

On Saturday afternoon, Laura Jo pulled her car into the drive of her parents' home. Allie sat in the seat next to her. Laura Jo had told her about her grandparents a few days before. She had asked Allie to forgive her for not telling her sooner, and had also told Allie that they would be going to visit her grandparents on Saturday. Later that evening, Laura Jo had called the number that she'd known from childhood. Her mother had answered on the second ring. Their conversation had been a short one but during it Laura Jo had asked if she could bring Allie to meet them.

"Mama, what're we doing?" Allie asked.

"I'm just looking, honey. I used to live here." That was

true but mostly she was trying to find the nerve to go further. The last time she'd been there, hurtful words had been spoken that had lasted for years.

A few minutes later, she and Allie stood hand in hand in front of her parents' front door. Allie rang the doorbell. Her mother must have been watching for them because the door was almost immediately opened by her mother herself. Not one of the maids. Her father was coming up the hall behind her.

"Hello, Laura Jo. Thank you for coming." Her mother sounded sincere.

"Mother and Daddy, this is Allie."

Her mother leaned over so that she was closer to Allie's level and smiled. "Hi, Allie. It's so nice to meet you."

Her father took the same posture. "Hello."

Allie stepped closer to Laura Jo. She placed a hand at Allie's back and said, "These are your grandparents."

Both her parents stood and stepped back.

Her mother said in a nervous voice Laura Jo had never heard, "Come in."

It felt odd to step into her parents' home after so much time. Little had changed. Instead of being led into the formal living room, as Laura Jo had expected, her mother took them to the kitchen. "I thought Allie might like to have some ice cream."

Allie looked at Laura Jo. "May I?"

"Sure, honey."

"Why don't we all have a bowl?" her father suggested.

When they were finished with their bowls of ice cream her mother asked Allie if she would like to go upstairs to see the room where Laura Jo used to sleep. Allie agreed.

Laura Jo looked at her father. "I don't know how to say thank you enough for your gift."

"We had heard that you were looking for support to buy it."

She should have known it would get back to them about why she'd been at the dance.

"It's a good cause and we wanted to help. Since we weren't there for you, maybe we can help other girls in the same position. I know it doesn't make up for the struggle you had."

It didn't, but at least she better understood her parents now. She had to share some of the fault also. "All those calls I made to Mom—"

"We thought we were doing what was best. That if we cut you off then you would see that you needed us and come back."

"But you wouldn't talk to me." She didn't try to keep the hurt out of her voice.

"We realized we had been too hard on you when you stopped calling. I'm sorry, Laura Jo. We loved you. Feared for you, and just didn't know how to show it correctly."

"You saw to it that I got the nursing scholarship, didn't you?"

He nodded. "We knew by then that you wouldn't accept if we offered to send you to school."

"I wouldn't have. It wasn't until recently that I realized that sometimes what we believe when we're young isn't always the way things are. You were right about Phil. I'm sorry that I hurt you and Mom. Kept Allie from you."

"We understand. We're proud of you. We have kept an eye on you both. You've done well. You needed to do it the hard way, to go out on your own. It took us a while to see that." Her strong, unrelenting father went on, with a catch in his voice, "The only thing we couldn't live with was not having you in our lives and not knowing our grand-daughter."

Moisture filled her eyes for all the hurt and wasted opportunities through the years on both sides. Laura Jo reached across the table and took her father's hand. Forgiveness was less about her and more about her parents. A gift she could give them. "You'll never be left out of our lives again, I promise."

Three weeks after the fact Mark still flinched when he thought of Laura Jo accusing him of being a jerk and not living up to his responsibilities. The plain-talking Laura Jo had returned with a vengeance when she'd lectured him.

She was right, he knew that, but he still couldn't bring himself to talk to Mike. That was the place he had to start. He'd spent over ten years not being able to face up to Mike and what had happened that night. Could he be a bigger hypocrite?

He'd looked down on Laura Jo's ex, taking a holier-than-thou approach when he'd been running as fast and far as Phil had when the going had got tough.

Every night he spent away from Laura Jo made him crave her more. He wasn't sleeping. If he did, he dreamed of her. The pain at her loss was greater than any he'd ever experienced. Even after the accident. He wasn't able to live without her. He'd tried that and it wasn't working.

He'd tried to call her a couple of times but she hadn't picked up.

Mark thought about Laura Jo's words. Didn't he want a family badly enough to make a change? Want to have someone special in his life? More importantly, be a part of Laura Jo's and Allie's world?

He'd been running for so long, making sure he didn't commit, he didn't know how to do anything else. It was time for it to stop. He had to face his demons in order to be worthy of a chance for a future with Laura Jo, if she would have him. How could he expect her to believe in him, trust him to be there for her, if he didn't believe it for himself? He had to get his own life in order before he asked for a permanent place in hers. And he desperately wanted that place.

Mark picked up the phone and dialed the number he'd called so many times he had it memorized by now. He'd been calling every day for a week and had been told that Mike wasn't available. Was he dodging Mark, as well?

He'd made his decision and wanted to act on it. It was just his luck he couldn't reach Mike. The devil of it was that he couldn't return to Laura Jo without talking to Mike first. She would accept nothing less. For his well-being as well as hers.

The day before, he'd received a call from Marsha. She'd told him how they had missed out on the house but then an anonymous donor had bought it outright and gifted it to them.

Mark was surprised and glad for Laura Jo. At least the dream she'd worked so hard for had come true. Marsha went on to say that she and Laura Jo no longer required a board but planned to have one anyway. Marsha wanted to know if he was still willing to serve on it.

"Have you discussed this with Laura Jo? She may not want me on it."

"She said that if you're willing to do it she could handle working with you on a business level. I think her exact words were, 'He's a good doctor and cares about people. I'm sure he'll be an asset.'"

Panic flowed through his veins. Laura Jo was already distancing herself from him. The longer it took to speak to Mike, the harder it would be to get her to listen.

Marsha said, "Look, Mark, I don't know what happened between you two but what I do know is that she's torn up about it. I love her like a sister and she's hurting. She can be hardheaded when it comes to the ones she loves. The only way to make her see reason is to push until she does."

"Thanks for letting me know."

The next day, when Mark had a break between patients, he tried Mike's number again. This time when a woman answered he insisted that he speak to Mike.

"Just a minute."

"Mark." Mike didn't sound pleased to hear from him.

"I was wondering if I could come by for a visit," Mark said, with more confidence than he felt.

"It will be a couple of days before I have time." Mike wasn't going to make this easy but, then, why should he. "I've been out of town and have some business I need to catch up on."

Mark wasn't tickled with having to wait, but he'd put it off this long so did two more days really matter?

"How does Thursday evening at seven sound?"

"I'll be here." Mike sounded more resigned to the idea than cheerful about the prospect. Mark couldn't blame him. His jaw tightened with tension from guilt and regret at the thought of facing him. He felt like a coward and had acted like one for years.

The next day an invitation arrived in the mail. It was to a garden party tea at the Herrons' mansion on Sunday afternoon. It was a fund-raiser for the new shelter. Had Laura Jo taken his advice and cleared the air with her parents? He looked forward to attending.

Two evenings later, Mark drove from Fairhope over the bay causeway to Mobile. Mike lived in one of the newer neighborhoods that Mark wasn't familiar with. He hadn't slept much the night before, anticipating the meeting with Mike, but, then, he hadn't slept well since the night he'd had Laura Jo in his arms. He drove up the street Mike had given as his address during their phone conversation. It was tree-lined and had well-cared-for homes. He pulled up alongside the curb in front of the number that Mike had given him. It was a yellow ranch-style home, with a white picket fence surrounding the front yard. Early spring flowers were just starting to show.

Mark sat for a minute. He'd prepared his speech. Had practiced and practiced what he was going to say, but it never seemed like enough. If Laura Jo were here, she would say to just share what was in his heart. To stop worrying. Taking a deep breath and letting it out slowly, he opened the car door and got out. Closing it, he walked around the car and up the walk.

He hadn't noticed when he'd pulled up that there were children's toys in the yard and near the front door. Mike had a child?

Mark winced when he saw the wheelchair ramp and hesitated before putting a foot on it to walk to the door. His nerves were as tight as bowstrings. He rang the doorbell. Seconds later, Tammy opened the door.

"Mark, how nice to see you again." She pulled the door wider. "Come on in. Mike's in the den with Johnny."

She closed the door and Mark followed her down an extrawide hall to a large room at the back of the house.

Mike sat in what could only be called the most high-tech of wheelchairs in the middle of the room. A boy of about three was handing him a block and together they were building a tower on a tray across Mike's knees. "Mark. Come on in. Let me introduce you to my son, Johnny."

Mark went over to Mike, who offered his hand for a shake. "Good to see you again."

Mike dumped the blocks into a bucket beside his chair and then set the tray next to it. "Come here, Johnny, I want you to meet someone."

At one time Mike would have introduced him as his best friend. By the way he acted he wasn't even a friend anymore.

The boy climbed into his father's lap and shyly curled into Mike. He looked up at Mark with an unsure gaze.

"Johnny," Mark said.

"I think it's is time for someone to go to bed." Tammy reached out and took Johnny from Mike. "We'll let you two talk."

Mark watched them leave the room and turned back to Mike.

"I admire you."

"How's that?"

"Having a wife and family. The responsibility. How do you know you're getting it right?"

"Right? I have no idea that I am. I make the best decisions I can at the time and hope they are the correct ones. Tammy and I are partners. We make decisions together." Mike looked directly at him. "Everyone makes mistakes. We're all human and not perfect. We just have to try harder the next time."

Was that what he'd been doing? Letting a mistake color the rest of his life? If he couldn't be sure he'd be the perfect husband or father then he wouldn't even try.

Before Mark could say anything more, Mike said, "Take a seat and quit towering over me. You always made a big deal of being taller than me. Remember you used to say that was why you got the girls, because they saw you first in a crowd."

Mark gave halfhearted grin. Had Mike just made a joke?

Taking a seat on the edge of the sofa, Mark looked around the room.

"Why are you here, Mark? After all these years, you show up at my house now," Mike said, as he maneuvered his chair closer and into Mark's direct sight line.

He scooted back into the cushions. "Mike, I need to clear the air about a couple of things."

"It's well past time for that."

Those words didn't make Mark feel any better. "I'm embarrassed about how I acted after the accident. I'm so sorry I left without speaking to you and have done little to stay in touch since. Most of all, I'm sorry I put you in that damn chair." Mark looked at the floor, wall, anywhere but at Mike.

Moments passed and when Mike spoke he was closer to Mark than he had been before. "Hey, man, you didn't put me in this chair. I did. I was drunk and not listening to anything anyone said."

"But I was the one going too fast. I'd driven that part of the road a hundred times. I knew about that ninety-degree turn. I overcorrected." Mark looked up at him.

"You did. But I wouldn't have been thrown out if I'd worn my seat belt. I don't blame you for that. But I have to admit it hurt like hell not to have your support afterwards. I can't believe you did me that way."

Mark's stomach roiled as he looked at a spot on the floor. "I can't either. That isn't how friends should act." He looked directly at Mike. "All I can do is ask you to forgive me and let me try to make it up to you."

"If you promise not to run out on me again, and buy me a large steak, all will be forgiven."

Mark smiled for the first time. "That I can do."

"And I need a favor."

Mark sat forward. "Name it."

"I need a good general practice doctor to oversee an experimental treatment that I'm about to start. Do you know one?"

"I just might," Mark said with a grin. "What's going on?"

"I just returned from Houston, where they are doing

some amazing things with spinal injuries. With all these guys coming back from war with spinal problems, what they can do has come a long way even from nine years ago. I will have a procedure done in a few weeks and when I return home I need to see a doctor every other day to check my site and do bloodwork. My GP is retiring and I'm looking for someone to replace him who Tammy can call day or night." He grinned. "She worries. Doesn't believe me when I tell her what the doctor has said. Likes to hear it from the doc himself."

"I'll be honored to take the job. I'll even make house calls if that will help."

"I may hold you to that."

For the next forty-five minutes, he and Mike talked about old times and what they were doing in their lives now. Mike had become a successful businessman. He had invented a part for a wheelchair that made it easier to maneuver the chair. As Mark drove away he looked back in his rearview mirror. Mike and Tammy were still under the porch light where he had left them. Tammy's hand rested on Mike's shoulder. That simple gesture let Mark know that Mike was loved and happy.

Mike had a home, a wife and child, was living the life Mark had always hoped for but was afraid to go after. All Mark owned was his car and Gus. He'd let the one special person he wanted in his life go. Ironically, Mike had moved on while he had stayed still. And he had been the one feeling sorry for Mike, when he had more in life than Mark did. He wanted that happiness in his life too and knew where to find it.

If he could get Laura Jo to listen. If she would just let him try.

CHAPTER TEN

LAURA JO COULDN'T believe the difference a few weeks had made in her life. It was funny how she'd been going along, doing all the things she'd always done, and, bam, her life was turned upside down by her daughter having a skinned knee. She'd worked Mardi Gras parades before but never had she had a more eventful or emotional season.

She scanned her parents' formal backyard garden. There were tables set up among the rhododendrons, azaleas and the dogwood trees. None were in full bloom but the greenery alone was beautiful. The different tables held canapés and on one sat a spectacular tea urn on a stand that swung with teacups surrounding it. People in their Sunday best mingled, talking in groups. The eye-popping cost to attend the event meant that the shelter could double the number of women they took in. Her parents had convinced her to let them to do this fund-raiser so that she could get the maximum out of the grant. She'd agreed and her mother had taken over.

How ironic was it that she had rejected her parents and they were the very ones who were helping her achieve her dreams? Her anger and resentment had kept her away from her parents, not the other way around. Forgiveness lifted a burden off her and she was basking in the sunshine of having a family again. She only wished Mark could feel that way, as well. She still missed him desperately.

Allie's squeal of delight drew her attention. Laura Jo located her. She was running down the winding walk with her new dress flowing in her haste.

"Mark," she cried, and Laura Jo's stomach fluttered.

She'd thought he might be here, had prepared herself to see him again, but her breath still stuck in her throat and her heart beat too fast. Each day became harder without him, not easier.

Already she regretted agreeing to let him remain on the board. Now she would have to continue to face him but he was too good an advocate for the shelter to lose him. At least, that was what she told herself. Somehow she'd have to learn to deal with not letting her feelings show.

When Allie reached Mark he whisked her up into his arms and hugged her close. The picture was one of pure joy between them.

Laura Jo had worked hard not to snap at Allie when she'd continued to ask about where Mark was and why they didn't see him anymore. Finally, Laura Jo had told her he wouldn't be coming back and there had been tears on both sides.

Mark lowered Allie onto her feet and spoke to her. Allie turned and pointed in Laura Jo's direction. Mark's gaze found hers, even at that distance. Her heart flipped.

He started toward her.

A couple of people she'd known from her Mardi Gras court days joined her. They talked for a few minutes but all the while Laura Jo was aware of Mark moving nearer.

He stood behind her. She'd know anywhere that aftershave and the scent that could only be his. Her spine tingled.

As the couple moved away Mark said in a tone that was almost a caress, "Laura Jo."

She came close to throwing herself into his arms but she had to remain strong. She turned around, putting on her best smile like she'd been taught so many years ago. "Hello, Mark, glad you could come."

"I wouldn't have missed it."

His tone said that was the truth.

"Marsha told me that you got the house after all. That's wonderful. With the grant and all the money you've raised, you'll be able to furnish it."

"Yes. My father was the one to outbid us. He then gave it to me."

His brow wrinkled. "You were okay with that?"

"I was. The women needed it too badly for me to use my disagreement with my parents against them. It really was a gift to me anyway. He wanted to make amends by helping other women going through the same experience I had."

Mark nodded. "It sounds like you and your parents worked things out."

"I wouldn't say that it's all smooth going. But I've forgiven them. We're all better for that. They want to see their granddaughter and Allie needs them. I don't have the right to deny any of them that."

"Mama, look who's here," Allie said from beside her.

Laura Jo hadn't seen her approach, she'd been so absorbed in Mark. She turned. "Who—?"

Allie held Gus's leash. Behind the dog sat Mike and next to him stood his wife. She looked back at Mark.

He smiled and turned toward the group. "I brought a few friends with me. I hope you don't mind?"

Did this mean what she thought it did? Mark had taken what she'd said to heart and had gone to see his friend.

"Hello, Mike and Tammy. Of course you're welcome. I'm glad to see you again."

"We're glad to be here. This is some event. And I understand it's for a very worthy cause. I think we'll have Allie show us where the food is." Mike winked at Mark. "We'll see you around, buddy."

Laura Jo looked between them, not sure what the interchange meant.

"You're busy. I think I'll get some food also." Mark captured her hand. "When this is over, can we talk?"

A lightning shock of awareness and a feeling of rightness washed through her simultaneously. "It'll be late."

"I'll wait."

Mark sat in Mr. Herron's den, having a cup of coffee while he waited for Laura Jo. Her father was there, along with Allie and Gus. Mr. Herron had apparently noticed Mark was hanging around after the other guests were leaving and had taken pity on him by inviting him in for coffee and a more comfortable seat.

The longer Mark sat there the more nervous he became. Would Laura Jo listen to what he had to say? Would she believe that he had changed? Would she be willing to take a chance on him? He broke out in a sweat, just thinking about it.

She and her mother finally joined them. He stood. Laura Jo looked beautiful but tired. Had she been getting as little sleep as he had?

As if her mother knew Laura Jo needed some time alone with him, Mrs. Herron said, "Why don't you let Allie stay with us tonight? We can get her to school in the morning. She can wear the clothes she wore from home to here today."

"Is that okay with you, Allie?" Laura Jo asked.

"Yes. Can Gus stay, too?"

"I think you need to let your grandparents get used to having you before you start inviting Gus to stay," Mark said with a smile.

Ten minutes later, he and Laura Jo, with Gus in the backseat, were leaving her parents' house. She had touched her seat belt when he'd looked.

"Old habits are hard to break," he said in explanation.

"Not a bad habit to have," she assured him in a warm tone. That was one of the many things he loved about Laura Jo. She understood him.

"I hope you don't mind me taking Gus home. I don't want you to think I planned to lure you to my house. I just thought Allie would be glad to see him. I didn't think it all the way through."

"She was, and I don't mind riding to your house."

As they traveled through the tunnel Laura Jo remarked, "I've never known my parents to let a dog in the house."

"Gus does have that effect on people."

She went on as if more in thought than conversation, "Come to think of it, I've never seen my father invite another man into his private space."

"Maybe that's his way of giving me a seal of approval."

She pieced him with a look. "Are you asking for a seal of approval from my father?"

"No, the only seal of approval I'm looking for is from you."

She studied him for a minute before asking, "Are you going to tell me about Mike and Tammy or keep me in suspense?"

"It took me a while to admit you were right. Actually, I knew all along that you were. I just didn't want to admit it."

"So what made you decide to talk to Mike?" She had laid her head back and closed her eyes.

He hadn't planned to go into this as they traveled. But as usual Laura Jo had a way of surprising him. "Why don't you rest and I'll tell you when we get to my house?"

"Sounds like a plan."

By the time Mark pulled into his drive, Laura Jo was sleeping. Here he was, planning to bare his heart to her after weeks of being separated, and she'd fallen asleep. He let Gus out of the car and went to open the front door.

Going to Laura Jo's door, he opened it, unbuckled her and scooped her into his arms. She mumbled and wrapped her arms around his neck, letting her head rest on his chest. He kicked the passenger door closed and carried her inside.

He loved having her in his arms again. After pushing the front door closed, he went to his favorite chair and sat down. She continued to sleep and he was content just having her close.

Sometime later Laura Jo stirred. He placed a kiss on her temple and her eyelids fluttered open.

"Hello," she mumbled against his neck. Then she kissed him.

The thump-thump of his heart went to bump-bump.

Her lips touched the ridge of his chin, while a hand feathered through his hair near his ear.

His hopes soared. His manhood stirred. Had she missed him as much as he'd missed her? "Laura Jo, if you keep that up, talking is the last thing that will happen."

"So talk," she murmured, before her mouth found the corner of his. "I'm listening."

"Maybe we need to go out on the deck."

"Mmm, I like it here." She wiggled around so she could kiss him fully on the mouth.

His length hardened. If he didn't say what he needed to say now, he wouldn't be doing so for a long time.

"I can't believe that I'm doing this…" He pushed her away until he could see her face. She blinked at him and gave him a dreamy smile. "Why did you agree to talk to me? Was it because you saw me with Mike? You haven't answered any of my phone calls in the past few weeks."

"I hoped…"

"Hoped what? That I had changed my mind? Hoped you'd gotten through to me? Hoped there was a chance for us?"

"Yes," she whispered.

"Do you want there to be?"

By now she was sitting a little straighter and her eyes had turned serious. "Tell me what made you decide to go talk to Mike. When you left my place I didn't think you ever would."

"I went because I discovered that I was more afraid of something else than I was of facing Mike."

Her gaze locked with his. "What?"

"Losing any chance of ever having you in my life."

"Oh, Mark. I thought I had lost you forever until I saw you with Mike today. I knew then that you thought we had something worth fighting for. I've been so miserable without you." She took his face in her hands and kissed him.

"We've both been running from our pasts. I think it's time for us to run toward our future. Together."

His arms tightened around her. Their kiss deepened. He had to have her. Beneath him, beside him, under him. Forever.

Mark lifted her off him and she stood. He quickly exited the chair. Taking her hand, he led her to his bedroom. Putting his hands on her shoulders, he turned her around and unzipped her dress. Pushing it off and letting it fall to the floor, he kissed her shoulder.

"I've missed you so much it hurt."

"I felt the same."

He released her bra and it joined her dress. There was a hitch in her breathing when he cupped her breasts. She leaned back against him. As his hands roamed, she began to squirm.

She flipped around to face him. "I want you." Her hands went to his waist and started releasing his belt.

"No more than I want you."

With them both undressed, they found the bed and the world that was theirs alone.

Sometime later, Mark lay with Laura Jo in his arms. Her hair tickled his nose but he didn't mind. All was right with his world if she was in it.

Laura Jo shifted, placed a hand in the center of his chest and looked up at him. "Hi, there."

He looked at her and smiled. "Hey, yourself."

For a few moments he enjoyed the feel of her in his arms before he said, "I've worked for years not to become emotionally involved with anyone. I didn't think I could trust myself. Then along came you and Allie. I've been miserable without you both. I've always wanted a family and when a wonderful one was offered to me, like an idiot I turned it down. I won't do that again if the invitation is still open. See, the problem is that I've fallen in love with you."

With moisture in her eyes Laura Jo stretched up and placed a kiss on his mouth. "I love you, too, but are you sure that's what you want? What you can live with? I can't take any chances. It has to be forever. Kids or no kids. Good or bad days. Sickness or health."

Mark leaned forward so that his face was only inches from hers. "Until death do us part."

"I can live with that."

Her kiss told him she meant it.

* * * * *